SONIA OVERALL

The Realm of Shells

HARPER PERENNIAL
London, New York, Toronto and Sydney

Harper Perennial
An imprint of HarperCollins*Publishers*
77–85 Fulham Palace Road
Hammersmith
London W6 8JB

www.harperperennial.co.uk

This edition published by Harper Perennial 2007

1

First published in Great Britain by Fourth Estate in 2006

ISBN-13 978-0-00-718411-8
ISBN-10 0-00-718411-5

Set in Sabon with Arepo Display by
Palimpsest Book Production Limited, Grangemouth, Stirlingshire

Printed and bound in Great Britain by Clays Ltd, St Ives plc

for the real grotto builders

          ERALL grew up in Ely and Canterbury, where she studied Literature and Philosophy. She lives in Kent with her husband, a fine artist. This is her second novel.

Visit www.AuthorTracker.co.uk for exclusive information on your favourite HarperCollins authors.

From the reviews of *The Realm of Shells*:

'Fanny proves an engaging and perceptive heroine ... Her life seems transformed when her brother Joshua stumbles on something magical: a mysterious grotto, its walls covered in a "twirling twisting" mosaic of fans and flowers and stars, all made from shells, that glint and shimmer in candlelight. Overall writes movingly about the children's excited pleasure, and traces their gradual, increasingly bitter disillusionment when they feel they must admit their secret to adults who, inevitably, exploit and ultimately destroy their discovery' *Sunday Times*

'Remarkable ... it takes a writer of rare ability to produce a novel as good as this' *Glasgow Herald*

'The details of a child's life in the early 19th century ... have the ring of complete authenticity about them, obviously based on meticulous research and a genuine love of history' *Daily Telegraph*

'A poignant, powerful novel with Overall lending a sense of horror to the gradual disintegration of the Newloves' dearly-held values by subjecting them to the scrutiny of a child brutally forced to re-evaluate her world' *Big Issue*

By the same author

A Likeness

Acknowledgements

There are several people I would like to thank for helping me during the writing of this book. Special thanks are due to Sarah Vickery, current owner of the Margate Shell Grotto, for her help and interest, and to her mother Pat for allowing me an out-of-hours candlelit visit. I am indebted to Mick Twyman of the Margate Historical Society, who generously supplied me with copies of his research into the grotto, and to Tony Snow and Colin Bridge of the Margate Civic Society, whose knowledge of the old town proved invaluable. I would also like to thank the obliging staff of the Canterbury Cathedral Archives, the University of Kent's Special Collections Library, and the local collections of the Margate and Canterbury public libraries.

I am very grateful to Simon Trewin and Philip Gwyn Jones for their continued support; to my friends and family for their patience and interest; to Duane Williams, whose innocent comment about a Margate junk shop unwittingly started this project, and most importantly to my husband James, whose unwavering assistance and encouragement made it possible. Thank you.

Seaward

'The Hero is a good start' Joshua says, eyes screwed up with rain. 'I wonder which.'

'I shall die of a monstrous fever' (*huffing Lizzy*) 'before we even get half-way there, I shall never set foot on the shore alive.' *Huff-huffity.* She wrings water from her shawl fringes. 'Ruined! The salt will ruin it and you none of you care.'

Mary pretends to, unmittens her fingers and combs combs soft and quick at the fringes. Peevish Lizzy shakes her off, horsetail fly-switching, cross head tossing. (*Shoo.*) The corners of my hatbox cold and sharp – hug them hard with my inside elbow softness, cold and sharp, feel plump purple bruises dimpling there.

Joshua rubs his dripping fringe, wet black V between his eyes grey and quick. 'I hope it is Napoleon.'

'That is unpatriotic, my dear' says Mama, soft-scolding. She shooshes trunks and cases into a circle, cooping chickens. The flock of trunks sit wetly shining and pooling water on the slip-slimed cabin floor. *They* do what they are told.

'Napoleon is a hero too' says Joshua. He flicks hair water at Lizzy. 'For the French.'

'Pooh!' *(huffing Lizzy.)* 'The *French*.'

Mary dabs at her own shawl, sadly.

'Will we have chickens in Margate?' say I.

Lizzy *hhhnn!* snorts. Mama looks at me strangely. Her face is badly drawn and blotched like a paper with Mary's coloured waterpaints.

'There will be seagulls' says Mama. She looks away quickly.

'They shriek like ghosts' (murmuring Mary) 'heralding the watery deaths of fishermen.' Eyes wide, black brows high, hushing scaring Mary. But smiling now. 'They scold the fishwives for throwing out cods' heads.'

'What nonsense' Lizzy snaps. 'You've never seen a seagull in your life. You've never even seen the sea.'

Mary's lip quivers. 'There are seagulls here, and we are seabound.' (*And I have seen as much as you*, but only her eyes say *that*.)

Squeeze Mary's hand: damp cold and wind-raw. The gulls shriek, but sweet compared to our Lizzy.

'Dismal' Lizzy grumbles. 'Why could Papa not send for us in the Spring? It is so cold and dismal.'

'Surely you don't want to be apart from Papa any longer?' say I.

Lizzy's eyebrows draw up high and disappear under her bonnet.

'I like it' says Joshua. Dab-dab-dabs his boot toes into the trunk-water puddles. 'The sea will be rough and icy.'

'Boys!' sighs Lizzy. She sinks down – *aaaargh!* – jumps up shrieking, squeaking 'Water, everywhere! These cushions are soaked! Oh! Wretched boat, I wish I had never been born!'

Mama *tut-tuts* quietly.

Joshua winks at me. 'We might all die on the seas today anyway' he says. 'They hardly ever keep a packet safe in this weather.' Shakes his head like an undertaker. 'I wonder that the captain has let us come aboard.' He turns, runs back up the cabin steps – *fhuuw-fhuuw-fhuuuuuw!* – all cheerfully tunelessly whistling. Wicked winking Joshua.

'Horrid little monster' Lizzy says. Grumble grumble. She turns about the cushions, stabbing and poking each one.

She should not speak so. Look at Mama, but Mama looks at the flock of cases. Her face is long and very white.

Huffing Lizzy sinks, drops between two cushions. 'Pass me the guide, Fanny.' Snap-snap fingers. She points at Mama's book, wrapped in the bookseller's paper.

Mama says nothing, sits on the padded bench by the steps. The bench is fixed to the floor planks with big nails. *And* the chairs. Everything nailed down tight. Mary's boots white with salt flutter-tap flutter-tap on the floor. Nail them down too.

'For goodness' sake!' shouts Lizzy, *smack-kapkap* clapping her hands.

'You oughtn't to speak so' say I.

'Frances dear' sighs Mama. 'Do not contradict your sister.'

Smug Lizzy smiles. 'Don't be a rude little girl, Fanny. Now, pass me the guide.'

'Mama –'

Lizzy demanding holds out her hand. Take the neat brown parcel crumpling crinkling, sea-damp but smelling new. Give it to *her*. She tugs, rips, pulls the string free, drops it by her feet. Grinding boot heels. It falls and coils there, little snake, shred of sailor's rope. Hokum? *Oakum.* O-A-K-U-M. Poor-man's pickings, workhouse trade, break your fingernails.

'Now, let us see.' Lizzy parts the paper and takes out the book. 'I hope there are good Assembly Rooms.'

3

Rescue the string from her heels.

'It is a very well-appointed place, my dear' Mama says.

Lizzy holds up the book. ' "Of all the watering places in England" ' (she reads badly – too quickly) ' "Margate has now become the most attractive, from the salubrity of its air, the variety of its amusements, and the short space of time . . ." et cetera.' She *ya*-yawns, thud-closes the book. 'That is promising.'

'The Assembly Rooms' says Mama, 'are called the Royal Hotel. The late King met his wife there.'

'Which one?' Sly Lizzy, spitefully aside.

'It will be like the novels set in Bath' Mary burbles 'where heroines befriend the glamorous daughters of baronets and are fallen in love with at balls by sea captains.' She breathes.

'There will be no captains of any sort for either of you' soft-scolds Mama. 'You would do well to remember that we go to Margate to work and be studious, and to support your dear father. We do not go on an idle errand of amusement.'

Huffing Lizzy huffs again. Mary looks at the salt on her boots.

Mama's long hands go lace-patting at their faces. 'I do not doubt, my dears, that my daughters will be the finest two girls Margate has seen for many seasons.'

Mama has only ever *two* girls to speak of.

'Margate will *never* see us if all we do is work.' Never-happy Lizzy, never satisfied. 'Father will never let us do anything fine.' *(Grumble grumble.)*

'Your father does not tolerate vanity, my dear, that is all.' Mama starts up the steps. 'I will get a little air above deck.'

'*Our father* would have us dry as the ink in a psalm book' mutters Lizzy, eye-rolling.

'Do not say unkind things of Papa' say I. 'He is only afraid that you will be dull and stupid from reading romances.'

4

'What would you know of romances? Cross little girl.' She makes claws with her grey glovefingers. 'How many balls were *you* seen at last season? How many sea captains have asked Papa for *your* hand?' She *haw-haw-haw*s.

'No more nor less than asked for yours' say I.

'Margate will remedy that' she hisses, preening. 'Margate will be in a great wave of shock at seeing such a creature as myself arrive.'

(A shock to kill all the fishes of the sea.)

'Indeed' smiling Mary says. 'The ladies will be in widow's weeds when they see the two of us among them.'

Sulk-lipped Lizzy pouts. 'Depend upon it, I will have broken at least ten hearts before Lent.'

It is well that she does not have one to break herself.

Almost there

Poke poke prodding at my arm. *Joshua?*

'Wake up, Fan. Are you sick?'

Sick? Room rocking, floor creaking tipping – not room, *cabin*.

'Sleepy' say I.

He grins. 'Lizzy's sick. Fearful sick. Stops her talking, though she moans and moans.'

Just us in the roo– *cabin*. And cushions and cooped-up cases. A piece of string by my head. 'Where are the others?'

'Above deck.' He stretches. 'Mama is talking, talking to everyone. Mary is tending Lizzy, she's been retching violently. Ha! Her grand entrance into Margate society.'

'Poor Lizzy.'

'Pooh! Poor Mary. Come up. You've missed everything, we're nearly there. The coast is close, you can see the cliffs and everyone walking about. Come and *see*.'

'Seagulls?'

'*Everywhere*. And the steam towers make *such* a smoke. I went down to look but they pulled me out. It was hot as hell.'

'Joshua!'

'What? *Too* good.' He shrugs, tugs my shawl. 'Get up. Come and see.' Tug tug tug – he will tear it. 'There were ruins back there, right on the cliff edge. *Roman* ruins. And ports and everything.'

'All right.'

Slip-slide floor all shiny with seawater. Joshua pulls himself up the steps by the rope rails. Wet rope hard with weather. Square of sky, grey with seagulls hanging there, wings not flapping not moving. Up into cold cold mizzle of air on the deck and the sea, *SEA!* – spreading out and out all grey and green and lumpy, thick as milk, fish soup salty and smelly. Wave-wave-wave rolling and folding and tucking one under the next. Hooshing and whooshing. I wave back. The *Sea!*

'D'you like it?' He grins and grins.

'It *moves* so much.'

'It's just monsters, *lurking* below. And mermaids, of course.' Shows me his pink curling tongue-tip. 'Come and see over the side. The boat cuts right through it.'

Over the slip boards and hold the rail (icy) raw knuckle tight and there the water, splashing slap-slapping against the side, long ribbon trims of wave ripples flying and trailing. Seagulls *aa-eeeek akk akk* swooping screaming and chasing us. Fish-pot, soup-pot, salt-pot smell, strong and thick in the air. Lick your lips.

Joshua tugs. 'Come on. Show you the coast.'

Over the deck again, rocking leaning weaving. Men staggering long-jacketed, long-armed against it. No ladies anywhere. Where is Mama?

Foot-stamping cold. No toes in my boots – no, there is *one*. *One* right *one* left. Not the others. Webfoot numb. Waddle after quick-toed Joshua.

Joshua points. 'There, see? In front there. That must be the edge of it.'

The coast? Big dirty bank of stone, grubby riverbank, a giant's ditch. The sea stops against it but pushes, pushes and rushes at it. Push it over, the land. So that is it, when the land stops, a tall field with a big white bite taken out – and then water. A big rock slab sticks up. The sea spits at it.

'The coast?'

'*On* it, silly. Look!' Fingerpoints again, up and along. 'Past the rock. The *town*.'

Ship sails, low walls, buildings. Blurry. People moving behind us before us.

Whistling icy air in my ear, cold folds in my clothes. Wish my shawl into blankets. 'Let's go in. Where's Mama?'

'*Go in?* You'll miss everything. You haven't even *looked* at the steam towers.' Black choke of smoke on board like big work chimneys. He loves it, wide grin full of teeth. 'Don't go in, Fan. Look, there's a lighthouse!'

'I'm cold' say I.

He frowns. 'We're getting closer.'

The rock floats away and the lighthouse grows. Tall torch on a long hooked arm coming towards us. Turning. *Cra-a-a*-creaking. The white-grey town spread out. Not like London – busy busy people streets shops carriages parks and trees. Muddy, grey and fish-soupy. Margate. Wide, low and smelling soupy, spreading tumbling over the edges and into the sea.

'Don't cry, Fan.'

Not. Margate will be home now. Papa is here.

'Come on, Fan.' Hand on my hand on the railing, cold and burning. 'Come on.'

Stumbling mumbling swaying people, pointing and waving. Mama's face, blotchy and red. Frowning.

'Why must you always wander off?' She tug-tugs at the knot under her chin, at Joshua's arm. At me. 'Where is your bonnet, child?'

'In the cabin, Mama' say I.

Her hand on my shoulder hard and bony. 'Out above deck without your bonnet. Where did you learn such behaviour?' Open my mouth to say but Joshua shakes his head. Not *really* a question. She pushes me, steering, walks me in front, shove shove through the people and down the cabin steps. 'You deserve an earache.'

Nothing in the cabin. Cases gone, Mary and Lizzy gone. Bonnet gone. Look under the seat – string, puddles, salty footprints.

'Hurry, child.' Mama snaps her fingers. Snap-snap, like Lizzy. 'Where did you put it?'

Point at the seat. Hot nose hot eyes stinging.

'Come along, the others are waiting.' She sighs. 'Silly girl.'

Back above and across to the side, people crowding out and on to a wooden road. Joshua waves. Mama pushes crossly. Lizzy and Mary stand at the side, leaning on the cases.

'Look' says Joshua. 'We have to walk along that platform, right over the sea.'

'It doesn't look safe' says Mama. 'Why do we not stop at the jetty? There is a jetty, is there not?'

'Pardon me, ma'am.' Man in a big grey coat, grey hat lifting, grey-whiskered. 'This is the landing place they use when the tide is too low to dock in the harbour.' He smiles, all white-toothed and whiskery.

'Indeed' says Mama, turning away. 'Well, then I am sure it *is* safe, my dears.'

'Hope not' says Joshua ever-so-quietly.

'You must be frozen, Fanny' says Mary. Holds out *my* bonnet. 'You left this in the cabin.' *See? See, Mama?* She puts it on me, soft-tucks the ribbon under my chin. 'Poor lamb' she says, tying. 'Your ears are quite blue.'

Mama says nothing.

'Let's get across' says Joshua. He scrambles to the steps.

Mama fusses with the cases. A man comes cap-touching, nodding. 'I'll take these for you, ma'am.' A porter. His cap salt-grimy, rusty-crusted brassy buttons. Like a copper pan, too many burned chops stuck to the bottom. His eyes red and seawatery. He picks up the cases like they're full of nothing, piles them up on a trolley. Joshua disappears over the boat side.

'He has run off already' Lizzy whines. She murmurs to Mary. 'Thank goodness *Papa* will be here to control him.'

'Come along' Mama says. 'We cannot keep your father waiting.'

She stands us in line to leave the boat, claw-gripping my shoulder again. Not pushing this time – pulling back. A woman, lace-shawled, shuffle-shuffles in front of me, too wide to balance, her skirts long and wet. Mustn't tread on them, on the wet brown train of them. The ship's captain at the steps, all braids and sashes, nodding, handshaking, *thank you so much sir, see you again madam, goodbye, God speed.* He bows to Mama, nods to Lizzy and Mary. A boy reaches to take the lace woman's hand, steady her on the steps. She pulls back rudely, nearly topples. The boy shrugs, reaches for me. Step up – swing-swaying steps – feel his fingers clutching. Rough fingers, they look, red and cold. Big against my glove. He smiles.

Straight wooden path to land, spread shiny with water. A stony road curls away from us out to sea, safer and wide but cold-looking. Like a London avenue. Our path high, not swaying but like a big wide bridge of tree-trunks and nails and tar. Joshua skips along it, weaves in and out, waving. Runs up to us, right against the railed edge – the lace woman topples again, hands out. Mutters.

Joshua grins. 'Come on.'

The wind whisks, lifts the lace shawl high and away from the muttering woman. She wobbles, grabs at the air – the shawl sails up, hangs like a seagull, sinks spinning down again. Flap – flap – flap, a lacy sail unfurling into the sea. The woman shrieks.

'Wait!' Joshua shouts, runs slip-sliding to the edge and lies down between the rail posts. The shawl spreads, swirls, starts to sink. Joshua reaches finger pointing, pushes and crawls right to the edge, arm stretching.

People stop. Mama murmurs. Lizzy huffs *for shame*!

Joshua crawls back through the posts, dragging the ragged sea-soaked shawl. He stands and waves it at the woman. She shakes her head.

'How am I supposed to carry it like that?' she says, *tut-tutting*.

Joshua wrings it between his hands. It makes a puddle on the wet wood. 'I'm sure it will dry' he says.

The woman shakes her head and walks off.

'Funny business' a man says behind us. 'Could have given the boy a shilling.'

The shawl woman mutters shuffles. *How am I supposed to? How?*

Joshua shrugs, holds up the wet shawl. 'I'm sure it would dry' he says.

Mama snatches at it. 'Making a spectacle of yourself!' she says whisper-hissing. 'Look at your clothes! Soiled all over!

Sliding about on the floor like that.' She shakes his shoulder. 'For an old rag like this?' She drops the shawl on the floor. 'I'm ashamed of you.'

Mama turns us, pushes us forward. Joshua frowns. His lip trembles. He looks back at the shawl, his shoulders all sad and low.

'Honestly!' Lizzy sighs loudly. (*Little heathen* she says too, but very low.)

'It would have dried all right' Joshua says.

Papa is not at the end of the platform. There are horses, carriages, boys with handcarts. A big fine painted coach. A black-bonneted girl standing smiling, smartly black, paper bills white in smart black gloves. She passes me a paper – MISSES BATSFORD, BOARDING AND DAY SCHOOLS – and one to Mama. 'A fine educational establishment' the girl says 'perfect for young ladies, a splendid start for any girl.' Mama nods politely. The paper whips rustles in my glove, tears across and flies away. Only a scrap left: *LISHMENT – a splendid start for any girl.*

Papa is not here. The man standing by the painted coach asks if we are *bound for any place within the isle*. Mama waves him away. The porter wheels our cases to the path and leans, scrape-scratching his head under the rusty-buttoned cap.

Joshua sighs, Mary frets with her gloves, Lizzy shivers noisily. The town is wide. Tall white houses, very fine, but not grand as London.

'What now?' Lizzy moans.

'Look at the arch' says Mary, pointing.

We all look up. The big arch *craa-eek* creaks crakes like a gatepost. Black iron, black lamp-post either side. Gold lettering on a swinging sign, bang-banging mouse-squeaking. JARVIS' LANDING PLACE. Squeaking swinging harder and harder in the wind like it wants to get loose, like a shawl. Like a piece of paper. Whip away and throw itself into the sea.

Mama strides up to a boy with a cart and starts talking. The boy shakes his head and shrugs. The porter whistles, unloads the cases from his trolley. Where is Papa?

'Hello?' says Joshua, elbow-nudging. 'Looks like someone.'

A man jumps down from a coach box and beckons to the porter. He nods at Mama.

'Are you for us?' Joshua says.

'Looking for a Mrs Newlove' says the man. Mama looks up quickly. 'Mrs Newlove, is it? Got to take you to the school meself, Mrs Newlove. And the youngsters.' He nods at us.

'Urgh' says grunting Lizzy.

'Thank you thank you,' Mama says, fussing. She tips the boy, tips the porter, tips the coachman. 'Come along, children' she says, pushing us into the coach. 'Your father will be waiting.'

'He might have come' whispers Joshua.

He might.

Dearest James,

We are arrived at last in Margate. The journey was passed tolerably well although I slept quite a lot on the way. Margate harbour is shaped like a crooked arm and Mary says that this makes it a bay. Next to the sea there is sand which is yellow. We walked along a long platform over the sea called the landing place. Papa sent a coach for us from the harbour and it was very grand to ride through the streets like that. Lots of people stopped to look at us. Do not think I was proud though for I know you would not like to think of me behaving so.

Papa is very busy. The pupils will be coming on Monday next. There will be boys living in the house as boarders as well as day pupils. Mama said that we will sometimes take our supper with them. I wonder if they will all be like Joshua is at table. I hope not for I shall never get anything to eat. Tomorrow we shall look at the new house that is to be Mama's school for girls. I will have lessons there too. If I am very good at lessons Mama may ask me to be a monitor. There is already a school for girls here but Mama and Papa do not seem to mind about that. I know because a lady gave me a handbill for it when we got off the boat. I hope that I will not have to do that for Mama. I do not think Papa would like me to. Of course I shall do whatever they say because they know what is best for me, even if it means giving handbills out to people I have never met before coming off the steamers.

The schoolhouse is quite large and black and grey. Papa said that it was once a farmhouse. There is a farm very near and fields. The house is that colour because it is made out of flint. I have my own room and do not have to share. It is very small but it is all for me. The boys that stay here will all sleep in beds in the attic. There is a housekeeper here and a maid that helps her called Anne. I cannot remember the housekeeper's name but I will be sure to find out so that I can speak politely to her if I need to ask her anything.

The weather is not as wet as it was in London but it is very cold. Mary says that it is the sea breeze. I think it is because it is January. The roads are very muddy and there are frozen puddles at the sides. I promise not to go near them.

I will write again tomorrow. I know that you are busy with all your studies so I will not ask you to promise to write to me soon. But I should like very much to get a letter directed to

your affectionate sister Frances.

I have brought lots of paper with me so that I may write very often.

Doors *bam* bang – different bangs in different places than before. Papa said there will be eight boys upstairs. Eight! (Lizzy said that one is enough for anybody, but I couldn't put that in the letter.) And how shall I like that? Not very.

Nap-nap tapping on the door – not Mama's knocking, nor

Mary nor Lizzy. It opens. The paper flutters, cold whoosh of air over the table. *Icy.*

'Cold, little miss?' The housekeeper. She looks hard at me. 'Brought you some more things.' Lifts her hands up: blankets, rugs. 'Your shawl's wet still. Will be awhile, I'd say.' Sighs, puts the things on the bed. 'The fire'll soon perk up, don't fret.'

'I wasn't' say I.

She looks at me, looks at the fire. 'You're not going to be a sulky little miss, are you now?' Poke-pokes the fire. It hisses, but not red, not warm. Just smoky. 'Because I can't abide a sullen child.'

'I'm not sullen' say I.

'Not sullen, indeed? With that great long face upon you?' The woman in *London* never spoke to me like that.

She sits down on the bed. 'And I don't suppose *you* want to be here either, do you now?'

A bit of wood jumps and spits.

'I know your brother doesn't. But he'll soon settle. There'll be lots of lads soon for him to lark about with.'

It starts to glow at the end, just a little bit. A little hot cinder.

'Still [*sigh sigh creak creak*] you'll find it hard, making friends. With that great long face and no tongue in your head.'

'I have got a tongue.' And I might show it her, soon.

She picks up a blanket, tucks it around me. It smells old. So does she, old and sweet together, like lamp oil, warm wool. 'You'll be all right, Fanny. I'll keep an eye on you.'

'My name is Frances' say I.

'Mine is Ann, but everyone calls me Mrs D.'

'Including Mr D?'

'He doesn't call anyone anything any more, child.'

'Oh.'

'I don't mind it, being called Mrs D. You can call me by that, if it please you.'

'Everyone calls *me* Fanny.'

'And you don't like it.' *NO I DON'T*. She nods. 'Then I shan't call you by it.'

Good.

'How do you do, Mrs D?' say I, ever-so-politely.

She laughs. 'Well enough.' She goes back to the door. 'Better come and get some supper if you want any. They'll be here soon.'

'Who will?'

'The teachers.'

'Why?'

'Why? Well, to meet your mother and say welcome, and to make pigs of themselves on my salt pork and chutneys.'

'Oh.' Salty pigs and pickles.

'Best not say that to your mother.' She taps the side of her nose. Her finger is very long. 'Come down quick, if you want something. You're to go to bed, soon as they get here.'

She pulls at the door, turns to the hall. Someone coming, creak-creaking the floorboards.

Is everything all right? Mama's voice.

'Quite all right, ma'am.'

Mama appears. Mrs D is gone.

'What are you doing, Fanny?' Mama says. 'Do take off that blanket, you look like a pedlar's daughter.' She rat-rattles at the fire with the poker. The little cinder goes black and grey. 'Get ready for bed now. Have you settled in? It's a nice little room, isn't it?'

'Yes, Mama.'

'But rather different from London.'

'Yes, Mama.'

She sits on the bed. 'Where is your brush? Why don't you bring it here?' Soft smiles and pats beside her.

'Will you do it? Really?'

'Yes, yes, if you find it quickly.'

Not on the table, *should* be. Tug out the case from under the chair; petticoats, stockings, wool rough, creased things.

'Fanny, dear, it is well that we are all together here.' *(James is not here.)* 'You will like it in time. We must all try our best to become accustomed to it.' *Handkerchiefs. The linen bag Mary made.* 'There are some people coming tonight, for supper. Your father has invited them, which is very civil of him. You can meet them another time, you know.' *Another petticoat, the patched one.* 'They are teachers. And – and a neighbour, I believe. Or perhaps two neighbours.' *My notebook with the lilac tree on it. The mirror!*

'I've found the mirror, Mama!'

She takes it. Frowns. 'A mirror is no use without a brush.' Holds it out. 'Really, Fanny, you should be more careful with your things. This is cracked.'

Only a *little*. I put it on the table. Another case, behind the door – Sunday shoes, Bible, the blue shawl with the fancy lining.

'Naturally, we will have much to occupy us. We must look over the garden tomorrow, and the new schoolhouse, of course.' *Linen, and my peacock feather, and something hard, smooth – the handle?* 'We must see what rooms there are. And we will need to buy fabric for curtains, perhaps.' *It is! The brush!*

'Here, Mama! I found it!'

'What, dear?'

The brush. 'Here, Mama!'

'Oh. Oh well, not now, dear, it's getting late.'

Door-slam below, noises. Papa's voice.

Mama?

'I'll do it tomorrow, dear. I promise.' She gets up, peck-kisses my head. 'Sleep well, then. Another busy day tomorrow.'

Creak creak she goes, down the hall, down the stairs. Bang bang again, more voices. Put the brush on the table. *There you are, Arabella* says Papa's voice. Said that when we arrived, too. Didn't come to say goodnight. Perhaps he has forgotten us all already, except for Mama. I think he only missed Mama. He did kiss us though, and said *how cold your face is!* and *how tall you've grown!* But I haven't. Joshua has.

Doors don't squeak if you open them fast. Joshua told me that. The handle is slide-slippery with polishing – hold on hard through my handkerchief. It swings open wide and quick and I am in the hall.

So glad you could come says Papa's voice. Murmuring rustling different voices all talking, Mama's laugh high and strange like it is when she meets people I don't know when we are out walking. *Murmur murmur – this way – murmur murmur – so pleased you could make it – really delighted – madam – how kind – please come through.* They are going into the big room. Lizzy will be there, will have been practising how to stand up elegantly and look surprised and sound clever all at the same time. Mary will be going red, from the ears in.

'What are you doing, Fan?'

'Sssh!'

Joshua, all scrub clean and hair-brushed. He tugs at his Sunday waistcoat. 'Are you to come down too?'

'No. Mama said not.'

'Pooh. That's too bad. Still, it'll be boring.' He kicks at the floor. 'I'd go to bed if I were you. Have you had any supper?'

'I want to listen.'

'I'm *starving*. They're all teachers, you know. You'll have to listen to them anyway, in lessons.'

'I won't, *you* will. I'll just have Mama.'

'That's one good thing about being a girl, I suppose.' Arm-swings on the banister top and slide-thumps down the stairs. 'I'd better get in there, I'm late.' Twirl-turns at the bottom. 'Go to bed, Fan' he whispers. 'You'll get cold.'

I *am* cold.

Joshua skips down the hall. He is late – he will be in trouble. He is always late and always in trouble.

Another doorbang – the outside door. Mrs D's voice very muffled, and a man's. Coming closer. Tuck curl chin-on-knees small on the floor, lean up tight against the banister rail.

All right, Mrs D says the voice. *I know the way.*

The voice comes right to the bottom of the stairs. *What is it, boy?* it says. The man that it belongs to comes next, older than Papa and not as tall. His hair is yellow and grey and he has a stick, clip-tapping and swinging. Not a stick like an old man has, but the sort that Lizzy says handsome men should carry, with a shiny top. A something else is with him, moving, scratchy scrabbling. A dog! A grey dog, skinny tail bat-batting at the wall and the man's legs. It snuffles and whines. *Huh-huh-huh* it says, *bang-bang* answers its tail. It looks up and sniffs, and it *sees* me. It comes up the stairs, up trotting, bang-banging the banisters, long mouth open and sagging all wet in the corners.

'Get away!' say I. It comes right up and sticks its long nose

in my skirts and huff-huffs wetly, horribly. 'Urgh! Get away!'
Its back is all arched and bony.

'Don't mind Wellesley' says the man below. 'That's just his
way of making friends. Come on, boy! Good job we don't
all go about it in the same way.' He laughs, walks up the
stairs. 'Although, of course, it would have its benefits.'

Would it? The dog pulls its nose away. My skirt is wet and
horrid from it. I wipe at it with my handkerchief. The man
laughs again. His teeth are very small and there are lots of
them, behind thick yellowy whiskers.

'Well now, don't be shy' he says. His eyes are very blue,
too blue, like they are stones or painted-on eyes. Nobody has
eyes that colour. 'What's your name, eh?'

'Frances' say I.

'How d'ye do, Miss Frances?' He holds the dog by its shiny
collar. 'I'm Easter.' *Easter?* 'As in Good Fridays, Lost
Saturdays and Holy Sundays. Well, and what are you doing
on the stairs? Sent to bed without your supper, eh?'

'Mama says I am not to come down, sir.'

'What? With all this ado going on? And I suppose you
think that a rough piece of justice.'

'*No*, sir –'

'Nonsense. Come on, the pair of you.' The dog licks his
hand and then looks at mine – I put them quick behind me.
'Come on' says the man, tugging the dog down the stairs.
'You're both coming with me.' He stands at the bottom of
the stairs and taps his gloves on the banister rail. 'Well, then.
Don't you want to?'

'Mama says I am not to, sir.'

'And I say you are *(bark bark)* and I'm your father's guest,
so that makes me right.' He sounds cross. 'You'd better come
along, then, hadn't you?'

Ever-so-slowly walk down – one step, two steps. He might change his mind and go away. The dog whines and he lets it go, lets it run off down the corridor. Three steps. *Well, here's the captain's dog* says Papa's voice. Four steps. The man looks hard at me and frowns. He snaps his fingers (*everybody* does that today) – five, six, seven steps.

'Jump the rest or I'll come up and *carry* you down.'

Eightninetelevenetwelvethirteen and back up – fourteen and down – fifteen – and there he stands, grinning. 'That did the trick' he says.

Where's your master, then? says Papa's voice, closer.

'This way' says the man. He holds me by the shoulders and pushes me along the corridor. He leans very low, his mouth whisker-tickling close by my ear. *Huh-huh-huh.* 'Let's surprise them all, eh?' He smells of tobacco. Moral Laxity.

The tall green door. They are all in there, talking, Mama is talking and laughing and the dog tail-thumps scratch-scrapes from inside. Thump-thump *huh-huh-huh* at the open crack, wet nose twitching. The man laughs *ahaw-haw-haw* shoves my back, the door very green and very close and shiny. The dog nose reaches for me. Yellow light inside spills out, bigger and bigger. *Krrrkuk-krrrrrruk-krruk* claws on wood, shoving, snuh-snuffling. He *haw-haw*s again, pulls the handle: wider, wider. The dog jumps up wet and scrap-scratching my skirts and hands licklicklick. Yellow light and faces in it and the dog everywhere wet and smelly like old damp straw and mutton.

'Fanny!' Papa says, *very* sharp.

'What are you doing out of bed?' says Mama.

The faces are all looking. Mama and Papa, and Lizzy, frowning, and Mary holding a tray, and Joshua standing beside her all sulky, and lots of men I don't know sitting and standing and rocking on their heels and staring, staring at me surprised and cross and disappointed. The dog whines and sticks its nose in my skirts again.

'This little hostess wanted to show me the way in' says the man, push-steering me into the room. 'I told her she was too young to be in mixed company but she assured me she was already out.'

Did *not*!

Mama frowns. 'Go back to bed this instant.' She looks away, up to the lying man. Her face goes all soft and nice-Mama-like again when she looks at him.

'Madam' says the lying man. 'Might I have the honour of introducing myself? Captain Jeremiah Easter, Twenty-third Light Dragoons.' He bows grandly.

Papa bows back. 'So glad you could come, Captain.' Waves at Mama. 'My wife, Arabella.'

Mama soft-smiles and holds out her hand. The lying man takes it over my head and kisses it noisily. 'Mrs *New-Love*' he says.

The dog jumps about. 'Sit down, Wellesley!' he says. They all start rustling and murmuring again. Mama sits down. The man makes a growling moaning doggy noise behind me. *Arabella* his voice says. *Hurruhhhmm*.

Lizzy frowns hard at me and her mouth says GO A-WAY but she doesn't say it out loud. Papa's hand thud-claps heavy and hard on my shoulder.

'To bed' he says, *very quiet*. (He is always *really* angry when he is quiet.)

'Oh, I don't know' says the lying man. 'Now we've seen the old girl, I think she could stay for a bit, don't you, Newlove?' His eyes are very blue and very very hard.

Papa lets go of my shoulder. 'You are too forward, Fanny'

he says. 'But if you want her to stay, Captain, I am at your command.'

'Oh, I do' he says. 'I want to become acquainted with all of your delightful family.' He winks at me. It is not a nice wink at all. His eyes are bad, even when there is only one of them open.

'Allow me to introduce you to my daughters, Captain Easter' says Mama. (Just the two of them.)

'With pleasure.' He leans down to pat the dog. His hand reaches over and ow! sharp-pinch nips at me. 'Now we are even' he says, but very low.

Not.

Mama fusses over Lizzy and Mary. Lizzy lets the lying captain's yellowy whiskers tickle the back of her hand. Mary bobs and wobbles shyly. He does not try to kiss *her*.

Joshua tells me to sit with him and pat-pats the dog, smelly tail slap-banging my legs. Papa makes the captain shake hands with everyone. Some of them smile, but some of them don't. One of them just nods – *he* looks quite rich. His hair and whiskers very black and neat.

'Who are they all?' say I.

'Told you' says Joshua. 'Teachers.'

'Yes, but who?'

'I don't know.'

'Didn't you hear their names?'

'Can't remember. But I think one of them was French.'

French?

Mrs D appears, purses her lips at me. Mama does not look at her. Papa goes instead.

'The supper tray's ready, sir' says Mrs D.

'Bring it in directly, please.'

She shakes her head, looks at us. 'Not with that there creature in here.'

'It is the *captain's* dog' says Papa.

'I don't care if it's the King's' says Mrs D.

Papa looks at us and at the captain, admiring Mama's dress. Joshua gets up and holds the dog's little collar. 'Come on, boy' he says. It goes with him through the door, *huh-huh-huh*. The captain does not see.

Mrs D and the girl bring in supper trays. Joshua comes back, *without the dog*, eyes big and hungry.

The men stand around the trays ever-so-carefully balancing plates. Mary and Lizzy cut things up and spoon things out. Mama smiles at them sweetly. Joshua picks up a plate and she smack-slaps his hand behind the table.

One of the men is tall and pointy, sharp-cornered, pointed elbows and knees and nose. He doesn't say anything to anyone. He holds his glass with lovely hands, long and white, beautiful long white fingers. His voice is probably beautiful too, too beautiful to use.

Everyone *else* talks, on and on. *More pickles? Another slice? Do take another glass.* On and on and on. Lizzy long-nosed looks down at her plate, the rich-looking man smiles and smiles at her and picks his teeth with a fork. The lying captain pat-pats Mama's hand. Joshua eats and licks his fingers, passes me a shiny plate with a gold pattern on it and salty pig pieces in the middle.

'Hello' says a man. He sits down, plate wobble-swaying, pickle pieces falling. 'Hope you don't mind my joining you.' Little nose, little chin, skin all creamy and freckle-dotted. He has *white* eyelashes, like there is frost on them.

'I'm not terribly good at this sort of thing' he says.

'Nor am I' say I.

'That's as well' he says and smiles. His white eyelashes flutter-flutter prettily. 'But I really ought to be, you know.'

'I'm Frances' say I.

'Charles Mills' he says. 'Very pleased to make your acquaintance.'

'Thank you' say I. 'Nobody else is.'

He laughs. A black pickled walnut rolls wet and slime-staining across the rug and underneath a chair. 'I gather you were not meant to be here' he says.

'The *captain made* me come.'

'Yes, he's rather a forceful fellow, isn't he?'

Worse. And he is patting Mama again.

'And how are you enjoying it, now that you are here?' Mr Mills points his fork at my plate. 'Don't you like your supper?'

'Not very.'

'Is that both your answers?'

'I don't know who anyone is and no one cares who I am.'

'Well, I care' he says. 'We must all get along, mustn't we?' *Wish my eyelashes were white.* 'May I?' He stabs at the salty pig pieces. 'Well, you know Captain Easter, of course. And now you know me.'

'Are you a teacher?'

'Yes. What do you think I teach?' *Don't know.* 'I shall leave you to guess at it before I have eaten all your pork. There is a challenge for you.' Stabs again, chew-chews quickly. 'Do you see the man with the dark hair and the terribly smart attire?' Points his fork at the rich-looking man, standing next to Lizzy. 'That is Mr Maurice da Costa, a wealthy foreign gentleman and a friend of the captain.' He cannot be very nice then, even if he is rich. 'The man talking to your father, with the handsome waistcoat, is our instructor of geography, Mr Partridge.'

Partridges should be plump but this one isn't. His waistcoat is long and has gold swirls down the edges.

'Has he travelled all over the world?' say I.

'Well, he has travelled Europe a fair bit, I dare say. But our Mr Davidson has been to India.'

'India? Which one is *he*?'

Fingerpoints at a man twitch-sitting by the fire, twirl-twirl-twirling his fork and jolting his knee up and down like Joshua does under the table. 'Mr Davidson teaches writing and Latin, although he knows Hebrew too, I gather. And Mr Ducheson' (the pointy man with the lovely hands) 'is the French master.'

'Oh.' *He* is the French. 'Does he have a beautiful voice?'

Mr Mills laughs, stabs the last pink pork piece. 'Yes, I dare say he does. Ladies like Frenchmen's voices. I'm afraid I don't have such a voice, although I sing tolerably well.'

'He has very nice hands.'

'Indeed?' He looks at his own hands and spreads his fingers. 'And what do I teach?'

'I don't know, sir.'

'Dancing.' His fork silver-flashes waltzes in the air over the empty plate. 'I play the piano, with these not very beautiful hands. I am the music and dancing master.'

'Oh! I like dancing.'

He stands up, bows ever-so-handsomely. 'Perhaps I shall have the honour of your hand soon, Miss Frances. But now I must face the throng again, alas, if I am to have any more of that splendid supper. I seem to have missed out on the pickles.'

He goes to the trays again, spoons and stabs. Everyone talks and talks. The rich man and the waistcoat stand together. Their voices get louder and louder.

'Captain!' says the rich man. 'Mr Partridge here claims that Wellington is finished.'

'What?' The captain drops Mama's hand. 'Damned fool thing to say!' *(Huff huff.)* He turns crossly to the waistcoat. 'Damned fool thing to say, sir.'

Mama *ahuh* coughs politely into her handkerchief.

They are going to quarrel.

MR PARTRIDGE: With all respect, Captain, your duke, fine military man as he was –

CAPTAIN EASTER: *Is*, sir. *Is* yet!

PARTRIDGE: – as he was, he put up a poor defence in the House. He thought reform the enemy of the people, and the people showed him his grave mistake.

THE CAPTAIN: The people be damned!

MR MILLS WITH THE WHITE EYELASHES, HOLDING THE CARVING KNIFE: If you'll forgive me for saying so, sir, the people are – are they not? – what the duke, and yourself, fought for the good of? *(Slice-slices.)*

CAPTAIN: King and Country, sir, King and Country. Never mind the mob. I didn't get my face near blasted off for the sake of your damned rabble.

MR DAVIDSON, WHO HAS BEEN TO INDIA: K-King and country, you say, C-Captain. Alas that they should yet be one in any man's m-mind. M-monarchy is the curse of our nation. *(Tap-taps his plate.)* History has repeatedly d-demonstrated, sir, here and across the water, the d-dangers of promoting Divine Right. Yet we continue f-foolishly on, as though we had never been shown the error of our ways, and, indeed, as though we had n-never tried the civil experiment ourselves.

CAPTAIN, GROWING RED: Talk, talk, talk. Unpatriotic, disloyal reformist wind and foolery. Bah! Talk isn't what made this country what it is today. Action! That's what makes the man. We'll have none of your Whiggish nonsense here.

MR MILLS: How do you find Margate, Mrs Newlove?

MAMA, LOOKING WORRIED: Oh! Oh, I hardly know, Mr Mills. We have not yet looked about.

MR MILLS, GETTING YELLOW MUSTARD ON HIS SLEEVE: There is a very fine stretch of coast hereabouts. Perhaps you might explore it. I'm sure that your children will enjoy the seashore.

MAMA: Yes, perhaps. We have much work to do, however.

CAPTAIN, NOW NOT SO RED BUT NOT VERY PLEASED EITHER: My dear Mrs Newlove! You cannot work all the time. *(Looks for her hand to pat.)* I know this part of the world well enough. Perhaps I might show you some choice parts for walking? *(Finds it, pats it.)*

MAMA: You are very kind, Captain –

MR PARTRIDGE: The cliffs here are not so promising as some of the more rugged English coastlines.

CAPTAIN: *(cross)*: It's a damned fine bit of land for a walk, man! *(Not cross.)* I'm sure that you, dear Mrs Newlove, and your two charming daughters *(yes, two!)* will find plenty to amuse you here. There is good rock and shell picking for the lad, too. *(To Joshua)* Fancy that, my boy?

PAPA: I trust that my family will take many healthful walks, Captain. Of course, the children will be inspired by the seashore and learn much from its diversity through their lessons in botany, et cetera.

MAMA, HER HANDS GRASPED FIRMLY BY THE CAPTAIN: To breathe sea air and to gather seashells, a perfectly innocent and pleasurable recreation for the children. *(Sweet and smiling Mama-like.)* After all, Captain, are shells not simple and elegant, like flowers? The very essence of natural beauty. It is only right that we should admire them.

MR DAVIDSON, WHO CAN SPEAK HEBREW: Shells are the h-husks of dead creatures.

CAPTAIN: I say –

MR DAVIDSON: Indeed, they m-may be b-beguilingly beautiful to the feminine eye. Yet certain of the Jews, who make a study of the hidden worlds as well as this more tangible one, w-warn against what they call the 'realm of shells'.

PAPA: My dear Davidson –

MR DAVIDSON: K-Kelipot, they call it – that is, the realm of shells – the h-hellish hidden world of the demonic that exists about us, yet cannot be seen. It is a recondite matter of g-great significance amongst J-Jewish –

PAPA (*dangerously quiet*): We are all *Christians* here, Mr Davidson.

MR DAVIDSON: It is everywhere, this d-demonic realm, all about us. Even here in M-Margate.

JOSHUA, HIS EYES EVEN BIGGER THAN WHEN HE SAW THE SUPPER TRAYS: Everywhere?

PAPA (*very very quietly*): Joshua, Fanny, what are you still doing here? You should be in bed. (*Almost a whisper*) Now.

Dearest James,

Today is our first full day in Margate. It is very cold this
morning but I am being sensible and wearing my warm shawl
while I sit up to write. It is early in the morning and still quite
dark outside. When I woke up I had forgotten where I was and was
surprised to hear cows outside and a cockerel crowing. I was a little
frightened in the night but I am quite all right now. I know that
you would tell me not to be silly and to be a brave girl. I am quite
happy really and we are all together. I would say that I wish that
you could be here too but that would be very wrong and selfish of
me, so I shall not say it.

I hope that you will tell me if I write foolish things or if I spell
badly. I try very hard to get things right and to have an elegant
hand. You know how Papa is always telling me how important that
is.

Last evening Papa and Mama gave a supper party. The teachers
from Papa's school came to welcome Mama. Mama and Papa allowed
me to stay up for a little while. The teachers are all very clever and

one of them has even been to India, which is on the other side of the world. The dancing and music master is called Mr Mills and he was very kind and came to talk to me. Some neighbours came too. I did not stay up very long because it was so late. It was a very pleasant evening.

Today we will look over the new schoolhouse. I will tell you all about it afterwards.

I have learned the housekeeper's name, she is called Mrs D. Even Papa calls her that so I am sure that it is quite all right for me to do so.

Write more later. There isn't much I *can* say.

Nap-nap tapping – Mrs D. Doesn't even open the door. *Come on, my girl* her voice says, hollow hall wood-muffled. *Your father wants you.*

Papa is waiting. Papa does not like to wait. Open the door quick and no-creakingly and Mrs D waves shoos at the stairs. On her head a white cap like a frilly handkerchief. Like it fell out of the sky and landed there.

Insides emptily aching. *Good.* Oats and milk and bread and ham and eggs drip-meltingly buttered, and maybe smelly bony kippers even.

'Is breakfast ready then?' say I.

'Breakfast? Bless you, child! They had breakfast an age ago.' She tap-taps on Joshua's door too. 'Go on with you then' she says.

The shiny green door is open. The fire smoke hisses. No Papa. The pickled-walnut stains are gone. The chair is heavy and twist-twists its legs into the rug but does not move. I lie flat, wriggle close and eye right up to the crack and *there it is*! Perhaps it will stay there for ever, little pickled-walnut pebble all hairy and covered with moss.

Where is everyone?

Fanny! Papa's voice.

Jump up quick. He is big and dark in the doorway, frowning.

'Good morning, Papa' say I, ever-so-carefully.

'Fanny. I am not at all pleased with you.' He does not say it quietly. *That is good.* 'You behaved very badly last evening' he says. He comes to the chair and straightens it. The rug lets it go.

'I am sorry, Papa' say I. 'The captain –'

'Do not answer back.' His shoes are shiny, little bright window shapes on the black toe pieces. 'I will not tolerate it.' *Sighs.* 'However, I understand that things may be a little strange for you at present and I am willing to overlook the matter. In this instance – and only this.' Fingers flutter-stroke the chairback. His eyes wrinkle-crease in the corners. 'You did not come down for breakfast. You will not linger in future.'

'Yes, Papa.'

'Doubtless the late hour of your appearance last evening is to blame. You were abed late, and over-excited by your bold and unseemly behaviour. You will not remain up so late in future. It breeds idleness.'

'I *was* awake early, Papa. I was writing a letter. To James.' *TRUE.* 'And I am very sorry, Papa, but I did not know where breakfast *was*, Papa.'

His lips twitch like he wants to smile but mustn't. 'You must not be so wilful, Fanny. You must promise to be a good girl.'

'Yes, Papa.' *Am.*

'You are to assist your mother today, along with your sisters. Until you begin regular lessons you are to remain available to your mother at all times. You are not to run off or hide yourself away. The housekeeper may also find tasks for you. You are to make yourself useful. There is no call for idleness. Do you understand me, Fanny?'

'Yes, Papa' say I.

'Good. That is all.'

'Papa? Is Joshua not going to help too?'

'Joshua is a pupil of Dane House Academy now. He will assist me. Lessons will recommence on Monday.' Frowns again. 'Joshua must also strive to be useful.'

Papa pulls at his waistcoat. Nods. Goes away.

The fire crackles. At least *this* room is warm.

Mrs D comes in, silly frilly on her head. 'There you are, child' she huffs. 'And did you find your father?'

'Yes, thank you. Might I have some breakfast now?'

'Children! Stomachs on legs.'

'*I* didn't have any supper' say I.

'That's your *own* fault. Come on then. I've cleared the table but you can have a bite in the kitchen.'

Mrs D walks ahead, big feet broad brown shoes scuffle-shuffling. Along the hall and into a little corridor. Wooden steps going down to a wide white door. 'Mind the steps' she says. Onetwothree-down. She opens the door.

Noisy and busy, black stove wooden table copper pots swinging. Cross-looking aproned woman, big arms hairy with rolled-up sleeves all smudge-smeary. Girl with pink face, big knife, nose like a pig snout. Pig butcher.

'Sit here, my girl' says Mrs D. Scrape-drags a chair on the floor, big squealing square tiles red like bricks. Stops by the stove.

'Huh!' huffs the apron woman. 'She can't sit in ere. I've

34

the dinner to do.' The big hands slam-bang a basin on the table.

'Come on, woman' says Mrs D. 'The child is hungry. Let her warm up a minute.'

'Should have got up for breakfast' says the apron. 'We've been awork for hours.'

'It's her first day' says Mrs D. 'Where's that loaf?'

'She's not gentry' says the apron. She pulls something out of the basin, something feathery, slams it on the table, hard mouth chew-chewing.

The pig girl watches me, ugly fat nose, fat piggy eyes. I hold on to the door.

Mrs D tut-tuts, opens cupboards, unwraps a loaf of bread. The apron woman stares at her, leans on the table. 'Give me a knife then' says Mrs D. The pig girl does.

'You can get on with your work!' shouts the apron.

My ears hot and tingling. They stare and stare at me. The pig girl opens the stove and pokes inside, clatter clatter, turns and stare-stares again.

Mrs D shakes her head. She puts something on a plate and comes to the door. 'Come on' she says. Turns me round, walks me out. Onetwothree-up.

Well, the devil! says the apron woman's voice.

Mrs D opens another white door. 'Take no notice' she says. 'Now, this is my room.'

Desk, bed, chairs, dresser and a little window, a fire. She puts a chair in front of the fire and throws on a piece of wood. Picks up china pot and spoon from the dresser – jam! *Jam!* Thick and dark and purple. 'Here, I made this' she says. 'It's better than the cook's old slop. Never you mind them in the kitchen. When you need anything, you come and find me.'

'Thank you, Mrs D' say I.

Mrs D spoons jam black-purple and shiny on to the plate. *Blackberry*. 'They're just jealous is all' she says, ever-so-quiet. *Why?*

Going to the new schoolhouse

Lizzy has her *good* shawl on, even though we are to work today. Flick-flicks the tassels.

Mama walks very quickly. 'Come along' she says, over her shoulder. 'It is just ahead.'

Papa said that Mama's new schoolhouse is adjacent to his. A-D-J-A-C-E-N-T, adjacent. It is only a little way along the road where the carts go. Mary points out holes. Lizzy grumbles.

'I cannot believe the state of this place' she says. *Moan moan.*

'It is only due to last night's storm' says Mary. 'It is not so very bad today.'

'Was there a storm?' say I.

'Yes' says Lizzy 'and an infernal racket it made too. Not that you'd know, all tucked up in your own cosy little room.'

'It is not *so* very cosy' say I.

'Well, don't get used to it' says Lizzy. 'It won't be yours for long.'

'What do you mean?' say I.

Lizzy shudders. 'I am quite frozen through.' *(Mutter mutter.)* 'I shall die of the ague.'

'What do you mean, Lizzy? About my room?'

'Not that anyone here will mourn me' she says. Moan moan moan. 'And I shall die a spinster for there isn't a man to be seen in Margate.'

'There were several at supper' mild-mannered Mary murmurs.

'Uh!' says Lizzy. 'What absolute bores. And not a single one of them worth looking at.'

'One of what?' say I. 'And what *about* my room?'

'Men' says Lizzy. 'Not a decent one among them.'

'Mr Mills was nice' say I.

'Pooh! That puddle of a man?' *(Scoff scoff.)* 'And he was positively ugly. Did you see his chin? I declare he scarcely had one.'

'He was nice' say I.

'*Nice*' says Lizzy, nasty pretend little-girl voice. '*He was nice*. I don't want nice, I want – *dashing*. You can keep nice. In fact, you can keep Mr Mills for yourself. He would suit you – *nicely*.'

'Lizzy dear' says Mary 'do not tease poor Fanny so.'

'Oh, I do not tease' says Lizzy 'I am quite in earnest. I am sure that Mr Mills would wait for you, Fanny. I shall ask Papa if he might arrange the match. I doubt anyone else will come along in the next ten years to steal him away from you.'

I hate her.

'Oh!' says Mama. She stops, turns. 'Here comes our neighbour, girls. Be polite, now.'

A man swing-swinging a stick. A dog too. *The lying captain.*

'Good morning, Mrs Newlove!' He comes whisker-curling smile-smiling, stick swinging, dog *huh-huh-huh*ing. 'Good morning, young ladies! What an auspicious coincidence.'

He bows. We bob-bob skirts minding puddles. He takes Mama's hand and kisses it – *again*. 'On my way to pay you my compliments. Fine supper yesterday evening.'

Mama soft-smiles back. 'You are very kind, Captain. I am afraid you caught us rather unprepared for guests. We are not yet settled in, of course.'

'Well, I shall come back another time then. When you're settled, eh?'

'Oh, yes' says Mama. 'Whenever you wish.'

'Splendid!' He lets go of Mama's hand. The dog snuffle-huffs at my boots. 'So, where're you off to? Come to look at my estate? You're a curious lot!'

'We are going to the new schoolhouse, sir' says Mary.

'Not seen it yet? Well, I'll come with you then.'

He holds his arm out and Mama puts her glove ever-so-slightly on it. They walk off. The dog trots behind sniff-nosing at the road.

'I'd rather see his estate than a dreary schoolhouse' says Lizzy, *very* quietly.

'He is our neighbour' Mary whispers 'so he's bound to ask us to visit some time.'

'At least we'll have some society then' says Lizzy. 'Even if he is a wheezing old soldier. But then, perhaps some *young and dashing* soldiers might come to visit him too!'

'That's *very* likely!'

They *tee-hee* at their gloves.

The house is tall, wide, grey-red brick and white and big-windowed. Gate, walls, muddy garden, twiggy trees, path, moss curling, up-growing ivy. The dog runs to the gate and lifts its leg.

'Wellesley!'

The captain pushes the dog away and opens the gate. Mama

nods, glovefinger at nose. Steps one-two-three-up on to the path. Mama walks up and rattle-knocks the doorknocker.

Papa's maid opens, white cheeks white cap white pinafore wide surprised look.

'Ah, Anne, isn't it?' says Mama. 'We've come to see the rooms. Captain Easter has kindly escorted us.'

Anne bob-bobs, round face sly-eyeing the captain.

'Well then, let's take a look, shall we?' the captain says, and stick-swing pushes into the house.

Narrow hall tall and wooden, doors and doors. Mama opens each one into rooms. 'Which is the largest room downstairs, Anne?'

'This un, mam.'

Big yellow room with long white windows, white iced ceiling, fireplace. Nothing else. Not even a *chair*.

'This is very pleasant' says Mama.

It is very empty and very very cold.

'Fine solid floorboards' says the captain, thud-thud foot stamping. 'Good place for a dance.' He winks at Mama. 'For a waltz.' The dog trots in and sniffs at the corners.

Mama *ahems* politely.

'I say' the captain says to Anne, 'take old Wellesley here into the back garden would you? There's a girl.'

She pulls the dog off by his collar, *huh-huh-huh-huh-huh*.

'This would make an excellent music room' says Mama. She pat-pats the curtains, yellowy white and poached-egg fluffy. 'A very fine space for music. What do you say, girls?'

'Yes, Mama' say we.

The next room small and green as a pea, green paper green chairs green and gold curtains. Fireplace *should* be green but isn't, stove black and shiny.

'A modest little room' Mama says.

'Very cosy' says the captain.

Along the hall, two doors side by side meeting in the middle. Captain tugs, doors squeak-*eek*-creak and shudder open. 'Get a spot of oil on that' he says.

'Ah!' says Mama. 'A perfect schoolroom.'

Long room of nothing, nothing coloured. Empty fire grate. Two little windows smeary green.

'Pardun me mam' (Anne at the door bob-bobbing) 'Mister Nulove askd fer buth the large rums t be cleered mam, so as you cud chuse tween um.'

'Thank you, Anne' says Mama. 'No furniture just yet. I would like the windows *cleaned*, however. As soon as possible.'

'Yes mam. A corse mam.'

'Where is the kitchen?'

Anne turns, scuffle-scuttles. Around a corner, big closed closets, through a door and there the red and white kitchen small and scrub-shiny. She stands in it shyly, hands in knots in her pinafore.

Mama nods her pleased nod. 'Is everything in order?' she says.

'S pots and pans aplenty mam an the stove works a vast heat but the kettle s cracked mam an we cud use a better.'

'Very well' says Mama. 'See that you get what you need from the housekeeper. What about linens?'

On on on. *Plates, cups, yes mam no mam*. Lizzy shuffles. The captain smiles yellow-whiskered smiles showing white and yellow teeth. On and on. Mama says *upstairs now!* and we all go (cupboards, hall) and the stairs, brassy woody and (one-two) up-sloping, square and tall (seven-eight) square landing square window tall skeleton tree (eleven-twelve) up-up brassy banister top (seventeen-eighteen) and out into wide wood-shiny hall.

'Splendid!' says the captain at nothing in particular.

Mama opens more doors: little white room, bigger blue one. More and more, and steps up. 'The attic room' says Mama. 'I will take a look, but there is no need to follow.' She goes up, swish-swishing. The captain watches. 'The maid sleeps up here' Mama says, not turning.

'I shall have the blue room' says Lizzy.

'Are you going to live here then?' say I.

Lizzy huffs. 'We all are, silly.'

Why?

Mary handsnatches at me and spin-spins us round and round, laughing and bonnet-bobbing.

Lizzy sighs. '*Do* stop!' she says. *Groan groan.*

We stop and the room stops. Lizzy nods to the captain, who is not looking at us but up the attic stairs instead. Mary shrugs.

'Why are we living here?' say I.

'Because' says breathing panting Mary 'we cannot stay at the boys' school.'

'Why not?'

'Because it wouldn't be right.'

'Why?'

'Well, because there will be boarders. And because boys are noisy.'

'I don't mind' say I.

'I do' says Lizzy 'and anyway there isn't enough room.'

'But we've all got rooms there' say I. *TRUE.*

'Papa is going to need those rooms' says Mary. 'We are going to sleep here.'

'What about Joshua?'

'Joshua will stay with the boys' says Mary.

'Thank *goodness*' says Lizzy.

'What about Mama and Papa then?' say I.

'They will sleep in the boys' school too, dearest' says Mary 'because they need to be there for the boarders.'

Not fair. NOT.

Hot ears hot eyes. The captain *fhuwww-fhuwww* whistles and tap-taps his stick on the stairs.

'I thought we were all going to be together' say I.

'Well, we are, dearest' says Mary.

'No, we aren't' say I. 'It's even worse than before.'

'Look, Fanny' cross Lizzy finger-stabbing 'you can't have everything your own way all of the time. None of us likes it, you know. You'll just have to put up with it.'

NOT fair. And I DON'T, not *ever*.

Mary's lips go tight together. 'There now' she says 'you shall have a nice room here and we shall look after you.' Tucks hair into my bonnet. 'Poor lamb.'

Mama comes swish-swish down the stairs, looks at me. 'What is going on here?'

'Nothing, Mama' says Mary.

'Fanny was complaining about her room' says Lizzy.

Wasn't.

'That is not a very good beginning, Fanny' says Mama. 'I hope you are not going to be difficult and selfish.'

'Child needs to get settled in' says the captain. 'Which room is hers?'

They all look at me.

'Mama' says Lizzy 'as I am the eldest I shall need the larger room. The *blue* one.'

'Yes, Lizzy dear, of course.' Mama looks at me but is not looking really. 'You can share with Mary, dear. Fanny can have the white room.'

Lizzy's mouth goes long and horrid. *Share?* it says but not out loud.

Mary smiles. 'There, Fanny' she says patting my bonnet 'we shall all be just as we were before.'

'Excellent!' says the captain. He holds Mama's hand again and kisses it. 'Do excuse me for one moment, Mrs Newlove. I must see what that old scoundrel Wellesley is up to.' Goes stick-tapping down the stairs. 'I shall await you in the garden, ladies' he says, bowing turning at the landing.

'Now, girls' says Mama 'as your rooms are decided upon, I think you should have another look into them and see what you might need. There is some furniture stored which you may choose from, and we shall get the man Woods to arrange bringing up the beds.' She crosses the hall, opens a door. 'I will have another look at this rather promising parlour.' *(Sighs.)* 'I fear we shall be forced to change the paper.'

'Well' says hissing Lizzy 'I hope *you*'re satisfied, Fanny.'

Not. 'I'd rather stay in the other house' say I.

'Spoiled little brat' Lizzy hiss-spits. 'Come on, Mary, let's go and look at *our* room.'

Nasty Lizzy leads off Mary tug-tugging her arm. Slam shuts the door.

Wish we were home again. Wish James was here. Wish we were in London, even without Papa. Wish Lizzy would go away and get married.

Skeleton tree *sssssscrap*-taps bony fingers at the landing window. Creak creak creak say the floorboards. The dog yap-barks outside, Lizzy's voice grumble-grumbles, Mama moves creaking, Mary murmur-murmurs. Open the door to the white room, *my* room now. Wish it wasn't. Little, littler than in the other house. White paper pink stripes white ceiling huge spiderweb huge long-needle-legged grey spider hanging in it. White window white curtains moving, icy wind blowing

44

through the cracks. Muddy garden through it, broken fence muddy field little skinny trees without leaves. Muddy-looking clouds moving quickly. The captain stick-tapping the ground. Poke poke. Poke poke. Like he's looking for potatoes. Mama will want to grow potatoes now, *too costly to buy* she says but she likes them. Squashed potatoes and dripping. Could have peas too and they grow on poles. Could keep chickens even. Poke poke goes the captain's stick, he bends over poke poke pokes again. The dog comes up tail bang-banging the captain's legs, nose at the ground. Scrabble-paws at the captain's feet. The captain looks up at the house. Doesn't see me. The dog digs, earth flying hitting the captain's legs. He doesn't move away just watches the dog and the earth dig-dig-dig.

Fanny says Mama's voice.

She is in the doorway. 'I trust you are content with your room' she says, not-very-nicely.

'Yes, Mama' say I, not-very-truthfully.

'Good. There is plenty of light and room enough for your bed and a small desk. Of course, you may keep your workbasket in the parlour.'

'Yes, Mama.'

'I will see that the beds are brought over soon. Let us go out to the back garden. Come along.'

Down the stairs (three-four) Mama leading, Lizzy chattering *new lining for curtains* (eight-nine) *I may make over a room upstairs as a study* Mama says, *what do you think, girls* (twelve-thirteen-fourteen). Lizzy and Mary say, *yes, Mama*, bonnets bobbing (seventeen-eighteen). Hall, back door, little path through the muddy grass and there is the captain and the dog digging.

'Here we are, Captain' says Mama.

45

He stands up ever-so-quickly, bows, tug-tugs at the dog's collar. 'Wellesley got a scent' he says. 'How d'you like the place then?'

'Very well, thank you, sir' says Mary.

Owwww-wowwww, the dog whines. It tugs and tugs to get free.

'What about you, missy?' he says, whiskery-grinning at me. 'Like your room did you?'

'Yes, sir' say I (but *he knows*).

Owwwww whines the dog.

'Forgive old Wellesley' says the captain. Pushes the doggy earth with his foot, stamp-thuds it down again. 'Got a sniff of a rabbit, I dare say.'

Rabbits make holes, not dogs. Only dog holes here.

Mama and the captain chatter chatter. They do not look at us any more. Wonder what is Joshua doing? Mama talks about the rooms, on and on. The captain bows and smiles. The dog *waaa*-whines and pulls and tugs.

'Yes' says Mama, 'it is very promising. I have great plans for it, Captain.'

'Good space for flowers and such' he says. 'Got quite a plot myself, ornamentals, kitchen garden, avenues. Put a fountain in a while back, most refreshing in the Summer. Come and see it, Mrs Newlove, come and see it.'

'I should be delighted' says Mama sweetly. 'Perhaps in the Summer, then.'

'Summer be damned, Mrs Newlove!' says the captain not-very-sweetly. 'I'll have you there before the week's out. Summer's months off. Can't wait for Summer you know.'

Lizzy smiles and elbow-nudges Mary.

'Well' says Mama, *ahemming* waving at the garden, 'we have a good deal of space for vegetables and pot-herbs, as you see. Mr Newlove will have use of much of the field, of course, for the boys. We must see that the fence is mended.'

'Field?'

'Oh yes, Captain Easter. My husband is leasing the whole plot, including the field.'

'Leasing it, is he? Well well.' He *thwack*-whips his stick against his boots.

'The boys need a little field to run about in, Captain. Mr Newlove says that they become restless and distracted without fresh air and play. Of course there will still be ample room for us to have an extended garden. I wonder if we couldn't have a little duckpond somewhere, at the bottom of the garden perhaps.'

'Fine notion' says the captain 'keep the slugs down.'

Duckpond? If we can have ducks we could have chickens too.

'Might we not keep chickens, Mama?' say I.

Everyone looks at me.

'Chickens?' says the captain. 'That would keep you busy, keeping the foxes off.' Turns to Mama. 'No, Mrs Newlove, I wouldn't bother with chickens here. They'd all be taken. Plenty of eggs to be had at the farm you know.'

Mama nods.

'But what about the ducks?' say I. 'Would foxes not come for ducks too?'

'Fanny!' says Mama.

'Ducks fly off' says the captain. 'Chickens aren't so nimble. Old Reynard would get 'em straight off.'

Chickens have wings too.

Lizzy shakes her head, Mama looks away frowning.

We will not have chickens, then, because *he* says so. He doesn't want me to have *anything*.

They talk again, on on on not looking at me because I am not here really. Wish I *wasn't*. Lizzy does it too, the not-looking. *Mary* looks at me, smiles. DO-NOT-SULK-FANN-Y her lips say. The dog scratches again and the captain pulls it away. Everyone goes over to the broken fence. They murmur and point, murmur and nod. *Old Stroud fine gardener – really, Captain? – got a son – could be useful – hardworking lad – put in some hedging.* On and on. The patch where the dog was digging is not so muddy now, white bits in it like broken white stones sharp-cornered. Like the cliffs from the steamboat when we came from sea. Pick a bit up, sharp wet and white, and white powder comes off in my hand, crumbly. The dog looks and *wowww* whines at me.

'Get away from there!' says the captain, *very sharp*.

They are all looking at me again.

'What *are* you doing, Fanny?' says Mama.

'Nothing, Mama' say I. Tuck the white powdery stone in my pocket.

'Get herself muddy playing about there' says the captain crossly.

What does it matter to *him*?

'Come away, Fanny' says Mama. 'Come and stand here.'

I do. The captain looks at me. His eyes are very hard and blue again.

'Want to keep away from those rabbit holes' he says. 'Don't want to go falling in, do we?'

'Are there hares too, Captain Easter?' says Mary, in her *ever-so-interested* voice.

'Hares? Why, yes, hares, rabbits, all good for eating. I'm still a fair shot you know, got plenty of practice in the wars, know how to get 'em without peppering 'em. Old Wellesley and I go off and bag a few now and then. Don't we, old chap?'

Everyone looks at the dog. It looks at me, pink tongue loll-lolling black shiny eyes bulging.

'Get some fine birds too' says the captain, 'a few phea-sants wandering this way, quite all right with the estate if I shoot 'em, plenty of partridge and pigeon of course. If you care for pheasant I can send you down a brace, Mrs Newlove.'

'Oh, that's very kind, Captain' says Mama 'but really –'

'No trouble, no trouble at all.' He looks at me, tap-taps his stick on earth and boot. 'Well, dear ladies' he says 'it is cold for idling. Allow me to escort you to Chateau Bellevue for some refreshment.'

'Oh!' says Lizzy, *very* pleased. '*Chateau* Bellevue?'

'That is very gracious of you, Captain' says Mama 'but I am afraid we must refuse you. We have so much work to do today.'

They talk and disagree but they are not quarrelling, not really. Ever-so-polite. *I insist – no really, Captain, you are too kind – I must insist.* Lizzy too please please please me me I want. *Sunday then – chapel – oh, Mama – afterwards – Sunday school – must insist – please may I?* He takes Mama's hand and she takes it back and says *let us get back to your father, my dears.* We all bob and bow and walk back to the front of the house, down the path, into the road.

'On Saturday then, Captain Easter' says Mama.

'I will think of nothing else until then, dear Mrs Newlove.' Bows grandly. Mama *a-hahahmm* laughs but I do not believe she really thinks him funny.

The dog huff-huffs pull-tugs and up-jumps at me – paws thudding claws muddy smelly wet nose hot *huh-huh* breath.

'Get down!' says the captain.

It does. My pinafore all mud-smeary and white powdery. Mama frowns.

'Really, Fanny' she says. *Sighs*.

Not my fault. *Not*.

Back along the road holey muddy water-trickly like a little stream along the middle. Papa's house seems bigger grander now, wider staircase wider hall bigger rooms. I go up-skipping thirteen steps (downfourteen-upfifteen) so it is not so tall as Mama's staircase but the banisters are brassy and shiny. No Joshua. Not in his room, not in mine (which is not really mine any more anyway), not in the front garden when we came in, not in the back garden from the windows. Down the stairs again but he is not in the schoolrooms or the hall. Papa strides about very quiet very quick, does not look at me. I go up again, change my pinafore. I will have to wash it out now. Mama is *not pleased*.

Lizzy, Mary, Fanny! Mama's voice calls up the stairs. *Come into the parlour this instant.*

Grey pinafore, not so nice as white but Mama says I am to wear one for we shall get dusty. Cleaned my boots on the scraper but clumps muddy and white fall off still on the floor-boards. Lumps on the stairs too. Tiptoe boot-toe, round the rugs along the hall through the green door into the parlour.

Mama sits hands in lap, Papa stands by the fire, hands behind him, up-down-up-downing rocking on his toes.

'Ah, Frances' he says.

'Papa?'

'Sit down, Fanny' says Mama 'and oh! goodness, child! mind your boots!' Points at the rug. *Deep sighs*. 'Really, Fanny, you are a dirty creature! You will clean those boots the moment your father has finished with you. Walking about the house with dirty boots on. What is wrong with you, child?'

Another Mama not-question. Lizzy's voice in the hall, *tea – Saturday – very smart*, and she comes in pleased-looking with pink cheeks. Mary comes in after.

'Good morning, Papa' says Mary bobbing. Lizzy bobs too.

'Sit down, girls' says Papa. 'Fanny, where is your brother?'

'I do not know, Papa' say I.

'Come along' says Mama 'don't be difficult. Is he in his room?'

Am not difficult. 'He was not there when I looked' say I.

Papa sighs. 'We will begin without him then' he says, *quietly*. 'As you know, girls, pupils will be arriving for the commencement of school on Monday. There will be boarders here. Some may arrive on Sunday evening. I need not apprise you of the reasons why you may not remain under the same roof as these boys. Suffice it to say that you will now be living for the main part in the new schoolhouse, your dear mother's establishment. You have been allocated rooms there, is that not so?'

'Yes, Papa' say we.

'You will sleep, school and take your daily meals there. At the end of school hours you will fulfil any tasks required of you by your mother or by the housekeeper. You may then visit here and spend your evenings in a useful and sociable manner with us. Is that fully understood?'

'Yes, Papa' say we.

'As the eldest Arabella-Elizabeth will be responsible for the new schoolhouse during your mother's absence.' Lizzy smiles a horrid pinched fish-face smile. 'Lizzy, you will assist your mother in managing the household, seeing to the maid and any trade enquiries that take place during lessons. It will be a manner of schooling for when you must run your own household, in the future. You will also assist with lessons when required.'

'Yes, Papa' says Lizzy, very important and grown-uply. 'I will do my best, sir.'

'You will do very well I'm sure, Lizzy dear' says Mama.

Papa nods. 'During all school hours you will refer to your mother as Mrs Newlove, and to myself as Mr Newlove. You may of course continue to call me *sir*. You will show the same level of respect and deference as other pupils. We expect you to lead the way.'

Bang – the front door. Scraping wiping of boots clatter *thump-thump-thump-thump* of running and bang-banging up the stairs. Papa frowns, fist clenching, sweeps out of the room.

Joshua Newlove! his voice says, hissing and very cross. *Come here.*

Slow soft-stepping back down the stairs, Joshua sniff-sniffing. *Yes, sir?*

Where have you been? Papa's voice says. *Come in here and explain yourself.*

Joshua comes in with Papa pushing shoving, dirty-kneed dirty-elbowed and scowling. Mama throws her hands into the air. 'Look at you now!' she says. 'You look like a crow-boy. Honestly! Cannot you or Fanny pass a morning without becoming filthy?'

'Sorry, Mama' says Joshua.

'Dirty slovenly boys are a slight to Christian eyes' says Papa. 'What were you doing to get so dirty?'

Joshua looks at me, looks at the floor, looks at his dirty hands. 'I was helping Woods, sir.'

'Doing what?'

'Um, chopping wood, sir.'

'Chopping wood?' says Papa in his *milksop and moon-shine* voice. 'And that required you to roll about on the bare earth, did it?'

'No, sir.'

'And did you chop much wood?'

'Quite a lot, sir.' Joshua swallows. *Liar.*

'I hope you will continue to be so industrious in future' says Papa. 'We will look at your marvel of a woodpile together shortly. Perhaps we can get some more logs for you to chop. You can finish them before dinner, as you are so good at it.'

Joshua hangs his head.

'Your father was instructing your sisters' says Mama. 'You have missed much.'

'I will summarise for you, Joshua' says Papa. 'How does one spell the word summarise?'

Joshua is very white. 'S-U-M-A-R, um, R-I-S-E' he says. *Wrong.*

'That is incorrect' says Papa. 'S-U-M-M-A-R-I-S-E. You will write it into your copybook this evening and bring it to me. I expect to find much work there from your past months of study.'

Joshua nods sulkily.

Mama tells Joshua about our rooms. He stands there looking at the floor in front of him, not-listening. Where has he been? *Not* chopping wood. He is such a very poor liar he really ought to give it up.

'So when you have finished with the wood chopping, Joshua' says Papa 'you may empty your room of belongings. I require the space for a study. Your bed will be taken directly to the attic, with the other boys' beds. I will hold you personally responsible for the cleanliness and order of the dormitory – and for the boys' good behaviour.'

Joshua's mouth falls open. *Dormitory* it says, not speaking.

'Your beds will be moved this afternoon, girls' says Papa. 'You may as well get used to your new home straight away.'

He nods. 'Well, dispose of yourselves usefully until dinner. You will attend promptly in the dining room at one o'clock. We will keep school hours from now on.'

'Well then, girls' says Mama. 'Run along now, tidy your things. We've much to do this afternoon. And, Fanny! See the housekeeper about your boots and pinafore.'

We all stand, bob and say *yes, Mama* and go to the door. Joshua turns to follow me.

'*Not* you, Joshua' says Papa, very quietly.

Look for Mrs D's room in the corridor. Not the white door down the steps (*kitchen*, don't go there) not the one with the latch on the outside (shelves, sheets, cloths) not the one with the lock (won't open) not the one with the handle half-way up the wall like a stable door (hooks, lamps, greasy oil smelling). Stand in front of the last one and *taptap* quiet as I can.

Come in says Mrs D's voice. Good.

She is by the window, sitting. Big book on the desk, spectacles on her nose.

'What can I do for you, Miss Frances?' she says.

'Mama says I am to clean my boots and wash out my pinafore' say I.

'Come closer.' I do. 'Well' she says 'your boots are caked right enough but your pinny looks fine to me.'

'Not this, the white one. Upstairs.'

'Go fetch it then, and I'll show you where the things are kept. And put on some clean house shoes while you're there.'

Hall, stairs, room, shoes, hook, white pinafore – not to say pinny Mama doesn't like it – and back down quick and quiet and hard breathing. Mrs D still by the window, door open where I left it and I go in.

'My, that was quick' she says.

'I didn't run' say I.

'I should hope not!' *He-haw* donkey laughs. 'Let's see this pinny then.'

Hold it up all dirty doggy muddy and white. 'Mama says I am to wash it out.'

'I would say so too. Come on then.' Takes off her spectacles, rub-rubs red rings on her nose.

'What were you doing?' say I.

'The accounts. They can wait. Take those boots off then, put your shoes on.'

I do, wobble-standing and unlacing. She bang-closes her big book and stands up. Put on the shoes black and shiny, soft-soft and like not wearing shoes, dry and cool inside on my stockings. Mrs D goes out. Follow her with boots and pinafore along the corridor out into garden (tiptoe careful) through a little door into a little low building on the side of the house. Big wooden tubs and drainers and brushes hanging on the walls, all wet-smelling, wet wood-smelling like rain and trees but cleaner, soapy. Mrs D opens a cupboard, brings out wooden stick legs with feet all different sizes.

'I don't know if we've got a right-sized pair for your little boots. The rest of us have fair hommucks. Give them here, then.'

I do. 'What are hommucks?'

'Bless you! These are.' She lifts her skirt up and stamp-stamps her feet. 'Great hommucks. You've only little feet. They aren't hommucks, though they may be yet, in a few years.'

She lines up the wooden feet and holds my boots on top, one pair, two pairs. She tucks the third pair inside and holds the leg tops. 'Near enough. Now we can hold on fast and clean the boots. Pass me that brush.'

I pass and she brushes, *swoosh swoosh*, and the dry

muddiness makes lumps and dust on the cupboard top. *Shee-uw-shee-uw-shee-uw*. Her elbows move very fast.

'Thank you' say I 'but Mama said I should do it.'

'No need to tell her you didn't,' says Mrs D. 'I've time enough today. There's only the family dinner to get up and I'm best out of cook's way.' *Shee-shee-shee*. 'How did you like the new schoolhouse?'

'Very much, thank you.'

'Is that so?' *Not really*. 'And what about your room? Which one have you got?'

'The little white one. Upstairs.'

'Oh. You don't sound too thrilled about it.'

'I am sure that I shall like it. And I *am* the youngest.'

'It's a good room' she says. *Shew-shew* (shoe-shoe). 'Good view of the garden, nice and light in the Summer.'

'It was very cold' say I. 'There are big gaps in the windows.'

'Indeed? I shall see to some new curtain inners then. Keep the frost off you.' She puts down one boot and picks up the next. 'You can rub some polish on that one now' she says. Pushes cloth and pot to me. 'Rub a little on all over then rub it hard off again. Woods normally does the shoes. Never gets it all off properly, I say.'

'Does Woods chop wood?' say I.

'Not as you'd notice' she says.

The polish is greasy like soft dripping but bad smelling. Goes smooth butter-spreading on the boot toe.

'Not too much now' says Mrs D.

Rub-rub very carefully not to get it on the laces or the sole or on me. Sticky not shiny. Is Joshua chopping wood? Wasn't earlier.

'How did you get so filthy anyhow?' Mrs D says. Just like Mama.

'I didn't *mean* to' say I. 'We were looking in the school-house garden and it was muddy and the dog had made a big hole.'

'Dog? What dog?'

'The captain's dog.'

She puts the boot down. 'Captain Easter was there?'

'Yes. We met him on the way.'

'Did you now? Hmmn.' She picks up the boot and *shew-shew-shew-shews* it hard and fast.

'His dog jumped at me and made my pinafore dirty. It wasn't my fault.'

'What's that old rascal hanging about for?' says Mrs D, very quiet.

'Is the captain a rascal?' say I.

'I didn't say that.' DID. *Shew-shew-shew*. 'I wonder what he wants with you is all.'

'He doesn't want anything with me' say I.

'I dare say.' *Shew-shew*. 'I suppose Anne was there, was she?'

'Yes. And Mary and Lizzy and Mama.'

Bangs the boot down. 'That's enough polish, girl, pass it here. You can start on this one.' She takes my boot and another brush and swoosh-swooshes so quick her hand goes blurry.

'I don't like him either' say I, quiet too.

'Well, it won't do to speak ill of him' she says cross-snapping 'though he might be a gambler and a debtor and a spoiler and Lord knows what else, he will have his way.' *Swoosh-swoosh*. She is *very* cross. Puts down the boot, picks it up again. *Sighs*. 'I shouldn't have said that, child. Don't take any heed.'

'He cannot be a debtor, though. He lives in a chateau.' C-H-A-T-E-A-U. 'That is French for castle.'

'Horse feathers. Give me that boot.' She swoosh-swooshes that one too.

The first boot is shiny-smooth, slippery-polished. Clean smelling but damp inside.

'The captain has very blue eyes' say I.

'So he has.'

'Is it vulgar to have such blue eyes, Mrs D?'

She looks at me sideways. Her eyes are not blue. 'I don't know about vulgar. Dangerous, maybe.'

'How?' Eyes are not dangerous.

'There. Boots are done.' She rubs her hands on a cloth. 'Let's take and wash out this pinny.'

I hold it out and she takes it, puts it in a tub, rub-scrubs it on a board.

'What's this here?' she says. 'You've left your pocket tied on.' Forgot it, the pocket. And Lucy Locket lost hers. 'What are you about, tying your pocket to your pinny? You should keep it on your dress.'

'Yes, Mrs D.' Don't *need* a pocket in the house.

She unties it, opens it. 'What are you doing carting this about?'

The white stone, powdery muddy.

'I found it in the garden. The dog dug it up.'

'Do you know what this is?' says Mrs D. *No.* 'Chalk, child. Like you use on a slate. That's what it looks like when it comes up out of the ground.'

Chalk. Dog dug it up. Papa will be pleased if there is more chalk under the schoolhouse. Perhaps he may use it for classes.

'You'd better run along with those boots' says Mrs D. 'This pinny'll need a good soak in some hot water and there's none in the coppers. I'll see to it after dinner. Go on with you, get yourself cleaned up.'

'Thank you, Mrs D' say I. Take boots and chalk and pocket and go to the door.

'No need to say aught' she says. 'About the captain. Understood?'

I go out into the cold mizzle-drizzly grey garden, foot stepping carefully.

And keep away from those puddles! says Mrs D's voice, muffle-damp.

Skip-step quickly back into the house. The corridor is warm, smoky and boiled-pudding steamy, onion smelling. *Hungry.* Noisy banging clattering from the kitchen. Wipe wipe my feet (no mud lumps) and go quick along the hall and up the stairs.

Is that you, Frances? Papa's voice. It is coming from the schoolroom.

'Yes, Papa.'

Hurry up and wash his voice says. *If you are late for dinner you will go without.*

'Yes, Papa.'

The door is open to my room that is not my room. Trunk gone, bed gone, mattress folded over in the corner. Put my boots by the other boxes, which have not gone. Have to put my things away, Mama said. The washstand is still there with water in the bowl, icy on fingers. Wipe them quick on my pinafore to dry.

Joshua is at the door, sulky-faced. 'Hello, Fan. Where've you been?'

'With the housekeeper. Cleaning my boots. Look, someone has taken my bed.'

'Mine too. They are coming for the mattresses later.'

'Who took them?'

'Woods, the manservant. And another man, a gardener.'

'Woods doesn't chop wood' say I. 'At least not as you would notice.'

Joshua shrugs, holds out his hands, cross red crossed lines on his palms. 'Papa found *that* out' he says.

'Why say it then?'

'What's the difference? He canes me when I say true and canes me when I don't.'

'Papa does not want you to tell lies.'

'So?'

He is cross too. 'I am not to live here any more' say I. 'I have to empty my room.'

'I know' says Joshua. 'It's too bad. But at least you *have* a room. I've got to sleep in the attic.'

'I don't understand why. Why can't I live here with you and Mama and Papa? I've got to do what Lizzy tells me now too.'

'She's very pleased about it. Oh, did you hear? Captain Easter has invited us to Chateau Bellevue. That's his house. On Saturday. Lizzy and Mary were talking about it.'

I know. 'He said so to Mama this morning.'

'I hope we can all go. A chateau!'

'I think he just calls it that. He said we should see his fountain.'

'It will be really grand. He might have his weapons on the wall, you know, like they do in castles. His sword and musket and helmet. With blood on them.'

'That's just in stories' say I. And anyway he's a rascal but I mustn't *say* so.

'He killed people in the wars you know' says Joshua, wide-eyed. 'The French.'

'He *was* a soldier, that's what they are supposed to do.'

'With his bare hands!' His wicked grin. 'I want to be a soldier. I should like to gore the French.'

'No, you shouldn't. Anyway, you can't be a soldier, you are going to be a schoolmaster, like James and Papa.'

'Am not.' Stamps his feet and swing-swings his arms. 'I'm going to have a red uniform and a helmet and shiny boots and everyone will call *me* captain too. *Not* sir.'

His feet are noisy. 'Do stop' say I. 'Papa will hear.'

He stops. 'All the same, I'm not going to be a schoolmaster.'

'We've got to go down to dinner' say I. 'We will be late.'

'Come on then.' He swings out of the door, arm-swing marches knee-lifting foot stamping *thump-thump-thump-thump* down the stairs.

Joshua Newlove! says Papa's voice. *Go back to the top and WALK down the stairs. Properly.*

Friday the Ninth day of January 1835
bedtime
Bellevue School for Girls
Margate

Dearest James,

I am very sorry not to have finished my last letter and not to have sent it to you until today. I shall put this one in with it, as so much has happened since then, and send them both together.

Lizzy, Mary and I have moved into Mama's new schoolhouse. I have put the address here so that you may write to me if you have time. We have been very busy with the new school. All of my things have been packed away and unpacked again. On Tuesday my bed and Lizzy and Mary's bed were taken from Papa's school and put in our new rooms. My new room is not as nice as the one in Papa's school but Papa needed it more than me. Mrs D (that is the housekeeper) has made new curtains that are very thick and blue and now it is not so cold as it first was. I like the curtains even though Lizzy laughed and said that they are probably made from Mrs D's old clothes and look like a duchess's pantaloons. (<u>Please</u> do not tell Mama that.) Mrs D is kind and she let me walk with her to the market and to the farm to buy eggs. The market is noisy and busy and there are a lot of public houses around it that sell beer, so I am not to go there on my own.

Mama has been getting the new schoolrooms ready. There will be a parlour upstairs for us to use. Mama is having it papered so we cannot go in just yet. It was very red and striped before. I do not know what colour it will be now but it will not be red. Lizzy is now to look after Mary and me and the maid Anne when Mama is not here. I hope I shall like that. We have had workbaskets full of things to make. My sewing is getting better but Lizzy says that I shall never be a seamstress, although I hope I shall never have to be. Mary's work is still the neatest, she has made covers for cushions and gave Papa a lovely handkerchief with his name on it and a Psalm embroidered around the edges. He was very pleased.

Papa is very busy with things for the school but today he walked with us into town. We all went together and he showed us where the important buildings are. We went into Bettison's Library. It was very grand. Lizzy and Mary have taken books and after Papa went they looked at pictures of ladies' clothes. Mama chose a book for me, it is called Life's Adventure but it does not look very exciting, I do not think that it is really about having adventures. Joshua did not choose a book but watched the boats instead. The harbour is very crowded and the boats bring fish and other things for people to buy. Mama was glad to see such nice fish just caught and bought some little silver ones which she and Papa ate for supper. I did not have any for there were many little bones in them. At the harbour we saw coal coming in big carts on rails along the stone jetty. The place where we walked across the sea when we arrived looks much safer when you are standing on the other side.

I will stop writing now as it is very late and I must blow my candle out. Lizzy does not come to make sure that I am asleep but Mama would not like it if I stayed awake. Tomorrow is Saturday and we have been invited to visit at our neighbour's house. I will write and tell you all about it as soon as I am able.

I miss you very much as I am sure we all do. I hope that you do not mind my saying that for I know that it is selfish of me to want you to come and live here. I hope too that we shall see one another one day quite soon. Goodnight dear brother and spare a thought for your affectionate sister Frances.

Skipping to Queenie Caroline

Queenie Queenie Caroline – dipped her head in turpentine –
'Faster!' says Mary.

I go faster turning faster jumping skipjump skipjump skipjumpskip too fast for singing and slip, slap-slapping the rope, tangle foot tripping. Stop and unwind it. Mary likes to skip still even though she is quite big now. When she doesn't skip she likes to watch me do it.

'I lost it' say I.

'We need someone else to help and then I can hold the rope for you' says Mary. 'Where is Lizzy?'

'Lizzy won't play' say I 'and anyway she has gone to see Papa.' *Good.*

'I will fetch Anne' says Mary. 'Anne will play.' She runs half-down the stairs and calls 'Anne! Anne!'

Queenie Queenie Caroline – dipped her head in turpentine – turpentine to –

'Come and hold the rope with me, Anne' says Mary.

Anne comes grinning. 'I hant skipt fer yers' she says. 'I can turn tho.'

Mary and Anne take the rope from me and turn it slap, slap, clumsy then even.

'Not too close to the stairs' says Mary. 'Come on, Fanny, you've got to jump in.'

'Turn it faster then' say I. Onetwo onetwo onetwo. 'Let's do apples and pears.'

'No' says Mary 'that's too hard. Do Queenie again.'

Onetwo onetwo jump-in skipjump skipjump skipjump. 'Do the rhyme too!'

Mary sings it –

Queenie Queenie Caroline – dipped her head in turpentine – turpentine to make it shine – Queenie Queenie –

Anne haw-haw laughs and drops the rope. 'I hant erd that un!' she says haw-haw-hawing.

'Can we go faster?' say I. 'I want to go faster.'

'Let's do a counting one' says Mary. 'They are faster.'

'Wa bout Sint Johns a chiming?' says Anne. 'That wa my favrit.'

'I don't know it' says Mary.

Nor do I.

'You go *Sint Johns s chiming chiming chiming* an then cownt *one-two-three* an on fast till you trip.'

'Like Big Ben!' says Mary. 'Let's do that, Fanny.'

They turn turn turn and I run skipjump skipjump skipjump.

'You start, Anne' says Mary.

Skipjump skipjump and Anne sings –

Sint Johns s chiming chiming chiming

and Mary starts –

Saint John's is chiming chiming chiming

and they laugh and Mary says 'ready?' and they turn fast *one-two-three-four-five-six-seven-eight-nine-ten-eleven*

'What on earth are you doing!' *Lizzy*, cross-faced arms folded.

Anne stops, rope stops, slap-clatters on the floor.

'I was up to eleven!' say I.

'What are you thinking of?' Lizzy shouts. 'Skipping inside the house?' (Like Mama, a not-question.)

'It's raining outside, Lizzy dear' says Mary mildly. 'She couldn't skip outside.'

'Then she shouldn't skip!'

'*Lizzy*, I *was* up to eleven. And Anne was teaching us a new rhyme.'

Lizzy nasty staring looks at Anne. 'Get back to work' she says.

'Yes mam' says Anne.

She is very red. Lizzy watches her hurry downstairs.

'Really, Lizzy' Mary says sweetly 'there was no harm. Fanny needs to play.'

'She can play in her room whenever she wants' says Lizzy. 'Quietly.'

'I wanted to *skip*' say I.

'Well that's too bad' says Lizzy. She picks up the rope, twist-twists it round her hand. 'You will do as I say from now on.'

Will *not*. 'You are not Mama and I shan't do as you say.'

Lizzy thunder-faced glares, reaches for me and twist-pulls at my collar. 'You are coming with me' she hisses. 'This instant. Papa wants to speak to you.'

Horrid hateful spiteful Lizzy push-pushes me down the stairs, pulls my ear, pinches my neck. Shove shove into the rain, cold muddy-puddle road, splashing shoving. 'Stop it!' say I, but she doesn't. Spiteful hateful Lizzy. Along the road and up to Papa's school and the door is opened by Mrs D.

'Bless me!' says Mrs D. 'What is going on?'

Lizzy pushes and says nothing. Push push along the hall and she stops and knocks on the green door.

Come in says Papa's voice. Lizzy pushes me pushes the door and Papa looks up.

'Fanny was skipping on the landing' says Lizzy. 'I told her to stop and she was very impertinent. Mary was with her. And Anne, the maid. She was holding the skipping-rope.' Lizzy shows Papa my skipping-rope. *Mine.*

'Is this true?' says Papa.

'Yes, sir' say I 'but Lizzy shouted and was horrid.'

Lizzy pinches *very* hard.

'Now then, Fanny' says Papa 'do not speak unkindly of your sister.' He looks at Lizzy. 'Thank you, Arabella-Elizabeth' he says. 'I will talk to Fanny now.'

Huffing hissing Lizzy is *not pleased*. She pinches me again and goes. *Good.*

'Now, Fanny' says Papa, smiling and not at all quiet. 'I should like you to read to me. I want to hear how you are getting along with your reading. Would you like that?'

'Yes, Papa.'

'Sit down at the table then, and read to me from the newspaper.'

I sit. The chair is very high and the newspaper page is long and black with tiny letters. *KENTISH GAZETTE* it says at the top and *general weekly journal for east and west Kent.* Why is Papa not cross?

'What is the matter, Fanny?' says Papa. 'Why do you not begin?'

I do. ' "Advertisement. An auc . . . auct—" '

'Auction' says Papa.

'Auction. "An auction of Muskets, Bay – Bayo—" '

'Bayonets.'

'Bayonets "and Light Calvary will—"'

'*Cavalry*, Fanny' says Papa. 'Read closely.'

'"Light Cavalry Swords will be held at the Queen's Arms in Margate."' *Queenie Queenie Caroline's Arms. What does she do with them?* '"On Monday the Sixteenth of February, at One o'clock".'

Papa nods. 'Very well, and some more.'

Turn the pages. Dredge's Heal-All. Kent elections. Arboretum Britannicum; or the Hard Trees of Britain, Native and Foreign. Weights and Measures. Money Wanted (that's usury, which is *bad*.)

Papa tap-taps his foot. 'What is wrong, Fanny? Am I to take it that you have forgotten how to read?'

'No, Papa.'

'Then why do you not read?'

He does not look very cross. 'Papa' say I 'are you not going to scold me for skipping?'

'I do not believe so.'

'Then, am I allowed to skip, Papa? Because Lizzy said that I am not to.'

'I see no reason for you not to skip, Fanny, as long as you do so outside.'

Oh. '"New Edition of London's *Ency-Encyclo—*"'

'Encyclopaedia, Fanny.'

'"*Encyclopaedia of Gardening*".' He will not scold me. '"Three Chron . . . Chronol—"'

'Chronological?'

'"Chronological Trees of English, Irish and Scottish History."' Turn the page, thin and ink-smelly, dirty corner dirty-fingered. '"Melancholy Accident at Tenby, fifteen persons drowned".' Deaths, Marriage. While sitting by the fire, Mr Hodden, aged 89 (that is very ancient). Public gardens for sale – the Wilderness and Belle Vue. (That is like the name of the captain's chateau. *And* Mama's school. Perhaps the captain will sell his chateau and go away.) ' "On Wednesday evening Mr Lushington, our highly popular candidate, visited the Catch Club. His health drunk amid three times three of the loudest—" '

'That will do, Fanny' says Papa. He closes and folds up the newspaper. 'This evening you may read to me from your book. Your mother selected a book for you from the library, I believe.'

'Yes, Papa.'

'Very well. I hope to hear you read more consistently from your book this evening. How do I wish to hear you read?'

'Consistently, Papa.'

'That is correct. And how is it spelt, Fanny?'

'C-O-N-S-I-S-T-E-N-T-L-Y.'

'Very good, Fanny. I am pleased to note that your spelling is as precise as ever. I had hoped that your reading aloud would be as confident. However, you may prove that to be the case this evening.'

'Yes, Papa. Thank you, Papa.'

'After dinner we will all attend our neighbour, as you know. As we have received a family invitation you may accompany us. Should you like that?'

'Yes, Papa. Thank you, Papa.'

'Good.' His hand reaches big and lays heavy and hot on my head. His hand! 'Bless you, you are a good girl, Fanny. Run along now, attend to your duties.'

Papa!

Down from the tall chair, stepping carefully, walk slowly to the door, not skipping. The clock whirs *bong* chimes for the half-hour. Half past eleven. *Saint John's is chiming chiming chiming one-two-three-four-five-six-seven-eight-nine-ten-eleven* and *nearly* twelve. Nearly. Papa did not scold me. Papa *blessed* me.

Miss Frances! Mrs D's voice. She comes pinch-faced frowning along the hall and touches my hand. 'Are you all right, child?' she says.

'Yes thank you.'

She peer-peers at me, eyes wrinkling frown-frowning. 'Are you sure?'

'Yes, Mrs D. Thank you.'

'Miss Arabella-Elizabeth. She's all right, is she?'

No. She is horrid but mustn't say so. 'Yes thank you.'

'Hmmn' says Mrs D, very quiet. 'Well, you be sure and tell me if you're upset about anything, you hear? You'll do that, won't you?'

'Yes, Mrs D.' *Promise.*

She opens the door and I go, skip-jump-step skip-jump-step. *Queenie Queenie Caroline – dipped her head in turpentine –* through the gate and into the road, puddle jumping. *Turpentine to make it shine.* Ha! I *can* skip if I want to.

Going to look at a fountain in the rain

The lying captain is in the parlour. *Nonsense, Newlove* his voice says. I can smell his nasty dog. Huh-huh-huh.

Mrs D closes the door and follows me along the hall. 'Better go and get the cordial out then' she says, mutter-muttering.

Lizzy tap-taps the green door and opens it.

'Ah!' says the captain loudly. He is standing by the fire in a smart red waistcoat. The dog trot-trots up and tail banging sniffs at us. The captain bows and smiles all yellow-whiskery. 'How are you today, young ladies?'

'Very well, thank you, sir' says Lizzy. She is trying *very hard* to sound grown-up.

'Come in, girls' says Papa. We do. Mary shuts the door and pushes the dog away with her foot but it still stands there huff-huff-huffing sniffing.

'My my, ladies' says the captain 'what a picture of loveliness you are!' We bob ever-so-politely but I know he doesn't mean it. Doesn't mean me. 'Handsome girls, Newlove' he says to Papa. Papa bows. 'And it's no secret where they get it from' the captain says. He winks at Mama. Mama looks rather hot.

Although it is Saturday Mama said that we were to wear our Sunday clothes to go visiting. Lizzy and Mary spent an hour after dinner taking shawls and ribbons out and sighing. Lizzy said she wasn't fit to be seen and had nothing to wear, but I know that she has lots more dresses than either me or Mary. It is silly to wear best clothes to go walking and looking at fountains because it has been raining again and we are only going to get wet and muddy anyway. Mama has her nice blue dress with bows on and even her locket. She does not wear her locket very often. I think Papa is afraid that she might lose it. Like Lucy Locket.

'Fanny' says Papa, 'go and ask the housekeeper to bring in a tray. Would you care for some cordial, Captain?'

'Cordial? *And* something to go in it!'

'I am afraid we cannot offer you that manner of refreshment, Captain' says Mama.

'We practise temperance in this house, Captain' says Papa.

The captain frowns. 'All things in moderation, Newlove' he says. 'If God hadn't meant man to drink port and brandy he wouldn't have made the grape. Ha!'

Papa does not look very pleased. 'Cordial, Fanny' he says, quietly.

'Yes, Papa' say I.

'Don't stir yourself, girl' says the captain. 'I've no thirst for your cordials. Let's begin our walk, eh? Before the rain gets any thicker.'

'Of course, Captain' says Mama sweetly. She stands and holds Papa's arm. 'Girls, put your bonnets on. And, Fanny, run and fetch your brother.'

'Yes, Mama.'

Out into the hall and up the stairs, past the room that isn't my room any more and up to the attic. Tap-tap the door and go in. Joshua, sitting on the bed, arms folded, sulky.

'What's the matter?' say I.

'I hate Papa.' Kick-swings his legs. 'I hate him.'

'No you don't. And you mustn't say that or you'll go to hell.'

'I don't care.'

'Of course you do.'

'*He* made us come here' says Joshua. (Pout pout, lip sticking out.) '*London* was all right.'

'You didn't like London.'

'Did. Anyway it was better than *here*. Now I've got to live in the attic like a servant. *And* share. With *eight* other boys. And Papa said that if they make noise in the night, or don't turn down their beds, he will blame *me*. And then I shall have the cane again.'

'Captain Easter is here' say I. 'He wants us to go now.'

'Go then. I don't suppose *he*'ll let me come.'

'Mama told me to fetch you' say I. 'I think you are supposed to come.'

'It's probably just so she can shout at me too. In front of everybody.'

'She seems quite nice today. She has even got her locket on. I think you shall come.'

Sighs, huffs, swings his legs. 'All right.'

'Mama said to wear Sunday things' say I 'so you had better put your Sunday coat on. And brush your hair.'

He goes foot-dragging to the press. 'I bet Lizzy's all ribbons and stuff' he says. 'I bet she's even got her best drawers on.'

'Joshua!'

'Well? So?' Puts his coat on, licks his palms and wipes them on his hair. 'Ready.'

'Come on then.'

Down the attic stairs down the hall stairs and Lizzy and Mary there tying their bonnet ribbons. Mary gives me my bonnet and Lizzy looks at Joshua and wrinkles up her nose.

'Little vagabond' she says.

'Lizzy dear' says Mary 'why don't you take the captain his cane?'

Lizzy does. Mary takes out her handkerchief and rubs at Joshua's face with it. 'Grubby boy' she says. 'You'd better run up and put your waistcoat on, Mama said Sunday clothes.'

'I'm all right' says Joshua.

'No' says Mary 'run up and put your waistcoat on.'

'Shan't' says Joshua (*grumpity-grump*) 'and stop telling me what to do, you're only two years older than me.'

'Come' says Mary hushing shushing 'I don't want you to have to stay behind.'

Joshua sulky goes foot-dragging boot-shuffling sighing up the stairs. Papa comes out and Mary helps him into his long coat. Lizzy and Mama and the captain and the dog all come and stand in the hall and Mrs D appears carrying a tray with glasses and the cordial bottle on it.

'You can keep your potions, Mrs D' says the captain 'we're off to Chateau Bellevue for a negus.'

Negus?

Mrs D's lips go tight.

'Thank you' says Mama. 'Perhaps we could have some tea when we return.'

'Very good' says Mrs D, although she obviously thinks it very bad. She scuffles away.

'Where's that maidservant of yours?' says the captain. 'With the big eyes.'

'Anne is at my school now, Captain' says Mama. 'She will be living in.'

'Ho!' says the captain.

The dog *ssscraaa*-scratches at the floor and *waa-woo* whines. Looks at me like it wants to swallow me up whole, bonnet and shawl and everything.

'All right, Wellesley' says the captain 'we're off now.'

'Where is Joshua, Fanny?' says Mama.

'He is coming Mama' say I.

We all look up the stairs and down comes Joshua, not smiling, Sunday waistcoat Sunday coat Sunday boots.

'Hmm' says Papa. Looks at Joshua's hands and face and waistcoat. 'Good.'

Mary smiles and opens the door and we all go out into the grey mizzly wet garden and down the path. The dog runs away and turns and lifts its leg against the gatepost. It is still raining.

Papa and Mama and the captain talk and talk. The fields are muddy and brown with nothing growing in them. Joshua walks long-faced long-stepping over the puddles. *Don't splash*. Lizzy listens to the captain like you should listen to a preacher.

'Good to get a walk in before dinner' says the captain, 'sound for the constitution. Staying for dinner, of course, eh, Newlove? Cook's as good as you'll get in Margate, I can tell you.'

'That is very kind of you, Captain' says Mama 'but we have already taken dinner.'

'What?' says the captain, very loudly. 'Dinner already? What d'you mean by it?'

'We keep school hours' says Papa. 'The children eat at one o'clock.'

'One o'clock? Damned uncivilised hour. Eat at four and not before. Always will.'

Eat at four and not before. We have, onion pudding all floury hot steaming and sausages peppery and horrid green things that Papa said I must eat so I did, even though they were slippery slimy and nasty. And mincemeat tart, which made it all better again. Joshua had two pieces he said, but Papa never lets him have two pieces so he *can't* have. Unless he stole it from the kitchen (and he wouldn't *dare*, not with Cook there).

'One o'clock is the correct time for a school dinner' says Papa. 'Children become restless when they are hungry, and a restless child is an unruly child.'

'A cup of broth and a clip of the cane' says the captain. 'That's all a boy needs.'

'There are schoolmasters' says Papa 'who would see their boys go hungry for the sake of economy. Not I.'

'Damned waste of money' says the captain. 'Boys are always hungry.'

'My husband's pupils are liberally boarded' says Mama 'but we do not indulge them unnecessarily. A good meal in the middle of the day is a healthy thing for a growing child.'

'Let their parents feed them,' says the captain. 'You're not in the business of running Charity Schools, are you, eh? Newlove?'

'I am entrusted with the welfare of my boys, Captain' says Papa (rather quiet) 'and it would be a sin not to uphold that trust. They are sons of honest men and my task is to see that they too grow into honest, useful Christian souls.'

Papa is getting cross.

The captain huffs and swing-swings his stick. The dog runs down the lane and stops, nose-nosing a puddle.

'We find, Captain' says Mama sweetly 'that when a boy has a plain, healthy meal he is better able to concentrate on his lessons.'

'Boys are greedy by nature' says the captain. 'I wonder you don't keep their appetites under control instead of giving in to them every day.'

'Captain' says Papa (whisper quiet) 'I do not give in to the will of children.'

'What d'you think, lad?' says the captain, swinging his stick at Joshua and poke-poking him in the side. 'I bet you're a greedy lad.'

'No, sir' says Joshua sulkily.

'Come now. I'd lay a sovereign on you sitting at your desk all day dreaming of roast mutton and puddings.'

'No, sir.'

'He does not' says Papa 'for gluttony is a mortal sin, Captain, and not tolerated in my house. But there is no more certain way of making a glutton of the man than by making a starveling of the boy.'

'Shall we see your garden, Captain?' says Mama. 'I fear that the rain has made it rather too wet underfoot.'

'What? Garden, oh yes, garden.' *Ahem* clears his throat. 'Yes, dear Mrs Newlove, of course you shall see the garden.' He takes hold of Mama's hand and tucks it under his arm. 'There's a particularly pleasant little avenue, Mrs Newlove, that I should like you to see. Very much to a lady's taste, I'd say. Shame not to have ladies walking in it.' He smiles white-toothed whiskery. 'You can come and take your walk there any time you wish, Mrs Newlove.'

'Thank you, Captain' says Mama. 'Perhaps in the fine weather.'

Turn the corner and there is the big stone wall, and the

road where the carts go carries on without us. 'Well, here's the bottom end' says the captain.

'Is all this yours, Captain?' says Joshua.

'Yes, this wall is at the bottom of my land. Bit rougher this end, made it a bit of a wilderness, you know, the usual estate way. Plenty of trees. Bit wet this time of year. We'll start at the top, you get the approach that way.'

We walk and walk, the road slopes up and the wall goes on and on. Lizzy smiles and Mary nudges and they look very pleased, even though it is cold and horrid.

'Well, you can see the top of her from here' says the captain, pointing.

Over the wall and there is the house, tall and white-looking with grey sky all round, up-down-up-down roof like the wall of a castle but not old or with ivy on it.

'Is it really a chateau?' says Joshua. He is not so sulky now.

'Built her like a fortress' says the captain. 'Nothing in the way between her and the sea, that was the plan. Put her on the top there so I can look out over the cliff.' He winks at Joshua. 'Like to keep an eye open for the French, you know. Can't trust 'em.'

'Goodness' says Mary.

'Take you round the front' says the captain.

We walk on and on and come to the top, icy wind blowing. Windmill with sails spin-spinning fast. Not by the sea but we can smell it salty, hear the *aak-ak* seagulls. The sea looks a long way away but we are high up now.

'This way' says the captain.

The dog runs up a path, sniffing stopping running again. Hedges prickly skinny short trees bare branches. The house gets bigger, closer.

'Other side looks out to sea' says the captain 'bit blowy this time of year. Good for the lungs, though, eh? We'll keep to this slope. Warmer.'

The house is grand, wide, little stones in front *scrash-scrunch* where we walk. Mama murmurs Papa nods Lizzy and Mary gasp and giggle and prod each other.

'Well' says the captain, stick swinging 'take you straight on.'

We follow and he walks very pleased past the windows past the big door *scrash-scrash-scrunch* and down a little path. Grass, little trees, more grass. Mama and Papa talk and point and the captain smiles nods *shrubs, fruit, really, Captain? neater that way, plenty of sun, avenue, further down.* Lizzy looks back at the house and grins.

'There is the fountain!' says Mama, very pleased.

Big stone fountain, not marble, not anything-shaped really just pointy at the top like a church. No water coming out but rain trickling pattering splash-splashing making my boots wet. Icy *icy* toes. Joshua looks at me and shrugs. *Not big enough to climb* his mouth says. Mama and the captain talk and talk and talk.

'Thought about putting in a lake' says the captain 'but of course with the sea and the river fishing it hardly seemed worth it.'

'This is quite delightful, Captain' says Mama. 'Really charming.'

'Glasshouse is pretty fine, up next to the wing. Nothing much to see now of course but you must take a tour with me, Mrs Newlove, in the Spring.'

'Oh yes' says Mama 'I should like to, thank you, Captain.'

The captain grins, points down to the skeleton trees. 'The walkway I mentioned is towards the bottom there, Mrs Newlove.

Do say you will come back when the weather is improved. When the trees are in leaf it is quite enclosed.'

'Indeed?' says Papa. 'I wonder it is not rather dark for walking, Captain.'

'Quite light enough' says the captain 'and sheltered from wind and sun. Good quiet place for a walk, Newlove. As a church man you must know what good a quiet walk does a fellow now and then.'

Papa is *not* church. Papa is *chapel*.

'Indeed' says Papa again, but differently.

Mary shivers. The captain looks at her and whisker-grins. 'Chilly, eh?' he says. 'Let's go back to the house.'

We do. The rain gets thicker faster wetter. The captain lifts and *squeak-crash-squeak-crash* raps the big brassy knocker and a woman opens the door. She bobs.

'Sarah' says the captain 'these are our neighbours the Newloves.'

'Good day' says the woman. She looks at the captain and takes his stick. 'Please to come inside mam, sir. Misses.' (Doesn't look at Joshua.)

We go in, boot-wiping bonnet-dripping shawl-shaking wet. The captain winks at the woman and she lifts her eyebrows and looks at Mama. They both smile. *Wipe your feet* the woman says to the captain, *very* quiet. He does!

Mrs D would not *dare* to say so to Papa, even in a *whisper*.

The woman walks along the hall and we follow, Mary and Lizzy bonnet-swinging peering prying. The dog pushes tail thud-thudding wet and smelly and stands in front of me. It shakes its head and then all the rest of it, shake-spraying dirty doggy-water splashing at me and at the wall.

The captain laughs. 'Go on, you two' he says 'into the parlour.' He kick-taps the dog with his boot and pushes me along in front, big heavy hand on my shoulder. 'Keep up, missy' he says, whisker-close and hot in my ear.

Tall hall all blue and silver papered and very long. The captain pushes and the dog leads and we all go into the parlour, lower and brown and with a bright fire spitting jumping at the end. Warm and nice wood-smoke smelling.

Ho! Joshua stops and points at the floor. 'A bear!'

A bear?

A *bear* lying down, spread out blanket flat, stretched out like a carpet with a head on it, chin on the floor and black eyes shiny and not-seeing.

'Oh!' says Mary into her handkerchief.

Joshua runs up to it, sits on the floor one knee on each side of the head. Poke-pokes the big bear teeth.

'Joshua Newlove' says Papa quietly 'desist from that rude behaviour and get up this instant.'

'What, found the old fellow have you?' says the captain. 'Don't worry, Newlove, he's quite harmless.'

'Is it *really* real?' says Joshua. He pushes fingers in the bear mouth. *(Snap.)*

'Real? I should say.' The captain *gra*-growl mumbles *real teeth real claws* at my ear, growling mumbling. Claw-squeezes my shoulder. 'Shot him myself' he says.

'Goodness' says Mary. She sits down carefully. Mama sits beside her and takes her hand.

'Yes' says the captain, not squeezing now. 'Quite some time ago, I dare say. But I'm still a square enough shot for the likes of him, Mrs Newlove.'

Mama smiles her not-very-happy smile.

'Where did you shoot it?' says Joshua. 'Can I see the gun?'

'Gun's in the gunroom, my lad.'

Joshua poke-pokes the shiny glassy black eyes. The bear

doesn't mind. 'Can I see?' he says, whining wanting. 'Please, sir?'

'Well, I could get it out for you. I suppose you'll want to see muskets and bayonets too, though, eh?'

'Oh yes please, sir!'

'Keep 'em in a locked case. Can't have guns hanging up on the wall for anyone to pick up and fire off, can we, eh?' He walks up to the bear and push-pushes the poor not-smelling bear nose with his boot. *(Snap snap)*. 'Dangerous enough in the kitchen with all those knives and spits. But what if the cook got it in her head to shoot me?'

'Why would the cook shoot you?' says Joshua, eyes big grin-grinning. 'Is she French?'

'French? Bah!' (Snort snort kicks the bear snout.) 'No, but she's a fury.' He looks at Mama, bows. 'And after all, I did tell her we would be eight for dinner.'

Eight? Papa-one Mama-two captain-three Lizzy-four Mary-five Joshua-six me-seven. Dog-eight.

Joshua strokes the bear fur. 'Please might I see the gunroom, Captain, sir?'

'Captain is good enough. Come on then.' Points at me. 'You come along too, Miss Frances.'

Look at Mama but she just nods waves me away. Joshua and the captain go through a brown door in the corner.

'Come along' says the captain.

I do.

'The gunroom' says the captain. He reaches claw-claw-squeezes my shoulder again, tugging pulling. 'Come on.'

Dark and woody and nasty ashy tobacco-smelling, and on the wall a deer head with sad glassy eyes and no deer body any more, wooden shield behind it. Deer head and big curly candlestick horns and a big ugly black pig looking down.

Hairy black face snarly black snout and pointy white tusks pushing out of the wall.

The captain looks at me and smiles not-very-nicely. 'What do you think of my old hunting friends up there, Fanny? Like 'em, do you?'

Big teeth bad bold eyes.

'Not very much' say I.

'Ha!' says the captain. 'Thought not.'

Stiff striped badger and polecat and little brown-red fox still trotting tail up in a glass box. Fox in a box. Big glass case, guns and more guns long and short, and shiny sharp-looking things for hunting and hurting with. Shooting hunting hurting bears and badgers and foxes and the French.

Joshua presses his face against the glass, steaming breathing wet against it. 'Which one did you shoot the bear with, Captain?' he says.

The captain points at a gun and laughs.

The deer looks down and the fox twitches his tail and the big black pig snuffles and snorts. *He shot me* they all say not-speaking and look at me and at the lying captain. Want to open the door and let them out and watch them trotting running snuffling away. (Not the deer though, not the pig, no legs to run away on. Bad captain.)

Turn away and go back to Mama and the fire. Mama and Lizzy touch their hair and their skirts and look at the wall-paper. Mary *fnah-fnuh* blows her nose into her handkerchief. Her nose is very white and red.

The woman who opened the door comes in. 'Pardon me' she says bobbing, 'I was looking for the captain.'

In here, my girl says the captain's voice.

'The captain and his guns!' says the woman to Mama,

smiling eye-rolling. Mama looks away. 'Captain' she calls not moving 'Maurice is here.'

Show him in then damn it says the captain's voice.

The woman goes out.

Papa *harumhrem* clears his throat very loudly.

The captain comes back in with Joshua, eyes big and very pleased. Joshua sits on the floor, puts the bear's head in his lap and stares up at the captain. Papa breathes in and out like a horse that has just stopped running.

The door opens and a smart black-haired black-whiskered black-eyed man comes in.

'Da Costa!' says the captain. 'About time too. You know the Newloves, of course.'

'Of course' says the man, bowing. 'Such a delightful supper party.'

The rich man from Papa's supper!

We all bob and bow back.

'Good day, Mr da Costa' says Papa.

'How delightful to see you again, Mr Newlove' says the man. He takes Mama's hand and kisses it. 'And what a pleasure to see your charming family again.' He bows to Lizzy and takes her hand too. 'Miss Newlove' he says to Lizzy's fingers 'a very great pleasure indeed.'

Lizzy sly-smiles and tries very hard not to show all her teeth. She will never look grown-up and pretty like Mama.

'This is an unexpected pleasure, Mr da Costa' says Mama sweetly. 'We came to view Captain Easter's splendid garden, but as you may see, the rain drove us to seek shelter indoors.'

'The garden is fine enough in the Summer' says Mr da Costa 'but I wonder at the captain dragging you about it in such foul weather.'

'They wanted to see it, da Costa' says the cross captain

(snap-snappity), 'and anyhow, it's better than your sorry pile at any time of the year.'

They are supposed to be friends, but they are going to argue anyway.

They do.

MR DA COSTA, RATHER UPSET: That's an unholy untruth, Easter, and you know it.

MAMA: Do you have a pleasure garden also, Mr da Costa?

MR DA COSTA: Yes indeed, my dear Mrs Newlove, and a finer one by far than old Easter's here. You must come and view it, whenever you wish.

CAPTAIN EASTER: Damned out-of-the-way place. You'll never find it, Mrs Newlove.

MR DA COSTA: I assure you, Mrs Newlove, you will have no difficulty locating Lausanne House. It is in the fashionable part of town.

LIZZY: Oh! *Lausanne* House.

As if she knew where *that* was.

MR DA COSTA: My estate is close to Addington Square, Miss Newlove, a most genteel quarter of Margate.

LIZZY: Indeed, Mr da Costa? Your estate?

CAPTAIN: Estate. Bah!

DA COSTA: I say Easter, what kind of a host are you, man? Miss Newlove looks positively faint with need of refreshment and Sarah has quite disappeared.

LIZZY, LOOKING PERFECTLY HEALTHY: Oh? Oh, thank you, Mr da Costa (*dabs her forehead*).

PAPA: Are you feeling unwell, Lizzy? We will escort you home directly.

MARY (SNEEZING): Oh dear!

LIZZY: I am quite well, thank you, Papa.

CAPTAIN: She'll be all right when she's had a drink.

DA COSTA: No doubt it was walking in your damp garden that has made her so pale, Easter.

CAPTAIN, GOING TO THE DOOR: Let be, man. Sarah! Negus!

MR DA COSTA, TAKING LIZZY'S HAND AND RUBBING IT BETWEEN HIS: My dear Miss Newlove, you are quite frozen through. A little port negus will thaw you, and then you may dine comfortably.

CAPTAIN: They aren't staying for dinner, Maurice.

DA COSTA: But surely, Miss Newlove? *(To Papa)* My dear sir, will you not dine with us?

PAPA: I thank you, but we have already dined, Mr da Costa.

CAPTAIN: School dinners, Maurice. They dine early.

DA COSTA (RELEASING LIZZY'S HAND): Oh. I see how it stands.

MARY, SNEEZING AGAIN TWICE: Oh dear!

LIZZY, VERY DISAPPOINTED: I am sure we would have liked *very much* to dine with you, Mr da Costa.

DA COSTA: And so you shall, my dear girl. Another time, you may be certain of it. You shall all dine with me, at Lausanne House. My estate is very close to the theatre, Miss Newlove. Perhaps when the season begins again you will be attending the plays there? It is but a step from Lausanne House.

LIZZY: The theatre? Oh –

PAPA: We do not attend the theatre, Mr da Costa. It is not an institution that I approve of.

DA COSTA: Indeed, I approve of very little theatre, it is so often badly played. But, Miss Newlove, at the Royal –

PAPA: We do not attend any theatre, sir. And Arabella-Elizabeth is not of an age to attend public expositions. She is still very young, sir.

MR DA COSTA, LOOKING LIKE THE BEAR WITH HIS BLACK HAIR AND HUNGRY TEETH: Not so very young, not so very young. But certainly a young lady.

Sarah the woman who is *not* a young lady comes in without knocking, with a tray of glasses and a bowl of something hot steaming and smelling spicy. She puts it down on a table, bobs to Mr da Costa, winks at the captain and goes out again.

CAPTAIN: Negus, ladies and gentlemen. Pray take some. A little for the children also, to keep out the cold.

PAPA: Forgive us, Captain, but we will not take any, thank you.

CAPTAIN, FILLING THE GLASSES: What, walking about in this cold weather? *(To Mama)* Mrs Newlove, take a drop against the cold.

MAMA: Thank you, Captain, but I do not partake of spirits.

DA COSTA, HOLDING OUT A GLASS: 'Tis nothing but port and water, madam. *(To Lizzy)* Come, Miss Newlove must have some, she is unwell.

LIZZY, TO THE GLASS: It does smell rather nice.

PAPA: A little cordial will suffice, Captain.

MAMA: Do not trouble yourself, Captain. We will take tea when we return home.

CAPTAIN: Cordial, eh? Tea? Well well. We'll have to set to then, Maurice, or Sarah will complain of the waste. You'll have a cigar at least, Newlove?

PAPA: I will not, Captain. Tobacco does not nourish the body, and therefore I see no point in consuming it.

CAPTAIN, LIGHTING A CIGAR: For pleasure, sir! That is the point. For pleasure.

DA COSTA, LIGHTING ANOTHER CIGAR: How do your arrangements progress at the new school, Mr Newlove,

Mrs Newlove? *(Looks at the captain.)* Have you exchanged the deeds for the property yet, sir? I trust you have had no difficulties there?

PAPA: I have the lease on the new school, Mr da Costa, and am to sign the paper shortly.

DA COSTA: You have not – purchased the property, sir?

PAPA: No, indeed. It would be a rash matter to buy such a place outright. We must work to establish the new school, then we might look to buy the deeds of sale.

DA COSTA: I believe it would be a sound investment, Mr Newlove.

CAPTAIN: Look here, Newlove, none of my business I know, but if I were in your place I'd buy it outright.

PAPA: That is quite out of the question, Captain. I do not have the funds to do so.

CAPTAIN: It's a valuable piece of land, Newlove. It would be worth your while.

DA COSTA: It would indeed.

CAPTAIN: They say the man who built the place – what was his name, Maurice?

DA COSTA: Bowles.

CAPTAIN: Bowles. They say the man Bowles who built the place found something buried under there. Local gossip, you know. Might be something in it, though.

DA COSTA: There might indeed.

PAPA: What manner of thing did he find, Captain?

CAPTAIN: Oh, I couldn't say. Something – worthwhile. Valuable.

JOSHUA, LETTING GO OF THE BEAR'S HEAD: Buried treasure?

CAPTAIN: Well, it's just local talk, of course. But then he did run off to the Americas a little while after.

DA COSTA: Bowles was not a wealthy man, but he somehow built a fine house on that plot of land.

CAPTAIN: And to leave the country like that – very odd.

JOSHUA: If there's any buried treasure to be had, Captain, I shall find it.

CAPTAIN: Well, it's probably all nonsense. I wouldn't go about digging pits in the garden, lad, upsetting the rabbits and moles. Eh, Newlove?

PAPA: Indeed not. Well, forgive us, Captain, but we will leave you now. We must detain you from your dinner no longer.

The captain nods and Papa nods and everybody bows and bobs. *So soon?* says Mr da Costa's black moustache to Lizzy's fingers. *Dear Mrs Newlove* say the captain's yellow whiskers to Mama's glove. Mama smiles and Lizzy smiles and Mary sneezes and *oh-dears*. Joshua pats the bear and the dog yawns and stretches and turns round in the corner. We go out into the hall, Sarah gives us our bonnets and shawls and looks at Mama with a tight cross face and smiles at the captain. She opens the door and we go out.

'I shall call on you again soon,' says the captain. He reaches and kisses Mama's hand again.

'We will be delighted to see you, Captain' says Mama. *Won't.*

We go *scra*-scrunching away from the house and through the gate and down the icy hill to the bottom. Joshua swings his arms and pretends to march.

'I want to shoot bears and boars' he says.

'I shan't like you any more if you do' say I.

Lizzy is horrid

Lizzy is very pleased to have a key and she opens the door without knocking. 'Mama will want to know if we catch the maid idling' she whisper-hisses to Mary.

Mary nods, sneezes, and shakes her head.

'Anne!' say I loud as I might 'we have come back!'

Lizzy scowls at me. 'You are not supposed to give her warning, Fanny. *Really*.' (Huffity horrid sister.)

Anne is not in the hall, not in the music room, not in the schoolroom, not in the kitchen. We go up the stairs, Lizzy untying her bonnet, Mary dab-dabbing her nose. Anne is not there either.

'I knew it' says spiteful spitting Lizzy. 'She has gone off somewhere while we were out visiting. She is probably in the arms of some – rough sailor.'

Which is really where *she* would like to be.

'Do not fret, Lizzy dear' says Mary, sniffing. 'She is probably at Papa's house. Or on an errand for the housekeeper.'

'She is in a public house' says Lizzy 'or *worse*.'

What is worse than that? Nasty spiteful Lizzy.

'I am not at all sure that I am well' says Mary sniff-sniffing. 'I think I may have taken a slight chill.'

'I am certain' says Lizzy quickly 'that *I* shall be the one to suffer. Did not Mr da Costa remark that I looked pale? I should have taken some of the port negus. Papa should have allowed it.'

'If Papa thought it right he would have allowed it' say I. 'So then it cannot have been right.'

'Shut up, Fanny' says Lizzy.

'Now, lamb' says Mary pat-patting my arm, 'run along and get dressed in something warm and dry. We cannot have you catching cold also.'

'I'm all right' say I.

Lizzy cross-sighs. 'Mama said we were to change our clothes and take our workbaskets to her. Do as you are told, Fanny.'

'You do it too then' say I.

Lizzy stroke-strokes her hair and shakes bonnet water at me. 'Nasty little creature' she says. Her mouth is a horrid shape and only horrid things come out of it.

Mary's fingers fumbling undo her bonnet ribbons and then mine. 'There' she says. Her round nose red as a cherry and shiny too. She takes my bonnet off and shakes it, but not at Lizzy. 'And what did you think of Captain Easter's splendid house, Fanny dear?'

Not much.

'She doesn't think anything' says Lizzy.

'*Do.*' (I think you're hateful and he's a horrid lying captain and you should marry him and go away for ever and make each other very miserable and wretched and cross. But I mustn't *say* so.)

'The captain is very – *aschoo!* – oh dear! very gallant' says Mary.

'He is tolerably so' says Lizzy 'but nothing *like* the gentleman his friend is.'

'Certainly' says Mary 'Mr da Costa is a very well-attired person.'

'He is quite dashing' says Lizzy. *He is quite rich* her eyes say.

'He seems a man of substance' says Mary.

'Yet he is not so very large as Papa' say I.

'Fie, Fanny!' snap-snaps Lizzy. 'What nonsense you talk.' She unbuttons her gloves and pulls at the finger-claws. 'He admires me, of course.'

Mary frowns.

Lizzy pouts.

'Did you not note it?' says Lizzy, very sharply. 'I am incredulous. How dull you both are! Did you not even hear him invite me to attend the theatre with him?'

'No' say I.

'I knew, of course' says Lizzy, pulling flicking her gloves 'that he was pursuing me the instant we met. He was quite devoted to me on the spot, I declare he was.'

'Really?' says Mary, very big-eyed and not very believing.

'Not that I really took much heed of him the first time we met' says Lizzy 'for although he was positively *ardent* he did not seem quite good enough for me to notice. Yet I did quite like him even then. He was certainly the only man there worth the catch.'

Lizzy sounds like a heroine from one of the novels Papa does not like her to read (which is what she has always wanted to sound like), only nastier.

'Did you meet him at Papa's supper?' say I.

'Of course!' says Lizzy. 'Honestly, Fanny, when else did you suppose I met him?'

'Oh' say I. 'But, Lizzy, after Papa's supper you said you didn't like any of the men there. And Mr da Costa was at Papa's supper. So I suppose you couldn't really have liked him then, could you?'

'Be quiet, Fanny' says Lizzy.

'Besides, Lizzy' say I 'I do not think that Papa likes him, for he smokes tobacco and drinks spirits. Papa would not let you marry him even if he asked very nicely.'

'Pah!' says Lizzy, snorting. 'And what would you know of it? Anyway, I said nothing about *marrying* Mr da Costa.'

'But, Lizzy dear' says Mary 'you did say – *catch*.'

'And so?'

'Lizzy!'

Lizzy raises her eyebrows very high and flick-flicks at her shawl tassels.

'Lizzy dear' says Mary 'you must not encourage his attentions if you do not want him to propose.'

'Don't be ridiculous, Mary' says Lizzy horribly 'I shall do whatsoever I like with him. He is *my* suitor after all. And *you*, Fanny – if you so much as whisper a word of this to Papa or Mama or anyone else I will skin you alive and boil you for soup. *Do you understand me?*'

Lizzy says that she has a suitor. I do not suppose Mama or Papa would believe me if I *did* tell them.

Lizzy goes rustling swish-swishing and slam-shuts the bedroom door behind her. Mary looks at me and soft-sighs and dabs her nose again.

'Oh dear' she says through her handkerchief. 'Well, Fanny, let us dress and go to Mama at once. Run along to your room, little dear.'

I do.

Lizzy and Mary talk and talk in the next room and Mary

sneezes and Lizzy sobs and then shouts *I shall* and then sobs again. Mary hushes shushes sneezes. Put on my grey dress again and the not-so-nice but clean grey pinafore. Wet shoes wet stockings roll them off and rub-rub red toes and pink feet and roll on dry stockings. Put on my house shoes. Take overshoes to put on top for the road puddles. Lizzy says *I shall* again and *I am the eldest* and then Mary sniffs sobs. Shawl, bonnet, out and across the landing and Mary snuffling behind the door and into the parlour, which is now green-papered and *not* red, and there is my workbasket and Lizzy's and Mary's. Mine has the most in it *of course*. Lizzy's is full of ribbons and trims and Mary is embroidering for cushions. Mama said I must do a sampler for the schoolroom but it is very dull and hard and I pull threads and must go back and do it again. I would ask Mary to help me but horrid-mouthed horrid-tongued Lizzy would only tattle-tale and tell Mama.

Take my basket and put it on the landing and then take Mary's and Lizzy's too. Lizzy opens the bedroom door and comes out and points at the baskets.

'What are you doing with my basket?' she says cross-faced red-eyed.

'Mama said we are to take them so I fetched them from the parlour.'

Lizzy comes quick snatches her basket and looks and pokes at it. 'Where is my taffeta ribbon? What have you done with it?'

'Nothing' say I.

'You've taken it, haven't you?' she says. 'You nasty jealous little girl. Show me your basket.'

I do. She pulls and pokes and throws my sampler and squares and threads all on to the floor.

'Where is it?' Lizzy says very loud very cross. 'Where have you hidden it?'

'Haven't!' say I. Sampler crumpled pulled threads tangled horrid *horrid* Lizzy. Face hot and eyes hot and nose tingling burning. *'Didn't.'*

Mary comes nose red eyes red too and looks at me. Lizzy drops my basket and grabs, shakes me hard and pinching.

'Lizzy dear, what is the matter?' says Mary. She pulls at Lizzy and Lizzy pulls at me and lets go, screaming.

'Little brat!' Lizzy cries. 'Little monster of a spiteful jealous thieving child!'

'What ever is to do?' says Mary. 'What have you taken, Fanny?'

'Nothing' say I.

'My taffeta ribbon!' says Lizzy.

'Well now' says Mary 'this pink one?'

Mary pulls at Lizzy's basket and out comes a long pink ribbon fine and broad and pretty. Too pretty for Lizzy.

Lizzy snort-snorts.

'Come along, Fanny dear' says Mary. She puts the sampler threads and tangles into my basket again. Picks up my basket picks up her basket and her cherry nose comes close and she soft-kisses my hot hot cheek. 'Don't cry, poor lamb' she says 'Lizzy did not mean it.' *DID.* Mild Mary sweeter than nice-Mama even when I am crying. 'Come along, put your bonnet on, child.'

I do.

Lizzy scowls at me. 'She hasn't even got boots on' she says.

'She has overshoes' says Mary. 'Do be nice, Lizzy dear.'

Lizzy does not know how to be nice so she picks up her basket and goes thud-thud-thud downstairs. We go too, down the stairs and through the door, and Mary closes it because there is no Anne still, and along the road puddle-stepping drizzle-mizzling to Papa's house.

Lizzy knocks and Anne opens the door. Lizzy scowls and snorts again and pushes past Anne into the hall. Mary follows with the baskets.

'Was up wi Miss Nulove miss?' says Anne.

'She said you were in the arms of some rough sailor because you were not in the house' say I 'and now she is cross because she was wrong.'

Anne's mouth goes very round and then grins very wide. *Haw haw* it says. *Haw haw haw*.

'I don't suppose you were in the arms of a rough sailor, were you?' say I.

Anne shakes her head. 'Naw, wurst luck' she says. 'Gaw awn in, miss.'

I do. Mrs D is in the hall, white cap on her head, looking peering listening.

'Come with me a moment, Miss Frances' she says.

We go along the hall to the schoolroom and she shuts the door very quietly behind us.

'What was that you were saying to Anne?' says Mrs D, whisper-quiet.

'Lizzy was cross because Anne was not in Mama's schoolhouse' say I. 'And now Lizzy is cross because Anne is here instead.'

'Oh?' says Mrs D, eyes big eyebrows big mouth small and round. 'And what else?'

'Nothing else, Mrs D' say I.

'Hmm' says Mrs D 'and are you quite sure of that?'

'Oh yes, quite sure,' say I. I smile my ever-so-sweet smile and Mrs D frowns. 'Mrs D, might I ask you something too?'

'All right, child.'

'Is Mr da Costa very rich?'

'Maurice da Costa? Why, he's richer than you or I, that's for certain.'

'And Bowles the builder' says I 'is he very rich too?'

'Bowles?' says Mrs D. 'Who's been on about Bowles?'

'Mr da Costa and Captain Easter' say I 'and they said he was not very rich but that he built Mama's schoolhouse and became rich and went away to the Americas with his fortune. And that he found buried treasure.'

Mrs D *ho-ho* laughs but quietly. 'That old rascal, bad as the captain. Mind you don't say aught, though, eh?'

I shake my head very carefully.

'Well' says Mrs D 'he was nothing but a plain bricklaying man, labouring and so forth, and he borrowed money and bought that land and built the house on it. And when he couldn't afford to pay for his bread any more he ran off, clean as you like. Folk say he went to ship and sailed to the Americas and some say he never made it past Ramsgate port and drank himself to ruin there. And some say as he had family in Canterbury and went there and took on a new name. But I can tell you, my girl, he didn't find himself any buried treasure. He found himself without a farthing and took off to escape the bailiffs.' She pinches her lips together.

'So did the captain lie then?' say I. 'And did Mr da Costa lie *too*?'

'Larloes and medlars' says Mrs D. She huffs sighs and shakes her head. 'I shouldn't like to say so I'm sure' she says.

(*I* should.)

'Well' says Mrs D, opening the door ever-so-softly 'there I go telling you all again. You just mind you keep your thoughts to yourself. Run along now.'

Dearest James,

Although it barely seems to be so little, we have been a whole week in Margate. I can only hope that you <u>must</u> have received my first letter by now. I do hope that you have got the others too and that they find you well and not studying <u>too</u> hard.

Papa's school has begun again this morning and so I am to spend much of my time here now, with Mary and Lizzy. The boy boarders arrived yesterday and the day-school pupils came today. I have not seen them yet although I did see two of the boarders. They were very pale and sad-looking and smaller than Joshua. Mama said we are to let the boarders become settled before we are introduced to them, although of course we shall not be much in their company at all. I hope that they are good and obedient to Papa and learn their lessons very well. I hope also that I shall be allowed to play with Joshua sometimes, even though he is a boy too.

Yesterday was Sunday. We went to the new chapel. I had not been to a service all week but we have had family prayers of course. Mama says that Lizzy and Mary and I and Mama are to go to chapel together in the evenings. We went twice with Papa and Joshua yesterday. The new chapel is very tall and grand-looking and is next to the burying ground. Papa is very important at the chapel as you might guess and he helped also with the Sunday school, which of course I do not go to, so we did not see him very much yesterday. We were to have had supper all together, but the new boy boarders came just before, so we could not. Mama had supper with Papa and Joshua and the new boys, and Anne the girl here brought our supper for us on a tray from Papa's school. Lizzy says that this is how we shall live now but I am certain that Mama said we might have supper at Papa's school sometimes. Lizzy and Mary and I had cold mutton and potatoes in the new green parlour, which was once the red parlour that Mama did not like and so changed the paper. It is not quite so green as Papa's parlour but it is not quite so large either. I do not know what the boys and Joshua had for supper but I think it was probably nicer than ours.

Mama has been very busy with making the new school ready and we are to have new desks made. Mama is giving me and Mary lessons just as before, except that we do not use the schoolroom yet for it is too big for just the three of us. Lizzy is not taking very many lessons with Mama but says that she is learning how to run the household instead. She has been with Mrs D the housekeeper all of this morning until dinner, which was very nice for us all, except perhaps for Mrs D. Do not be cross with me for saying so dearest brother about my eldest sister but she has been very cross and not nice to me at all since we have been here. I know I should bear it with good grace as you and Papa would both tell me, but it is very difficult to bear with good grace being called a thief when you are not one. (Do not say anything to Papa I beg you as I have not said anything to him about it myself. I shall pray that Lizzy becomes nice and good and kind one day so that she is not punished too much for her pride and vexatiousness on the Day of Judgement.)

Mama had dinner with us in the green parlour today. There is a table in the parlour which folds up very small and is not like a proper dinner table. We had mutton again only this time it was in a stew. I do not like mutton. Anne carried the pot of stew from the kitchen in Papa's school right up to us in the parlour. Mama says that kings and queens have their dinner carried in on salvers and that their dinner table is always a very long way from the kitchen. So we are living like people do at court. Anne said she had to wrap the pot in her shawl on the way to keep it warm. I think that is what she meant. I cannot think that our good King and Queen have their silver soup tureens looked after quite so well as that.

I am grateful of course that I am not cast out and hungry and always say grace properly before dinner and supper, even when it is mutton. So please do not think so very badly of me, dear brother, or believe that I have forgotten how fortunate I am.

On Saturday we visited with our neighbour Captain Easter, as I wrote before that we were all invited. Captain Easter has a very large house and a garden which he has made Mama promise to visit in the fine weather. We were asked to stay to dinner but had already had ours. There was also another man there who lives in a big house, he has a foreign name and very black moustaches. He and the captain both smoked tobacco and drank spirits but Papa was very civil with them anyway. I suppose that this is because they are our neighbours and need saving. Perhaps Papa will ask them to chapel soon.

My dear brother I must now go back downstairs as Mama has called me to read to her in French. I hope that the days are not so very long for you as they are for me until I hear from you, and so you must believe that even without your sending me any letters at all for ages I remain

your affectionate sister Frances.

Fetching Joshua

Not raining not icy just grey grey, grey sky grey path grey muddy puddles. Mary might have come but Lizzy would not let her. Mama said I must not go alone. Papa would not like me to.

Shiny brassy knocker squeak-knock-squeak-knock and Mrs D opens.

'Bless me, child' she says 'come in, come in.'

'Can I have Joshua?' say I.

Mrs D closes the door, shuffle-rustles along the hall. 'And how are you this afternoon, Miss Frances?' she says not turning.

'Very well thank you' say I 'but I want very much to go to the harbour and to the libraries and may not go alone.'

Mrs D calls *JOSHUA!* up the stairs. 'Well, I am sure Miss Mary would go with you' she says 'or Miss Arabella-Elizabeth.'

Won't.

Joshua does not come.

JOSHUA! calls Mrs D again. 'Where is that boy?'

'Shall I go and see in the attic?' say I.

'Bless me, my girl!' says Mrs D. 'On no account shall you go up there. Your father would never let me hear an end. No, no, I shall go up and see.'

She does, shuffle-shuffling one step two steps three steps four steps very slowly up the stairs and on and on for ever. Where is Joshua?

Door slam-bangs along the hall. Kitchen? *Garden.*

Talking thumping muffled man noises. Coming closer and there at the corner Woods, heavy-footed big-headed big-flat-nosed comes *kra-ump-kra-ump* along the hall. Big hands full of logs. *Pat-pat* stepping behind him too – not Anne, not the cook, not the cook's girl. A *boy,* coalscuttle swinging, long loose-armed like a monkey. Too *too* heavy for him to carry.

'Miss Frances' says Woods nodding although he is never pleased to see anybody.

'Good day' say I.

The boy pinch-faced stare-stares at me. He is not one of Papa's boys.

'Hello' say I.

'Come on, lad' says Woods.

The boy does.

They go *kra-ump* and *pat-pat* into the parlour. Woods's voice growl-grumbles. *Careful with them logs* it says. *Mind the floor.* Papa is not in the parlour then.

Mrs D comes down the stairs head shaking. 'Joshua's not there, Miss Frances' she says. 'Lessons are over and the boys are off somewhere. Step out the back and see, he may have gone over the field.'

Down the passage through the door out into the grey garden. Soil all clumpy muddy in brown dirt squares, shovel in one of them. No Joshua. Not in the garden not in the field not anywhere. Never anywhere any more.

Not there? says Mrs D's voice.

NO.

Go back in and follow her along the passage and past the schoolroom to the door. The boy that was with Woods comes and nods at Mrs D and nods at me and goes out past us.

'Where are you off to then?' says Mrs D.

The boy stops takes off his cap puts it on again. 'Town' he says.

'What for?' says Mrs D.

'Blacking for the stove polish for the boots oysters for the cook.'

'Oysters?' says Mrs D. 'What does the cook want with oysters?'

'Supper for the dancing master' says the boy.

'Mr Mills?' say I. 'Is he coming for supper?'

'And his mother' says the boy 'both windmills a-twirling.'

'Mr Mills is a very nice gentleman' say I. *Rude boy.*

He bites his lip.

'Well then' says Mrs D 'Miss Frances here wants to go to town too. You shall go with her.'

'Oh!' say we.

'Be off then' says Mrs D 'before it starts a-raining.'

The rude boy slump-slouches to the gate and I follow. He walks and I walk and he says nothing and starts *fhuw-fhuw* whistling.

'Must you whistle?' say I.

'Ye'm' he says and does. *Fhuw-fhuw-fhuw.*

'What is your name?' say I. 'You are not one of Papa's pupils.'

'No'm.'

'Who are you then?'

'George.'

'George who?'

'Gardener's son.'

'Oh' say I 'Mr Stroud the gardener.'

The boy grins. 'Mr Stroud? Most call im Stroud.'

His face is long pointy bony but his smile makes it look round and nice. I smile too and he smiles even bigger and we both laugh.

'You're the youngest then' he says.

'I'm Frances' say I. 'Do you know Joshua my brother?'

'Course I do.'

'Where is he?'

He shrugs. 'Goes off all the time, looking for the French. Looking for something.'

'Buried treasure' say I.

'Pirates' says he.

'Captain Easter told him that there was some' say I.

'Pirates?'

'Treasure. But Captain Easter is a –'

Don't say. *Mustn't say.*

George stops peers at me. 'A what?'

'Mustn't say' say I. Walk faster turn the corner jump-stepping puddle-minding.

George runs splashing up. 'I know what he is right enough' he says.

'Do you?'

'My pa says he's a gambler and a – oh, a something-monger but I can't remember what. I think it was about liking women.'

Women?

'Where do you want to go to?' says George. 'I've got errands.'

'To the harbour to see the boats and to the library to see the books and notices.'

'What for?' says George.

'Because.'

'Liberry first then' says George.

Past the farm past the gardens and down down towards the theatre and where Mr da Costa lives. Not that far. Hawley Square the tall houses very grand and the gardens all cut in patterns with the paths and no flowers yet. George *fhuw-fhuws* then looks at me. Stops and grins.

'Here's the library' say I.

'Right' says George standing leaning arm-crossing. 'I'll wait here.'

Pull-tug his arms apart. 'Come in with me' say I. 'I don't want to go in on my own.'

He frowns and I smile and he says *all right then just for a minute*. Grumble grumble. We go in.

Bettison's Library. Tall and wide and shining even though it is grey and horrid everywhere else. Mirrors bright-polished and lamps and gentlemen with tall hats and newspapers and ladies with flat bonnets and fine shawls. Books and books and books, shelves and glass and carved people coming out of the ceiling. George stares and his mouth goes all long and loose and silly like a horse's.

'Have you never been in here?' say I, whisper-quiet.

Shakes his head.

'Let's read the notices' say I.

Posters bills advertisers' cards and the newspapers smooth-folded hanging like curtains.

NOTICES for the Month of FEBRUARY.

AUCTION of plate.

ELECTIONS.

STEAMBOAT sailings.

TIDE TIMES.

SEA BATHING – the healthful cure for all ailments.

MAGICAL DANCING FIGURES.

'Look!' say I elbow-nudging George. 'Look at this one!'

Magical Dancing Figures –
Enthusiastic Violoncello Players, Changeable Cards,
with a variety of amusing tricks and deceptions.
Easily performed.

George nods, shrugs, looks away.
'Wouldn't you like to see them?' say I.
'See what?' says George.
'The figures!'
'What figures?'
'Look! *Magical Dancing Figures*. And these. *A variety of Fancy and Novel Ornamental Articles likewise on Sale*. Oh, I wish we could go! Do you think my papa would let us go?'
'Where is it?' says George.
'As it says' say I, pointing 'in Dover, and then in Ramsgate and then –'

'Then where?' says George, staring peering.

Not seeing. I point to MARGATE. He shrugs.

'Can you not see it?' say I.

He shuffles takes off his cap puts it on again. Shrug-shrugs.

'I can see it right enough' he says soft-sad. 'I can't make it out though.'

Can't make it out? It is black and tall and easy enough and very nicely printed.

'Why not?' say I.

'Because . . . because I cannot read' he says. Bite-chews his lip.

'Can you not?' say I. 'That is very odd for you are at least as old as I and almost as old as Joshua.'

'I've not learned it' says he. 'Come on, I've to buy oysters and all sorts.'

We go without books without newspapers without even looking properly at the magical dancing figures. Papa would not let me I am sure even though it is in the library and so cannot be such a very bad thing. Although they do allow raffles there, which *is* gambling.

Past the fine square where the duke lived past the Assembly Rooms (no dances for Lizzy) and on and on. Through the market square noisy smelly push-shoving and round and there the sea, cold fishy-blowing wind and the water all grey and lumpy.

'There's your boats then' says George not smiling any more.

Down to the harbour and the big black clouds coming fast from the sea and the boats up-down-up-downing in the water. George goes to a boat fish-smelling horrid and asks for oysters and the woman asks for his basket but he hasn't one, so she puts them in a box with string round it. The black clouds come up to us and stand over the sign that says

ROYAL YORK HOTEL and the sky *cra-aaak ra-raaaaaaaaaaa*-rumbles and everybody begins to walk *very* quickly.

'Come on' says George pull-tugging 'it's going to storm.'

We go fast walking up the slope past the market through the town and the sky *raaaaaa*-rumbles again and the wind stops.

'Come on!' says George skip-running. 'Here it comes!'

Plat-plat-plat thick drops falling wet on the path on my bonnet on the box of oysters. George runs and I run and we go up puddle-jumping and the rain comes loud falling in big hard drops *prum-prum-prumming* the stones. Running skipping jumping hard-laughing over the roads puddles past people shops houses, up the long lane (windy icy) past the old houses, rain running streaming down along the road racing us and on and on, skeleton trees shaking and through the gate and up the path to Papa's door. George laughing dripping knock-knocks and grins at me and we laugh.

'I'll teach you' say I.

'Teach me what?' he says.

'To read' say I.

'I'm well enough' he says. 'Don't say aught, will you?'

Thin cheeks thin pointy chin long and wet rain-dripping.

'All right' say I.

Mrs D opens and looks at us and shakes her head. 'Come on, you two' she says 'and mind you don't wet the rugs.' We go in and she *tut-tut-tut*s. 'Anne's just polished the hall too. Go on with you, Miss Frances. There's a good fire in the parlour.'

Go to the green door but George doesn't. Mrs D mutter-grumbles pushes him along and round the corner. *What about that blacking and the polish?* says Mrs D's voice and George's voice sighs and says *had to get back couldn't let Miss Frances wait in the storm.*

Papa is not in the parlour. (Good.) The fire is big with logs that Woods carried and the coal from the too heavy coalscuttle that made George's arms look long. George cannot read but he is not stupid like people who cannot read should be. He is nice for a boy, nicer than Papa's boys who eat all the supper and giggle at Mama and put out their tongues at me when Papa is not looking.

Hello. Joshua! Joshua, muddy dirty wet scowling at the door.

'I looked for you' say I. 'Where have you been?'

'Did you see the storm?' says Joshua coming to the fire. 'A real crasher.'

'Where were you?' say I. 'I wanted to go to town.'

'Stop hogging the fire' he says. 'I'm frozen.'

'Where *were* you?'

'I went to see Captain Easter' he says.

Didn't.

'You're all dirty' say I.

'So?' he says. 'You're all wet.'

'I went to town anyway' say I 'but you didn't go to see the captain.'

'Did' he says cross-scowling 'and you're not supposed to go into town alone.'

'Didn't' say I. 'And you're a bad liar and Papa will find you out.'

'I came back over the fields and fell over. That's why I'm muddy.'

'Pooh' say I 'that's a poor story. There aren't any fields to go over.'

'There *are*. And what are you doing going to town on your own, then? Papa will find that out directly too.'

'I went with George' say I. 'He's the gardener's son. He says he knows *you*.'

'So?'

'He's nice' say I 'and he took me to the library and the harbour, but it rained horribly and we ran back.'

'So?' says Joshua (again). He rubs his hands at the fire. He has *not* been with the captain.

'George said you were probably off looking for the French' say I. 'Have you found any yet?'

'Only in the Grammar' says Joshua 'and Mr Ducheson.'

'He has beautiful hands.' Joshua's hands are muddy streaky. 'Are you still looking for buried treasure?' say I. 'For you won't find any, you know.'

Joshua pout-pouts. 'Captain Easter says that there is some and I shall find it.'

'The captain tells stories' say I 'and so do you.'

'What do you know about it?' says Joshua. Just like *Lizzy*.

'Lots' say I 'and why does everyone always think I don't know about things when they are doing something silly and don't *want* me to know? Lizzy does it and you do it and even Mama does it too. I'm *not* silly and I *do* know things. And you weren't in the fields because I looked and you couldn't go to see the captain today because it is Saturday and he has gone to London. I heard Lizzy say so to Mary. He has gone with Mr da Costa and his friends.'

'So?' says Joshua cross-faced loud. 'And why should I tell you where I go? You are not Mama.'

'You shall have to tell Mama' say I 'and Papa too when he comes in and sees how dirty you are.'

'I shall get clean.'

'Papa will know anyway, he always does.'

Joshua huff-huffs and rubs his hands and bits of mud fall

off and on to the floor. He takes off his boots and puts them by the fire. They are muddy and there are white scratches too and white powder on his arms like the dog put on my pinafore. Chalk, Mrs D said. Joshua rub-scrubs at them, frowning.

'Anyway' say I 'there *isn't* any treasure because if there *was* it wouldn't be there any more. Bowles the builder who made the house would have had it and so would the captain and so would Mr da Costa, if they knew about it.'

'They know about it because it is real' says Joshua 'but they don't know where it is, that's all.'

'Well, they could dig for it' say I 'if they think it is in Mama's garden.'

'I shall find it' says Joshua 'and when I do I shan't give you any.'

'I don't care' say I 'and even if you did find treasure Papa would take it and it wouldn't be yours any more.'

Shuffling tap-tapping at the door and Mrs D comes in. 'Look sharp, you two' she says 'and get yourselves cleaned up before your mama and papa come in.'

'Yes, Mrs D' say we.

'Master Joshua!' says Mrs D. 'Look at that mud everywhere! Where have you been to get so filthy?'

Joshua huffs shrugs and looks at the fire.

'Mrs D' say I 'what does George the gardener's son do? Does he work for Papa now?'

'He is to work for his father' she says 'garden labouring. Mrs Newlove has asked for him to help with the new school garden.'

'Digging?' say I.

'I should say so, digging and planting and such' says Mrs D. 'Come along now, you look like a pair of deekers in all that muck. Don't go catching a chill.'

She goes and Joshua picks up his boots and goes to the door too.

'*Well*, brother' say I 'if there *is* any buried treasure in Mama's garden, it will most likely be *George Stroud* that finds it first.'

(He does not like that.)

Friday the day before the Fourteenth day of February 1835
Ten o'clock in the morning
Bellevue School for Girls
Margate

Dearest James,

Your letter arrived this morning and you may imagine how delighted Mama was to open it. She read it to us over breakfast. I was very pleased too to have a message from you, although it is not <u>quite</u> the same as getting a letter all of my own.

So very much has happened. The new schoolhouse is almost ready, there are desks and books and Mama has made some bills to advertise it. There is a notice in the town hall and the library, which makes it very proper. Mama says that we shall have the first girls in soon. The gardener's son George has been sowing vegetables behind the house so we shall have our own kitchen garden as well as Papa's. I have asked Mama if I may grow peas for they have such pretty flowers. The piano from Papa's school is now downstairs. The men carried it along the muddy path in the rain and a dog from the farm came and barked at the piano and chased them all the way. The room it is in is now the dancing and music room and there is a class in there this morning, which is why I am not having a lesson but am writing to you instead. Mama has gone to help for there are so many boys. They are dancing and I can hear the piano even though they are like a herd of cows stamping about. Mr Mills is the dancing and music master and he and his mama came to supper on Saturday last. I hope they shall come again for they are very nice and we had baked apples <u>and</u> rice pudding.

Lizzy and Mary are in the parlour for they are not to help with the dancing lessons. When the piano was moved Mr Mills came to tune it and then said we should try out the dance floor. He and Mary and Anne the maid and I all danced a country dance and Mr Mills sang the tune. Mama came in and danced too so that Mr Mills could play the piano. It is the first dance we have had. Lizzy said that she would not dance until a gentleman asked her, so Mr Mills asked her for a waltz and she was quite rude to him. She said she was waiting to be asked to a ball at the Assembly Rooms. Mr Mills did not say anything after that. Lizzy said later that there will be a ball for her at Mr da Costa's house. He is the man with the foreign name who is friends with our neighbour the captain. He is very rich and has a fine house so it is quite likely that he will have a ball one day, even if it is not for Lizzy. Lizzy and Mary have been hoping for a ball so that they may make new dresses and eat white soup. I do not know if I should like white soup, for soup should be brown, unless it is green like pea soup, which Joshua does not like. When I grow peas I shall make green soup with them and eat it all myself.

The music has stopped now and Mama will be asking for me soon so I must finish now. Perhaps when you are not so very busy you will think of me and send a letter especially written to

your affectionate sister Frances.

Papa is quiet

Joshua grubby-kneed grubby-handed dirty-faced scowl-scowls and kicks with his boot toes.

'Stand up straight when I speak to you' says Papa. *Very* quietly.

Joshua does. His eyes are small and dark and sulky.

'You are too old for this childish behaviour' says Papa. 'You are not a street urchin. If you wish to look like a beggar and a starveling I shall see to it that you feel as one. Is that your wish, my boy?'

'No, sir' says Joshua. (Shuffle sniffle.)

'If you wish to be covered in mud there is plenty of rough work to be done' says Papa. 'The gardener's boy has been very dutiful and diligent. I shall release him this afternoon and put you in his place. You shall begin directly. Is that understood?'

Joshua's eyes big and worried. 'Doing what, sir?'

'Digging, Joshua' says Papa. 'Digging and hoeing.'

Joshua hangs his head and Mama takes hold of him and pushes him to the door.

'Find the gardener's son and send him to us' says Papa. 'He will inform you of what to do. I will speak to him myself to be certain of it.'

Joshua looks at me and I say BUR-IED TREA-SURE with my mouth but not out loud. He tries to shrug but doesn't dare.

Mama opens the green door. 'Although you have quite ruined these clothes' she says (tugging prodding) 'you will change into something coarser for digging.'

'Yes, Mama' says Joshua.

He goes. Mama looks at Papa, who looks at me. Look down at my sampler and there is the letter J in blue silk with a big loop too long on it. Pick pick pick it out and start again.

Mama and Papa murmur mutter *chapel meeting – very shortly – stay with the girls* and Mama comes and sits beside me, looks at my sampler. I hold it up. She frowns and looks away again.

Door knock-knocks and Mrs D shuffles along the corridor past us and opens. *Not* George yet – Lizzy and Mary. They come in, baskets ribbons gauzes linens rustling and sit by Mama, talk-talking fussing shushing. Mama looks at Papa, and Lizzy and Mary make faces and nod and stop talking. Papa picks up a book but does not read it. His hands are very big and still.

Knock-knock *again* – Mrs D's voice and another, a man, *still* not George. Mama and Papa look up and Mary elbow-nudges Lizzy. Lizzy smiles and pat-pats her hair and skirt and the things in her workbasket.

Mrs D taps on the door. 'Mr da Costa to see you' she says.

Mr da Costa, tall hat long coat long waistcoat very smart and his whiskers black and curl-curling as he smiles. 'Good afternoon' he says, smiling bowing.

We stand and bow and bob back. Lizzy sly-grins, eyes all lashes and peering as if the sun was in them. Papa shakes Mr da Costa's hand and Mr da Costa kisses Mama's hand and smiles at Lizzy and sits down.

'So delightful to see you all again' he says.

Papa nods, Mr da Costa smiles and Mama and Lizzy talk and talk. Papa is to go to chapel soon and now we shall have to stay here with Mr da Costa. Lizzy rustles and fusses and cannot keep still in her chair. Mary is quite red. Look at my sampler and pretend to sew. J K L M. Where is George?

Talk and talk, on and on. Lucky Joshua to be outside, digging for treasure, finding worms and beetles and planting things that grow. Not sewing. Stab-stab the cloth and the needle goes down and through and back up and *ow!* sharp-pokes. The blood comes up, wet red bubble on my thumb where all the swirls meet. Put it in my mouth, *not* on the sampler.

'Fanny dear!' says Mama, frowning. 'You are not a baby.'

'I pricked it' say I.

Lizzy laughs. Papa frowns, but not at me.

Tap-knock soft on the door and there he is, *George*. He must have come in through the back door, like Woods does. Like a tradesman.

Papa stands up. 'Come in, boy' he says.

George looks at Papa, looks at Mr da Costa, looks at me. I smile and he comes in, very shy and scared-eyed. Lizzy makes a not-very-nice face and turns back to Mr da Costa.

'Are your ears cold, young man?' says Mr da Costa to George.

'N-no, thank you, sir' says George.

'Then perhaps you might take off your cap' says Mr da Costa. 'There *are* ladies present.'

Lizzy snort-laughs. George mumbles shuffles and takes off his cap.

'Please, sir' he says to Papa very quickly, 'Master Joshua said I was to come in and say that I have left im to hoe the cabbages behind Mrs Newlove's school, sir.'

'Hoe the cabbages' says Papa, 'that is well. Thank you, George.'

George bows drops his cap and picks it up again. Lizzy soft-snorts and giggles. He goes out long-faced, not smiling not looking at me. Horrid Lizzy.

'Forgive me, Mr da Costa' says Papa. 'I am expected at the chapel and must leave you now.'

They stand and bow and Mr da Costa says that he is happy to be left in such delightful company. Mama and Lizzy smile and laugh. Papa goes out. He is still very quiet.

Talk and talk and then tea, and sewing and more talk. Lizzy chatters and smiles and shows Mr da Costa her teeth (like a frightened horse). I try not to stare at her but she sees me looking anyway.

'Fanny dear' she says not-very-nicely 'how is your embroidery coming along?'

'Very well thank you, sister' say I.

'Fanny is something of an apprentice, Mr da Costa' says Lizzy.

'Do show Mr da Costa your lovely tapestry, Lizzy' says Mama. 'It is quite wonderful, Mr da Costa. Quite a marvel.'

'Oh, shall I?' says Lizzy.

'I am afraid' says Mary softly 'rather, I *believe* it is in the other house.'

'Fanny will fetch it' says Mama. 'Won't you, Fanny?'

They look at me.

'Yes, Mama' say I.

'Be *careful* with it then' says hissing Lizzy.

Oh yes I *shall*. 'May I bring Joshua back also?' say I.

Mama looks at the window and then at the clock and puts her head on one side.

'It will be quite dark soon, Mama' say I.

'And Joshua has not had any tea, poor lamb' says Mary.

Mama nods. 'Very well, Fanny, but make sure he washes his hands and takes off his boots before he comes in.'

'Yes, Mama.'

Down the hall and through the door and skip-jump-skip-jump the path. Darker now, harder to mind the puddles, not too deep but still muddy. The lamp is lit above the new sign white and black-lettered and very smart. BELLEVUE SCHOOL FOR GIRLS. Scrape-knock the knocker and Anne comes, round-faced smiling.

'Hallo' she says. 'Come fer the nu gardner?'

'Is he still out there?' say I.

'He hant come in yet.'

Down the hall and out into the dark garden. Not by the cabbages, not by the rubbish pile. Not in the shed where the shovel is kept. Not in the privy. 'JOSHUA!' say I. Not anywhere.

Back in and up the stairs five-six-seven and the skeleton tree tap-taps at the window. It has a light hanging swinging in it. No – not the tree, *outside*. Out, behind the glass behind the tree, a light swinging moving. A lantern. Press my face up against it, cold glass steaming tree tapping. A light moving across the garden, low like someone carrying it, lower and lower and darker. Gone.

Hop-run up into my room and swing open the window quick and not-creaking. No one in the garden, no light any more. Dark now, all blue and black and the shapes of things disappearing, even the cabbages and the roof of the shed. No lantern any more. No Joshua either.

Into the parlour and there all Lizzy's things piled up on a

cushion. Take the tapestry and spread it out, sit on it, put it on the floor and put my boot on it (ha!) and shake it out clean again. Horrid Lizzy's horrid tapestry with trees and sheep and ladies in big silly dresses and bonnets sitting on swings. Not as nice as Mary's tapestries with flowers and birds in, but Mama never says so. *I* shall.

Down the stairs again and Anne at the door and *Papa*!

Papa comes in black coat black hat black shoe-wiping.

'Frances' he says 'where is your brother? Has he finished outside?'

'I have not seen him yet, Papa' say I. 'I came to fetch a tapestry for Lizzy to show to Mr da Costa.'

'Is he still there then?' says Papa (a not-question). 'Very well, child. Give me the tapestry and I shall take it to them. Find Joshua and bring him along directly, he has done enough penance today.'

'Yes, Papa.'

He takes the tapestry and puts his other hand on my head and smiles. 'Good girl, Frances. Come back quickly to the house. I do not want the two of you to loiter here.'

Run to the garden door and shout *JOSHUA! JOSHUA! PAPA IS HERE!* at the dark and run back in again. Papa is gone. Into the music room, sit on the piano stool tall and red-velvet-cushioned. The piano is dark and smooth-shining and smelling of polish. I open the lid and touch the keys ever-so-softly, *pflunk-pflunk-pflink*. Wish *I* could play, properly. Like Mr Mills.

Stamp-thumping in the hall and there is Joshua, dirty and dusty and face-smeary. 'Don't play the piano' he says. 'You know you're not supposed to.'

'I'm going to learn' say I. 'Where were you?'

'Hoeing the cabbages.'

'Liar.'

'Was.' Huffity-huff.

Soft-shut the piano lid. 'We're to go back now. Mr da Costa came and he won't go away again. Papa has been and said he wants us.'

'What are you doing here anyway?'

'Fetching you.'

Joshua wet-snuffles and rubs his nose. 'Come on then.'

'You're to wash first.'

'I'll wash later.'

'*Fine.*'

Out of the door and along the path. Shan't wait for him, *shan't*. He is a *liar* and as bad as the captain and if Papa scolds him for not washing his hands I shan't care a bit for it. Not a bit.

'What's the matter with you?' Joshua says.

Not saying. Not a *word*.

Along the lane and through the gate and knock on Papa's door. Joshua stands arm-crossed on the step, huffity-huffing. *Don't care.*

'You're in a fine mood' he says.

(Don't care.)

Mrs D opens the door and rolls her eyes at Joshua. 'You get dirtier every time I see you' she says.

Go in and along the hall and they are still in the parlour, murmuring laughing. Joshua runs up and tug-pulls at my hair from behind. Not hard, though.

'Let go' say I.

'Made you speak.'

'You should be glad that I don't speak *more*' say I.

The green door opens. Mama and Papa and Mr da Costa come out.

'Oh!' says Mama. 'You are very messy, Joshua. But Mr da Costa is leaving now. Get his hat and coat, Fanny.'

I do. Mama and Papa talk to Mr da Costa in the doorway. Joshua watches them, big-eyed long-mouthed.

'What was that supposed to mean?' he says, whisper-quiet.

Mr da Costa comes out and takes his things. Mary and Lizzy come too. We all go to the door, Mr da Costa kisses Mary's hand and then Mama's and shakes Papa's and then looks at Lizzy. She holds out her hand and he takes it and smiles and squeezes and kisses.

'Goodbye, Miss Newlove' he says.

Joshua sharp-nudges me. 'What was that supposed to mean?' he hisses.

'You are lucky that I don't tell Papa how you went off walking' say I ever-so-quietly. 'With a *lantern*.'

Mama opens the door and Mr da Costa goes out. He looks at Lizzy.

'Mama dear' says Lizzy *very* sweetly, 'might I go back to the schoolhouse quickly? I should like to fetch some more green silk for my workbasket.'

'I have some green silk here' say I.

Lizzy looks narrow-eyed and horrid at me. 'I can't use *your* silk, Fanny' she says. 'It is too coarse for *proper* embroidery.'

'Very well, Lizzy dear' says Mama. 'Come directly back again.'

Lizzy smiles and steps out beside Mr da Costa. 'Allow me to accompany you to the gate, Miss Newlove' he says.

'Why!' says Lizzy in her best ever-so-surprised voice. 'That is very kind of you, Mr da Costa.'

They go together along the path and Mama shuts the door behind them. Mary white-faced bites her lip. Joshua stare-stares at me.

'Go and get cleaned up now, Joshua' says Mama. 'You are

a disgrace to your father. The boarders will soon be back for supper.'

Mama and Papa and Mary go back into the parlour. Joshua is staring and pinch-mouthed and trying not to look worried.

'I thought I saw a fox sniffing about' he says. 'So I chased it off.'

'With a lantern?'

He shrugs.

'You're a bad liar, Joshua Newlove' say I.

'You're a cross little sister, Fanny Newlove' says Joshua. He pinches his lips tight together. 'Promise you won't tell?'

'Promise.'

'Swear it on Papa's Bible.'

'I swear.'

'And on Mama and Papa.'

'And on Mama and Papa. What is it?'

He grins all toothy and grimy. 'I've found the treasure.'

'That's silly' say I. 'There isn't any treasure.'

'There is. It's a secret underground palace.'

'Liar.'

'It's true. I've found it, the place Mr Davidson was talking about. The underground place.'

He puts his hand in his pocket and brings out a lump of something, white with shiny bits of pink and grey and blue. *Chalk*, with seashells stuck into it, curved and cupped like a flower. He grins again.

'What is that?' say I.

'Just a tiny bit of where I've been.' He puts the flower back into his pocket. 'I've found the realm of shells.'

Coming back from chapel

Joshua is being good-Joshua today. Soft *one-and-two-and-one-and-two* walking, not stamping stomping arm-swinging. Smiling carrying Mama's books. (Not even puddle-splashing.) Know why he is being not-Joshua. *Our secret.*

Papa said that Joshua must finish working in the garden after chapel, and I said *may I help please, Papa?* and Mama said *no* for I was still *belabouring my workbasket*. B-E-L-A-B-O-U-R-I-N-G. That is to make a lot of work out of nothing, which is not true. Mama thinks that working in the garden is punishment for Joshua, but when I ask if I may, it is a treat like syrup or playing on the piano. Which does not make sense. My workbasket is full and I am only up to P on my horrid horrid sampler. Mama will not let me help Joshua and if I do not help I shall *never* see the shells.

Papa staying behind until dinner. Dinner and then prayers and then evening service and *then* it will be too dark to go. *From the sixth hour there was darkness over the land.* Night time begins at five o'clock now. Papa will be home for dinner and then he might let me but Mama will not.

Past the corner along the road and Mama's school sign smart shiny. The boy boarders do not go to our chapel but they will be back for dinner. Better to go before that. Joshua says that they might want to see the shells too but I said not to. They might tell Papa. Joshua Sunday coat Sunday shoes shining hurries (*not* running) to Papa's school to get ready for digging.

'Go in and change your clothes too, girls' says Mama.

Lizzy and Mary go in. Mama looks at me. 'What is it, Fanny?'

'Please, Mama' say I ever-so-nicely and not-grumbling 'please may I help in the garden until dinner? Only until dinner, Mama.'

Mama looks at the sky and my pinafore and the grass. 'Why do you ask again, Fanny? I have already given you my answer.'

'Please, Mama' say I. 'I have not played outside *all week*.'

'That is because I will not have you rolling in the mud like your brother.'

'I will not roll' say I 'I promise. Ma*ma*.'

'Do not plead with me' she says crossly. 'I will not tolerate it.'

'Yes, Mama.'

Hot nose tingling hot eyes. No shells today and then lessons again tomorrow until *next* Saturday. Swallow hard. Not sniffing, *not*.

'Oh, very well, Fanny.'

'Mama?'

'Change your pinafore. You are not to do any digging but you may stand and watch if you wish. If you have a smudge upon you at dinner you will not go outside again for another week. Is that clear?'

Mama!

She goes and I go up-skipping along the hall up the stairs into my room. Fold and put my Sunday pinafore and shoes (very *very* careful) into the press and the grey pinafore from the hook over my head. Grey a no-smudging colour. Lizzy and Mary on the landing chattering moving fetching things. Mary tap-taps and peers round the door. 'Come along, Fanny dear' she says. 'Bring your basket.'

'Mama said I may stay here with Joshua' say I. *Did*.

Mary's eyebrows go high up and she smiles. 'Wash your hands before dinner then' she says 'and don't get dirty. Joshua is outside already. I believe he quite likes gardening after all.'

She goes and Lizzy's voice says *thank goodness* and they walk chattering clattering down the stairs and the door bangs.

Mary gone, Lizzy gone, Mama gone. Papa at chapel Anne at church Mrs D helping the cook. All gone. Just Joshua and me and the shells and nobody else but God who sees everything anyway.

Down the stairs and out and there Joshua, grinning in the cabbages (his proper Joshua grin) leaning on the shovel.

'You got away with it then?' he says.

'Mama said only until dinner.'

'Have they gone? All of them?'

I nod and he grins and *sthwiiiick* sticks the shovel into the earth. It stays there upstanding handle sky-pointing.

'Come on then' he says.

He goes mud-striding to the shed and I hopscotch step-jump-skip over the dirt and cabbages.

'There's a tunnel first' says Joshua. Puts his hand in the dusty spiderwebbiness under the shed, pulls out a tin box.

'What's that?'

'Lantern.' He opens the tin and there the lantern that I

saw, with a piece of string on it and a tinderbox. A candle too. 'Got the tinderbox from Woods's cupboard' he says.

'That's stealing' say I.

'Only borrowing.'

Joshua looks round at the garden and the house, and at the wall and the field behind. There isn't anybody but us and the cabbages and the shovel, so he opens the tinderbox and lights the lantern and turns it down ever-so-dimly.

'Where do we go now?' say I.

'Follow me.'

Past the vegetables past the big empty pots (Mama said we might have one each to grow flowers) on to the piece that is not dug yet, stony and bumpy. Joshua kneels, puts down the lantern and lifts up big stones that are not stones but white and dusty.

'I found it' he says 'under these chalk blocks. They've been cut like big bricks, look.'

White lumps, like my old building blocks but bigger. My tummy fluttering grumbling and not for dinner. Sick feeling, like when Papa is cross and not saying anything.

'Perhaps we didn't ought to' say I. 'Perhaps we should tell Papa.'

Joshua scowls frowns. 'Don't you *dare* tell' he says 'you *swore*. And if you're going to be silly and frightened you might as well sit with Mama and start *sewing*.'

Not frightened, NOT. 'I'm not sewing any more' say I 'I'm going in.'

'Good.'

Chalk pieces piled up and Joshua points into a hole, grey-and-white dusty. 'You have to go through there' he says 'and put the lantern round your neck.'

'Aren't you coming?' say I.

'I'll keep watch.'

He puts the lantern string round my neck and I kneel and my hand is in the hole. Cold damp dusty and smelling funny like old paper, like wet straw. Joshua turns up the lantern and the hole goes orange. Black at the end, black and dark. Long, long and twisting with nothing at the end like a big chalk tomb.

'I'm not going in there' say I. 'You can't make me.'

'Silly' says Joshua, 'don't be scared.'

'Not.'

'Yes you are. Oh, come on, I'll go first. Here, you take this for when we get in.'

He gives me the candle and I put it into my pocket. He takes the lantern, puts it round his neck and goes in on his knees and hands like a dog. Put my hands in again. Cold and chalk dusty. Roll up my pinafore and follow Joshua's grubby grey bottom and *don't look*. Don't look at the sides where the insects live and the spiders are. On and on and Joshua scrabble-scratching and my knees sore through my stockings and the chalk all rough and cold and then smooth.

Now says Joshua's voice. His feet stop moving. *In there.*

Wet-smelling and horrid. Joshua sits, shuffles forward. *You have to swing your legs in* his voice says, all flat and funny. Like talking into a well. *It's a bit wet.* He turns and there are his legs knees bent scuffled dusty and the lantern near my face. He is *inside*, in the darkness. *Come in* he says *mind your feet.*

Sit and push out my feet and they go dragging-scraping out and out and then down. Curl up and go pushing through the hole and my feet go *pla-ish plssh* splashing and stop. Stand up, *right* up, straight. Not a tunnel now.

Well done! Joshua's voice says haw-hawing. *Right in a puddle.*

The lantern light on the floor. Not a tiny tunnel hole now. Big, big and dark.

Joshua picks up the lantern, holds it to my face. 'Pass me the candle then' he says.

Feel in my pocket and bring it out. He takes it and puts it to the lantern to light it.

'Ready?' he says.

'Ready.'

He passes me the candle and turns up the lantern.

Shells!

White shapes shining in the black above us beside us. Hold up the candle and there, white shapes, white shining shells in shapes everywhere. *Walls* of them, all over the walls everywhere twirling twisting shell shapes, brown blue orange grey. And the white. Put out my hand and there a big fan of shells brown and yellow shining, shining like they are wet. Like they are under water. Not a fan, a *fish*. And stars. Shell stars, shell flowers, all different colours.

'Oh!' say I and the *oh* goes round and round, like *we* are under water too.

'What do you say to this?' says Joshua wide grinning.

'It's beautiful!'

'That's just the first bit. Look, it's round. There are passages and this one goes round in a circle. I'll show you.'

Turn and turn and the shells are everywhere, high up and behind me and on either side of the tunnel hole. The walls all shaped go up and up, pointed like the arches of chapel windows and all close together in a row. Prettier than chapel windows, bright and shining like church windows with picture glass. Hold the candle and the lantern higher and the light gets bigger wider and the roof shows up all covered in shells swirling joining making lines and shapes. Shell flowers, a whole *garden* of them.

'It's enchanted!' say I. 'It's an enchanted shell garden.'

'Come on' says Joshua, 'look round here.'

Follow him and the lantern light. The first big wall curves round like a pillar and the rest a corridor that goes round it. Shell flowers shell swirls making shapes like plants and all in arches. Hold the candle high and the white shells sparkle bright and watery. Joshua holds the lantern over his head. 'Come here, Fan' he says walking on 'this bit is really good.'

'Wait for me' say I.

Shells and shells coming shining out of the black where we walk and then bright and white, a big wide splash of white. White walls up and up like a tower with rows and rows of silvery white shells.

'It's so lovely!' say I.

'This bit is a dome' says Joshua. 'Like in a palace or something. There's another corridor here.'

He points into the dark. Not one, though, two – two corridors like a crossroads.

'There are two' say I. 'Look, either way.'

'No' he says 'that's the other bit where we came in. It goes round in a circle.' He holds up the lantern and the shadows go big and stretch out. More shell shapes, more arches with white shell lines on. 'See?' he says. 'That's the bit that goes back, back to the way in.'

'It's so dark' say I. 'What if we get lost?'

'Don't be silly, Fan' he says. 'I've been in before. It's all right.'

He goes on again, into the dark. Keep close behind him and hold up the candle. Our light splashing on to the sides and the shells are thick here too, the roof closer and lower but still all shells, arches reaching up and pointing. Joshua quick-walks and the dark comes behind him again, closing up.

'Slow down, Joshua!' say I.

Come on! His voice all odd and disappearing, like when the schoolrooms were empty. Hollow.

On and on. Shell flowers. Shell plants in shell pots. Hearts – big hearts with more shells inside, and a row of small ones too. The shells sharp and smooth-polished. Stuck on and sticking out, glossy shining. Cold, and some of them wet and some of them dusty.

So dark. 'Joshua!' say I. 'Joshua, come back!'

I'm just here.

Scraping shuffling and the light and shadows spreading out again. The lantern and a hand and Joshua's face, grinning.

'Don't leave me like that!'

'It goes round the corner' he says. 'That's why you couldn't see me.'

'It's so dark' say I. 'Please don't run away.'

'I'm not running' he says 'you're just taking an age.'

'I want to *look*.'

'Come on. It gets even better round here.'

He goes on. Follow him and the path goes bumpy and the sides move and we go round a corner. The shells still stretching up and up and round and round into the darkness. Joshua holds up the lantern. A big black arch at the end. Broken bits of shell wall on one side and the floor lumpy and puddle-wet.

'It's damper here' says Joshua 'and some of the wall has come off. Look, here's the door.'

Door? He holds the lantern out and his hand goes through the black arch. *Not* an arch, an *entrance*.

We shouldn't be here. It isn't ours. Head fluttery ears noisy and watery sick feeling inside. My shadow big on the shell wall.

'I don't think we should' say I. 'I don't think we should go in there.'

The big black space empty and hollow and the lantern disappears into it. Joshua's feet scuffling and mine fluttering splashing.

'Don't, Joshua! Don't go in!'

Don't be silly his voice says all muffled *it is wonderful in here*.

Step and step. One two. What if there is a pit, like in a dungeon? Three four. Hold up my candle and *don't look down*. The arch goes up over me and then a room – *a room!* Four walls and roof all glowing orange and yellow and *beautiful*. Beautiful! Shell suns and shell stars shining, pink and orange. Long dark shells too, dark blue drops fanning out, sticking out around the suns. A shell shelf in the middle with a little arch over it, and two little posts with tiny white shell lines on them.

'See?' says Joshua. 'Wonderful, isn't it?'

Lumps of chalk and slate and broken things on the floor. The walls are bright and pretty but with ugly gaps where the shells should be. Not finished like the rest. *Not ready!*

'Joshua' say I whisper-quiet 'this bit isn't done yet!'

'What do you mean not done?'

'Not finished! What if they come back to finish it and find us in here?'

'Who?'

'The shell fairies!'

'Don't be *silly*' says Joshua 'there's no such thing. It's just old and falling apart, that's all. Nobody is coming back.'

Big flat slates with pictures on, like the shapes on the walls. *Not finished.* 'I don't care' say I. 'These are pictures of the walls and the fai– the ones who are making it must use them to copy out. It *isn't* finished.'

'It *is*' says Joshua. 'It's just that they have taken bits off again.'

'Why?'

'I don't know.'

Arches and posts and the shell shelf, patched and bits missing. 'If it isn't a fairy house then perhaps it is a church' say I. 'It is a bit like a church.'

'I don't think it can be' says Joshua. 'Even *Catholic* churches don't have flowers on the walls.'

'How would you know? You've never seen one.'

'Nor have you.'

So? 'You said the tower bit is a dome. The cathedral in London had a dome.'

'It's too small for a cathedral, silly' says Joshua 'and anyway who would want an underground cathedral?'

'Maybe it's a palace.'

'I thought that' he says 'but it's too small.'

'A fairy palace then.'

'*Silly.*' He kick-pokes the floor lumps. 'It's a treasure house. There must be some treasure left here. I bet they came back for the treasure buried behind the walls and didn't bother putting the shells back.'

They? Even with the suns shining it is dark. We turn and the light turns and the shadows move. Hold the candle very high and bright and it *ow!* burns splashes hot and dripping on my hand.

'What's the matter?' says Joshua.

'My candle. It dripped.'

He looks at the candle and pulls a face. 'We should go' he says. 'We've been here for ages.'

Have not. 'We only just came in.'

'Look at your candle' he says. 'It's burning right down.'

True. Can't go yet. Mustn't let it burn out, though. Then it would be even darker, *too* dark.

'If someone did come back for the treasure' say I 'then there won't be any treasure left.'

'Bet there is though.'

Suns and stars and flowers. The little posts with rows and rows of broken blue and white and yellow. It is *not* because it isn't finished. *Someone else has been here.* Someone else has been here and spoiled it.

'Do you like it?' says Joshua. 'You do like it, don't you?'

'Oh yes!'

'You're not scared?'

Yes. 'A bit. Maybe we shouldn't be here. Not if it is someone else's.'

'It *isn't* someone else's' he says. 'It's *ours* now. Nobody else has been in, not for years probably.' Puts his hand on a shell sun. 'Didn't I tell you Captain Easter was right?'

'He's not right, because there isn't any treasure. But it *is* lovely. Ever so lovely.'

Joshua grins. 'And *I* found it.'

'I know' say I 'so I suppose it *is* yours, really. But I don't think we should tell anyone, do you?'

'No, no, we shouldn't.'

'*Especially* not Captain Easter.'

'All right.' Poke-kicks at the fairy slates again. 'Come on, Fan, we'd better go.'

'Not yet' say I. 'Let's see if there are any secret doors. There are always secret doors in magic places.'

'Papa will be back for dinner soon. We'll have to look another time.'

'He won't be back for ages.'

'He will, because we have *been* ages. *Look!*' Points at the candle again.

'When?' say I. 'When can we come back?'

'Oh, I don't know. Tomorrow.'

'We *can't* tomorrow' say I. 'It's Monday.'

'Next week then.' He goes lantern swinging to the big archway. 'Come *on*, Fan. Papa will look for us and if he finds the tunnel we'll never be let back in again.'

'All right.'

Through the arch and puddle-splashing shadow-flickering into the dark again. Along the corridor close together hands out against the cold smooth bumpy shell walls. Hearts and flowers and trees and plants. Back through the beautiful white silvery dome and stand at the crossroads. Joshua goes along the other path this time, back to the tunnel hole. Shell plants shell trees and the big shell fish again, the beginning. Little fishes too, below it. The dark closes up behind us.

No shell people. Not anywhere. No crosses like in chapels and churches and no treasure chests. Suns and stars and hundreds and hundreds of lovely little shells, all stuck on. Stuck on by *somebody*. Or by magic.

Blow out my candle and Joshua turns down the lantern.

'I'll go first' he says 'in case there is anyone at the top.'

He puts his head in and the light goes dim and he crawls up. His feet wiggle and disappear. Follow him quick into the hole again and along the tunnel, scraping scratching. Away from the dark. Away from the shells.

Maybe there are ghosts. Maybe ghosts made it, but ghosts don't have hands that can pick things up, not like people when they are alive. It doesn't feel like there are ghosts there. Chest thud-thumping. Goodbye, shells. Goodbye. Joshua going faster and faster and then disappearing out. Beautiful shells. Cold air and grey sky again and Joshua puts in his hand and pulls at me.

Mama's garden. Rainy muddy puddle and earthy. Joshua puts the chalk lumps back over the hole.

'Quick, Fan' he says. 'It's been raining. They'll come to get us.'

'I don't care' say I.

'You're a terrible mess' says Joshua. 'You'd better get cleaned up.'

Pinafore smeary and white-dusty and my shoes all mud and my stockings torn with big grey holes where the knees go, showing through. Left knee scratched and blood-smeary but it doesn't hurt, not really.

'You'll have to say you fell over' says Joshua.

'I don't care' say I. *Don't.* 'Promise you'll take me back again. Promise, Joshua.'

'All right. Promise. *Hurry up!*'

Back to the house not skipping not mud-minding now. Not anything minding. Knee throbbing chest thumping hands and tummy all prickling burning fluttering. Not caring about anything any more.

There is a fairy shell garden under Mama's field. *Is.*

The Morgan girls are coming

When Mama looks at me she is not-pleased but when she looks at Lizzy she is very very happy. The Morgan girls are coming to be pupils at Mama's school. Mr Morgan is a tradesman but that does not mean that he is not nice or that his daughters will be stupid. Mama said that I am a disgrace. D-I-S-G-R-A-C-E, that is to not be a grace. Which is what Lizzy is supposed to be, only she isn't, because she looks as though she has just swallowed a mouthful of nasty medicine.

Mama goes out frowning.

'Leave us alone, for goodness' sake' Lizzy says hiss-spitting.

'Fanny dear' says Mary 'run along and clean yourself up, before the Morgan girls arrive. You want to make a good impression, don't you?'

Up the stairs and the skeleton tree *tap-taps* and there is the place in the garden where the shells are buried. Cannot tell from here, not even high up. Cannot see the chalk blocks. Nearly didn't hear Mrs D when she came out, calling shouting. Joshua was playing ghosts and whistling and saying *ooooooooo-oooooooooooooooooooo!* from the end of the tunnel and I listening laughing and trying to put the shell flowers back on the shelf wall. And then Mrs D's voice above my head saying *bless me!* and her feet scrabble-scratching. Ran to Joshua and said *sssh stop making ghost noises* but she hadn't heard us. *Bless me where are those children?* and then gone. Joshua was quite white, like he had heard ghost noises back. We came out ever-so-quickly and then Mama was there, frowning at Joshua's knees and my dirty stockings and calling me a disgrace.

Up the stairs and to the press and put on clean stockings, *again*. Mrs D said she will teach me how to darn if I soil another pair. That is good, for Mama will never know how many holes I make. Ha!

Two Morgan girls are coming and so is another girl who is not a Morgan but a Lucas. Mama said they will come for tea in our upstairs parlour, not to the green one at Papa's. They will be the first girls at Mama's school and will not ever need to go to Papa's school for anything. They are not to live here though, Mary said. They are only to be here in the daytime.

Tappity-tap on the door. Mama's face, frowning.

'Fanny' says Mama 'I will have no more of your playing in the dirt with your brother. Is that understood?'

'Yes, Mama.'

'The girls will be here soon and I want you to set a good example. They are more of your age than of Mary or Lizzy's, and they will look to you for their pattern of behaviour. I expect, therefore, that your behaviour will be exemplary.'

Exemplary. 'Yes, Mama.'

'They will begin lessons on Monday. We must ensure that we are all prepared.'

'Yes, Mama.'

'Very good.' She almost smiles but then remembers and does not. 'Brush your hair and come to the parlour, then. They will be here at any moment.'

She goes and I turn and brush-brush-brush my hair. It does not feel as nice as when Mama brushes it. The brush is white-dusty with chalk and *eeukh!* a piece of *spiderweb*.

Clean and Sunday-smart for the new girls. Mama downstairs talking to Anne about tea things. Lizzy and Mary already murmuring in the parlour. Go towards the door and it opens and George comes out quick-walking. *George!* Big-eyed surprised and pushing a piece of paper into his pocket.

'George' say I 'what are you doing here?'

'Nothing' he says, fast-walking and not smiling.

'I didn't know you were allowed upstairs' say I. 'I am not allowed upstairs in the boys' school.'

'That's different' he says. He goes to the stairs, still not-smiling, walks down quickly quietly on his toes like he is not supposed to be there after all.

'George!'

'Not now!' he says hissing whispering tippity-toeing.

Gone.

George does not know about the Morgan sisters, or the Lucas girl. Or the shell fairies. Busy busy busy and not stopping for me to tell him anything.

Back to the parlour door where George came from and Lizzy's voice hissing and Mary's voice shushing. Mary's voice says *it is not safe, sister, how could you be so imprudent?* and Lizzy's voice says *I know what I'm doing thank you, Mary.*

They are quarrelling.

MARY'S VOICE: I cannot believe that you would act so hastily!

LIZZY'S VOICE: Really, Mary, you make such a fuss. It is very low of you to be so easily perplexed.

MARY'S VOICE: Easily perplexed! How can you say so? It is not a mere nothing! You will be exposed, Lizzy! Think, sister, how would Mama and Papa stand such a thing?

LIZZY'S VOICE, VERY LOUD: Really, Mary, you are ridiculous. Exposed indeed!

MARY'S VOICE: But sending a letter! And how will you keep him quiet?

LIZZY'S VOICE, LAUGHING: It is no different from sending a parcel by a donkey. Honestly! Surely you do not think I would send it unless I knew it quite safe? The boy will keep quiet for a shilling.

MARY'S VOICE, SOUNDING VERY ANXIOUS: But he may open it!

LIZZY'S VOICE: Well may he open it, for the good it will do him. The simple idiot cannot read!

MARY'S VOICE, WHISPER-HISSING: Cannot read?

LIZZY'S VOICE, VERY PLEASED WITH HERSELF: Not a word. He is completely illiterate. No better than a mule.

MARY'S VOICE: Even so, sister, you run a fearful risk. He might say where he is taking it.

LIZZY'S VOICE: Who would he prattle to? The cows in the field? No one would listen.

MARY'S VOICE: It is a fearful risk. Besides, sister, you should not behave so, it is so very indiscreet. (Sighs.) You should not run after him. You should wait until he speaks to Papa.

LIZZY'S VOICE, VERY HARD: Speaks to Papa? And what if he never speaks to Papa? Do you think that I will sit and wait and make sheep's eyes under my parasol like a little fool until some other girl comes along? Certainly not.

I shall get what I want for I shall go after it myself. You will never get what you want. You take no chances.

MAMA'S VOICE, FROM THE STAIRS: And this is where my daughters live. Do come up to meet them.

Mama's feet on the stairs and more feet walking climbing coming closer. Turn the handle of the door and open it and there is Mary pale and Lizzy red and neither of them sewing.

'They are here!' say I.

Sit down quickly and we all pick up our workbaskets and make pretend busy noises. Mama comes to the open door and smiles (even at me!) and comes in.

There are three girls standing shyly looking at us and at Mama and at the floor.

We all stand up.

'Well' says Mama smiling pointing 'here are my daughters Arabella-Elizabeth, Mary Ann and Frances. Girls, meet Frances and Mary Morgan, and Elizabeth Lucas.'

We all bob and they bob back. They come in and Mama makes them sit and we sit too. Anne comes and puts down tea things on a tray and winks at me and goes out again.

Important Lizzy bustle clatter pours tea, passes cups. The girl who is not a sister has long curling pretty golden hair. Pink ribbons pink Sunday dress black shiny Sunday shoes. Looks at me and at my sampler. She is Mr Lucas's daughter. Mr Lucas is *not* a tradesman.

'Now' says Mama 'we must make sure that we all have our names aright. For as you have heard, my dears, our new girls have the same names as you. Isn't that a curious thing?'

'Yes, Mama' say we.

The girls stare and stare. Put my nose in the teacup, strong tea-and-milk-steam-smelling, too hot for sipping. One of the sisters wriggles in her chair.

'We shall all get along very well together' says Mama. 'Firstly, we must ensure that we can tell one another apart by name, for if we cannot we shall be in a muddle!' (To the wriggling girl) 'Frances Morgan, you may remain Frances, for our little Frances here is always called Fanny. Isn't that so, girls?'

'Yes, Mama' say we.

Frances wriggle-wriggle Morgan smiles at me. She has two teeth missing and black hair and eyebrows. I do not like her. Why can't *she* be called Fanny instead?

'Mary Morgan' says Mama (to the other black-haired girl) 'do you have another name? For we already have a Mary here.'

'If it please you, ma'am' says Mary Morgan very softly, 'my ma calls me May.'

'That's very well indeed' says Mama. 'We shall call you May also. And you shall call me *Mrs Newlove*.'

'Yes, Mrs Newlove' says Mary-May.

Our Mary smiles and Mary-May smiles back ever-so-nervously. Mary-May-Morgan. She has black hair too but no teeth missing. Black hair green ribbons green eyes green dress white pinafore. Frances has a white pinafore too. Her dress is grey and it wriggles. She kicks her feet.

'Frances dear' says Mama *but not to me* 'please try to sit still. Stillness is essential to good manners. Ladies do not swing their feet – that is the behaviour of ill-mannered little boys.'

(Like Joshua.)

Frances Morgan goes very red and looks down. Her feet stop swinging. She is trying not to cry. Her eyes go small. Her nose wrinkles up. She pretends to drink her tea.

'Elizabeth Lucas' says Mama (to the pretty-haired not-sister) 'we shall call you Beth, if you do not object to it. Arabella-Elizabeth is called Lizzy.'

'Yes, Mrs Newlove' says Beth Lucas.

She is not soft and shy like Mary-May but very very sweet and pretty. She has all her teeth and they are neat and small. She does not smile with them though. She holds her teacup nicely, like Mama does. She is *very* grown-up.

'And how do you like your names, girls?' says Mama.

'Very well thank you, Mrs Newlove' say they.

Mama does not ask me. Mama never asks me.

Sip-sip hot tea. Shiny cups shining tinkling clattering. Mary-May looks at me and I smile and she smiles back. Mama asks the girls questions and they say *yes Mrs Newlove no Mrs Newlove nine in April Mrs Newlove I am ten already Mrs Newlove.* Frances Morgan is ten and Beth Lucas is eight but she seems older and more grown-up than all of us. Except for Mama. May is eight like me and soon she will be nine. Lizzy is seventeen so she is nearly old enough to marry and go away. Perhaps she will marry Mr da Costa and move to London. George Stroud has a note from Lizzy and Mary is cross with her for it. Lizzy called George a mule. He is not a mule, just because he cannot read. I would teach him if he would let me. I will ask him. I will find him and ask him.

'Well, girls' says Mama 'thank you for coming to meet us all. We will see you for your first lessons on Monday morning. You may go now. Fanny will see you out, won't you, Fanny?'

'Yes, Mama' say I.

'Thank you, Mrs Newlove' say the girls. They put down their cups and I put down mine and we stand up and bob. Across the landing and down the stairs past the skeleton tree seven-eight-nine-ten. Frances Morgan without the teeth is ten years old but she is more like a baby. She comes *thump-thump-thump* grumpity-grump down the stairs and May comes behind her soft-stepping and Beth Lucas does not seem to walk at all but floats down the steps with her lovely pink dress on.

Out to the door and Anne comes into the hall and bobs.

'It's all right, Anne' say I 'I can do it.'

'As you like Miss Fransuss' says Anne.

'I am Frances' says Frances Morgan. '*She* is just Fanny.'

'I am Frances *too*' say I 'and *I* was here first.'

'I am older than you, Fanny Newlove' says Frances Morgan 'and your ma said to call me Frances and you Fanny.'

Anne's eyes go very wide. 'Ull call you *Miss Nulove* thun' she says to me and smiles.

Open the door and Frances no-teeth Morgan goes out and flounces trounces off up the path. May looks at me sadly. 'Goodbye, Miss Newlove' she says.

'You can call me Fanny' say I 'but I don't think I shall let your sister.'

She goes and grown-up Beth Lucas goes too. She curtsies properly on the doorstep (not bobbing) and offers me her hand but I am not a man so I cannot kiss it. Touch her fingers and she smiles a very small smile like her lips are stuck together and takes her hand away and puts on her lovely white gloves.

'Goodbye, Fanny' she says. 'I am very pleased to have made your acquaintance.'

'Goodbye' say I. I am very pleased to have made her acquaintance too but I do not want to say it wrong.

She walks to the gate and a girl in a white cap like a maid's appears and they walk off together.

Anne comes and shuts the door for me.

'Wull, miss' she says, 'that other Fransuss'll give you sum trubble, I lay.'

'I shan't mind *her*' say I.

Shan't. She can never be as horrid as Lizzy is, even if she tries.

Anne *haw-haws* and goes down the hall.

'Anne' say I, 'have you seen George?'

''S in the gardun miss' she says.

Through the house and out into the back garden and there is George, kneeling on the ground with his hands in the earth.

'What are you doing?' say I.

'Planting' says George. Grubby knees grubby jacket with sleeves rolled back and tied with string.

'Planting what?'

'Bread-and-butter trees.'

'Silly.'

George might still have the paper in his pocket. Even if he has opened it he couldn't have read it.

'George' say I 'what were you doing upstairs?'

'Errands.'

'Who for?'

'Woods.'

'You were taking a note for Lizzy' say I. 'Where were you taking it to?'

George turns and looks cross-faced at me. 'Don't make trouble, miss.'

'Don't call me miss, George' say I.

'Don't make trouble then' says George. He picks out little stones from the ground and puts them in a pile.

'Why is Lizzy giving you notes?' say I.

'I don't know what you're talking about, miss.'

'I'm not stupid' say I. 'I know you took a note for Lizzy. I heard them talking in the parlour. Have you taken notes for her before?'

'What notes, miss?'

'Notes. Letters.'

'I don't know what you mean.'

'Show me' say I 'or I shall tell Papa.'

'You won't.'

'I will. Show me.'

'I han't got it.' He stands up very cross. 'I han't got it, all right?'

'*Have not*' say I 'though I know you *have*. Lizzy was horrid about you. You might as well tell me everything.'

'There's nought to tell.'

'*Is.*'

George sighs arm-folds huff-huffing. 'It's none of my business and none of yours neither.'

'Lizzy said she gave you the letter because even if you opened it you wouldn't be able to read it. She said you were a simple idiot.'

'So I am.'

'No you are not' say I, 'but if you learned to read you would know what she was hiding. *Secrets*. Wouldn't you like to know?'

'No'm.'

'I would. Maybe she is doing something bad' say I. 'If she is doing something bad then you are doing something bad too. Papa would be very cross with you.'

'I han't done nothing.'

'*Have not* done *anything*' say I 'but you *have*. And you took money for it. Like Judas Iscariot.'

'Not so.'

'*Is* so. You are an accomplice. If you show me the letter I can tell you if it is bad or not, and then you will know if you have done something bad too.'

'I don't have it.'
'Why not?'
'I already took it to him.'
'Who to?'
'Can't say.'
'To Mr da Costa?'
George huffity-huffing picks up a shovel and walks away to the shed.
'George! Tell me!'
'No.'
Donkey.

Joshua said we can go after dinner

Because it is Saturday. Mama and Lizzy and Mary said they shall walk into town after dinner and Papa is to go to chapel meeting and the boys have their half-day. No teachers and no Woods being everywhere when you don't want him, and no Mrs D for she is going with Mama to see about things for the linen cupboard. Only Anne who is busy busy polishing and sweeping and she will want to clean in our rooms anyway while we are out. And she is to get the schoolroom scrubbed before the Morgan girls and Beth Lucas come on Monday. *And* the music room, which Mrs D said is *in a shocking state*. (But that was the painting master's fault, *not* Mr Mills's.)

So Joshua said that we can go. Anne tappity-taps and comes in to take the dinner things away. (Couldn't eat dinner for fluttering thinking about the shells, even though there *was* onion pudding.) Anne looks at my plate and frowns and goes clatter-banging away again. Mama saw the pudding there when we had finished and said I looked unwell, and I said I had a headache, which is *almost* true.

I shall watch for Joshua from the parlour window. Lizzy

will not want me to go into town with them anyway. She complains that I drag along and never keep up, and that I stop and stare at things like a simpleton. She said to Mama that if I am unwell I should stay behind and Mama said that was very considerate of her, and that I may, and to sit quietly while they are gone. Joshua will come soon, when Papa has left. I do not know what he will say but he always thinks of something.

Mary smiles at me and Lizzy looks at the clock and sighs.

'Well, my dears' says Mama 'run along and get ready for town.'

'Yes, Mama' says Mary.

Lizzy jumps up and goes out quickity-quick but Mary stands and stops and puts her hand ever-so-gently on my head.

'Poor lamb' she says. 'I hope you will feel better soon.'

'Oh yes thank you, Mary' say I. 'I am sure I shall.'

Mary goes and Mama looks at me and pinches her lips together.

'You ought not to be suffering from headaches at your age' says Mama. 'I trust you have not caught a chill. Perhaps I should ask Mrs D to give you some medicine.'

'Oh!' say I. 'Oh no, Mama. I am quite well really.'

'We shall see' she says. 'Sit quietly while we are gone, Fanny. I shall come and see how you are when we return.'

'Yes, Mama.'

She stands bends and peck-kisses my head and goes out. Walks down the stairs lightly one-and-two stepping and mutter-murmurs to Anne and the door thud-shuts softly.

Mama is gone.

Out on to the landing and Lizzy and Mary bustling fussing come out of their room. Lizzy stands bonnet-tying and looks at me.

'Behave yourself while we are out' she says. *Grumpity grump.*

'Do take good care' says Mary. 'Sit nice and quietly, like Mama says, and read a book.' She frowns. 'No, perhaps you had better not read a book, Fanny dear. It might be too much for your poor eyes.'

'Oh, *do* come along!' says Lizzy (*whine whine*). She goes *thump-clump-thump-clump* down the stairs, pulling on her Sunday gloves. *Sunday* gloves, even though it is only Saturday.

'I'm sure you will feel better in a little while, poor lamb' says Mary.

Mary goes down the stairs too and her voice says *goodbye, Anne* and the door opens and bang-shuts. Into the parlour again and up tiptoe at the window. Mary and Lizzy at the gate and Mary turns and looks up and waves and I wave back.

They are gone. *Gone!*

In my room under the bed behind the trunk with Summer things in it and there it is – my bundle. Untie and unwrap and take out the torn stockings muddy with holes for knees, and the little candle pieces and the broken shell flower. Pull the dirty stockings over my clean ones, and the grey pinafore from the hook instead of my white one. Candle pieces into my pocket. Shell flower under my pillow. (Anne will clean today but she will not look *there*.)

Back into the parlour. Where is Joshua? Not at the gate. Papa will be gone now. Anne goes out on to the path with a broom and swoosh-sweeps. No rain today, *good*. No mud no puddles just dull dull cloudy and cold. Anne stops and looks up. Someone comes through the gate.

Joshua?

George.

George (*hee-haw*) does not know about the fairy shell garden. Anne opens the door and he comes thud-stepping in.

Cross the landing and hop-jump five-six-seven-eight down the stairs and he is in the hallway.

'George!'

George turns and looks at me but does not stop. Puts his hands in his pockets and *fhuw-fhuwww* whistles.

Into the hall and he still walking not waiting. 'Where are you going, George?' say I.

'Garden.'

'What for?'

'Putting in the early peas.'

'Oh. Are you doing it now?'

'Yes'm.'

George opens the back door and goes out. I go too. He is going to be in the garden putting in peas and he will see us fetching the lantern and going to the shells, and we shall be found out. George is rude and does not like me any more. He will probably tell Papa, and then I shall *never* get to see the shells.

'George' say I ever-so-nicely 'must you put the peas in now?'

'Yes'm.'

'Why?'

'Makes them come early.'

'Wouldn't you rather go to the harbour?'

'No'm.'

'Or for a walk?'

'No'm.'

'Or to sleep?'

'No'm.'

George goes to the shed and fetches a little hand shovel.

He comes back and kneels grubby-kneed and scrape-scrapes little earth trenches.

'George' say I 'wouldn't you rather play a game?'

'No'm.'

'We could play hide and seek.'

'What for?'

'I bet you couldn't find me if I hid.'

'Wouldn't want to.'

He is not going to help. He is not going to go away.

'George' say I 'why are you so cross?'

'I'm not cross, miss.'

'Don't call me miss' say I. 'You would have played with me before.'

'You shan't want my company any more' he says. 'Not now you've got young ladies to keep with.'

'What do you mean?' say I.

'You'll have them Morgan girls soon' says George. 'You shan't want anything to do with me. Quite right an all.'

'I shall' say I 'and anyway, I'd rather play with you than with Frances Morgan, even though she *is* a girl.'

'Hmmn' says George.

'Truly.'

George puts down the little shovel and looks at me and then at my stockings.

'Miss Frances!' he says laughing pointing. 'What *are* you wearing?'

'Play things' say I.

'You look a fine sight in those. Like a Bo-boy.'

Bo-boy?

He does not know about the shell garden. He should like to though.

'George' say I 'have you taken any more notes to Mr da Costa?'

'That's none of your business, miss.'

'If you tell me about the letters I will tell you a secret too.'

'I don't care for secrets.'

'You will care for this one. Have you?'

'No'm.'

'Have you taken any from him to Lizzy?'

'No'm.'

'Liar.'

'Not so. I han't taken one.' He sly-grins and touches his cap. 'I've one *to* take though.'

'Where? Let me see!'

'No.'

'Who is it for?'

'For Miss Newlove. But she's not here to give it to.'

'Show me instead then.'

'No.'

'If you show me, I will take you to a secret place. Wouldn't you like to go?'

'No.'

'It's a secret underground place. Only Joshua and I know about it. No one else knows about it in the whole world, not even Papa.'

'I don't care for secrets.'

'Why keep them then?' say I. 'I bet you don't even *have* a letter for Lizzy.'

'Do.'

'I don't believe you.'

'Here then.' Puts his hand to his cap and takes it off and there inside a square of paper, folded very small. 'See?'

'Show me' say I.

'No.'

'Lizzy called you a mule and a donkey.'

'No.'

'I'll take you to the shell place. And I'll teach you to read.'

George twist-wrings his cap and looks at me. 'What shell place?'

'Show me the letter.'

'Do you mean the lime pit?'

'It's not a pit, it's a palace.'

'Where is it?'

'The letter, George.'

George stands and I stand and he holds out his cap. Take the paper quick and there is no seal on it. Open it out. It is very small.

'What if someone comes?' says George.

'Let's go into the shed.'

We do, me carrying the letter he the little shovel. There are spiderwebs and it smells musty. George looks at me big-eyed scared and shakes his head.

'It's all right, George' say I. 'Lizzy won't find out. Don't you want to know what it says?'

'Maybe.'

'I will read it to you.' Mr da Costa's handwriting very neat very small and elegant, but not so nice as Papa's. Not many lines either. ' "Dearest girl. Urgent matter arisen. Cannot be at pump as planned. Try to find you at Bettison's. Sending this by the boy, do give him a shilling for it, my dove. M." '

'Hemm' says George grin-grinning.

'What does it mean?'

'What does it sound like?'

'I don't understand' say I. 'Why can't Mr da Costa just come here to see Lizzy? Papa always lets him in.'

'It's not like that' says George.

'Why not?'

'Because. You know.'

'No I don't.'

'He says "dearest girl", see?'

'Mama calls her "dearest" too. She even calls *me* "dearest" sometimes.'

'That's different. And he calls her his dove.'

'Lizzy isn't a bit like a dove' say I. 'Anyway, all I can see is that he was supposed to meet her in town and now he can't. *That*'s not very secret.'

George laughs. He takes the paper and folds it and puts it into his cap. 'I don't suppose she'll give me a shilling for it now. She'll give me what-for instead.'

'Don't tell' say I.

'Don't you tell then' says George.

Scuffle-rustling outside and Joshua's face appears. *Joshua!* He has come for the lantern.

'What are you two doing?' he says.

'Looking for tools' says George.

'Joshua' say I 'George is coming with us.'

Joshua stare-stares and shakes his head.

'I said he might' say I 'and he said he will make it easier for *us* to go *other* times. He said he will tell Papa that we have been helping him in the garden. Didn't you, George?'

George shrugs shuffles. Joshua cross-frowns and folds his arms.

'We *agreed*' says Joshua. 'You said you wouldn't tell *anyone*.'

'I know about the pit' says George. 'Everyone knows there's a lime pit round here.'

'It's not just any old pit' says Joshua 'and anyway it's mine. I found it.'

'My pa knows about it' says George. 'He told me ages ago that there's a pit here somewhere.'

'Ever been down there?' says Joshua. His face is very red and cross.

'No.'

'Well, you'd better keep quiet about it, or else.'

'I shan't tell' says George.

Joshua looks at me and then at George and shakes his head. 'You'd better not.' He goes out and *scra-scraa*-scrabble-scratches under the shed for the lantern box.

'Miss Frances' says George whisper-quiet, 'don't tell about the letters. I've been getting shillings for them. I need them shillings.'

'I won't tell' say I 'if you bring me all the letters they give you.'

George shakes his head. 'Can't do that.'

'Promise' say I. 'Promise you will and I'll teach you to read. Then no one will ever call you a donkey again. *And* you can visit the shells, too.'

Joshua comes with the box. 'Come on then' he says. He is *not* pleased.

'What about Anne?' say I.

'She's gone.'

Follow him over to the chalk blocks and George watches us move them. Joshua lights the lantern and puts it round George's neck. He looks wide-eyed surprised and puts his hand in the hole and looks at me.

'It's all right' say I.

'You go first then' says Joshua. 'You have to crawl.'

George puts his head in and pulls it out again.

'Go on, George' say I. 'It's lovely in there, really it is.'

He goes ever-so-slowly in. His boots scuffle-scrape along the tunnel.

'Shall I go next?' say I.

Joshua huffs. 'What did you bring him for?'

'I had to' say I. 'He was supposed to be working in the garden and he would have seen us anyway. We wouldn't have been able to come.'

'We could have done it another time. *Really*, Fan.'

'Don't be cross' say I. 'George is nice.'

'Well, if you are going to bring people then so am I.'

George's voice calls out *hallo aren't you coming too?*

'Don't tell Papa' say I 'or Captain Easter.'

'Don't tell Mary or Lizzy then' says Joshua '*or* any more *servants.*'

George is not a servant.

Miss Frances! says George's voice.

'All right, George!' say I.

'I shall tell John Fassum' says Joshua 'and then he might stop being such a pig and making trouble with Papa. And I might tell Tom Gore. *He*'s all right.'

'Don't tell any teachers' say I.

'No I shan't. Come on then, before he gets scared and makes too much noise.'

Joshua puts his hand into his shirt and pulls it out. *Candles.*

'Look' he says 'I got more. Take one, then.'

I do, put it in my pocket. Joshua puts one back in his shirt and the rest in the lantern box.

'For next time' he says.

He goes into the hole and I go too, close behind. Joshua stops half-way and his voice says *keep moving for goodness' sake* and George says *I thought you'd gone and left me in here.*

'Go on, George' say I. 'It's lovely!'

Joshua's boots move and I move and then the boots disappear and Joshua's voice says *pass it here*. The lantern goes up high and the light spreads and George gasps.

Lor his voice says. *Lor.*

Swing my legs over and in and there are the lovely lovely shells, and Joshua very pleased now holding the lantern, and George with his mouth open stare-staring.

'Lor' he says (again).

'This way' says Joshua and goes round to the dome.

'Isn't it lovely, George?' say I.

'Ever so' says George.

'George' say I 'you won't tell, will you?'

'No, miss.'

'Please don't call me that. Call me Frances.'

'All right.'

'*Don't* call me Fanny, though.'

'All right.' George grins and puts his hand on the big shell fish. It goes dark.

Come on, you two says Joshua's voice.

'Wait' say I 'you didn't light the candles! I can't see a thing, Joshua.'

Come here then says Joshua's voice.

Frances says George's voice *when you learn me my letters, shall we do them down here?*

'*Teach* you' say I. 'I'm going to teach you your letters.'

Can we though? It's a good place for meeting. Secret.

'All right.'

George said he didn't care for secrets. He does now.

Dearest James,

Thank you so very much dear brother for writing to me and for sending the lovely animal cards. The pictures are so pretty and they are very educational, as you said. I have read your letter over and over many times. I am sorry that I have written so many foolish things to you before. I shall try very hard to be sensible in my letters. I am sorry also that Mama thinks I am becoming wild. I promise you that I am being as good as I can be and that I only get a little dirty some-times from playing in the garden. Mostly I am <u>working</u> not playing. The gardener's son George is showing me how to grow vegetables and Joshua and I are helping him to make Mama's garden nice. I am also trying very hard to make my writing neater, like Papa's. I am <u>always</u> trying to be better.

It is the first Sunday of Lent today and we have just been to chapel. Papa is at Sunday School telling the children all about Easter. I asked Papa if we should observe the fasting of Lent because I read that people should not eat much in the weeks before Easter. Papa says that we are not Catholics or superstitious and

161

that he knows best about our spiritual welfare, which is true of course. Mrs D the housekeeper does not fast but she did make pancakes on Tuesday, which is almost the same thing. I think she is very superstitious. She made pancakes to share with Anne the maid and let Joshua and me have a pancake each with lemon and sugar on. It was really lovely. Mrs D says that there are special cakes that she makes for Easter too, they are called pudden-pies. I think that is what she said. They are traditional here, Anne told me.

We have three girls at Mama's school now. They are called Beth Lucas and Frances and May Morgan. Beth is the same age as me and very grown-up. Mama says that I should strive to be more like Beth Lucas. She can already speak French and play the piano. I should like to play the piano too. Mr Mills the dancing master says he might teach me to play in the Summer holidays. Mama has been teaching us arithmetic and dictation and it is very hard but I am trying to get it right. We have a new drawing master who uses the music room on Fridays. He is here to teach the boys how to draw plants and statues but Mama says that he may give us lessons as well. His name is Mr Toogould but Mary and Lizzy call him Toogood. He has curly hair which is quite black and which he has to look through because it is long at the front. Mary says that he is Byronic, which means that he looks like a poet. Lizzy says that he may want to paint her but I do not think Mama will let him, for only bad women and duchesses ever have their portraits painted. Mary is pleased about us having lessons. She draws very well as you know.

I am to go now for we are being called for dinner. I hope that it will stop raining soon so that I may go into the garden. Papa says that the fresh air is very beneficial.

Thank you ever so much again for writing to me and for pointing out my mistakes. I hope that you will soon see a little improvement in

   your affectionate sister Frances.

George is getting better

A is for apple. B is for boat. C is for camel. George has never seen a picture of a camel before but I have one in the cards that James gave me. It is yellow and has a lumpy back and a face like a goat, but it is taller than a goat. It lives in the desert in the sand. Goats live in fields, on grass. Or mountains. George stares at the camel and frowns.

'What is D for?' say I.

'Dungeon' says George.

'That's a bit too hard' say I.

'Write it for me though.'

I do. D-U-N-G-E-O-N.

'Oh' he says.

It *is* too hard.

D is for duck, and for drake, which is a he-duck. And for *donkey*. E is for elephant, which is in the cards too, and in the circus that came to London. Mama would not let us go but we saw the elephant, huge grey long-nosed *thud-thud* walking. The elephant had red cloth on its back with gold tassels and a man walked behind it with a shovel and a bucket. *For the mess*, Joshua said.

F is for flower. George touches the shell flowers in the arch.

'F is for Frances' he says. I write F-R-A-N-C-E-S on the slate.

G is for George, which he can spell anyway, and for gardener, which he can't. H is for heaven. That is a hard word for it does not look like it sounds. I is for insect.

'What sort of insect?' says George.

'Any sort.'

'Like spiders?'

'I suppose so.'

'Spider is with S' he says.

'Don't be difficult' say I. 'S is a long way off yet. What is after I?'

'Me.'

'*J*, silly.'

J is for jam, and for James, who gave me the cards, and for Joshua, who is not here now but was earlier, with two of the boarder boys. He shows them the shells now. We must take it in turns to visit or it is too noisy, especially when he brings John Fassum. He is loud and horrid. I shall show May Morgan but not Frances, who is very rude. Her voice is common and I told her so and she said that Mama and Lizzy and Mary and I had *below-London voices*, and that really we were *from the Sheers* and no better than anyone else, especially proper Margate people like *her* family. I wanted to say that her family was common and her father is just a tradesman, which is not even as good as being a proper shop-keeper. But Frances's father is May's father too. May is nice. Beth Lucas said that we shouldn't quarrel about such things, which is true but I didn't start it. I might show Beth Lucas the shells, even though she is rather serious.

J is also for jaguar, which is a very large cat, and for jungle, which is where the jaguar lives. George rubs his eyes.

'How much can you remember?' say I 'We did some of the words last time.'

George puts his hand into his shirt, pulls out a piece of paper. A letter!

'Show me the words in this' he says. 'I think I can tell some of them.'

Mr da Costa's writing, *again*. Longer this time, almost a whole page.

'How many have you taken this week, George?' say I.

'Four. Five with this one, but this is the biggest by far.'

'That's nearly twenty notes altogether' say I. '*That*'s a lot of secrets.'

'None so good as ours though' says George.

'I shall read it out' say I.

I do. ' "Dearest girl" (*he always says that*) "Dearest girl, cannot a – *abide* so long without your being here." '

'What's "abide"?' says George.

'I'm not sure. "Arranged with your mother for visit Saturday next but must see you before." '

'I *knew* Saturday' says George. 'I read that aright.'

'That's good' say I. 'Write it on the slate.'

He does. S-A-T-U-R-D-A-Y. It is clear and neat. 'Saturday' he says.

'Do the other days of the week too.'

He does. They are all right, except for Wednesday which he writes as WENSDAY. I write it again. W-E-D-N-E-S-D-A-Y.

'That's very good' say I.

He grin-grins, pleased. Points at the letter again. I read it.

' "– must see you before. Say you shall get away. You know my house. Your sister will cover." *(That's Mary.)* "Come tomorrow while they are at their books and I shall teach you far better lessons. The messenger-boy" *(that's you, George)* "is becoming careless, look to him."'

'I'm not careless' says George.

'What does he mean about better lessons?'

'You know. Courting.'

'Why should I know about that?'

'Show me the bit about me' says George.

'Here' say I. *Careless.*

'There's more after that' he says. 'Read the rest.'

'"Do not refuse me as you did before, <u>cruel one.</u> I know you do not wish to. Say we shall be together very soon. I am devotedly yours, M."'

'Well well' says George.

'"Cruel one"' say I. 'That is good. At least he knows that she is cruel and not a dove.'

'I don't think he means it' says George. 'It's just love talk.'

'How would you know?'

He shrugs, picks up the cards. Elephant, camel, donkey, jaguar. Rhinoceros (that is very hard). Tiger. There are no animals in the shell pictures, only fish. Fish are animals too though, in a watery way. All God's creatures. Even Lizzy is God's creature but sometimes it is hard to believe it. Nasty spiteful sneaking Lizzy. She thinks that nobody knows but *we* do and so does God. Hiding the letters doesn't make any difference. She has already met him twice this week, in town. She said in the note she gave to George on Tuesday T-U-E-S-D-A-Y that it is easy to meet in town, *easier now that the weather is improving.* I hope it rains and storms and snows until A-U-G-U-S-T.

George takes the letter and stare-stares at it. Mr da Costa wants Lizzy to go to his house. In secret. Mama and Papa would lock her in her room for ever if they knew.

'Perhaps I should tell Papa' say I.

'No' says George. 'He wouldn't let us come back here if he knew.'

'Not about the shells' say I 'about Lizzy and Mr da Costa. I think I ought to.'

'If you do she'll know it was me that told. Then they'll both give me a lacing.'

'I don't know why she wants to meet him' say I. 'He's not even very nice.'

(But then nor is Lizzy.)

'Well, she thinks different.'

'He won't marry her' say I. 'Papa is not rich enough.'

'It's not always about marrying' says George. 'Folk don't always marry.'

'Why do they do it then?'

'Because. It feels nice.' George shrugs. 'You're too young to know about that.'

'I'm very grown-up for my age' say I. 'Even Papa says so.'

'Not grown-up enough for kissing.'

'I am' say I. 'If you are, I must be.'

'I'm older than you.'

'Not much' say I.

'Four whole years.'

'You can't read though.'

'I can kiss' says George crossly. 'You don't have to be clever for *that*.'

George is quite red. Didn't want to make him cross.

I wipe the slate. 'Try your words again' say I.

He takes the chalk and *skeeeeeeee-skreeeeeeeep* scrapes the slate. *George. Frances. Cammel.*

'Only *one* M' say I.

Flowr. Flow<u>e</u>r.

'Let me write something' say I 'and see if you can read it.'

George watches and I write the words and he screws up his eyes to see them better.

' "George – is – a – boy. He – li – li –" '

'Likes.'

' "Likes – flowers. And – trees. He – is – not – oll." Oll?'

'Old.'

George shakes his head. 'I'm a right loghead' he says. 'I can't make the rest out.'

'You're much better than before' say I. 'You've got all the letters and lots of words already.'

He shrugs. His face is still very red. 'What does it say?'

Point at the words. ' "George is a boy. He likes flowers and trees. He is not old enough for kissing." '

'*Am.*'

'Not.'

'Here then.'

His face comes very close and red-shiny and he peck-kisses my cheek and moves away again ever-so-quickly.

'You're like Mama' say I. 'When she kisses me she does that.'

'Does what?'

'Moves away again. Like she didn't want to do it.'

'All right' says George. 'Hold still then.'

His eyes close together puzzled-looking and his nose and his long chin bony pointing. It comes right up to my cheek and his nose bumps on my nose. Peck-kisses my lip and two teeth show in his mouth, like a rabbit. Wet and tickling and his eyes and eyebrows huge and close and funny. I laugh.

'That's just silly' say I.

'You're meant to close your eyes' says George.

I do. Wet warm smudging tickling on my mouth again.

George smells of milk and earth and green things growing. Open my eyes again and George sits back and wipes his mouth on his sleeve.

'It just feels silly' say I. 'It must feel even sillier with Mr da Costa.'

'Why?'

'He has such thick moustaches.'

George laughs. 'When I start shaving I shan't have moustaches.'

'Lizzy thinks they are handsome.'

'I shouldn't want to kiss Miss Lizzy.'

Good.

George looks at the jaguar picture and his finger goes slow-pointing under each word. His mouth moves like he is saying them but he cannot read them all.

'You are getting much better' say I. 'You could go to Papa's lessons soon.'

'I'd rather you learned me.'

'*Taught* you' say I.

I would rather teach him too but I *can't*, not for ever. George will start reading things and writing and someone will notice it. Papa would not like it if he knew and he would stop us. And then Lizzy would know about the letters too.

George picks up the rhinoceros card. He copies the letters on to the slate. R-H-I-N-O-C-E-R-O-S.

He grins.

Papa will find out soon anyway. Papa always finds out.

There is to be a governess

'Well, girls' says Mama 'I will be back in a while with Mr Newlove and you shall all meet Miss Roke. You will have some time to yourselves, so be sure to spend it wisely. Stay clean and presentable, and do not tire yourselves out.' She looks at Mary. 'You will mind them, will you not, Mary?'

'Yes, Mama' says Mary. 'I shall be very pleased to.' She smiles at us.

Mary *must* mind us, for Mama will be with Papa, and Lizzy has *gone to town*. Even Anne is out this afternoon. Mama looks at the tea things.

'I will take them, Mama' say I.

Mama nods and opens the door. 'Thank you, Fanny.' She smiles at Beth and May and Frances. 'I will see you later, girls.'

'Yes, Mrs Newlove' say they.

Mama goes out.

'Well' says Mary sweet-smiling pleased 'I think it would be a good idea for you to play a nice quiet game in the schoolroom. Don't you agree, Fanny?'

'We could play Golden Goose' say I.

'That's a silly game' says Frances Morgan.

'No it isn't' say I.

'It's a lovely game' says Mary. 'It's your favourite, isn't it, Fanny?'

Frances Morgan looks at me and pulls a face.

'I would like to play' says Beth Lucas 'if that is agreeable.'

'So would I' says May. She looks at her sister.

'All right' says Frances 'if we really *have* to.'

Take the tea things rattle-clattering on the tray and go careful one-and-two stepping down the stairs and into the hall. May Morgan comes too.

'I will help you, Fanny' she says.

Beth and Frances Morgan stop in the hall behind us and Beth's voice says *let's set up the game* and Frances huff-sighs. They go into the schoolroom.

'I'm sorry that Frances is not nice to you' says May. Her eyes are big and green and worried-looking. Her lips pinch together like she has done a very bad thing and is about to tell someone strict.

'It's all right' say I.

'Don't pay any mind' says May.

Into the kitchen and lift the tray on to the table and the cups saucers teapot spoons *clitter-clatter* into the sink. May takes the milk and pours it *klug-klug-klig* back into the jug and puts it into the cupboard. She is nice. I shall tell her about the shells.

'May' say I 'if I told you a secret would you tell?'

'No' says she 'not if it was a real secret.'

'If it was a real secret and a wonderful one would you tell Frances about it?'

'I don't know.' She frowns. 'She *is* my sister.'

'Lizzy's my sister but I wouldn't tell *her*.'

May's forehead goes all screwed-up and worried and her eyes are very sad. I shall not tell her although I should very much like to. She will only tell Frances no-teeth Morgan.

'Let's go and play Golden Goose' say I.

We go skip-jumping into the schoolroom and there are Beth and Frances waiting with the board and counters. Frances says *I shall go first* and Beth passes her the die. I am red but I would rather be blue. Frances is blue, *of course*. Frances (blue) then Beth (green) then May (yellow) then me. We roll and count and I get six! and go up the bridge to number twelve.

'That's not fair' says Frances.

'Yes it is' says Beth. 'It's the rules.'

Frances goes and gets one (ha!) and Beth gets five and is on the same as me. May lands on eleven and I roll and get one, which makes thirteen. Miss a turn. Frances laughs snatches the die rolls it.

I *shall* tell May. She looks sad-faced sad-mouthed at me and her eyes say *never mind*.

And I shall tell Beth.

Beth lands on the inn and has to lose *two* turns.

'Poor Beth' says May.

'I shall win' says Frances.

She shouldn't win for you are only supposed to win if you are good. May counts her turn out and gets an extra turn and then lands on the well, which is very bad luck. I get four and Beth gets four. Miss Roke will not really be *our* governess. She and Mary are to teach the younger girls who will come after Easter. Mama said that Miss Roke may take us for some lessons, when Mama is busy. Eighteen-nineteen-twenty and twenty-one, which is the orchard, and roll again and one-two and I am on twenty-three.

'Oh dear' says Beth. She has landed on the maze.

Papa is meeting Miss Roke to make certain that she is suitable. I am sure that she will be, for she is a clergyman's daughter. That is not quite so good as coming from chapel but Mama said that such things are of little consequence as long as she is godly. I am not sure that Papa would say so, though.

Thud-thud-thud at the door and I get up to answer.

'We will wait for you' says Beth.

Into the corridor and open the door for there is no Anne. There *the Toogood* with his hair all flying blowing about in the wind and no hat on, and boys and boys all around him with big rolls of paper and bags and big eyes staring and nudging.

'Oh' says the Toogood. 'Hallo.'

'Hello, Mr Toogould' say I in my best grown-up voice.

Who is it? says Mary's voice on the stairs.

'Mr Toogould' say I 'and lots of boys.'

Open the door wider and he comes in and Mary comes *pat-pat-pat* stepping quickly along the hall. Her cheeks are very pink and she opens her mouth and puts her hand up to it.

'Oh! *Hello*, sir' she says ever-so-sweetly.

'Good day, Miss Mary' says Mr Toogould. 'I have a class waiting, as you see.'

'Of course' says Mary. 'Do go in.'

They do. The boys go clattering banging thumping rustling chattering into the music room. The Toogood shuts the front door and bows to Mary. She smiles.

'Go back to your game, Fanny' she says.

The Toogood goes along the hall to the music room and Mary follows him finger-combing her hair. She turns to me and makes little shooing waving signs at me and I go back to the schoolroom.

They all look up.

'Fanny' says May sadly 'Frances has won.'

'Won?' say I. 'Already?'

'I landed on the prison' says Beth 'so I am unable to move.'

Frances sickly-sweet smiles. 'May landed on quicksand and got stuck and I landed on Charity and got two more goes and now I'm on the golden egg.'

'I thought you were going to wait' say I.

'You were ages' says Frances.

'No I wasn't.'

'Was.'

'*Were*, you mean' say I 'only I *wasn't*. Anyway you can't have won fairly. It's not playing properly if you keep having turns when someone is missing.'

'Well' says Frances huff-huffing, 'we couldn't wait *all day* and if you *must* get up and answer the door like a *servant* how are we supposed to play the game properly at all?'

'I'm not a servant' say I.

She wouldn't know what a front door is for. She should come to school through the back door. Like her *father*.

'You even took the tea things like a servant' says Frances.

'Why are you so stuck-up?' say I. 'Anyone would think you were a *gentleman*'s daughter.'

'Whose daughter are you then?' says Frances. She sticks out her tongue. 'My father pays *your* father. And your mother. My mother doesn't work for a living, like a school dame.'

Get up and she gets up knocks the board over and the pieces go up and come down *klat-kli-kli-klaaaat* rolling. My hand up jumps smack-claps her cheek. She *aieeee-eeeee!*

screams yells and finger-claws at me and pulls my hair and
Beth Lucas pulls-tugs and says *stop it stop it at once!*

I do.

Chest hurting face hot throbbing nose tingling and Frances
hateful slap-face Morgan *owww!* howls and runs off. The
door bang-shuts.

'Oh' says May. 'Oh dear I *am* sorry.'

'*You* did nothing wrong' says Beth. She looks at me.

Don't care. *Don't.* Frances said horrid things about Mama
and Papa and she *should* be slapped. *And* worse. She is gone.
Ha! Nasty stuck-up slap-face Morgan. *Good.*

What is going on in here girls? Mary's voice.

She comes and stands in the doorway.

'If you please, Miss Mary' says May 'Fanny and Frances
had a quarrel but it is all right now.'

Mary looks at me eyebrows arching. 'Is this true, Fanny?'

Mary not cross not scaring. 'Yes' say I 'but she started it.'

'Fanny' says Mary 'I am very disappointed. You will have
to talk to Mama about this when she comes back.' Cross-
folds her arms. 'Now run and play outside. *Nicely.* You are
disturbing Mr Toogould's drawing class. Go into the garden.'

We do. Cheeks burning scratch sore and May sob-sniffing
and Beth Lucas looking down at the ground and sighing.
Hope Frances Morgan's face is apple red plum purple and
sore shining. Ha.

'What shall we do now?' says May snuff-sniffing.

'Sit and wait for Mrs Newlove' says Beth.

'I wonder where Frances went' says May. She looks at me.
I can think of places I would put her.

'Well' says Beth 'I hope Frances has not gone to Mr
Newlove.'

'She wouldn't dare' say I. *Wouldn't.*

May sad-faced touches my arm. 'It's all right' she says. 'I don't think you hurt her very much.'

Hope I *did*.

Beth walks along the garden and looks at the big pots of soil. 'What's over there?'

'Vegetable garden' say I 'and the shed.' *(And then the shells.)*

'We could play on the grass' says May. Points to the tunnel place. 'Is it all right to play over there? We could play tag.'

'Oh' says Beth 'did we ought to?'

'I've got a better idea' say I.

I shall show them the shells.

Thank goodness for George's sacks

For otherwise we would *all* have torn stockings.

Beth *ahem-hum* coughs, almost as nicely as Mama.

'Are you all right?' says May. She is not crying any more. First she was trying hard not to cry because of slap-face Frances and then she was sobbing smiling because of the shells. She is just smiling skipping now.

'It is rather cold and damp' says Beth. *Ahem*s again. 'Thank you for asking.'

Lit all the candles so the shells are very bright. George brought two more lanterns last time and trimmed the wicks. He is very good at things like that. Put all the pieces on the shell shelf in the square room. John Fassum (bully-boy) has left all his things in a box in the corner – storybook skates peg-and-ball fishing-nets toffee tin. He should bring his bed too and sleep here (*why not?*).

'I cannot quite believe how large it is' says Beth.

'Let's count the arches' says May.

'All right' says Beth.

'From the start' says May.

Back through the flowers hearts shiny tall dome and to the tunnel again.

May stands at the tunnel hole and goes one-two-three-fouring along the arches disappears round the circle comes out again. She stops at the dome and looks up.

'How many?' says Beth.

'Twelve.'

'There's lots more than that' say I.

'Oh' says May. 'I forgot to do both sides.'

'Never mind' says Beth.

May goes through the dome shell-stroking sighing. 'It's so lovely' she says. 'Oh! I've found a little girl.'

'There aren't any people' say I 'only flowers and things.'

'Here' says May pointing next to a tree 'it's a little girl.'

We look and she fingerpoints and says *head body arms legs* and makes the shapes in the shells.

'I'm not sure' says Beth. 'I think you could probably find anything you wanted to, if you looked hard enough.'

Head arms body legs. Not quite a girl, not quite real-looking. A doll? Feel the shells shiny and dusty and smooth round flat. 'It could be' say I. 'It's more like a doll than a girl though.'

'My ma has a corn dolly' says May. 'Her pa made it, ages ago. It looks a bit like that.'

Beth points at the white shiny dome shells. 'Those are oyster shells' she says. 'And there are mussels too. My father likes to eat those.'

'My pa likes cockles' says May. 'Are there any of those?'

Beth takes a candle and holds it up high. 'There must be some here, they are the – *oh*!'

Thud-thud-thudding above the dome. Someone walking. Someone big.

'What is it?' says May.

Sssssh!

Thud-walking stamp stops. *Well* says a voice. A man's voice. *Girls!*

Papa!

Beth clatter-drops the candle May gasps hand-claps her mouth. Stop stand statue-still. *Don't breathe don't move.* Papa walking thudding his feet very very near above our heads.

Where are those girls? his voice says. *Fanny!*

Thud-thud-thud-stamp.

Frances Newlove!

Thud-thud.

Humm.

Thud-thud-thud-thump-thump-thup-thup-thup.

They must be inside, dear. (Mama's voice.)

Mary said they had come out here. (Papa's voice.)

Let us go in, dear. (Mama.)

This looks very poor, Arabella. (Papa.) *Very poor indeed. Miss Roke is waiting.*

They will come. (Mama's voice.) *I will show her the upstairs rooms.*

Thud-thud-thud-thud-thup-thup-tup-tup-tup.

Gone.

'Quick!' say I whisper-hissing. 'In the tunnel!'

'But the lights!' says Beth. 'We cannot leave them.'

Clever Beth.

Shuffle-running quick quiet into the room candle-blowing-snuffing lantern-dimming and back into the passage and the tunnel entrance. May and Beth squeezing scraping into the tunnel and I pushing shoving. Dark dusty and no lantern now.

Oh! says May's voice. *I cannot see!*

'Keep moving' say I 'quickly quickly!'

Did he hear us? says Beth's voice hush-scared. *Did he?*

'No' say I 'you can't really hear from outside only inside.'

Beth's feet moving scuffling. Stop.

'What's the matter?' say I.

I can't says May's voice. *I daren't go up.*

'Why not?'

He might be there. He might see me!

'Get out quick' say I. 'Sooner out sooner safe. He'll come back otherwise.'

Go on! says Beth's voice. *We are all together, May.*

Scraping scuffling and Beth's feet move again and then the tunnel end. Sky and clouds and Mama's garden. Pile up the blocks quickly and stand up and there is no one here but us.

'Thank goodness' says May. She is shaking trembling.

'Oh my!' says Beth to her skirt. 'Look!'

White powder chalky dusty dirty on her skirts and on mine and May's and on our faces and arms. Brown smudges too. We stand shaking wiping dust-brushing and face-rubbing and hand-clapping clean.

'Quick' say I. 'We'd better get inside.'

'I daren't!' says May wailing sobbing. 'Oh, don't make me!'

'Do stop' says Beth crossly. 'We will be all right. Won't we, Fanny?'

They look at me and I look at their grubby faces and knees and at the house. Papa will be very very cross.

'We will say we were playing in the lane' say I 'near the farm. Come on.'

Over the grass past the shed past the vegetables and to the door.

'But we are coming in the wrong way for the lane' says Beth whisper-hissing.

'I know that' say I 'but the maid isn't here to open the door so we thought we'd come in from the *back*.'

'Oh!' say they. Beth smiles.

Open the door soft-stepping not talking into the corridor tippity-toeing past the kitchen and into the hall and *there is Frances Morgan*. Hand-fisting face-slapping scratching Frances Morgan. She smiles.

'*Here* they are, Mr Newlove!' she says.

Papa, black Sunday coat black shoes cross-frowning. He stands big and arm-folding in the doorway to the schoolroom.

'Where have you been?' he says. VERY quiet.

'Please, Papa' say I 'we were playing in the lane.'

'Why?'

Don't know. Papa stares cold-eyed cross-faced at me. Lips tight eyebrows pinched.

'Mr Newlove sir' says Beth Lucas very softly 'I am sorry to say, sir, that it is my fault that we did not stay indoors.'

We look at Beth. Frances Morgan bites her lip.

'Why?' says Papa. He says it a little louder than before. 'Were you not instructed to remain inside and be quiet?'

'Miss Mary did say that we might play quietly in the garden, sir' says Beth. 'But please, sir, I was to blame. I was not feeling very well and I asked Miss Fanny if we might go for a walk.'

'You were not in the garden' says Papa.

'Oh no, sir' says Beth 'for I wanted to walk about and Miss Fanny said that we might disturb the drawing class if we did so. Then, sir, I said that we might go into the lane. I am very sorry, sir.'

Beth Lucas is an *angel*.

Frances Morgan narrow-eyed stares at me and at Beth.

May gasping barely breathing looks trembling at Papa and Papa nods slowly and looks at Beth.

'You are a well-spoken girl' he says. 'What is your name?'

'Beth Lucas, Mr Newlove.' She hangs her head ever-so-modestly. 'I am truly very sorry, sir.'

'You should be' says Papa. He looks at me. 'You, Fanny, will explain yourself later.'

'Yes, sir' say I.

'You are very dirty. Your clothes are in a very sorry state.'

'Papa' say I 'a horse and cart passed us in the lane and the horse took fright and reared up and we had to climb the bank.'

'You are not to play outside again' says Papa. 'Miss Roke the governess has been waiting for you. She is upstairs with Mrs Newlove. You will not disturb them now. You are not fit to be seen.'

Papa looks into the schoolroom and at me and at Frances Morgan. 'It is late now. Go home, girls.'

'Yes, Mr Newlove' says Beth. 'Thank you, sir.'

'Thank you, sir' says May ever-so-softly.

'Frances Newlove' says Papa whisper-quiet, 'come in here.'

'Yes, Papa.'

He goes into the schoolroom. Beth and May look at me and Beth rolls her eyes.

THANK YOU BETH my lips say but not out loud. GOOD LUCK says Beth's mouth. May pulls on my arm and smiles sadly.

Frances Morgan comes skipping sickly-smiling up.

'I told him' she says. 'I told him you slapped me just because you lost the game. Like a *baby*.'

'Hope it hurt' say I.

Frances sticks out her tongue. 'You weren't in the lane' she says 'because *I* was. I shall tell.'

Now Frances says Papa's voice.

Frances Morgan jumps, turns to the door.

'Not you, stupid' say I.

'Good' she says thumbnail biting 'because he has a cane and he will whip you till you cry.'

Frances suck-a-thumb slap-face Morgan. She will *never* see the shells.

I am not allowed

Clattering chattering and the door bang-shuts. They have gone. *Good*.

Mama in her nice blue shawl that she only wears for proper visiting. *And* her locket. Mary Sunday smart with her red ribbon and Lizzy all fringes and feathers and silly frilly things. Her best bonnet too.

Hope it *rains*.

Sitting boring sampler-sewing. *Not* going, for Papa said that I am not to leave the house except for chapel. He is very *very* angry. Frances Morgan told him that I had slapped her, and *I* told him that she had said horrid things to me to make me cross, but I couldn't tell Papa what she had said, for it was about him and Mama. Papa said that I should *not give ear to ignorant abuse* and that I should *turn the other cheek*. Frances Morgan didn't turn the other cheek. If she had I probably would have slapped that too.

I do not want to have tea with Mr da Costa anyway, even though he is rich and has a big house. *Don't*. They will be sitting talking ever-so-politely with their tea things and Mr da

Costa will sly-smile at Lizzy over his teacup and *that* will make her behave like a goose. Mary said that it was a shame I could not go for the gardens would be very pretty. She thinks that Joshua and I are *proper little gardeners now*, just like George. Joshua is not allowed either, even though the lying captain will be there. Joshua was cross and lip-pouting, wanting to hear soldier stories. (Don't believe the captain's stories anyway, even if Joshua does.) But Joshua is not to go either, for he has spoiled his clothes and encouraged the boarding boys in *rough play*. Mrs D says he is just being a boy and doing what comes natural but she does not know that it is because of the shells. The shells are making a lot of trouble for *everyone*.

Joshua said that he will come when Papa has gone to chapel. He is supposed to stay indoors but he is bringing logs in the barrow, which *is* allowed. He said that we must have a secret meeting. Not in the shells, though. It is too dangerous.

Sitting sewing the silly sampler verses with silk. Mama says I am not to do the flowers or animals until I have finished the verses. *He did make the garden green and all the things that grow therein.* Dull dull dull dull dull. Stupid sampler.

Tappity-tap downstairs and Anne opens the door.

S Master Joshua Miss Fransuss her voice says. *Shall e come up?*

'Yes please, Anne' say I.

He does, *thut-thut-thut-thut-thuttuty-thut* up the stairs and over the landing and door-swinging crashing banging in.

'Hello, Fan' he says *fthud* sitting. 'What are you doing?'

'Sewing' say I. 'I hate sewing.'

'Pooh' says Joshua. 'So should I.'

'Has Papa gone to chapel? Is he still very cross?'

'You're so lucky you don't have to be there with him, *all*

day. He's got such a face.' Joshua scowls frowns pinches his lips, just like Papa. 'And he's been making me wash dishes with Woods since dinner. Woods kept telling me not to break things and Cook muttered about me being a runagate and a tear-rag spaddler the whole time. Whatever *that* is.'

'I had to sweep the kitchen' say I. 'And Mama told Anne that I should help her clean out the fire in the schoolroom, but Anne said not to. She said she would do it and not to tell.'

'Lucky you.' Joshua huff-sighs. 'What happened with that Morgan girl?'

'I slapped her face and Papa says I am no better than a heathen that has never been taught the Christian difference between right and wrong.'

'Phew' says Joshua, 'that's a bit far.'

'Frances slap-face Morgan went off in a horrid mood so I took May and Beth Lucas to see the shells. And then Mama and Papa came with the new governess to look for us and we had to get out quickity-quick and clean up.'

'What's she like?'

'I don't know. Papa wouldn't let us see for we were such a mess. And Frances Morgan *told*, and Papa gave me the cane. Now I have to stay in and sew.'

'I got the cane too. Tom Gore put a hole in his jacket and John Fassum tore his shirt trying to climb up the dome. They got extra Latin. I got extra Latin *and* the cane.'

'That's not fair.'

'I know.' (*Sulk sulk.*)

'John Fassum has left so many things in the shell room' say I. 'I think he wants to live in there.'

'He's taking over so' says Joshua. 'He thinks it's *his* secret place now. He's been saying who can come in and who can't.

Yesterday he let two of the day pupils in. They're not even in the same class as me.' Hangs his head swings his feet. 'And – and, Fan, he said that girls aren't allowed any more.'

'He *can't*' say I. 'He *can't* say that!' Horrid horrid horrid. 'I shall throw all his things out into the lane, I shall put them in the ditch where the cows go. *And* I shall eat his tin of toffee.'

'There isn't any toffee' says Joshua. 'I looked. Anyway, he's telling about it, all the time. Boasting. He'll tell a teacher or someone soon. *Then* we'll be for it.'

'He can't do that!' say I. 'He *mustn't*. You mustn't let him, Joshua!'

Joshua boot-swinging lip-pouting looks at me and shrugs. 'I'm sorry, Fan' he says. 'He's bigger than me.' *Sigh sigh.* 'I wish I'd never let him in.'

'So do I.'

'Fan' says Joshua 'I've been thinking. Maybe we should tell Papa.'

'That won't work' say I. 'It didn't work with Frances Morgan.'

'Not about Fassum' he says 'I mean, tell him about the *shells*.'

Put down my sampler. Joshua's eyes very sad and worried, very sorry and his face all long and white. Papa would be cross if he knew. Papa *will* know, soon. Someone will tell him.

'Papa will know we kept it secret' say I. 'That will make it even worse.'

'Not if we pretend to find it' says Joshua.

Find it?

Joshua gets up points to the door and we go to the stairs and one-two-three down and stop at the skeleton tree. It is a green skeleton now. Joshua puts his face flat and steamy breathing on the glass. Points at the grass and the tunnel place.

'I heard Papa talking to Stroud the gardener this morning' Joshua says. 'Papa said that he wants Stroud to cut the grass down. He said that there is to be more garden there, maybe with a pond.' He looks at me big-eyed sad-faced. 'You see, Fan, if they start digging to make a pond, they will find it. And they'll know that we've been down there.'

'How will they?' say I. 'Even if they find it then it will be the same as when *you* found it.'

'We will have to empty it' says Joshua. 'Take out the sacks and everything.'

'When?'

'Soon. Soon as we can.'

'We could still go in even if there is a pond' say I. 'We could go when Mama is out, just the same.'

'No' says Joshua. 'If they make a pond on top all the water will go through. Then the roof will fall in and there won't *be* a shell place any more.'

'What do you mean?'

'I asked George. He said that it is made of chalk, and water goes through chalk.'

George said. George knows about things like that. If we let them make a pond then the shells will be spoiled, and if we tell them they will never let us in again *anyway*.

'What should we do then?' say I.

'Dig the pond ourselves' says Joshua. 'Right over the top.'

'But what about the water? I don't want it to go away even if we *can't* ever see it again.'

'We don't really make a pond, silly' he says 'we just make a hole. Then we get to the tall bit, the dome, and drop something in. That way we can pretend to find it.'

'Papa will know' say I. 'Papa always knows.'

'No he won't' says Joshua. 'Not if we are *really* clever.'

'Will we never be able to go in again, then?' say I.

He shrugs. 'Papa *might* let us. He won't be able to go in, he's too big. But he will want to know what it's like.'

'What about the others? Won't they tell?'

'They can't, and anyway, if *we* pretend to be surprised, Papa will never believe them if they do tell.'

I don't know how to dig a pond. George will know, he will help us. We will have to hide everything. Lamps. Candles. Fassum's things. Sacks. Tinderboxes.

'They won't be our shells any more though' say I.

'Yes they will' says Joshua. 'We found them first. We just have to find them again.'

They won't though. *Won't*. They will be Papa's shells.

Easter Day the Nineteenth day of April 1835
After dinner
Bellevue School for Girls
Margate

Dearest James,

I hope that you are having a very joyful Easter Day.

We had a special long chapel service this morning and sang lots of hymns. Papa stood up at the lectern and read from the gospels. The sermon today was all about how Jesus suffered for us and is the lamb of God. It was very sad and it made Mary cry. She was still crying when we walked home. Mama told her to stop sniffing but Papa was pleased, he said that it was the zeal of the Lord and that the spirit of Jesus was moving her. I hope that is why and not that she has got another cold. She has a very red nose even now.

We have had a lovely dinner all together in Papa's house. The boy boarders are not here because it is a holiday. They will be back later though. We had roast lamb, which made Mary cry even more. There were onions too and potatoes, and parsnips. I do not like parsnips but I did eat one because I must learn to suffer in silence for the greater good, like Jesus did. Mrs D made the special pudden-pies which have custard with raisins in. They are lovely. We said prayers after dinner and I prayed that you would come to visit in time for tea, but Papa said that is wishing not praying, and that I should not ask God for such things. I know that I am very selfish and bad, so I said extra prayers in my room, and told God that I was sorry, which I am, and prayed that you had had a nice dinner too. I hope it worked.

I am very busy with lessons. This week we have been learning all about the Old Testament and where Jerusalem is. Mama has found a new governess, she is called Miss Roke. She is coming tomorrow. She is going to teach the little girls who will be starting lessons soon. They are too young to be in the same class with me, for they are only five and six years old. That is too little to do Old Testament history. I will be <u>nine</u> this year.

We are to go for a walk now so I cannot write very much more. Mama says that we may go down to the harbour to see the ships, as it is a special day. The last time we went to the harbour there was an odd-looking man sitting on the end of the pier staring at the sea. Papa said that he was painting a picture. He must have been very cold though, for he did not move even when it began to rain. It has rained very much this week but it is quite fine today.

Mama is calling for me so I shall finish now. I hope that you are not studying too hard and that even though you are very busy you sometimes have time to spare a thought for

your affectionate sister Frances.

Mama and Papa send you their Easter blessings.

Finding them, again

I was afraid that Mama would say I am not to help but she has gone out with Lizzy and Mary. I have been so good all week, no shells no mess no skipping in the lane not even any fighting with Frances Morgan, even though she pulled my hair and said *you Newloves are pikey foreigners*. I turned the other cheek instead. She didn't like that. She would not dare to call anyone else names. She just likes to fight with *me*.

George already in the garden near the tunnel place, shovels barrow big stick in the ground where the shells are. He smiles but he does not want to really. Nor do I.

'Hello, George' say I.

'Hello.'

'What's that stick for?'

'Marker. Me and Joshua found the place where the dome is and put it there, so as we'd get it right. Don't want to dig the wrong bit.'

'No.'

'Got all your things out?'

'Joshua did.'

(*I* haven't been in for *ages*.)

'Pa took the grass down' says George. 'I had a job keeping im from finding the opening.'

'He didn't see though, did he?'

'No'm. I cut that bit.' George looks up. 'Here it comes.'

Joshua dragging walking sulky-faced over the garden. He flop-sits and pulls at the cut-grass. It smells nice but the ground looks funny without it. Bumpy.

'I had to hide the sacks under the shed' says Joshua. 'I don't know what we'll do with them.'

'I'll burn them' says George. 'Pa said to get the bonfire going.'

'Fassum wanted to come' says Joshua huffing-sighing.

'You didn't tell him?' say I. 'He's *not* to come.'

'He thought I was just going in' says Joshua. 'I said I couldn't today because we were making a pond. He doesn't know I've moved all his things out.'

Good.

George stands picks up a shovel and *tsthwick* slices pushes it into the grass. 'Best get on with it then' he says.

Joshua stands too and takes another shovel and poke-pokes the ground.

'Wait' say I. 'We should make a pact first.'

Joshua nods and they drop the shovels and we stand hand joining round the stick where the dome is. Standing looking down not moving not saying anything. Joshua sighs.

'Swear' say I 'never to tell. Not ever.'

George nods and so does Joshua.

'Swear' say I.

'I swear' say they.

'Not ever to tell the truth about finding the shells so help you God' say I.

'I swear' say they.

So do I.

Drop hands pick up shovels and they start. Dig dig dig. Cut out mud slices with grassy tops and George lays them in a pile ever-so-carefully. Joshua dig-digs earth stones snail-shells glass-pieces bits of broken pot and worms all pink and muddy wriggling. George digs and the stick falls over and I take it, throw it away.

Poor shells.

'Today is the last day they will ever be secret' say I.

They don't say anything. Dig dig scrape scrape. Earth and earth and then white pieces, white chalk in the hole. Joshua looks at George but he shakes his head. *Thut-thut-ssslik-thut.* Scrape scrape. George makes the hole wider and I take the little hand shovel and scrape the earth *kre-kre-kreee kre-kre-kreee* from the chalk and up the muddy sides. Whiter bigger wider. Papa will know soon. *Thut-ssskreeeee-thut-ssslik-thut.* Dig and dig and dig and the chalk pieces splitting coming out in lumps and the hole bigger wider deeper. Joshua puffs wipes his face on his sleeve.

'Stop!' says George. 'There it is.'

Not digging not scraping. George waves shoos us back. Holds his shovel over the muddy white. *Tup-tup-tup* knocks.

'Like a drum' says Joshua.

George nods. 'Make a wish' he says, eyes closing.

Dear God do not let them hurt the shells and do not let Papa be cross with us and please do not let George fall into the hole. Amen.

George thud-pushes the shovel at the chalk and the muddy white moves and *kreee*-creaks and he *tup-tup-tup* hits it again. 'It's going!' he says. 'Keep back.'

The chalk crumble cracks and he hits it one-two-three-four

and it starts to fall and *craaaaaaaaak* rumbles and the earth begins to roll and a *hole*! Dark hole falling in, soil tumbling chalk crack-crackling loose and shells, white shells and lumps like plaster and George wobble-stands and leans back and *thud*-sits on the grass.

'There' he says.

Joshua lies down pokes the hole and scrape-pushes at the edges. Earth and chalk and shells all falling tumbling in. He stops and the hole clatter-rumbles and the earth pieces roll in. *Plit-plit pla-it-plit. Plit.*

Lie on our bellies and wriggle-creep to the edge. Like a rabbit hole, long and dark but with the silvery white shells in the sides, some shiny some chalky and earth-dusty. George's head bent peering in and Joshua's face all pale and earth-smudgy.

'It's done then' says George. He sighs. 'I'll fetch your pa.'

'All right' says Joshua. 'He's in the study. No chapel meeting today.'

George stands wipes his hand on his trousers. 'Thanks' he says, ever-so-quiet. 'For showing me, before, I mean.' Puts his hand out and Joshua puts out his and they shake hands quickly.

'Good luck' says Joshua.

George looks at me and sad-smiles. 'I won't be long' he says. 'Don't forget the shovel.'

He goes over the garden to the house and round the side. To Papa.

Joshua stands, picks up a shovel and holds it over the hole.

'Don't!' say I. 'Don't break any more shells.'

'I've to drop it in' he says. 'I'll drop it straight, so it doesn't hit the sides. It's the only way, Fan.'

Joshua lets go of the handle and the shovel drops smack-clattering through the hole. Peer down but too dark to see it. The silvery shells all bare and dusty white under the sky. Poor shells. Please don't let it rain on them.

'It looks so different from here' say I.

'I don't suppose anyone's ever seen it from the top before' says Joshua. 'It's only right that *we* should.'

'I hope we didn't break too many.'

'Some of them were already down. We can always put them back up.'

Papa may not want us to. Papa may not ever let us in again.

'Don't cry, Fan' says Joshua.

Not.

The hole very dark damp-smelling. Worm wriggling pink long-bodied from the earthy side flops wriggles and falls in.

'Maybe I should have gone for Papa' says Joshua. 'Maybe it wasn't fair to send George.'

'It's better for George to do it' say I. 'Papa would know if we told him, he'd know we were lying. George is always scared when he talks to Papa so it's harder to tell.'

'That's true. Mama isn't inside, is she?'

'No' say I. 'She went out with Lizzy and Mary. Shopping.'

'Good.'

'Joshua' say I 'it won't ever be the same now, will it?

'No.'

'Do you think John Fassum will tell?'

'He won't dare to.'

Roll over and the ground is bumpy damp cut-grass and earth-smelling. The shells are there, under me. Trees flowers fishes hearts, pink yellow orange white and blue. Put my hands out and feel the ground cold lumpy. The sky cloudy fast-moving. Beth Lucas said you could see anything you wanted if you looked hard enough. Like faces' shapes in clouds. Clouds thicker sky darker. Hope it doesn't rain. Please don't make it rain yet O God.

'Get up, Fan!'

Joshua up-jumps and I roll-stand and there is Papa coming across the cabbages, cross-faced in his big coat and boots and no hat. Where is George?

'What is going on here?' says Papa. (He does not say it quietly, at least.)

'Please, Papa' says Joshua scared-eyed, 'we were digging the pond out and there was a noise and this hole came.'

'And the shovel fell in, Papa' say I.

Papa looks at me. 'What are you doing here, Fanny?' he says. 'Where is your mama?'

'Shopping, Papa. With Lizzy and Mary.'

'Why are you not inside? This is not girl's work.'

'Sorry, Papa.' Hot nose tingling swallow hard. His eyes very cross especially for me. 'I only came out to watch, Papa. I did not dig.'

'I asked Fanny to come out, sir' says Joshua 'for she knew best where Mama wanted the pond to be.'

Thank you Joshua. Papa frowns, nods. Goes to the hole. Bends over.

'What is that?' he says pointing to the shells.

'I'm not sure, sir' says Joshua 'but I think they are oyster shells.'

'I can see that, boy' says Papa. 'What are they doing in the hole?' (a not-question). 'Hmmn. An old rubbish site perhaps.' He *ah-hrem* coughs and the *hrem* goes on and on into the hole and disappears. He stands stretches his back shakes his head. 'It must be an old well' he says. 'Is there water in it? Did you hear a splash?'

'No, Papa' say we.

'Just an old chalk pit then' he says. 'I was preparing for tomorrow's service, children. I do not wish to be delayed by trifles.'

George! George coming carrying a piece of rope and *a lantern.* The lantern is already lit. It is the one from the box under the shed. George stops red-faced in front of Papa, holds up the rope.

'Good lad' says Papa. 'Give me the end. Who is the smallest?'

'Me, Papa' say I.

'You are *not* to go in, Fanny' he says. (Huff huff.) Looks at George and then at Joshua. 'You are the shorter, Joshua' he says. 'As there is no water it should be safe to go down.'

Joshua nods, tries not to grin.

George puts the lantern round Joshua's neck and he goes to the hole. Papa and George hold the rope and drop the end in. It rolls coils disappears.

'Be careful, Joshua' says Papa.

Joshua lantern swinging, ever-so-slightly smiling, goes down the rope into the hole. Papa and George hold the end and lean backwards. Papa frowns. 'Move quickly, boy!' he says.

Joshua is in the hole. *Oh!* his voice says all muffled strange. *Oh!*

'Have you got it?' says Papa. 'Come up now, it might give way.'

Joshua *oooooing aaaaaaa*ing and scratch-scrabbling in the dome. *There are passages Papa* his voice says *and shells.*

'Come up at once' says Papa. 'I shall not hold this rope any longer, boy.'

Rope tugging and scratching scraping noises and George

and Papa pulling walking backwards with the rope. Joshua comes up with the lantern, dirty-faced wide-eyed. He pulls up the shovel throws it on to the grass.

'Oh, Papa!' he says. 'It is a shell cave!'

Papa and George drop the rope and Papa huff-grunts. Joshua climbs out and stands, puts his hand into his shirt. Pulls out a piece of shell flower. *Clever Joshua.*

Papa stare-stares at the shell flower. Joshua turns, points, holds the lantern over the hole. We peer in and Papa comes and stands leaning with his hands on his trouser knees.

'Well' he says. 'Not just an old pit, then.'

Joshua takes the lantern string and lets the lantern down into the dome hole. There the shells all silvery white and blue and chalk-dusty, and the fallen chalk pieces white in the earth at the bottom. Papa makes a funny *harrum* noise. Joshua lets the lantern down a little more and there is the shell wall shiny pretty with the tree shapes on and the arch that goes to the passage all dark and shadowy.

'It is like a tower inside' says Joshua 'and there are passages going off it. At least two passages, sir. All shell-covered.'

Papa rubs his hands rubs his chin. 'George' he says 'find your father.'

'Yes, sir' says George.

Mr Stroud, now. *Another* grown-up.

'Tell him to find something to cover this hole' says Papa 'a slab or piece of slate. Quickly now.'

'Yes, Mr Newlove, sir.'

George goes jump-running over the garden.

'Do not tell another soul, boy!' Papa says after him. 'Well, Joshua' (*not* cross not quiet) 'this is quite something, is it not, son?'

'Yes, Papa.'

'I want you to go directly to Chateau Bellevue. Find Captain Easter and bring him here.'

Papa!

'Yes, Papa' says Joshua. His eyes are big shiny.

'Please, Papa' say I '*please* don't tell the captain!'

'Do not stop or speak to anyone else' says Papa. 'Is that clear?'

'Yes, sir' says Joshua. 'What should I tell the captain, sir?'

'Only that there is a hole' says Papa. 'We will see what he has to say when he arrives.'

Joshua tight-smiles at me runs off across the garden. Papa picks up the piece of shell flower and rubs it. It is very small in his hand. His big thumb is all black-ink smudges and chalk-dusty.

'The captain' he says bending speaking into the hole 'it must be what the captain had heard of.'

'*Please*' say I 'oh please, Papa! *Please* do not tell the captain.'

'Do not be foolish, Frances' says Papa. 'Captain Easter had some notion of this. He will tell us what it is all about.'

Will not. He will spoil it break it not let me in it.

I know what it is but cannot say, cannot tell. Sit on the grass and look down deep into the shell dome dark and damp-smelling. George gone Joshua gone, only me and Papa now but others soon. Stroud the gardener and the captain and Mama and Lizzy and Mary. And then who else? Who will Papa tell? Lizzy will tell Mr da Costa and Stroud the gardener will tell the neighbours and Papa will tell the teachers and the teachers will tell the boys and the boys will tell their fathers and mothers and they will tell the whole town. Not secret any more, not our shells any more. Papa's shells. And then *everyone's*.

Poor shells. I am sorry so sorry. I did not mean for the captain to come.

Papa puts down the shell flower. He is frowning but pleased. 'Of all the things on God's earth' he says. 'Such a curious thing. And in my own back garden.'

Mama's back garden.

Papa holds the lantern in the hole. He is smiling. The shells look sad and cold and lonely. It is already getting dark.

What's all this, Newlove? The *captain*.

He comes quick-walking stick-swinging. His horrid dog too, trotting tail-wagging cabbage-sniffing. Joshua is shiny red-faced and panting.

'Captain Easter' says Papa 'thank you so much for coming out. We have made a singular discovery.'

The captain smiles all whiskery, shakes Papa's hand. The dog comes *huh-huh-huh* and sniffs at the hole and at the shovel. *Sthlop-sthlop* licks my hand. Hot wet and horrid.

'Young Joshua here tells me he's found the buried treasure' says the captain.

Joshua grins.

'As you see' says Papa 'there is a hole with some manner of tunnel beneath.'

The captain and Papa and the dog peer in with the lantern huff-puff breathing murmuring. *Shell mosaic – boy brought up a piece – go down and look – getting dark. Cover the hole. Well well well.*

The captain stands and stick-pokes at the hole.

'I say, Newlove' he says 'this *is* a surprise.'

He does not look surprised. He looks pleased and worried and out of breath all at the same time. He does not look surprised. His eyes wrinkled cold thinking and very blue. They look at me.

'What do you know about this, young missy?' he says.

'Nothing, sir' say I.

'Is that so?'

Papa looks at me, looks at the house. 'They have just this moment found it' he says.

'Have they?' says the captain. Eyes very hard mouth whiskery lip-chewing.

'The maid is lighting the lamps' says Papa. 'Your mama will be home soon. Go inside, Frances. And you, Joshua. Wait in the parlour.'

'But, Papa –'

'Now.'

We do. The dog *huh-huh-huh* hot panting follows with its nose sniffing at Joshua's hand. Joshua push-kicks at it. It stops, sniffs, *scraa-scraa*-scratches at the ground under the shed where the sacks are.

Ask Anne to make some tea says Papa's voice.

Up to the back door mud-kicking boot-wiping and Joshua opens.

'Should we have done it?' say I. 'Why did the captain have to come? I wouldn't have done it, not if I'd known *he* would be here.'

'We had to' says Joshua.

Into the house along the passage and Anne standing peering from the kitchen door.

'Missus Nuloves come in' she says 'an s asked fer tea.'

'Papa is here' say I 'and Captain Easter.'

'See th captin' says Anne. 'Spose ll want tea n all?'

'Yes please, Anne' say I.

Into the hall, up the stairs and the green skeleton tree tap-taps. Almost dark now. Too dark to see Papa or the captain or the dog.

Hello, children! says Mama's voice.

Mama at the top, shawl-shaking. 'I didn't expect to see you, Joshua' she says. 'I've asked Anne for tea. You can tell her to bring another cup if you like.'

'I saw her, Mama' says Joshua.

'I left your sisters at Parker's' says Mama. 'Lizzy is choosing a new bonnet. Come up, then.'

One-two-three-up slow stepping and Mama smiles and then looks at our hands faces shoes and frowns. 'My, you *are* dirty' she says. 'Go and use Fanny's washstand.'

Mama goes to the parlour and we go into my room to the basin. Joshua hand-washes face dab-dabs quietly, not splashing even. Finger-flick cold jug water from the morning. He rubs his face.

'What do we say to Mama?' say I.

Door-bang downstairs and the captain's voice murmur-mutter and then Papa's. They come feet thud-thudding and dog-claw scratching padding *pat-pat-pat* up the stairs.

Oh! says Mama's voice. *What a delightful surprise.*

'We don't *need* to say, now' says Joshua. 'Come on, we don't want to miss anything.'

They talk and talk

On and on and on. Mama pours the tea and the dog huff-sniffs at all the table legs and then the chair legs and then *my* legs. *Huh-huh-huh.*

'Sit down, Wellesley' says the captain.

It does, leans its head on my foot and *hynnn-huynnn* whines. Horrid smelly wet thing.

'Is it quite safe, my dear?' says Mama.

'Stroud has covered the hole' says Papa. 'There is no danger of anyone falling in.'

'Or finding it, more to the point' says the captain. 'My *dear* Mrs Newlove' he says leaning smiling at Mama 'you must appreciate what an extraordinary discovery this is.'

'Oh yes, Captain' says Mama. Smiles, spoons the sugar out. 'What do you think it is, exactly?'

'Hard to say' says the captain 'rather dark to see. But the boy here says there are passages and there certainly seems to be a doorway.'

They look at Joshua. Joshua looks at the milk jug.

'How much did you see, my boy?' says the captain.

'Just as I said, sir' says Joshua.

'Tell me again' says the captain. Mama passes him tea and he whisker-grins over the cup.

'I went down the hole sir and there are shells in the sides, like you saw' says Joshua. 'And then at the bottom there were walls with more shells and they went off to the sides. Like passages.' He swallows, looks at me, looks at the tea things. 'And where there was earth and bits at the bottom there were broken pieces of shell stuck together in patterns. So I brought one up.'

'I see' says the captain. His eyes are shiny-pleased, like he has just said something very funny. 'So this piece of mosaic was part of the floor, was it?'

He holds up the shell flower but it is *not* the shell flower that Joshua had. *Not.* Another piece, brighter pinker not dusty not earthy but clean polished. Joshua shrugs.

'I picked the piece *up* from the floor, sir' he says 'but I don't think there were shells stuck *in* the floor.'

The captain has a shell flower and it *isn't* Joshua's. Isn't mine either for that is in the bundle under the bed with the torn stockings. Isn't mine, isn't Joshua's, didn't come from the hole today or from the tunnel for there aren't any there. *Where* then?

The captain looks at Joshua, looks at me. His eyes are *not* shiny-pleased now but hard and blue and horrid. Picks up the teacup, sips, puts it down. Little tea drops hang wet brown on his moustache whiskers. *Ssstheeuk* sucks them off.

He holds the shell flower out to me. 'I don't suppose you've ever seen anything like this before, have you, missy?' he says.

'No, sir' say I. Not frowning not smiling not moving at all just looking at his eyes all hard and blue and thinking.

'And you've never seen that hole before either?'

'No, sir.' *Not* a lie.

'I don't suppose you could see what was down there, could you?' says the captain.

'I could see shells, sir' say I 'but it was very dark.'

'Not that dark though, eh?'

'No, sir.'

'So you could see shells?'

'Yes, sir.'

'In patterns?'

'I think so, sir.'

'You think so.' He smiles, a not-very-nice smile. 'What colour were the shells you think you could see?'

Not the very orange ones for they are in the room not the very pink ones either. All silvery-white and blue in the dome. Not the shell-tree colours, for it was too dark to see those properly even *with* the lantern.

'White, sir' say I. 'They were oyster shells, Papa said.'

'Hmmn' says the captain. 'Well well.' Nods slowly, sips his tea. 'Well, this is quite a surprise to us all, I dare say.'

I don't believe you his eyes say. *Don't believe you either* say mine back. He is not surprised any more than me or Joshua or George. Joshua is a bad liar but he is doing very well at it today for Papa has not told him off for it once.

'What do you propose now, Captain?' says Papa.

'We'll need to have a good look at it first' says the captain. 'That hole will need widening, of course, so we can get in.'

No!

'If you please, sir' says Joshua 'I could go down first and see if there is another way in.'

'Secret entrance, eh?' says the captain. He *haw-haw* laughs at Mama and Mama *aha-ha*s back.

'I was just wondering, sir' says Joshua 'that there might be another way in, as there are passages.'

'I do not want you to begin crawling about down there, Joshua' says Papa. 'It might not be safe.'

'Your father is right' says Mama. 'We cannot have you getting trapped underground.' Puts her hand to her face and gasps. 'Imagine!' she says, very quiet. 'How *awful*.'

'It is quite safe, Mama' says Joshua. 'I mean, I am sure that it is.'

Joshua!

The captain smiles nods. 'Even so' he says 'I think a party of explorers would be a good thing. Don't you agree, Miss Frances?'

Looks at me very hard. I look very hard back.

'Yes, sir' say I, ever-so-sweetly. 'If you say so, sir.'

'I wonder' says Papa 'if it might be some manner of smuggling hole. I understand, Captain, that such activities were quite common hereabouts.'

'Still are' says the captain 'if you know where to look. But no, Newlove. I doubt smugglers would go to such trouble as to stick shells on the walls. Too busy drinking rum and giving each other the cutlass, eh, lad?'

Joshua grins.

'What do you truly think, Captain?' says Mama. 'You did suggest to us that there might be something buried here. What had you heard?'

'Oh' says the captain leg-stretching boot-crossing 'nothing certain, just local gossip. You know the kind of thing, old lime pits used for hiding booty, burying the family silver, church cups turning up in fields. The usual stories.' Cup-and-saucer clatters. 'I've found a few bits and pieces in my time too, things dug up when I built Bellevue.'

'Treasure?' says Joshua.

'Not the sort you mean.' He winks. 'Still, they fetched a fair price at the auctions up in town. Yes, Mrs Newlove, I wouldn't be surprised if that hole of ours doesn't lead to some sort of treasure trove.'

Ours. So it is his too, now.

'I bet there *is* treasure' says Joshua.

There *isn't* though, for he has looked. Only the shells and the walls and the big slate pictures.

'Well, Joshua' says Papa 'let us not get carried away. We have yet to see what is down there.'

'Of course' says the captain 'it could be some sort of cave, like the one Forster had.'

'Who was that, Captain?' says Mama.

'Old Forster, queer sort. He built Northumberland House, found some caves in his back garden. Odd place, I hear, huge caverns. Got some sort of tunnel that went out to sea. Forster got it all painted up but he never let anyone down there. He's on his last legs now, might even be dead already.'

'Are there shells there too, sir?' says Joshua.

'Not that I know of.'

Ours is a fairy shell garden. Not a cave not a pit not a treasure house. Not for smugglers who drink rum either.

Papa looks at Mama's clock and at Mama. Puts down his teacup. The dog *huyum-hums* and wet-snorts at my boot.

'I must return to the school' says Papa. 'The boarders will be back shortly. We do not want to create any excitement amongst them.'

'Indeed' says the captain winking smiling at Joshua. 'Excitement is a very bad thing for boys.'

'Perhaps you might be so good as to return tomorrow, Captain' says Papa 'so that we might investigate further. Would five o'clock suit you?'

'Admirably' says the captain.

'The boys will be out for the afternoon' says Papa 'and it will still be light enough. Arabella, be sure to let Anne go after dinner.'

'Yes, dear' says Mama. 'Captain, I shall be delighted if you might stay on for an early supper.'

'I shall look forward to it' says the captain.

'We could have a family supper tomorrow, could we not dear?' says Mama. 'Just this once.'

'Of course' says Papa. 'I will leave the boys under the house-keeper's care.'

'A doubly fine reason to return' says the captain.

He stands and we stand and the dog stands. The captain kisses Mama's hand and shakes Papa's hand and we bob and bow. He looks at me and smiles not-very-nicely and I smile ever-so-sweetly back. He says *come on, Wellesley* and the dog *huh-huh-huh* tail-banging goes to the door. Papa opens it and says *I will see you out, Captain* and they go thudding pat-patting down the stairs.

'Well well' says Mama. 'What a curious thing this is.'

Door banging and muttering chattering and Lizzy and Mary's voices downstairs. They come clattering up to the door and in, boxes and baskets swinging and bonnet-untying.

'Hello, Mama' says Mary. 'We just met the captain and Papa going out.'

'Yes' says Mama 'they stayed for tea.'

'I have found *such* a bonnet, Mama' says Lizzy. 'Really it is quite the most remarkable thing ever. Is it not, Mary?'

'It *is* lovely' says Mary. 'Do show Mama, Lizzy dear.'

Look at Joshua and he looks at me and shrugs sighs. The captain is coming back tomorrow.

The captain *knows*.

Lizzy clattering pushes the tea tray aside and puts down her hatbox. 'Look at this' she says untying unwrapping. 'It must be the best in the whole shop. Charlotte Parker has the nicest things, some of them come all the way from Paris. There, have you ever seen such a lovely bonnet?'

Straw and pink silk and pink ribbons and little silk roses. Mama says *oh, my dear!* and Mary sighs and Lizzy holds it up and fusses with the ribbons.

The captain had a shell flower. He had it in his pocket.

'Is it not the nicest bonnet, Fanny?' says Mary.

'Yes' say I.

Lizzy looks at me, looks at Joshua. 'Whatever is the matter with you two?' she says.

Look at Mama to say but Mama looks smiling at the bonnet.

'Honestly' says Lizzy huffing tissue-rustling. 'Anyone would think you'd *never* seen a pretty thing in your *lives*.'

The captain is back

And he has brought Mr da Costa with him (*bad*) but not his dog (*good*).

'Good afternoon, Newlove, ladies' he says.

'Good afternoon' says Mr da Costa.

We bob and Papa shakes their hands.

'Thought I'd bring Maurice along' says the captain 'useful chap, been about, you know.'

'Of course' says Mama.

Lizzy sly-smiles puts her head on one side. Her eyes go flutter-flutter. Mr da Costa looks away.

'Maurice was quite taken with the whole thing' says the captain. 'He thinks we might be on to something.'

'A most interesting matter, Mr Newlove' says Mr da Costa. 'I could not help but come along to see for myself.'

'I have removed the slab, as you see' says Papa 'and the gardener has given us the use of this rope-ladder. I have tested the rope and it is quite safe.'

The ladder curls drops down into the hole. There is a big

stone on top of it and George came to put pegs in, too. Mama lights the lanterns.

'Are we all going down?' says the captain.

'I am not certain, for myself' Mama says 'or for the girls.'

'I should like to go, Mama' say I.

'Oh, Fanny dear' says Mama sighing head shaking 'I do not think that is wise.'

Mama!

'Oh, I don't know' says the captain. He boot-taps the rope ends. 'Let the old girl go down. I'll keep an eye on her.'

Papa looks at me, looks at the captain.

'May I go first, Papa?' says Joshua. 'I can stand at the bottom in case Fanny falls.'

'Oh, very well' says Papa. 'You may both go. But do be cautious, children.'

Mama puts a lantern round Joshua's neck and one round mine. Joshua goes to the edge and climbs down into the hole. I go too and Mama holds my hand *like a baby* and says *be careful there do not slip* and *hold on tightly, child*. My boots on the ladder rungs and I go down *one two three four* very slowly. The ground goes away higher and higher and Mama's face peering down goes smaller further away.

The shell sides all silvery dusty and beautiful. Please do not let there be *too* many broken.

'Come on, Fan' says Joshua.

Are you all right, Fanny dear? says Mary's voice.

'Yes thank you' say I.

I think she is stuck says Mama's voice. *Are you stuck, Fanny? Shall we pull you up? I knew she should not have gone down.*

'I am quite all right really, Mama' say I.

Eight nine ten and my boot *skree*-scrapes on the floor.

Joshua standing grinning puts out his hands. 'I didn't think they'd let you in then' he says.

'Me too.'

'Let's go into the room. Before the others come.'

Murmur-murmur above and Mama's voice says *you do not have to go, my dears* and Mary's says *it is very dark*. Big boots turning stepping down, Captain Easter's boots. Mr da Costa's face above them peering in.

I shall go down too says Lizzy's voice.

Oh, Lizzy! says Mary's voice.

'Come on, Fan' says Joshua 'quick.'

Along the passage past the hearts and flowers and into the sun room. Scraping foot-stepping in the dome and the passage, voices murmuring. *Which way?* says Mr da Costa's voice. *Down here* says the captain's voice very close in the passage.

Joshua leans on the shell shelf and sighs.

'They will break it, you know' say I, whisper-quiet.

'They might not.'

Touch the sun shape on the wall, lumpy shiny, put my face against it. Cold, damp. Dusty. Won't let them hurt you. Poor shells. Promise I won't. Kiss the sun shape's middle, pin-cushion round and smooth. Lovely beautiful shells, they *shall not* hurt you.

Scuffling foot-thudding and light spreading in the archway and the captain comes stick-swinging in, holding up his lantern. 'Here, Maurice' he says.

Mr da Costa comes in lantern swinging wide-eyed wide-mouthed. 'I say' he says. 'I say, Easter, it's a damned altar!'

'What did I tell you?' says the captain.

Don't look at us don't look at the shell shapes. They go up to the shelf and Joshua steps back, looks shrugging at me.

'Damned well is' says Mr da Costa. 'That's an altar if ever I saw one.'

Not an altar, not like in a chapel. Mr da Costa puts his lantern on the shelf, puts his hands all over the shell wall.

'This recess must have something in it' he says. 'It even looks like it's been opened.'

'That's the thing' says the captain. 'Probably already emptied.'

'Do you think there's treasure in there, sir?' says Joshua.

'Who knows, boy?' says the captain (snappity-snap). 'Why don't you two run along and tell your father what's in here, eh?'

No. Not leaving the shells, not leaving the captain in here with them. He puts his finger under the shell shelf and pick-pick-picks at the shells. 'Reckon this piece might come away' he says.

The captain puts his lantern down and they put their hands on the wall under the shell shelf and tug tug tug at it.

'Don't!' say I. 'Don't, you'll spoil it!'

They tug and tug and Mr da Costa kicks at the bottom of the wall. Joshua looks at me big-eyed sad and shakes his head.

'Come on, Fan' he says 'let's look in the other bit.'

'No.'

Shan't go. They are spoiling pulling tearing. Joshua won't stop them and Papa will not come either for he cannot get in.

Are you in there? says Lizzy's voice.

Tap-tap walking and lantern-light and Lizzy comes stepping up to the arch. Mary behind her too, coughing eye-rubbing.

'My goodness!' says Lizzy. 'What are you doing?'

'They are looking for treasure' says Joshua.

'I don't think we should be in here' says Mary. Her voice

215

soft and tremble-quiet. 'I think we should go out again before something happens.'

'Good idea' says Mr da Costa.

Lizzy eye-rolling looks at Mary. 'Really' she says. 'What superstitious nonsense. I suppose you think it's haunted, Mary?'

'Yes' says Mary 'it probably is.'

'Pooh' says Lizzy. 'Maybe there isn't any treasure. Maybe there are only dead bodies behind that wall.'

'Maybe so' says Mr da Costa.

Lizzy pulls a face.

'I do not like it, Lizzy' says Mary. 'It does not feel right.'

The captain pushes prods stick-taps the walls and the roof. Poke poke. Poke poke. Little white chalk pieces fall *plit-plit* down where he pushes. *Taptaptuptup. Craaa*-crack *kreee.* Dusty shell flower pieces cracking *craa*-thumping falling down.

'Do stop!' say I. 'Stop it!'

'Really, Fanny' says Lizzy. 'What is the matter with you?'

They are spoiling it, *spoiling* it. Mary stare-stares and Joshua shakes his head again. Lizzy shrugs, turns, goes out. *It smells horrid* her voice says.

'Come on, Fanny' says Mary. 'Come with me. It isn't nice here.'

It is. *Was.*

'Don't cry, Fanny dear' she says.

'They are breaking it! Don't let them break it.'

'Come on, Fan' says Joshua.

His hand hot on mine, pulls-tugs me to the door. 'Come on' he says whisper-quiet 'don't let them see you cry.'

Mustn't leave them mustn't let them. I promised.

Papa says to come out says Lizzy's voice.

Mary sighs turns goes back along the passage. The captain

looks at me. 'What are you making such a fuss about, child?' he says.

Shan't say, can't. He *knows*, anyway.

Joshua drops my hand, goes out along the passage. Mr da Costa wipes his hands on his trousers, picks up his lantern.

'Well' he says 'it's plastered in pretty tight but I'd say there's something there. We'll have to get something flat behind it, wrench it off that way.'

'Crowbar' says the captain. 'That should do it.'

'What about these plinths then?' says Mr da Costa. Boot kicks the shell post.

'Must have had something on them' says the captain.

'I wonder about these slates. Copies, eh?'

'Pretty useful' says the captain. 'At least we'll see how to put it back if we need to.'

'I should say. Suns and stars. Rather complex designs, all the same. That roof is coming down.'

'Might as well break the whole thing off and be done.'

'No!' say I. 'You can't!'

'Not today we can't, missy' says the captain, whisker-smiling. 'We'll have to take a pick to it, I dare say.'

Joshua comes quick-stepping back from the passage. 'Captain Easter' he says 'and Mr da Costa, sir, Papa is asking for you to come back up. I think you'd better come, sir.'

'Do you indeed?' says the captain.

'*Yes*, sir.'

Pick up their lanterns, eyebrow-arching boot-kicking stick-swinging, past me into the passage. Captain Easter's hand comes up, tap-taps under my chin. 'There now, missy' he says. 'No need to get so upset.'

Hateful horrid lying captain. He has seen it before. He knows all about it.

Follow them along the passage murmuring wall-knocking. They stop at the dome and look up the ladder.

Come out now, Captain says Papa's voice *it is beginning to rain.*

Look up too and there *is* rain, very thin very fine falling ever-so-softly through the hole. Joshua at the bottom of the ladder turns and nods. 'It's getting thicker' he says. 'We'd better go up quick.'

He goes boot swinging up climbing and Mr da Costa puts his hands on the rope and goes up too. The captain looks at me.

Rain faster heavier *plat-plat-plat-plat* through the hole on to the ladder plashing splishing on the floor.

Hurry up down there says Papa's voice. *It is getting worse.*

'Up you go then, missy' says the captain. 'I'd better go behind you. We don't want you to slip, do we?'

Horrid hateful captain. He puts his hands out takes mine puts them on the ladder. His face whiskery-smiling close to mine and his mouth at my ear. 'That's it' he says. 'One step at a time.'

Pull out my hands and go *one two three* up-stepping and the ladder wet swinging and the rain warm *plat* splashing on my cheeks. Not crying, *not.* The captain's boots shuffle scuffle. He tugs on the ladder.

I'm right behind you, Fanny Newlove his voice says. *Don't forget that.*

Back to the house

Cold hands muddy-boot-wiping and shawl-shaking. Mama in the kitchen, plates clattering trays rattling. *You should not feel compelled to do these things* her voice says. *It is not lady-like.*

Fanny went says Lizzy's voice. (Huffity-huff.)

Fanny is a little girl says Mama's voice. Clatter clatter. *And we are in company.*

I do not like it says Mary's voice. *I think we should cover it up again.*

Papa tap-knocks on the kitchen door. 'We are going up, Arabella' he says.

Very well, dear says Mama's voice.

They go mutter-muttering up the stairs, Mr da Costa and the captain and Papa. Joshua goes to the stairs too. Mama comes from the kitchen.

'Come here, Joshua' she says. 'Lizzy and Mary are fetching the supper trays and I want you two to get yourselves cleaned up. Your father and I will be in the parlour with our visitors.'

'Can we come to the parlour too?' says Joshua.

Mama goes skirt-swinging *one-two-three-up* stepping.

'May we, Mama?' say I.

'I will call you when it is time for supper' she says.

Mary and Lizzy come noisy bustle-busy from the kitchen.

'I shall look no better than a serving girl' says Lizzy.

'Mama does not mean it that way' says Mary.

'It is not how it is *meant*, Mary' says Lizzy spiteful spitting 'it is how it *looks*.'

They go hissing shushing along the passage and out. The door bangs and the parlour door thud-closes and Joshua looks at me.

Now.

Soft-stepping tippity-toeing mouse-quiet up *five-six-seven-eight*. Joshua scowl-frowning.

'I told you they would spoil it' say I whisper-quiet.

'*Shush!*' says Joshua.

Sixteen-seventeen-eighteen. The parlour door closed and Papa's voice low murmuring. Joshua puts his fingers on his lips and nods and we go not-creaking not-shuffling to the door and kneel down.

THE CAPTAIN'S VOICE: There's no doubt about it, Newlove. You must buy it outright, straight away.

MR DA COSTA'S VOICE: Quite so. Do not delay, sir.

PAPA'S VOICE: I do not think that possible, gentlemen. I cannot raise such an amount.

MAMA'S VOICE: We did *plan* to buy, dear, eventually.

PAPA'S VOICE: We do not have the capital, Arabella. Gentlemen, our funds are entirely involved in expanding the schools.

THE CAPTAIN'S VOICE: You cannot do otherwise, Newlove. This isn't just an investment in a piece of land, you know.

MR DA COSTA'S VOICE: Consider, sir. You would be gaining not only the land and the house, which you had already planned to purchase, but all that is buried beneath. This grotto, whatever it is, will be a source of income in itself. And then there is the publicity, sir, the notoriety.

PAPA'S VOICE: I do not seek notoriety, Mr da Costa. I run an educational establishment.

THE CAPTAIN'S VOICE: Damn it, Newlove! Your educational establishment won't be worth a flea if this gets out. Listen here. Buy the land and worry about the money afterwards. There's stuff worth having in there, mark my words.

Joshua nods, foot shuffles. *Don't breathe don't move. Skwee-ee* squeaking of chair springs and Mama's voice says *was that the girls coming back already?* Skirt-rustling boot-shifting *ahem-hemming* noises. Joshua looks at me. *SOR-RY* his lips say, not-speaking. Must be very *very* quiet.

THE CAPTAIN'S VOICE: Look here, I'll put up the funds. An investment. Find out what the brokers want, and I'll lend it to you.

MAMA'S VOICE: You are very kind, Captain, but we could not possibly –

PAPA'S VOICE: That is quite out of the question, Captain. We cannot allow ourselves to be indebted to anyone.

THE CAPTAIN'S VOICE: Devil take it, Newlove! This is bound to get out, you know. Then what, eh? Bowles left this place without settling for even *half* of it. His debtors want this land. Think what will happen when they know what's here! They'll have you out, Newlove, you and the damned girls' school. The end of your *educational establishment*, sir. The end of dear Mrs Newlove's livelihood.

MAMA'S VOICE, SOUNDING VERY UPSET: Oh my! Oh, think of it! The captain is right, my dear.

THE CAPTAIN'S VOICE: No more Bellevue School for Girls. No more home for the Misses Newlove. What then, eh? Back to London? Or the *North*, perhaps?

PAPA'S VOICE, DANGEROUSLY QUIET: Thank you, Captain. You have made yourself very clear. *(Ahems sighs.)* I will consider your proposal.

MR DA COSTA'S VOICE: Whatever your decision, Mr Newlove, the land must be bought.

MAMA'S VOICE: Oh my dear, yes.

THE CAPTAIN'S VOICE: I say let's start having a damned good look about. Then we'll know what we've got on our hands.

MR DA COSTA'S VOICE: What I propose is this. Let us begin looking behind those mosaic panels. There is a room, a square room, very like a chapel. Vaulted roof, arches, everything. There's an altar in there. My bet is that if there's anything to be had, we'll find it in that room, and most decidedly behind that altar.

PAPA'S VOICE: If it has an altar, gentlemen, it may well be some manner of church. If it is a holy place it must not be desecrated.

THE CAPTAIN'S VOICE: Holy place! Heathen shrine more like. Look Newlove, you're a sensible fellow so let's be serious about this. There are slates in there with copies of the mosaic patterns on. We can rip those panels off, see what's behind and get the damned things put back again, easy as you like.

No!

Joshua shakes his head, puts his hand on my mouth and soft *sssh!* shushes. *Must not say must not move must not speak*. Horrid horrid hateful captain.

MR DA COSTA'S VOICE: I know a fellow, a plasterer. Very

discreet sort. He's a fair craftsman himself, he could easily repair the panels, put the shells back up. Stephen Wales. *Prinny* Wales they call him.

THE CAPTAIN'S VOICE, HO-HOING: Good notion, Maurice.

PAPA'S VOICE: Gentlemen, please! Let us not be hasty. It is imprudent to speak of who may or may not repair any damage. I have not yet seen what we have here, and if there is any chance that it has been, at any time, a place of Christian worship –

THE CAPTAIN'S VOICE: Damn it, Newlove! What does it matter?

PAPA'S VOICE, VERY QUIET: With all respect, Captain, I wish to have a further, considered opinion. Our writing master Mr Davidson is a very serious gentleman, extremely well travelled and liberally educated. I would like him to see the site before we carry out any major excavations or alterations.

MR DA COSTA'S VOICE: Do you really think it wise to involve your staff, Mr Newlove?

PAPA'S VOICE: I believe I can trust the discretion of my assistants, sir.

THE CAPTAIN'S VOICE: I remember the man Davidson. Rather an excitable fellow. Seemed exactly the sort to start blathering about it. Couldn't keep the tongue still in his head, as I recall. What if he tells the boys? It would be all over the county in a matter of days.

MAMA'S VOICE: Oh, I am sure he would not tell the *boys*, Captain.

THE CAPTAIN'S VOICE: The fewer who know, the better, I'd say. Look here, at least keep a lid on it until you've got the deeds.

MAMA'S VOICE: Perhaps it would be better, dear, to wait until the boys have their midsummer vacation. That might be the best time to speak to Mr Davidson. The boys are very curious you know, Captain. They do pry and poke about so! They are almost certain to find it out. Midsummer is not so very far off, dear. Mr Davidson could be prevailed upon to look at the place then, could he not?

THE CAPTAIN'S VOICE, VERY LOW: My *dear* Mrs Newlove, a most *excellent* suggestion. When are the holidays, Newlove?

PAPA'S VOICE: From the end of June, Captain, and into July. There are three weeks in total without lessons.

MAMA'S VOICE: The weather will be *so* much better by then. You do not want to go poking about underground in the cold. You must think of your poor chest, dear.

THE CAPTAIN'S VOICE: Quite so, Mrs Newlove. Well, Midsummer it is, then, eh, Newlove?

Cree-eek door creaking downstairs and Lizzy's voice says *do hold it open, Mary* and they are back! Foot-scuffling tray-rattling door-banging. Mama's voice says *oh, here come the girls* and Papa's voice says *no more now, gentlemen, please, not in front of the children.*

COME ON Joshua's lips say.

Lizzy and Mary moving chattering along to the kitchen and back again. Lizzy's voice says *I don't see why we should have to* and Mary's says *it is only once, Lizzy dear*. Creaking boot tapping *one-two* up the stairs. Joshua tugs-pulls my arm and we go soft-stepping across to my room. Joshua quick not-creaking swings and soft-shuts the door.

'We should never have told!' say I. 'Never! They are taking over now and spoiling everything!'

'They always do' says Joshua. 'Anyway, we had to tell. At least now if there is any treasure, the captain will find it.'

'But there isn't!' say I. 'And they will spoil it looking. The

224

captain said he would break the roof and pull the walls down and *everything*.'

Joshua's lips tight shut and his mouth all down-turning.

'I'm sorry, Fan' he says. 'Papa knows best. He will look after it for us.'

Won't, though. Papa *did* know best before but he doesn't, not here, not any more. He does whatever the captain wants him to do now. Sometimes he doesn't even notice that he's doing it.

Telling them in the music room

May is very sad. She nods and says *that is all right* but her eyes really say *how could you, Fanny Newlove?* I didn't want to but we *had* to.

Beth smiles her not-smile with closed lips. 'Of course we shall do whatever you think best, Fanny' she says. 'We do not want to make trouble with your father.'

'Papa would know, you see' say I.

May nods again.

'And then he would never let any of us go in' say I. 'And he would give us extra sewing and everything. We'd never even be let out into the *garden*.'

'It's all right' says May. But it *isn't*.

'Promise you won't tell, still' say I 'even though Papa and Mama know. Because Anne and Mrs D the housekeeper, and Woods and Cook and everyone else, *they* don't know yet.'

'Promise' they say.

'And, May' say I whisper-quiet 'don't tell Frances, either.'

'All right.' She nods sighs. 'Does your pa know that the shell fairies made it?'

'No' say I. 'He thinks it is a church, or a temple. An old one.'

'That is very likely' says Beth.

She *never* believed. She is too grown-up to believe in anything except angels.

'When Papa has bought the land he will take the slab away again. Then we will be able to go in, just like everyone else.'

'Will Frances be able to?' says May. Her eyes are very wide.

'I don't know about that.'

'She *ought* to be able to' says May 'if it is open to the town, I mean.'

I ought to be able to go in NOW. Frances Morgan!

Frances Morgan at the door standing glaring staring at me and May and Beth. Her hands on her hips just like Cook when she is cross and her lips all pouting. She comes up and push-shoves May and *ow!* pulls my hair. *Tug tug tug.*

'If you [*tug*] don't take me this minute [*tug tug*] Fanny [*tug*] Newlove [*tug*] I shall *scream*.'

'I don't know what you are talking about, Slap-face' say I.

'Yes you do' she says. 'The shell fairies.'

'There is no such thing' says Beth Lucas. (Ha!)

Frances Morgan tug-tugs pinches pulls. 'Take me there right now' she says 'or I shall tell your [*pinch*] pa and [*pinch*] ma what a horrid little [*tug tug*] liar you are.'

'They would never believe *you*' say I (although they would).

'Take me there. Now.'

'No.'

Frances scratches and I pinch and she pinches and I push.

'Oh' says May 'oh, don't fight, please!'

Not fighting. Not. Frances Morgan will *never* see the shells.

'Take me right now or I shall bite you' she says.

'Bite then, Rat-face' say I.

She hair-pulls and I hair-pull and her head goes to my hand and *oww!* sharp burning snap-bites my fingers. Hateful hateful Frances Morgan. Slap her hard and her head tugs tears and *aarghh!* lets go.

She is very very red. 'That's it' she says stamping to the door. 'I'm telling.'

'Don't tell!' says May wailing sobbing. 'Don't tell or we shall all be in trouble.'

'That's not my fault' says hateful Morgan. 'If you are all punished it will only be *her* fault.' Points her horrid rat paw at me.

May looks at me white-faced big-eyed and Beth looks at the floor. Frances Morgan is right. Frances Morgan will tell because she is spiteful and horrid and bites like a rat, and we shall all be in terrible trouble with Papa.

'All right' say I. 'All right. You can go after dinner, when Mama lets us out.'

'No' says Frances. 'Now.'

'If you go now' say I 'you shall have to go in alone for Mama is expecting us soon and she will look for us. She will know *where* to look, too.'

'Just me and you then' says Frances. '*They* can go to lessons and you shall take me to see the shell fairies.'

'What about Mrs Newlove?' says May.

'Tell her Fanny is in the privy. Tell her she is not feeling well and I am waiting for her and will bring her back in, and not to worry.'

May nods. Beth sighs and goes out.

'Do be careful' says May. 'Don't get caught.'

'Go away' says Frances. She does, very sadly.

'Come on then' say I 'but we shall have to be very quick.'

Out and along the corridor and into the kitchen for the

tinderbox and candles. Frances Morgan's hateful rat mouth says *hurry up* and I find a candle and put it into my pocket. We go out through the garden door and quick puddle-step over to the tunnel. It has been raining *again* and it will be all wet and damp-smelling and puddles inside. *Good.* The slab wet shiny over the dome hole and the earth all muddy where we were standing looking climbing in and out. The rope-ladder is gone. Papa rolled it up and put it in the shed so we might not use it without him.

'You will have to go into the tunnel' say I.

Move the chalk blocks and there is the tunnel hole dark and smelly. No sacks no lanterns. Only one candle. Light it, hold it out to ratty Frances. Point at the hole. 'You have to crawl in there' say I.

'What about you?'

'I'll be behind you. Here, you hold the candle or you won't see to go in.'

She does.

Frances rat-tooth Morgan grins bends over and goes into the tunnel. She shuffle-scuffles along with the candle in one hand. *It is very dark* her voice says. *Where are the shells?*

'Keep going' say I 'they are only a little way along.'

White pinafore brown boots moving disappearing. Good. Pick up the chalk blocks and ever-so-quietly pile them on. The candle light almost gone and then one block and another and it is all closed up with hateful Frances slap-face rat-toothed hair-tear Morgan in it.

Ha!

Look at the house and there is no Mama at the window. No Anne either for she is with Mrs D. Sit down next to the dome slab and listen.

Scraa-scraa-scratching scrabbling of Frances in the tunnel entrance. *Where are you?* her voice says. *Come here this minute!*

Why? She bites and scratches and is even more horrible to May than Lizzy is to me. Papa says to turn the other cheek but Frances does not know how to do that. I shall show her.

Put my mouth very close to the slab.

'Ooooooooooooo!' say I, even more scary ghost-sounding than Joshua. 'Ooooooooooooo!'

Oh! says Frances's voice. *Fanny? What is that?*

'Ooooooooooooo!' say I. 'Fraaaances Moooorgan, yooooou are a wiiiiicked girrrrl. Ooooooooooooo!'

Stop it this minute says her voice. *Let me out!*

'Yooooou are a seeeeelfish naaaaaughty girrrrl, ooooooooooooo! Yooooou do not deserrrrrve to seeeeee the skyyyyyy everrrrr agaaaaain, ooooooooooooo!'

Let me out! Fanny! I know it's you. Let me out!

'Yooooou bite and scraaaaatch liiiiike a raaaaat, Fraaaaances Moooorgan, ooooooooooooo! Yooooou shall staaaaay uuu-uunder the grooooound for foooorty daaaaays and foooorty niiiiights. Ooooooooooooo!'

Let me out her voice says. It is not cross now. It is *scared*.

'Yooooou shall be eaten by the woooooorms, ooooooooooooo! If the ghoooooost doesn't get yooooou fiiiiirst. Ooooooooooooo!'

No! Please let me out, please! Please!

Get up and stamp stamp my feet like I am walking away. Frances scuffles sobs wails.

I won't tell! her voice says. *I won't! I promise. Come back, Fanny!*

'If you tell' say I 'I shall drop you down the hole and you will stay there for ever. As *my* prisoner.'

I won't tell!

'Swear.'

I swear. Please, Fanny. Your ma will come and look for us, you said so.

'Swear you will never pull my hair again.'

I swear.

'And that you will never be horrid to me or May or Beth again.'

Frances shuffles. Sniffs. Sob-sobs. *Let me out* her voice says. *It is so dark.*

'Swear' say I.

I swear. Please.

Go to the tunnel and move the chalk blocks one two three four and leave the rest. Frances sobbing shuffling back along the tunnel. Her candle in front coming closer and closer *scraa-*scraping flicker flickering. Put my mouth to the hole and *fwoo!* blow.

The candle goes flicker flicker flicker and out. Ha!

Oh! her voice says. *Oh!*

'Keep going, Frances' say I. 'I'll see you in class.'

Get up and walk towards George's pea sticks. *Don't go!* her voice says wailing. *Don't go, Fanny! Don't leave me!*

'Goodbye, Frances' say I turning shouting. 'And don't forget to cover up the hole behind you, *or else*. Oooooooooooooo!'

Dearest James,

No more lessons for me!

As you may guess today is the very last day of school. We have just had our last school dinner time for *three weeks*. Three weeks seems like such a *very* long time, until I remember that I have not written to you since Easter. I do hope that you are not angry with me for this, dear brother. It is not because I am lazy, but because something wonderful has happened and I have not been able to think about anything else (except when I am in lessons or at chapel, of course.)

It is a very great secret, but Mama and Papa have said that I may tell you about it. I did not write before because I would have wanted to tell and was not sure if I may. You must promise not to tell a soul, though.

We have found a shell palace under Mama's garden!

I shall tell you how. Joshua and I and the gardener's son George were digging a duckpond in Mama's garden when it happened. We had made a pit and Joshua was digging when there was a big rumbling noise. A hole came and all the earth began to fall in. Joshua lost his shovel down the hole and George ran to tell Papa. Papa came and said it was probably an old well, but there was no water in it, so he sent Joshua down on a rope to fetch the shovel. (It was quite safe for Papa was there.) Joshua came back with the shovel and said that there was a palace under the ground covered in shells. The next day Papa let us go down to see inside. It is so lovely! There are shells all over the walls and the ceiling. The shells are pretty colours and make such clever flower patterns. You cannot imagine how lovely it is! You must come and see it very soon.

Papa covered the hole up with a big stone, but now that we are having our Midsummer vacation he will open it up again. Our neighbour Captain Easter and his friend say that the shell place is a treasure house but I do not think that it is, for there is nothing inside except for the shells. Papa is going to let them look for buried treasure but they will not find any. He has told Mr Davidson the writing master about the shells too. Mr Davidson is a very clever man, Papa says, and he might know about shell palaces and what they are for. Mr Davidson has been to many foreign places, even to India, which is very far away. Papa is going to buy the school and the land so that it will be our shell palace, but he has not told anyone about it yet, so you must swear not to tell.

So you can see why, dear brother, I have been so very excited and cannot think of anything else to tell you about. We will be allowed to look at the shells again after the boy boarders have gone home, which is this afternoon. I do not think we shall be allowed to go in until tomorrow, though. Lizzy and Mary have been inside but they did not like it. Mama said that it was not lady-like to go down a rope-ladder, so she has not seen the shells yet. Papa cannot get in for the hole is quite small, but Joshua has found another way in. It is a tunnel that goes into the shell palace but it is very small. Papa has asked the gardener Mr Stroud to dig it out and make it wider. Then Papa will be able to go inside and see the shells too.

I must go now for Mama said we are to walk into town this afternoon. The weather is very fine and the roads are dry so we shall have a pleasant walk to the harbour. It is pretty by the sea when it is not cold. Lizzy and Mary asked if they may go sea-bathing during the holidays, but I do not think Papa will allow them, even though it says in the Gazette that sea-bathing is a healthful cure for all ailments. There are a great many people in Margate now because it is the visiting season and there are crowded steamboats every day like the one that brought us here. They come from London and bring ladies and gentlemen to see the shops and take the sea air.

Mr Mills the dancing and music master has said he will teach me to play the piano.

I hope that I have not written too many foolish things in this letter and that if I have you will smile and not be cross about the silliness of

your affectionate sister Frances.

Mr Mills says that I am not concentrating

And he is right.

Plink-plink-plink. La-la-la.

'You *know* this now, Frances' he says. 'Try again.'

Eight notes and the first and the last are the same but different. *La-la-la-la-la.*

The captain is in the shell palace. He has tools and sacks and Mr da Costa is with him. Lizzy passed Mr da Costa a note in the hall. They thought no one could see them.

'*Listen* to the notes, don't just tap at them.'

Mr Davidson said that the underground shell place is demonic. D-E-M-O-N-I-C. That is, to be devilish. *Our* shell palace is not devilish though. When Mr Davidson saw it he waved his arms around and then started crying. He says that it is an ancient temple, and that the shell flowers are *not* flowers but secret code, secret shell writing.

Joshua laughed at Mr Davidson later and said he *cried like a girl*. He looked happy and sad at the same time. I had never seen a man cry before but that is not how *I* cry and *I* am a girl.

'Frances, please! This is an instrument of music, not torture.'

Mr Mills's eyelashes are white and so are his cheeks. They are pinched and cross.

'I am sorry, sir' say I.

'You have not practised, have you?'

'No, sir.'

Mr Mills sighs, soft-touches the keys. 'Move along, Frances' he says, 'and *listen.*'

I do. Mr Mills plays and his hands go quick-stretching finger-rippling over the white and black and white and black. 1-2-3-4-3-2-1. 2-3-4-5-4-3-2. 3-4-5-6-5-4-3. It is beautiful. I shall never be able to do that.

The captain asked Mr Davidson what treasure there should be in an ancient shell temple. He said that if the shell palace is what he believes it to be, it is *w-worth more than any t-treasure.*

'Listen to the scale, Frances' says Mr Mills.

La-la-la-la-la-la-la-la. La-la. The captain pulled at the panels and Mr Davidson told him to stop. Ha! Mr Davidson said that if there is any treasure behind the shells it *w-will require c-careful unearthing.*

'Do you hear, Frances?'

'Yes, Mr Mills.'

1-2-3-4-5-6-7-8. 1-8. It sounds easy when *he* does it. Mr Davidson says that the shell palace is a very special shape, and that he has seen the same shape in a book somewhere. He said he would look for the book again. He also said that next time he goes in he will make sketches of the shell panels. It would be better if Mary or Mr Toogould did that though because they both draw very nicely.

Mary does not like the shells. She says that they do not

feel safe. They *are* safe for we played in them, but I cannot say so. Mustn't. Mary asked Papa why he is buying a heathen shell temple and Papa said *Matthew thirteen verse forty-four*.

'You try again now' says Mr Mills.

1-2 3 4-5-6 7 8. La-la. La-la. 8-1 1-8.

'Much better' he says. He smiles and his eyelashes all lovely and frosty-white go flutter-flutter. 'Now try to get the rhythm. All the notes should be even.'

1-2-3-4 5 6 7-8. *The kingdom of heaven is like unto treasure hid in a field, the which when a man hath found, he hideth* 8-7-6-5-4 3-2-1 *and for joy thereof goeth and selleth all that he hath, and buyeth that field.* Heavenly shells.

'All right, Frances' says Mr Mills. He soft-sighs. 'We shall have a little break now.'

He gets up, stretches and goes to the door. *Cannot* let him go into the garden, *must not*. Mama said he must not see.

'Mr Mills' say I 'would you like some tea in the parlour?'

'Oh no, Frances, thank you. I should just like to get some air.'

'Go into the front garden then' say I 'for there are men working in the back. They are digging. A pond. For the ducks.'

'That's all right.'

'No, no it isn't. It is very messy and muddy and Papa said we should not go out there.'

Mr Mills's eyelashes flutter and his eyebrows make big arches. 'Muddy, in July?'

'Oh yes' say I 'because of filling the pond with water.'

He nods.

'Very well, Frances. I will just take a little air on the doorstep.'

He goes and his shoes *pat-apat-apat* and the door creaks squeaks open. Good.

Get up and soft-thud close the piano lid all shiny and polish-smelling. Out into the corridor and Mr Mills with his back to me up-down-up-downing on his heels in the doorway. Go soft-stepping along and round and to the back door and quick not-creaking open it.

Hot bright sunny and green Summery-smelling. George's peas fat and pale and the beans too, pink and red-flowery. Mama's potato plants tall and the carrot tops furry and my lavender pots full and not woody now, straight and blue and *zuzzzzzzzzz*ing with bees. Mary said we could make lavender bags. I will cut and she will sew them for me. *Not* sewing, not in the holidays.

Papa at the dome hole, hands on trouser knees, bending looking in.

'Hello, Papa' say I.

'Have you finished your lesson, Fanny?' he says, not-looking. 'Has Mr Mills gone?'

'No, Papa, he is in the front garden.'

'Go back inside then!' He stands looks points at the house. 'As we agreed, Fanny.'

'Yes, Papa. Sorry, Papa.'

George and Joshua at the tunnel hole, piling up chalk pieces. George's papa must be in there, digging. George sees me, waves. I wave back.

'I shall come out soon' say I. He does not hear though.

Back into the house and into the kitchen for the cordial and cups. No Anne for two weeks, so it is safe for the shells. Cordial in the cold cupboard but no ice, not like at Mr da Costa's. Mr da Costa has an ice-house, which is very grand, but he cannot need so much ice unless it is to have in his *whisky*. Mama and Lizzy and Mary gone too, at the harbour and the market, shop shop shop, Lizzy in her white muslin that is *very* thin and her

238

white straw bonnet. It is not *so* hot. She did not want to go until Mr da Costa came and then there was the note in the hall and they both smiled. *Secrets*. Then Lizzy and Mary and Mama went out and Mr Mills came in.

Two cups and a tray and the cordial bottle. Mary said not to pour it in the kitchen but take it on the tray. *It is more genteel* she said. G-E-N-T-E-E-L. That is from the French for 'nice'. Carry it ever-so-carefully into the music room and there is Mr Mills, *pflink-pflink* standing soft pat-patting the white piano keys. He looks sad.

'I have brought some cordial, Mr Mills' say I.

'Good girl, Frances' he says. 'I am excessively fond of cordial. Please tell me that it is raspberry.'

Oh. Not red but pale cloudy and sharp-smelling.

'I am afraid it is probably lemon, sir' say I.

Mr Mills smiles. 'That is even better.'

He pat-pats the stool and I put the tray down ever-so-gently-and-genteelly on the little side table.

'I shall pour it, Frances' he says. 'Sit down and practise that scale again.'

I do. 1 2 3-4 5 6-7 8. 1-2-3-4 5-6-7 8. The captain is down there and so is Mr da Costa and there is no Mr Davidson, not today. Papa at the top Joshua and George at the tunnel me at the piano. 8 7-6 5 4-3-2 1. 8-1 1-8. No one with the shells, no one to stop them breaking and pulling. Mr Davidson said not to, but when he had gone they did it anyway. Pull tug break. The captain said there must be treasure-hunting to help pay for the land, but *he* is not buying it. Papa was very quiet. 8-1-8-1. Papa said yes though, even so.

'What is wrong, Frances?' says Mr Mills. He holds the cordial cups and smiles, but ever-so-sadly. 'I thought you wanted to learn.'

'I *do*, Mr Mills' say I. 'I do, really.' *True.*

'Yet you do not listen and do not practise.' (Huff-sighs.) 'I suppose you would rather be outside, wouldn't you? Playing in the garden.'

Yes.

'Drink this' he says. Gives me the cordial. 'I suppose we would all rather be outside on such a day.'

Take the cordial and it is lemony cold and sip, sweet and sharp. Mr Mills sits too with his cup and *pat-a-plink-pflink* touches the keys with one hand.

'Run along and play, Frances' he says. 'I think we have done enough for today.'

Into the garden, at last

Papa's voice says *do be careful, gentlemen* into the hole.

They are still in there, then.

George with a wheelbarrow comes *fhuw-fheeeeeew* whistling and stops by the shed, tips up the barrow. Chalk pieces and shells rumble-tumbling out on the grass.

'Want to help me?' he says.

'All right.'

Mr Mills has gone but he will be back tomorrow. 1-2-3-4-5-6-7-8. George grinning sits next to the chalk pile and starts sorting.

'Chalk on this pile shells on that' he says. 'Broken shells into the bucket.'

'Are they all busy?' say I.

George nods.

'Lizzy gave a note to Mr da Costa in the hall' say I. 'We didn't see that one.'

George sighs, pushes at the chalk pile. 'I've got one from im to Miss Lizzy. I was going to show you.'

Another one. 'Come on then.'

George looks around. Joshua going into the tunnel, Papa peering down the hole. George puts his hand into his shirt, pulls out the note. 'I read *some*' he says. 'I could make out enough. It looks bad.'

Take the note and there Mr da Costa's writing, not neat like before but quick messy and leaning over, like when Mama gives us dictation. Read it to George, whisper-quiet.

'"Dearest girl. [*Always that.*] Was longing to hear from you and then your note at last." When did he give you this, George?'

'This afternoon. Said I was to give it to Miss Lizzy when she got back from town, said he was going off before then.'

Oh.

'"So delicious in that white dress, little temptress."'

T-E-M-P-T-R-E-S-S. Don't know that one.

'What is temptress, George?' say I.

'A doxy, a mawk. A bad woman' says George.

Oh. That *is* Lizzy.

'"Now an excellent time. Let me know when best for you. Thank God the maid is out of the way. [*That is Anne!*] Night is best but you will need to handle the sister. [*Me or Mary?*] You are right, grotto is perfect place."'

'Ho!' says George. He *haw-haw* laughs.

'What does he mean? Perfect for what?'

'Secrets' says George sly-grinning. 'Secret meetings. Like us before, with the reading.'

That was different. George nods slowly slyly.

'He doesn't mean that sort of meeting though, does he, George?'

'No'm.'

'He wants Lizzy to meet him in the shells. At night.'

'Yes'm.'

'For – *courting*.'

'That's it.' George sighs, points at the letter. 'There's more. Even I could make it out.'

' "Longing for more of you, devilish girl. Yours in rapture M." '

Rapture. That is new. Look at George, smiling nodding.

'George' say I, 'could you really read that bit?'

'Yes'm' he says 'I knew "devilish" from the tract you gave me. I didn't know "rapture" though.'

'That's very good' say I. 'You could go to classes now.'

George picks up a chalk piece, throws and catches right-left-right-left.

'Frances' he says 'I think we should stop it now.'

'Stop what?'

'Reading the notes. It's gone *on*, so.'

'What do you mean?'

He swallows, drops the chalk lump. His hands white-powdery, rubs them on his knees.

'I mean, they are sparking now, courting hard. I don't think we should read about what they get up to.'

'I'm not going to let them use the shell place' say I 'not for that.'

'Well then' says George 'you shall have to stop them, Lor knows how.'

They shan't use it, *shan't*. It is not *their* secret meeting-place.

'I can't tell about us reading the *notes*' say I 'but I *could* tell Papa about you *learning* to read.'

George stare-stares and his mouth opens like a fish.

'Don't worry' say I. 'Papa will understand.'

'He won't like it' says George big-eyed scared. 'He'll lace me good and well.'

'He won't if I say I was helping you to read and write so that you could have lessons at the school.'

George shakes his head. 'I don't want em.'

'You could read and write properly' say I. 'You are very good. I won't be able to teach you much more. You need proper classes now.'

He shrugs. It is *true*, though. He could tell "devilish", which is really quite hard.

'I don't want to go to school' says George 'and anyhow, my pa can't pay for it.'

'Papa won't care for that' say I. 'The boys at Sunday school don't pay. The important thing is that Lizzy will know that you can read, and she won't send notes by you any more. Then we won't have to read them. That's what you want, isn't it?'

'I don't know.'

'*And* she won't be able to write to Mr da Costa, so they won't be able to meet in the shells in secret.'

'They can still give each other notes' says George 'like today.'

'Not really' say I. 'Not as *easily*.'

'Miss Lizzy will skin me alive when she knows' says George. 'She wrote some rare things in her notes.'

'She won't dare to' say I. 'It will only make her look *more* guilty.'

'I don't know.'

George pokes and prods at the chalk pile, pulls out a piece of blue shell, puts it aside.

'Mussels' say I.

'My pa knows how to get them at the bay' says George. 'And cockles.'

'Did you know?' say I. 'Mr Davidson found the book he

had said about, the one with the picture in it. He says that there is a place in Wiltshire that is the same shape as the shell palace.'

'Wiltshire. Is that *in* the Sheers?'

'Of *course*' say I. *Silly*. 'You shall get geography lessons too, you know.'

'What does the book say?' says George. 'Have you read it?'

'No, Mr Davidson has it, but he brought it to show Papa. He told Papa that the tunnels and the dome in our shell palace are the same shape as this place in Wiltshire. But it is all silly really, because the other place isn't underground or made of shells, it's huge and there's a village in the middle of it and it's made of old stones. So it's nothing like it at all.'

'I thought Mr Davidson was supposed to be clever' says George.

Me too. Papa didn't say *milksop moonshine* when he saw the picture, but his eyes did.

'Anyway' say I 'the silliest thing is that this book is all about snakes. It's called *Serpent Worship*. It's written by a Reverend Somebody, but it's idolatry.'

'What's that?'

'I-D-O-L-A-T-R-Y. Praying to snakes.'

'Lor!' says George. He *haw-haw-haws*. 'What does your pa say?'

'He thinks Mr Davidson is very clever but he doesn't like the thing about snake worship.'

'I should say.' George smiles. 'Some of the shell patterns *are* wiggly, though. Some of them look a bit like snakes.'

Don't. They are just wiggly. *That* doesn't make them snakes.

'They are vines, George Stroud' say I 'like your peas and

beans and like grapes and ivy. *Plants.*' He is a gardener, he should know that. 'Besides I don't believe that the fairies *or* people that made such lovely shell patterns would ever be silly enough to pray to snakes.'

George lays chalk pieces on the grass in a wiggly line, makes a snaky tongue for it with his fingers. 'Are you going to tell?' he says.

'Shall I?'

'All right.' He huff-sighs. 'I'm sorry for it, though. *You* shan't be able to teach me my letters and *I* shan't get any more shillings for them notes.'

'I will still be able to help, sometimes' say I.

Won't though. Papa will not let me, when he knows.

George shrugs. 'Even so.'

He pokes at the pile, picks out a broken shell flower. Holds it up, all chalk-dusty and sad-looking.

'It's a real shame about the shillings' he says.

Telling Mama and Papa

Papa's spoon *tap-scree-ee* scrapes the dish. Gooseberry fool. Mrs D made it especially for Mama and Papa. She says it is only for grown-ups really, so I have apple pie from yesterday. Cold buttery yellow and appley. Papa's gooseberry fool sharp sweet with little hard berry bits in. Papa likes gooseberry fool *very much*, which means it is a good time to say.

Mama says *pass the sugar, Fanny dear* and I do. Little silver dish we do not use when the boys are here. Mama likes family suppers. It is a good time to say to her, too.

'Mama' say I shiny silvery sugary dish passing 'how old was I when I learned to read?'

'That is an odd question, Frances' says Papa. 'I hope you are not becoming proud.'

'Oh no, Papa' say I. 'I just wanted to know.'

'You were a very good pupil' says Mama. 'You could tell your letters when you were less than five years of age.'

She smiles her nice-Mama smile and spoons the sugar. *Good*.

'You read to me from your Christmas book' says Mary.

Smile-smiles sweetly. 'That was the Christmas after your fifth birthday. Do you remember that, Lizzy dear?'

'No' says Lizzy with pie in her mouth.

'When we came here, Mama' say I 'George Stroud the gardener's son could not read. He is twelve.'

'Frances!' says Papa hushing whisper-quiet. 'There is no shame in that. Not all children have been blessed with the same opportunities as yourself.' He sighs, puts down his spoon. *Bad.* 'Mr Stroud has brought his son up to be conscientious and God-fearing. George has had an unfortunate history and has not enjoyed the love of a mother and support of brothers and sisters, as you have. I am disappointed to hear you speak so.'

'I am sorry, Papa' say I.

'I should think so too' says Lizzy.

(She does not know yet but I shall tell her.)

'But, Papa' say I 'it is just that, I wondered if you might not give George Stroud a place in the school, so that he might learn like other boys. He *is* twelve, Papa.'

'Pooh' says Lizzy. Spiteful Lizzy stab-stabbing her pie piece. 'What good would schooling be to a gardener's son, Papa? Really, Fanny' she says not-very-nicely *at all* 'you spend far too much time in that boy's company. She follows him about like a dog, Papa. I have often remarked it.'

'You have not remarked upon it to me, Lizzy dear' says Mama. 'I would have noted such a thing.'

Lizzy *tappity-taps* at her plate. 'Papa' she says 'I do not think Fanny should hang upon that boy so. It is not natural.'

'I do not hang, Papa' say I.

'You do' says Lizzy. 'You are always together.'

Are not.

'George is all right' says Joshua. 'He helps ever so much with the shells and things.'

'There is no harm in the boy' says Papa *not* quietly 'but I would prefer it if you passed your time with your fellow pupils, Frances. The girl Beth Lucas is a good example for you.' Picks up his spoon again. *Good.*

'I believe, dear' says Mama 'that Fanny has reconciled her differences with the older Morgan girl.'

'I am glad to hear it' says Papa. 'There should have been nothing to reconcile at all.'

Don't want to talk about Frances rat-face-slap-face Morgan. Want to tell about *George.*

'Papa' say I 'George would be a very good student. He is quite clever really.'

'I am sure he is a very able fellow' says Papa 'but if he cannot read and write, I cannot admit him to my lessons. No, Fanny, he must go into some simple class. Perhaps the charity school would take him, or if his father were not against it he might come to my Sunday school.'

'He is not chapel, Papa' says Lizzy.

'Not all of my Sunday school children are, Lizzy' says Papa. 'I welcome all of God's children.'

'Yes, Papa' says Lizzy. Fork and yellow appleness go up to her lips. Only nasty spiteful things come out of there. Why does Mr da Costa want to kiss *those?*

'Papa' say I 'George *does* know his letters now, quite well. He can write the days of the week and the months of the year, and he can write his name too, and my name, and many other words. Yesterday he read and wrote out most of Our Father and only got "hallowed" and "trespasses" wrong.'

Lizzy's fork *taa-ting* clatter crashes to her plate. *Don't* look at her. *Mustn't.*

Joshua stare-stares and then grins. Mary *aha-ha-harrem* hems. She is trying very hard not to get her pie stuck.

'Well, Fanny' says Papa not quiet not crossly 'what are you telling us?'

'I have been teaching him, Papa' say I. 'I have been telling him his letters.'

'Oh, Fanny!' says Mary.

'I hope I did not do wrong, Papa?' say I ever-so-sweetly. 'George said that he wanted to learn, he asked me.'

Look at Lizzy. Lizzy looks very hard very angry at me. Her mouth is small and horrid.

'Did he?' says Mama. 'That is singular.'

'Oh yes, Mama' say I. Look at my plate and the pie crumbs. 'George said that he wanted to learn to read because he did not want anyone to call him a silly *donkey*.'

Ha!

'Oh *really*!' says Mama *almost* laughing. 'I am sure no one would be so uncharitable as *that*.'

Papa puts his spoon in the gooseberry dish again. *Scra*-scrape. 'That is kind-hearted of you, my girl' he says. Spoons. *Smiles!* 'It demonstrates true Christian behaviour, Fanny. I am proud of you.'

Papa!

Joshua grin-grins and his mouth goes SLY LIT-TLE THING but he doesn't say it.

'I hope, Fanny dear' says Mama 'that you have not forgone your other duties in order to teach the boy? Your needlework in particular is very sadly lacking.'

'Oh no, Mama' say I. 'I have only ever taught George when I have been allowed out to play.'

Papa nods but Mama does not. Lizzy's fork flick-flicks silver shiny and empty in her hand. *Don't look.*

'Please would you give George a place, Papa?' say I. 'I promise that I will do more needlework.'

'I do not like to be bargained with, Fanny' says Papa. He is not cross though. He looks at Mama. 'It is gratifying – is it not, Arabella? – to see Fanny take such an active interest in those less fortunate than herself.'

'Indeed' says Mama 'but I do not think it appropriate that she should teach the boy. He is a good deal *older* than her, my dear.'

'Only four years, Mama' say I.

Mama *oh dear*s sighs.

'There is that, of course, Arabella' says Papa. 'Fanny, I will speak to George and to his father. If the boy is as good at his letters as you say, we might come to some arrangement.'

'Thank you, Papa!' say I.

'You are not to teach him any more yourself though' says Papa. '*I* will see to it. Is that understood?'

'Yes, Papa.'

'Very well. Have you finished with your meal, children?'

'Yes, Papa' say I. Joshua looks big-eyed at the pie but doesn't say anything.

'You may get down' says Mama 'and Mary and Lizzy too, if you wish.'

We do. Mary waits folds her hands and looks at me. Lizzy goes out quickity-quick and so does Joshua. Papa puts his hand out to me and I go to his chair.

His hand comes up and he puts it big heavy on my head. 'Bless you, little Frances' he says. 'Run along now. I will speak to George, have no fear.'

I do.

I have *told*.

Papa very nice Mama not cross and Lizzy very very angry. Mary turns goes out along the hall, opens the door, head shaking, disappears. Joshua goes running *thud-thud* stepping up the stairs. Where is Lizzy?

Go to the door and out and she is *there*. Pulls bang-shuts the door and stands there all red-faced hard-eyed claw-handed.

'You conniving little minx!' she says hiss-spitting. 'You wretched, hateful little brat!'

Must not smile must not. Must not show that I know why.

'What is the matter, Lizzy?' say I ever-so-nicely.

'Why do you *always* have to interfere?'

'With what, Lizzy?'

'You know very well what with. Teaching that boy.'

'But, Lizzy' say I in my best surprised voice 'why do you mind about George? You never speak to George, do you?'

Lizzy's face all red and screwed-up. Her hand comes up-clawing to my face but she does not hit me, dares not.

(I read your letters and Mr da Costa's too, and so did George. Ha ha ha.)

'What is the matter, Lizzy?' say I. 'Why are you so upset?'

'I'll teach you' she says. 'I'll teach you, you little menace.'

She goes off stamping *huff-huffing* up the path to the gate, creaks thud-shuts it behind her. She will tell Mary that I am a minx and Mary will want to say *I did warn you not to, Lizzy* but she won't dare to. Lizzy didn't dare to hit me and Mama was only cross about my needlework and Papa *blessed* me. George is going to learn at school like a proper pupil and I won't be able to teach him any more.

Lizzy cannot hurt me. Lizzy cannot teach me anything, either. *Spiteful hate-spitter.*

Mama does not know everything

Sticky hot and sick feeling. Mama puff-fans and looks at us.

'Whatever shall we do with ourselves?' she says.

A not-question.

'You do look sorry for yourself, Fanny' says Mama. 'Why don't you go outside and play?'

Shan't play. Head hurting and heavy inside and sick.

Lizzy came sneaking creaking up the stairs and I saw her. I saw her and *I knew*. I saw her and she saw me and smiled her horrid smile. Her hair was down and her nightgown chalky-dusty and she was pleased and scared and shaking shivering at the same time. *It is not your secret place* said I and she said *it shan't be yours either*. She is nastier than ever since the letters stopped. *They are my shells* said I *you can't stop me* and she laughed and said *you can't stop me either, Fanny Newlove, and nor can anyone else*. And then Mary came out and saw us and started crying.

'Really' says Mama crossly 'whatever is the matter with you all?'

Hot hot hot and sticky. Opened the windows but they only

make it worse. Lizzy and Mary sitting pretend-sewing. Mary's eyes red-sad and Lizzy's not seeing not looking like she is staring out to sea. Mama sighs, stands up, sits down again.

'We need a little walk' she says. 'It will cool us, perhaps.'

'It would be cooler by the harbour' says Lizzy.

She has not said anything for ages. Mama looks at her and smiles. 'That is an excellent idea, Lizzy. Your father suggested that we might go to the sands and gather some shells for repairs. That would be a fine thing to do today, would it not? We could ask your father and Joshua if they would like to accompany us. What do you say, girls?'

Mary nods but she does not say anything.

Lizzy sits stiff sewing needle flicking not looking up.

'It is too hot to dig today' Lizzy says. 'I am sure they would rather go to the sea.'

'Very well then' says Mama standing fanning 'that is what we shall do. Change into your walking clothes, girls. I shall see you in your father's parlour in a quarter of an hour.'

Don't want to. Shan't go walking chattering shell-gathering. Pretending. Papa will know and even if he doesn't Joshua will guess and he will ask and Mary will start crying again.

Lizzy and Mary put down their sewing and stand smooth-smoothing at their skirts. Mama goes to the door and looks at me.

'Whatever is the matter, Fanny?' she says. 'You are not ill, are you, child?'

'Yes, Mama' say I.

'It is the heat' says Mama. 'The air will soon make you better.'

'Please, Mama' say I 'may I be excused? I feel sick.'

'Sick?' Mama's eyes go small-cross and her eyebrows try to join together. 'What do you mean, sick?'

'It is the heat' says Lizzy. 'She is just making a fuss.'

'Mama' says Mary very quiet 'perhaps she should stay behind. The sun might be too much for her.'

'I imagine she has had too much sun already' says Lizzy sharp nasty. 'She spends far too much time in the garden.'

'That is true' says Mama.

She looks at me, fan-fanning and frowning. She is not cross, though, not really. She is just hot.

'All right, Fanny' she says. 'You may stay behind, so long as you do not go outside or wander off.'

'Thank you, Mama' say I.

'Shall I ask the housekeeper to sit with you?'

No.

'I should just like to lie down in my room' say I.

'Perhaps she needs some sleep' says Mary. She looks red-eyed at Lizzy. 'We are all rather tired today.'

'I am perfectly all right thank you' says Lizzy *very* quickly.

Mama nods sighs says *very well* and goes out. Mary and Lizzy go too.

Lizzy turns in the doorway and stare-stares at me. 'Sick indeed' she says. 'I only hope that you *are.*'

She bang-shuts the door.

Hateful spiteful Lizzy. She is a doxy like George said. A bad woman. I wonder that *she* does not feel sick too.

Sit on the cushions and puff-puff-puff with the straw fan that Mary made. Wait. They are dressing not chattering not talking like usual. Mary is very sad and Lizzy is very proud and Mama does not know. She does not know everything.

Wait and wait. They will go soon.

Papa spoke to George's papa and George shall have lessons now. He does not have to pay, as long as he helps with the shells and chops wood for the stove. George does not really want lessons but he should, for he has already paid for it, really. Hateful Lizzy boxed his ears. George said that Lizzy said she *knew what we had been up to*, but George pretended not to know what she meant. She does know, though. Her eyes say so, all the time.

Never should have told Papa about the shells. Never should have made the silly silly duckpond.

No more shells no more George. I am not to play with him not to teach him. Lizzy will watch and so will Mama and Papa now. Joshua said *why did you teach him to read?* and I said *because I could*. Joshua does not know everything, either.

The door soft-opens and there is Mary's face, white-cheeked and sad red-eyed.

'Are you all right, Fanny?' she says.

No.

Mary sighs sniffs puts her fingers to her nose. She has been crying again.

'Try not to be too upset, little lamb' she says. Her voice is all thick and wet.

Come on for goodness' sake says Lizzy's voice.

Mary smiles a very thin not-smile. 'Sit quietly and rest' she says.

She goes, soft-closes the door. Their feet go soft-shuffling down the stairs and out and the door thud-closes behind them. Not chattering, not giggling. Not talking at all.

Gone.

Mary's workbasket not tidy not put away under her seat. Little blue and white squares and blue ribbon and silk. Mary is making bags for my lavender but she cannot sew today. Her stitches all long and messy and thread pulling, just like mine. Not *just* because it is hot, either. It was hot yesterday too.

Get up, go to the window and they are gone now, along the road to Papa's and then out to the sands. It is so hot that Mama will want to walk slowly. They will be gone a long time, long enough.

Down the stairs along the hall hot hot and the walls and the floor and everything sticky with it. Open the door and outside even hotter even stickier and wet, thick sweet flowery-smelling. Sun big and blurry like it is looking through water. No clouds. Not even blue really, just heavy heavy sky trying to touch the earth, trying to push everything into the ground. Pushing me too. *Zuzzzzzzzzzz* of flies and bees and nothing else moving, not even the grass.

No chalk blocks in front of the tunnel any more, just an old sack that George said is to stop dogs or foxes getting in. Mr Stroud said he could not make the tunnel bigger yet. Too much chalk coming out. *What am I supposed to do with all that chalk?* he said, and Papa said, *we shall wait.* Papa goes down on the rope-ladder now. The captain made the dome hole bigger. He stood at the hole and kicked and kicked until the shells fell in. Then Papa could get his shoulders through the hole and he went down.

The sack hard stiff and heavy and horse-smelling. Light the tunnel lantern and put it round my neck and go in.

Dark and cool and dusty-smelling. Bigger than before but still only big enough for crawling. Not smooth-polished but lumpy, scratchy. Knees scrape shoes scuffle scuffle but cool, cool and dark and *almost* like before.

Tunnel end much bigger wider now. Chalk lumps shell pieces and then the opening. Swing my feet down and in and the first lantern is there on the floor. Light it and the wick goes *pfzzz* hissing smoky and then bright and the walls go yellow.

Fishes flowers trees – the same. Not hurt, not broken!

Round the passage with both lanterns and the shells are there, bright and shiny and not chalk-dusty, even. Vines and sunflowers and tree-branches and ferns, swirling up-growing and star-shaped. *Not* snakes. The first shells. Mr Davidson says that they tell a story. He says *the f-first p-panels are the key* but there cannot be treasure there for they have not hurt them.

On and round and there the dome and the rope-ladder hanging and the sacks over the hole. They must have come in that way, him and Lizzy. The shells not silvery shining any more, not at the top. Broken and muddy and scratched and kicked and pieces on the floor.

Down the passage (Mr Davidson says *the s-serpent*) and the little girl that May found is still there, still whole. Hearts flowers shells and shells. Lumps on the floor and nearly all right up to the end and there – *there*! Broken broken spoiled and torn, holes in the shells holes in the floor and tools and chalk and the roof hardly there at all.

Wicked wicked captain.

Hold up the lantern and more holes and lumps and step step ever-so-carefully into the room.

Not a room any more. Big open broken hole. No shell shelf. White chalk and pink and orange and yellow shell pieces sticking out round the edges. Cut and smashed and sore and sad, poor shells, poor *poor* shells. Broken stars broken suns broken sky where the roof should be and lumps of shell pattern dusty cracked in the corner. Slates all piled up too and cracked and the little pillars kicked and spoiled. Tools and sacks, big angry ugly metal thing with pointed ends white and chalk-dusty. Like a scythe for cutting grass but *not* a scythe – thicker stronger and the handle wooden in the middle. A *pick*.

Sorry I am sorry I am so sorry.

Hot again, hot and burning and cannot help it. They have spoiled it killed it robbed it and they don't care. Papa has let them. How can Papa let them? *Please make it better again, dear God, please. Papa does not mean it it is not his fault.*

Wet nose and eyes and the shells watery blurry broken. Sit on the lumpy floor in the yellow lantern circles.

'No.'

Say it out loud and it goes round and round *no-oh-oh*.

'No.'

No-oh-oh.

'No!'

No-oh-oh.

Say it and the shells say it back and the *no-oh-oh* goes on and on round and round and out and down along the tunnel.

It comes back again, *scraa-scrup scup*.

Scraa-scrup. Scup scup scup.

Not the *no*, something else. Some*one* else.

Mustn't see me, *mustn't*. *Whooh whooh* huff-blow at the lanterns and they flicker smoke and *pfut* go out.

Scup scup scup coming closer along the tunnel.

Black dark, cold. Hands on floor and behind and ever-so-carefully stand. The shells and chalk smooth and dusty cold.

Scup scup scup and yellow light coming spreading along the shells and at the arch and into the room.

Bright yellow spreading and the shells and chalk yellow white pink and something dark. Some*one*, holding up a lantern.

Him.

I could hear your snivelling from the top of the ladder his voice says.

Scup-scup and he comes closer, puts down the lantern. The

shells darker and the floor brighter and there his boots, his trousers.

What are you doing here?

Not his business, not. Not his shells whatever he thinks.

'What are *you* doing here?' say I.

He *haw-haw-haw* laughs. Comes closer. Boots, trousers, belt. Arms and hands big and a hand comes up towards me.

No! Step back and my feet scrape scuffle trip but don't fall. Don't fall mustn't fall.

You're a sharp little fox aren't you?

No. Not a fox but he is, sly sneaking and whiskery.

'Leave me alone' say I.

I won't hurt you his voice says pretend-nice. *Come here, little missy.*

'You hurt everything' say I. 'You hurt the shells and Papa and now you want to hurt me.'

Don't be silly.

'Go away!'

Back and back but only the corner there and his shadow big in the yellow light.

What's the matter?

'Let me out! I want to get out!'

You know the way. You know this place better than anyone, don't you, Fanny Newlove?

Feet scuffing slipping scraping and the chalk pieces rolling *craa*-crunching. Hands out behind and the wall there, no floor left no space. Not cold now, hot. Hot and sobbing and broken.

'I shall tell Papa you were here' say I.

Tell him then.

'You shouldn't come when he isn't here.'

Nor should you, little missy his voice says. *Lucky for you*

you're not your sister's age. I should teach you then. Haw-haw-haw. I hear the eldest Miss Newlove likes to learn.

'Lizzy is bad but she will *never* be as bad as you.'

Is that so?

'You break things' say I. 'Mr Davidson said not to and Papa said not to but you do it anyway because you don't care. You don't care about anything!'

Davidson is a fool and so are you. So is your father.

'I hate you!' say I. 'I hate you I hate you! There isn't any treasure, there isn't! Leave us alone!'

His hands big out of the dark his face hateful whiskery. Push at them clawing kick-kicking and his hands big strong pushing me, tearing shoving shells sharp in my back and his eyes hard and small and very close.

'I shall do what I like with this place' he says. 'I shall do what I like with your family.'

'You can't!' say I. 'I hate you!'

His hand quick up and at my throat and pushing squeezing. 'I can' he says whiskery-spitting 'and I will, little missy, if I *ever* see you down here again. Now get out.'

'No' say I. 'No!'

No-oh-oh. No-oh-oh.

Dearest James,

I hope that you have not had <u>too</u> dull a time this Summer preparing for your examinations. I cannot imagine that you will have done anything other than study very hard, so please do <u>stop</u>! and go outside for a little while to read this.

There. I hope that you are sitting under a tree and that it has not lost too many leaves yet. Our big sycamore is almost a skeleton again already and the wind is whistling about my window as I write. How quickly the Summer goes.

You will be delighted to learn that Papa has the papers for Mama's school at last. It has taken so very long to do and Mama is very pleased, as you may imagine. Now that the land and the house belong to Papa, he has uncovered the shell grotto and taken away the big slab that the gardener put over it. Now we are allowed to speak about it, and do not have to pretend that it is not there. The boys and girls that did not know about it are very excited, and Joshua has had quite a time trying to keep them all from running over to our school and jumping in. The gardener is going to make the tunnel bigger so that people can walk in and out easily without having to crawl or stoop.

Mr Davidson, who is the writing master that I told you of, said he will finish his repairs to the shell patterns in time for next season. It is such a very long time since I went into the shell place that I cannot imagine how it will look when it is finished. Of course, the boys are able to fetch shells by the wheelbarrow full now that it is all known about, which will make it quicker. Papa said that I may choose some special shells from the souvenir shop to go in, too. I am not sure if that is right somehow, but of course if Papa says it, it must be. Papa also said that he will ask Mr Wales, who is the workman, to put in some places for lanterns, for visitors to see by. He says that it will be in the newspapers and people will come from miles about to see it, and will pay to go in. I am sorry that you have not yet seen the shells for you cannot know how wonderful they are. Perhaps you will be able to, if you come at Christmas. It will be cold then and damp but you might be able to go in for a little while. It would be nice if you could see them before everyone else comes, for soon it will not seem like it is our shell place any more. There are already so many people looking at it. Poor Mama's garden, there are holes all over it where silly people keep digging for treasure.

Mama is very pleased with her school for there are such a lot of girls this term. Mary has begun to help Miss Roke with the junior girls for there are so many, and of course she is the best to teach needlework for she is so good at it. I do not even know all of the junior girls' names, I am glad that there are not so many pupils in my lessons. Lizzy was asked if she would like to help Mama but she does not want to teach, so she will be Mama's housekeeper, at least until she marries somebody and goes away. Papa's school is very busy and Joshua should really be a monitor, but Papa will not have him. His spelling and arithmetic are still very poor, but please do not be angry with him for it, he does not mean to be bad.

I was very sorry not to be able to see you in the vacation. Papa says that we cannot spend money, especially on travelling. It seems like such a very long time since any of us have been out of Margate and an age since I saw you, my dear brother. I shall be eleven soon, imagine that! You shall not recognise me for I am quite tall now.

I must go now for I am to help Anne with the supper things. Do write and tell us all about your examinations when they are over. You may go back inside now and study all you like. Do forgive my teasing and remember

your affectionate sister Frances.

Hateful hateful

Mama smiles nods and says *oh yes, Captain, oh yes quite so*.
Hateful hateful. She looks at the tea things when she is not
looking at him or at da Costa. Cups and saucers and the
milk sitting settling with a skin on it and a wasp (a *wapse*
May would call it) cross *zing zing* buzzing about, diving and
paddling in the sugar bowl. Want to stand up take the tray
but Mama would not like it. Mama says that it is uncivil to
clear away the things while there are guests talking but that
is silly, for when else is it to be done and who is to do it?
Not Anne for she is out and not Lizzy or Mary for they are
young ladies. Pooh. He and da Costa are not guests anyway.
They might as well be living here and paying board like the
boys do. They drink more tea here than they do at home.

'I shall take away the tea things, Mama' say I.

Stand and clatter-stack the saucers and cups and don't look
at her. The wasp *za-zing zing* angry, flick at it with a napkin.
Lizzy sighs. She thinks it is low of me to do the maid's work
but she dare not say so. And if not I then who?

'Let's smoke a cigar, Maurice' he says.

'Oh' says Mama feebly 'would you mind terribly—'

'My *dear* Mrs Newlove' he says *very low* 'we would not dream of offending you.'

'It is quite fine out' says da Costa. 'Let us take a turn in the garden.'

'Excellent notion.'

They stand, bow, go out. Their boots on the stairs. Mama huff-sighs.

'Fanny' she says 'how many times must I tell you not to behave so in front of the gentlemen?'

They are not gentlemen they are Philistines and they should be cast out into the wilderness. They should be smitten with fire and with plagues. Hateful hateful.

Lizzy sighs (again).

'She cannot help it, Mama' she says. Lazy Lizzy arm stretching bosom up-pushing. Da Costa not there to look at her so why bother? Maux, Mrs D says. M-A-U-X. Draggletail. Slattern. *Doxy.*

'I cannot help it if I do not want the milk to go sour' say I. 'Papa says we are to be careful with everything.'

'*I* am the housekeeper here' says Lizzy crossly 'do not tell me my duty.'

'Do not argue, girls' says Mama 'it is shameful. And, Fanny, you are grown too forward.'

'Sorry, Mama' say I.

Somebody has to be forward, though, somebody must. Lizzy lazy sluttish, Mary mooning spooning about, half in love with the art master half with *marvellous Miss Roke.* Mope mope. I should have been a boy. I would have told them, then. Mama too frightened to see or to tell them to go away, and Joshua can't. Even Papa is frightened now.

Foot the door open and closed behind me. Another maid's

trick, yes, opening and closing doors with a tray full. Why not? Anne's a good teacher even though she does not say her *aitches*. Not the worst sin in the world – is it, Lizzy? – not saying everything that should be said. We are all grown very good at that.

Down to the kitchen and take the things off the tray. Quietly and not clattering, not chipping. Milk into the cold cupboard, a thick yellow on top already. Empty the pot, leaves into the bowl for soaking raisins. Anne always says *no point wastin em gud tee leefs*. Good enough for stewing fruit. Strong tea warm stove smelling and clean, take the cups and rinse them, put them ever-so-carefully and quietly on the lead drainer. No cracks no chips. *Yud be a gud maid, Miss Fransuss* Anne often says, teasing. I would not mind that. I would rather be a maid than a *maux*.

Back door creaking and boots sounding. Woods?

Them, nasty smoky bonfire cigar-smelling.

Curse this bloody rain! the captain's voice says.

Good. Hope you are wet through. Hope it put your nasty cigars out.

She won't notice if we keep the door open says da Costa's voice, and the captain's voice says *what of it if she does?*

They are going to smoke anyway. In the corridor.

Should go out there, should say no. He will laugh though, puff-huff horrid smoke at me. Hateful hateful. Too late to go out, they will see me. Quiet. Sit on Anne's stool and wait, then. They will go away soon.

Puff puff and da Costa's voice says *this is all very tedious, Easter.*

THE CAPTAIN'S VOICE: Out with it, Maurice.

DA COSTA'S VOICE: I have to get out of here, that damned creature is near smothering me!

THE CAPTAIN'S VOICE: Tired of her, eh?

DA COSTA'S VOICE: Tired of her months ago. Couldn't very well throw her off though, could I? Didn't know how it was all going to pan out.

THE CAPTAIN'S VOICE: Well, she doesn't come into it now. Cut loose, man. *(Puff puff.)* Plenty more, Maurice, plenty more.

DA COSTA'S VOICE: What about the mother? *(Grunt, haw-haw.)* I fear you're losing your touch, old fellow.

THE CAPTAIN'S VOICE: Biding my time, Maurice. They owe me. *(Haw-haw-haw, puff puff.)*

DA COSTA'S VOICE: How's Sarah?

THE CAPTAIN'S VOICE: She keeps me busy.

(They both haw-haw-haw for a long time.)

DA COSTA'S VOICE: I've been thinking. I say it's time I found myself a wife.

THE CAPTAIN'S VOICE: Devil take it! You're not serious?

DA COSTA'S VOICE: Good God, man, no! What, marry that? No no. *(Puff puff.)* As it happens I've my eye on a piece in town. Glover, Gracechurch Street.

THE CAPTAIN'S VOICE: Trade? I thought you'd want breeding.

DA COSTA'S VOICE: Wouldn't we all, but what's a fellow to do these days? *(Puff puff.)* Anyway it's a decent trade, not just any old thing. Plenty of money in it. People will always want *gloves*, Easter.

THE CAPTAIN'S VOICE: So, out with the *New*love and in with the newer, then, eh? *Haw-haw-haw.*

That is Lizzy, then.

Thud-shutting of the door and their boots past the kitchen along the corridor. *Get going shall we eh?* says the captain's voice, and da Costa's says *ages before the show, how about a bottle at the York?* That is the good hotel but Papa says it is no better than a common drinking tavern. Then they are going to the *theatre*. Put the tea tray back not thunder-crashing but very gently. Out quietly and along the corridor and they have gone up.

Wait. Shan't go to the parlour. They will come down soon. Go into the music room and play.

Piano lid still up from before. 1-2-3-4-5-6 down-2-3-4-5-6 up-2-3-4-5-6, 1. 6. I should like to play a jig but Mama says *concertos are more suitable*. Anne and Mary used to like a good country dance but Mary always asks for *something romantic* now. I am tired of romantic things. I am getting better, though. Mr Mills is right.

Men's boots thudding and soft shoe stepping on the stairs. Mama does not like me to play when there are *visitors*. How am I supposed to get better if I do not play? She is just sorry that I am not better *anyway*.

We'd gladly stay says the captain's voice *but I'm afraid Maurice here accepted an invitation from Sir John and we must go.*

Thud thud thud.

Oh of course says Mama's voice, and da Costa's voice says *a dry old sort Sir John but one must be gracious.*

Lies lies lies. They are going to the tavern to drink brandy.

Fanny! Mama's voice. *Fanny, the captain and Mr da Costa are leaving now!*

Good.

Get up and into the hall and there they stand, waiting. Get his horrid hat for his hateful head and da Costa's too. Pass them, not looking.

'My!' he says. 'What a surly young lady Miss Frances has become.'

Don't look at him, shan't. *Hate him hate him hate him.*

Lizzy standing puts her hand into her pocket pulls it out

again. *A note.* She looks at da Costa but he looks at his hat, turns to Mama.

He is ignoring her.

'My dear Mrs Newlove' says da Costa 'I am afraid that I shall not see you again for some little time. I am travelling up to town tomorrow.'

'Town!' says Lizzy.

'I trust it is for pleasure, then' says Mama 'and not some irksome business matter.'

'Oh indeed' says da Costa smiling 'it is definitely a matter of pleasure.'

Lizzy white-faced makes a fist with paper corners poking out. Mary leans against the wall.

'Goodbye, my dear' says the captain, whiskery-kissing Mama's hand. 'Goodbye, young ladies.'

We bob and bow and da Costa kisses Mama's hand too. Lizzy steps forward and he steps back and bows.

'Goodbye, gentlemen' says Mama.

Open the door and the rain *pat-pat-patting* on the step. They go out bowing hat-lifting up the path and open the gate. Mama waves. I shut the door.

Lizzy stare-stares at the door, puts her fist back into her pocket. Her lip goes all twitching trembling and pouting.

'Really, Frances' says Mama crossly 'you are so very rude to the captain and Mr da Costa. I am certain that Captain Easter took offence.'

Good.

Mama huffs sighs reaches for her shawl. 'I must go to your father now, girls' she says. 'I shall see you after supper.'

'Yes, Mama' says Mary.

Open the door and she goes out too, *tut-tutting*, not kissing not smiling.

'Why must it always rain?' she says.

A not-question.

Mama goes up the path *drip drip pat pat*. Shut the door behind her.

Lizzy stare-stares at the door, not moving. She stares at the door and we stare at her and she opens her mouth and *aaaaaaaaaaaaaaaaaaaaaaa!* wails. Not crying not sobbing not even like a person wailing. *Aaaaaaaaaaaaaaaaaaaaaaa! Aaaaaaaaaaaaaaaaaaaaaaa!* like a bird that a cat is teasing.

'Hush now' says Mary, very scared.

Mary puts her hand out to Lizzy and Lizzy stares at it like it is a monster's.

Aaaaaaaaaaaaaaaaaaaaaaa! Big mouth big nostrils round as saucers and twitching quivering.

'Hush now' says Mary. 'Come upstairs.'

Lizzy turns runs up the stairs and her door thud-crashes and she sobs sobs and *aaaaaaaaaaaaaaaaaaaaaaa!* wails right through the floorboards. Mary looks at me and turns, runs up the stairs after her. The door thuds again. *Oh my poor Lizzy lamb!* Mary's voice says and Lizzy *aaaaaaaaaaaaaaaaaaaaaaa! aaaaaaaaaaaaaaaaaaaaaaa!* wails and makes the house move about with her sobbing.

Go back into the music room and sit at the piano. Mama is gone now.

I shall play a hornpipe.

Thursday the Second day of November 1837 – my birthday!
Bellevue School for Girls
Margate

Dearest James,

Thank you <u>so much</u> dear brother for your lovely lovely letter and for the ribbons. I shall wear them at church every Sunday for they are too fine for every day. I am so happy that you will be able to visit for Christmas too. We are all very excited.

I have had many nice presents. Mama and Papa gave me a new bonnet and Lizzy and Mary a petticoat. Mary did the embroidery on it, it is very fine. Joshua gave me some candied violets and they are almost too pretty to eat. Anne has made me a cake to have at supper with plums and raisins inside. May and Frances Morgan and Beth Lucas are coming back for supper, even though they are not boarders, for Mama said that they might. They can have some cake.

I am sorry to hear that you are working so hard and not having fun. Papa says that a schoolmaster's life is difficult but rewarding and I am sure that you will find it so too. I think I should like to be a governess like Mama and Miss Roke. Perhaps one day I shall be. Mary says that it is a marvellous profession. She is very popular with the junior girls, as you can imagine.

I know that I must be more grown-up now that I am eleven, but I shall not keep telling everyone how old I am like Joshua does. He says 'I am <u>sixteen</u> you know' all the time. (He says that to make the younger boys take notice of him.) I promise to try my very best to be kind and considerate to others, as you say. I am sorry that Mama says I am being difficult for I do not mean to be.

It is very cold here now and already the garden is completely white with frost. I hope that it snows on the beach again this year, so you may see it. It is so pretty. Mary is calling me now for she says the supper table is ready, so I shall finish. Thank you very much for remembering

your affectionate sister Frances.

(Papa has put the big slab over the shells again, but he says you may look when you come, if it is not too wet.)

They rejoiced with exceeding great joy

Cold frosty white and boot-crunchy but no snow. Still no snow. Mama and Papa walking quickly, talking and nodding. Big clouds of steamy breath over them, *puff puff. Puff puff.* James very tall very serious nods and frowns in his long black coat. He is so grown-up now. He is just like Papa.

Joshua bony elbow-nudges my arm. Elbow-nudge him back.

'I'm ravenous' he says, very low. 'I hope Papa doesn't make us pray again before dinner.'

He would be like a cow if he could with many stomachs and always chewing. Chew chew chew. Chewing the cud. The *quid*, May would say. May has a nice way of saying things, softer than Mama and Papa. Frances Morgan says things the same way as May but it never sounds as nice. She says they say 'quid' instead of 'cud' because they are *Margate people proper and not like them with funny voices from the Sheers.*

'I thought the sermon would go on for ever' says Joshua. 'Why is he always so long about it?'

'It *is* a holy day, Joshua' say I.

And they fell down and worshipped him.

Roast goose and potatoes and plum pudding. Prayers and dinner all together and then games, perhaps. Mama said that Miss Roke was to come for dinner even though she is not family. I said *why?* and Mama said *be charitable, Fanny* and then *Miss Roke does not have any family to have dinner with.* But she does for she is a clergyman's daughter. Papa said so.

Miss Roke will have gone to church. She will come walking up the path in her lovely cloak with the rabbit fur on it. Poor rabbit. Miss Roke is *not* chapel.

Mary is pleased though and so is James. He and Miss Roke talked and talked and smiled for an age together in the parlour. I can't imagine what he said to make her smile for he has grown so very serious. He doesn't tell funny stories like he used to. I have worn his birthday ribbons every day since he got here but he hasn't noticed. He hasn't even seen the shells yet, even though I often said that I would show him. It would be all right to go in if James was with me. Last time I said we might look he just said *not now please, Fanny.* I went to my room and Mary came and asked me why I was sad, and I told her. Mary said *he is a man now, Fanny, he does not want to play like he used to.*

I have not seen the shells for such a long time either.

Joshua *fhuw-fhuw* whistles and then sings *I saw three ships come sailing.* Mama looks at him and frowns and he stops. James looks at us over his shoulder and turns away again.

Mama does not like us to sing in the street, even carols. She says it is *rowdy behaviour.*

'It is nice to have James here, isn't it?' say I.

Joshua shrugs. His feet go *crunch squeak crunch squeak* on the path.

'Do you think there will be bread sauce?' he says.

(Chew chew chew.)

I am eleven and James is twenty-two. That means that he is exactly twice as old as I am, for $11 + 11 = 22$.

And when they had opened their treasures they presented unto him gifts. Papa said that he could bear very little expense at Christmas this year. He said that the birth of Our Lord is richness enough and that we do not need material tokens when we have the wealth of His Spirit. Mama said later that we might have our stockings even so, but that I should not expect very much in mine for I had so many things for my birthday. But there wasn't a stocking this morning. There was a picture of the Wise Men and the Shepherds at the crib, which Mary had drawn. *Unto us a child is born.* She left it on my bed. And there is plum pudding. Mrs D said that there wasn't enough sugar left for sweets or she would have made some, but she must have known that there wouldn't be. I haven't been sent to buy sugar for ages.

Papa did not say why we could not have stockings, but I know. Papa owes the captain money. He gave Papa money to buy Mama's school, but it was really for the shells.

Mary is pleased that Miss Roke is coming. They are friends now. Lizzy does not like Miss Roke very much, probably because she is pretty and has golden hair. Lizzy does not care for anything today except that she did not get new gloves for Christmas. She kept groaning and grumbling about how badly she needed new gloves and I wanted to say *ask da Costa then for he knows a glover in London.* But I didn't. I held my tongue, because it *is* a holy day.

And when they were departed, behold, the angel of the Lord appeareth to Joseph in a dream. And they ran away to Egypt. E-G-Y-P-T. There would not have been any snow there either, which is better for the poor old donkey. Egypt is hot and full of sand, and there are camels and lions and crocodiles. They would eat the donkey if they could. There will be lions and camels at the Menagerie but probably not crocodiles. Mary said she would take me, for it is not such a very long way in the coach, but Papa says we may not. He says it will cost too much.

Up the path and Mrs D smiling opens and we go in. *And when they were come into the house they saw the young child with Mary his mother*. Papa's hall all goose and spice-smelling and steam on the windows. We take off bonnets and shawls and James and Papa give me their hats. James does not say *thank you, Fanny* but his eyes go peering peeking along the hall. He is looking for Miss Roke.

'The parlour fire is good and stoked' says Mrs D 'and your visitor's come already. I've seen to her, don't worry.'

'Has she?' says Mama. 'Thank you, thank you.'

Papa and James and Lizzy and Mary all go to the parlour. Hang up the shawls, cold and heavy and chapel damp. Miss Roke's cloak is there too, soft and rabbity. It smells of roses and soap, just like Miss Roke.

'How are matters in the kitchen?' says Mama.

'Oh, you know' says Mrs D 'she puffed and made a fuss but she's done it all right. Shall I let her go?'

'I'm not sure if we can manage' says Mama.

Looks at me.

No cook's girl today. No Anne for she is having Christmas with her father. Mama is looking at me and thinking that Miss Roke will find us very poor if we carry the dishes ourselves. Silly silly silly.

'I will help Mrs D' say I.

'Oh, Fanny!' says Mama. 'I am not sure.'

She wants me to, though. She does not want to pay Cook the extra to stay over dinner.

'I don't mind, Mama' say I. 'I should like to help.'

'There's a good girl' says Mrs D. 'You come and find me when you're ready and I'll show you what to do. The table's all set and done.'

'Very well' says Mama (*sigh sigh*). 'Please let Cook go.'

Mrs D goes shuffling back along the hall to the kitchen. Mama looks at me.

'I do not approve of you always acting like a maid, Fanny' she says.

(She does not approve of me acting like a maid when there are people *watching*.)

'No one else will do it, Mama' say I. 'I do not mind doing it.' I smile ever-so-sweetly. 'And it is Christmas for Cook too.'

She sighs, pat-pats her hair and goes along the hall to the parlour. Disappears. *My dear Miss Roke!* her voice says in its best *what a delightful surprise* way. Not a surprise though, because *she* planned it.

Go along and into the parlour too and there is Miss Roke, sitting in Mama's chair. She sip-sips from a glass and smiles. Pretty Miss Roke with a lovely blue dress and a shiny silver locket. Mary stands fusses at her and at the fire. Lizzy sits not smiling, looking hard. Looking *green*.

'I trust you had an enjoyable service this morning, Miss Roke' says James. He leans long-armed long-legged against Papa's mantelpiece.

Twenty-two *is* very grown-up.

'Oh, yes, thank you, Mr Newlove' says Miss Roke. 'We had a very moving sermon, and much singing. I do so enjoy singing a good carol, do you not, Mr Newlove?'

'My father is Mr Newlove' says James *almost* smiling. 'Please do call me James.'

'Oh' says Miss Roke. She looks at Papa and back at James and her eyes go very wide and brown. 'Well, if you insist, Mr Newlove.'

'Oh dear no!' says James.

They *ahee-tee-hee* titter titter laugh. Even Papa smiles. He is in a good mood because it is Christmas.

'I do like to sing too' says Mary 'especially sacred songs. It is so good for one.'

'It is not good for *me*' says Lizzy. 'My ears are still roaring from your "O Come All Ye Faithful" this morning.'

Mama *ah-ha* laughs. Mary smiles but her eyes say *please don't, Lizzy*.

Papa looks at Mama. 'It is a pity that our pianoforte is in the girls' school, Arabella' he says. 'We might have had a little carol-singing before dinner.'

'Oh, Papa!' says Mary. 'That is such a lovely idea. And we could have our very own Christmas ball! We are enough for a country dance. Fanny would play for us, wouldn't you, Fanny?'

'Perhaps we could have a dance after dinner' says James. 'Do you like to dance, Miss Roke?'

Miss Roke smiles and looks at her glass.

'There is a *proper* ball for New Year' says Lizzy slyly 'at the Royal Hotel. I should very much like to go.'

She looks hard at Papa.

'That is impossible, Lizzy dear' says Mama. 'Your father and I are expected at Mrs Mills's for supper that evening.'

'My dear Mrs Newlove' says Miss Roke 'please permit me to make a suggestion. If she would not mind my company, I would gladly accompany Miss Newlove.' She leans towards

Lizzy. 'I have so longed for a ball myself, Miss Newlove, but lack a companion. I understand that it will be a very proper occasion. Everyone will be there, even the admiralty!'

'I should like to go too' says Mary, very quiet.

'That is very kind, Miss Roke' says Mama 'but I cannot allow Lizzy to attend without an escort. Mr Newlove will not be at liberty to go with her.'

Lizzy pulls a face.

Lizzy told Mary that she wanted to go to the ball to dance and flirt with all the naval officers. She wants to make da Costa jealous, which is silly, because he may not even be there. He is still away in London. The captain went to visit him. *Good.* Hope they stay there. They are probably drinking whisky with the glover and his daughter and the *huh-huh* dog in a tavern somewhere. Anyway, naval officers swear and drink rum.

'Forgive my intrusion' says James. He *ahem* clears his throat, looks at Mama. 'I certainly think it unwise for the young ladies to go to such a gathering without a gentleman to escort them. Perhaps, then, I might take Lizzy and Mary to the ball, Mama? And Miss Roke, of course, if she would permit me.'

'Oh, James!' says Mary. 'Would you really? That would be wonderful!'

The ball is on Sunday and James is supposed to be going back on *Saturday*. He said so. I asked him to stay for New Year and he said *Fanny, I may not stay a moment longer than I have already promised.*

'Can you spare the time, James?' says Papa. 'I understood you would return before the New Year.'

'With your permission, sir' says James 'I would gladly remain another day or so with you all.'

'Oh, do!' says Mary.

'Very well' says Papa 'if you wish it. You may go, girls, on that condition.'

Mama smiles sighs and says *what a delight!* Mary claps her hands. Miss Roke looks at the floor and then at Lizzy. Lizzy not green any more smiles at Miss Roke and turns, sighs, frowns at the fire. 'I shall need a new dress' she says. '*And* gloves.'

'You are welcome to borrow a pair of mine, Miss Newlove' says Miss Roke. 'I have *two* pairs of white kidskin.'

Lizzy's eyes go very big. She will also say that Miss Roke is *marvellous* now, but if Miss Roke and James go to the ball she will not be able to flirt with all the naval officers.

'Papa' say I 'if Mary and Lizzy can go to the ball please may I go to see the lions?'

'Lions?' says Miss Roke. 'That sounds frightening!'

'There are lions at the Menagerie' say I. 'May I, Papa?'

'I have already given you my answer, Fanny' he says.

'I did not know there was to be a Menagerie' says Miss Roke. 'I am not sure that I like the idea of lions prowling the streets of Margate!'

Silly. 'It is Mr Wombwell's Royal Menagerie' say I 'visiting from London. It is in Canterbury for a regrettably short period only.'

'Fanny has been studying the newspaper, Miss Roke' says James.

They all laugh.

James is not staying for us. He is staying for Miss Roke. And now they are *all* going to the ball, which will cost *far more* than one ticket for the lions. *Not* fair.

'I should go to the kitchen now' say I.

Papa frowns. 'Whatever for, Fanny?' he says.

'Oh' says Mama. 'Fanny is to help with the dishes, for I have allowed Cook to go home.' She leans towards Miss Roke. 'It is Christmas for her *too*, after all.'

Saturday the Twentieth day of January 1838
Bellevue School for Girls
Margate

Dearest James,

I hope that you are well. We are all well although Mary has had a terrible cough which is much better now. She caught it after getting wet at the ball. We have begun lessons again and the art master and Mary are teaching us drawing. Mary says that my pictures are very promising.

Boring boring boring. He doesn't care about our lessons or my pictures or Mary's cough. He made her stand and wait in the rain, he was only worried about seeing Miss Roke home. *Scra*-scribble it out and tear it up and start again.

Dear James,

Mary has had a terrible cough and we are all very concerned about her. I believe it is from standing in the rain after the New Year ball you took her to. She should not have worn short sleeves, even if the new queen always does. Miss Roke did not catch cold, however. You will be pleased to know <u>that</u> I am sure.

The wind *whoo* whooshes and *rat-at* rattles the window. Cold cold and drizzling but Lizzy and Mary went out even so. Shopping. With Miss Roke.

Dear James

Do not be alarmed but Mary has the consumption. The doctor says that she is at death's door and will not last out the night. Miss Roke was so distraught and guilt-stricken that she has thrown herself into the sea and drowned. Lizzy is joining a convent. Joshua is to run Papa's school, for Papa and Mama are running away to Egypt. I can stay here and look after the shells if I like but I may be forced to flee like a convict for I ran Captain Easter through with a cutlass.

He has come back again (bad) but *without* da Costa (good). Lizzy pretended very hard not to mind whenever Mama or the captain said his name.

Whoo-whoosh. Rat-at-at.

No Lizzy no Mary. No Mama for she is visiting Mrs Mills again. No Joshua even, for he has gone off with John Fassum. Anne at Papa's and me at the desk and nothing to say to James. Nothing.

Dear James,

Lizzy and Mary are up to something. I can tell. Nothing has been right since you came for now they are fast friends with Miss Roke and always having tea with her. They are all out now shopping and looking at magazines of the new court fashions, and buying bonnets and gloves and cakes that Papa cannot pay for. Papa cannot pay for anything any more because he bought the shells but you didn't even see them did you? so what would you care about it. I am all alone in the house and it is cold and the wind is noisy. Mary and Lizzy have secrets and won't tell. I hate it when they do that. Nobody tells me anything any more because they think that I am just a little girl and they are all grown-up now. Even you were like that at Christmas and you never used to be.

Rat-at-at-at-at.

I know that you are writing to Miss Roke. You never write to me. Miss Roke is taking everyone away. I am not fooled by her pretty hair. She is a witch.

Woooooo. Woooooooosh-shush-shush.
Tear it in half and then the halves into squares and roll the squares into little balls. Mama says you cannot make a circle out of straight lines. You can. You can make a ball of paper and throw it at the wall.
Rat-at-at. Craa-eeek creak.
The front door opens and Lizzy's voice says *oh! you do fuss so*. They are back and they are quarrelling. Get up and go to the door and their voices come up the stairs louder and louder.

LIZZY'S VOICE: Miss Roke is my friend and I shall tell her what I like.

MARY'S VOICE: But Lizzy! To tell anyone such a thing—

LIZZY'S VOICE: I shall tell whomever I like. It is my business.

MARY'S VOICE (*sighs*): It is a foolish business.

LIZZY'S VOICE: You are a jealous creature, Mary Newlove.

MARY'S VOICE: Oh, Lizzy! That is unfair.

It *is* unfair but so is Lizzy. They are coming up the stairs, *thud thud thud.*

LIZZY'S VOICE: You can't hook the Toogood and so you are spiteful about my affairs.

MARY'S VOICE: Oh, Lizzy, you know that isn't true.

Mary is not spiteful, Mary is *never* spiteful. That is for Lizzy to do.

They come up and pass the door rub-rubbing their hands. Mary looks up. Her face is very white except for her nose, which is red with cold.

'Oh, Fanny!' she says. 'What have you been doing with yourself, my dear?'

'Spying' says Lizzy. 'Listening at doors.'

'I don't need to' say I 'for you are loud enough for anyone to hear. You always make a lot of noise when you have secrets.'

'You are always prying' says Lizzy, sniffing. 'You are always sneaking about.'

'I am good at secrets' say I 'and I know that you have one. You never tell me anything, but you always make sure that I *know* you are not telling.'

'Pooh' says Lizzy 'that is a queer bit of reasoning.'

'I *know*' say I. 'You told Miss Roke and Mary said you shouldn't have.'

'Sneak' says Lizzy.

'Now, Fanny dear' says Mary 'this is not like you. Do calm yourself.'

'Oh it *is* like her all right' says Lizzy. Her nostrils go all big and quivery. 'She is always stamping her foot and saying *I shall*. I suppose you will threaten to tell Mama now?'

'Yes I shall' say I. 'If you don't tell me I shall tell Mama.'

'See?' says Lizzy.

'Fanny' says Mary 'there is nothing to tell. Really there isn't.'

'Yes there is' say I.

'Yes' says Lizzy 'there is. But I don't see why I should tell a little girl like you.'

'You shall!'

'Now now' says Mary. Her eyebrows are very high and her eyes are big and watery. 'Be a good girl, Fanny, and calm down. Lizzy doesn't have anything of importance to tell you or anyone else.'

'Liar!' say I.

'Oh, Fanny!' says Mary.

'I have!' says Lizzy squealing 'I have and you, Mary Newlove, are too jealous to admit it because *nobody* has ever asked for *your* hand in marriage and nobody *ever will*!'

Mary shock-faced puts her hands to her mouth and begins to sob.

So that is it! He has asked her.

'When are you marrying him then?' say I. 'Will you move to London or live in Lausanne House? I would move to London if I were you.'

'Not Mr da Costa' says Mary wailing sobbing. 'It is not him!'

'No it is not' says Lizzy very pleased. 'It is a handsome young *captain*.'

Not *the* captain then, for he is not young or handsome.

'That is wonderful, Lizzy' say I. 'When are you going?'

'I haven't decided whether or not I shall marry him' says Lizzy. She pat-pats her hair. 'I may make him wait a little.'

'But you said yes!' says Mary sob-sniffing. 'You told him you would!'

'I agreed to an engagement, Mary' she says. 'That is not the same thing.'

It is though. Lizzy will get married and then she will not live here any more.

'What is his name?' say I.

'Never you mind' says Lizzy.

'You might as well tell her' Mary wails. 'You have told her all else so where is the harm?'

'His name is Captain Francis Meuer. Frank Meuer.'

He has my name and then a mew like a cat. Lizzy will be Mrs Arabella-Elizabeth Meuer. Ha!

'Where did you meet him, Lizzy?'

'At the New Year ball.' She looks at her gloves, which are *not* new. 'Of course, I had seen him before. But he began pursuing me after we danced together. He is quite ardent, you know.'

One of the naval officers then. Lizzy cannot have done it to make da Costa jealous, though, for he cannot know. Not if he wasn't there. Not if it *is* a secret.

'Have you told Papa yet?' say I. 'He should speak to Papa, shouldn't he?'

'It is a *secret* engagement, Fanny' says Lizzy. 'You said you were good at secrets, didn't you?'

'Oh yes. But what is the point of it if it is secret? You cannot marry him if it is secret.'

'I told you' says Lizzy 'I *may* marry him, I may *not*.' She leans down close to my ear. *Listen to me, Fanny Newlove* she says whisper-hissing, *if you breathe a word of this to anyone I will make your life more miserable than you can possibly imagine.*

She straightens, smiles, looks at Mary. Mary dab-dabs her nose with her handkerchief.

'How could you, Lizzy?' she says. 'Why did you agree to it?'

'For goodness' sake' says Lizzy '*do* be sensible.' She sighs, shakes her head. 'If you would only do as I say, Mary, you would have that long-haired scribbler on his knees before Lent. Really, you are quite hopeless.'

Mary *oh! oh-oh-ohs* and begins to sob again. Poor Mary. She goes handkerchief-rustling nose-blowing into her room and slam-shuts the door. Lizzy goes off queenly and important-looking into the parlour. Go back in and sit at the desk.

Dear James,

Lizzy is secretly engaged, Mary is in love with the art teacher and neither of them are very happy about it. Please do not write to me again. I am quite worn out by all of those long heartfelt letters that you send me.

Wa-oooo woosh-ush-ush. Rat-at-at.
If I throw lots of paper balls at the window all at once, it sounds like hailstones.

Dull dull and dreary

Mama said that Joshua may go out but when I asked her if I might she said *it is too wet, Fanny*. It was raining when Lizzy and Mary went but that did not stop them.

Sit and sit and sew and knit. Mama mending a petticoat and me my stockings, baskets of them. Mama says that I must learn not to spoil my things for I shall not have new ones, and until I *cease this persistent hole-making* then I must mend them myself. Dull dull. She would not let me stay at home and play the piano. She said I must sit with her and work. Dull dull. Dull and dreary.

Papa next to the fire, reading his book. It is black and serious-looking but not a psalm book, not a Bible. Mama sews and the clock ticks and the rain starts and stops and starts again.

Tap-tap knocking at the door and Mama looks up. Mrs D's feet shuffle along the hall.

'You are not expecting anyone, dear?' Mama says.

Papa shakes his head. Mama puts down her sewing.

Door noises and stamping-boot noises and voices. It is *him*.

In there are they? his voice says and his feet come clumping thumping along the hall. He opens the door.

'Oh!' says Mama. 'Good afternoon, Captain. How delightful to see you.'

'Is it?' he says, very sharp. 'Is it indeed?'

He looks at Papa. Papa sighs, puts down his book. Stands up.

'Good day, Captain Easter' he says, *not* bowing.

'*No*, sir' says the captain (not bowing either). 'No it is not, sir. It is a very ill day indeed.'

Mama's mouth makes an *oh!* shape but nothing comes out. Papa stands, rocks on his heels, puts his hands behind his back. He would not bow and he does not want to shake hands either.

The captain looks about the room but not at me. He drops sits on to a chair and the chair stuffing sighs and grumbles. He looks at Papa again. His eyes are very hard.

'It is rather wet' says Mama feebly. 'You did not get wet, Captain, I trust?'

'I did.'

Good.

'There appears to be something troubling you, Captain' says Papa, rather quiet. 'Do tell us if we may assist you.'

'Bah!' he says. *(Snort snort.)* 'You? *You* assist *me*, Newlove? A fine notion.'

Papa looks at the captain, looks at Mama. Mama's eyes are very wide.

'Kindly explain yourself, Captain' says Papa.

'Fellow called Holtum is causing trouble' he says. 'Claims he made the blasted grotto. Claims he dug it out himself years ago, before Bowles's house was built.'

'Oh my dear!' says Mama. 'How can that be?'

'It is *simple*, madam' he says *snap snap*. 'He is telling the whole of Margate the place is a fake.'

'That is ludicrous' says Papa. 'Who is this Mr Holtum?'

'Holtum is a conceited fellow and a braggart' says the captain 'and he was digging lime pits about here when I built Bellevue. God knows what he expects to get out of this nonsense.'

'Captain Easter' says Papa looking very grave 'this Mr Holtum cannot possibly have built the grotto. He may have happened upon it before we did, perhaps before the house was built. However, if that was the case, why did he not say so at the time?'

'Looting' says the captain. 'He was looting it because he couldn't buy the plot.' Rubs his nasty whiskers with his thumb. 'Now you've got your hands on it, Newlove, and he can't bear the thought he never made something of it himself.'

Ha! Mr Holtum got the treasure first, then. *That* is why he is so cross.

'But surely' says Mama 'we cannot allow this person to claim he made the shell mosaic? Why, who would pay to visit it then?'

'Quite!' says the captain, all cross and bristling. 'Quite.'

'Forgive me, Arabella' says Papa. 'This man cannot interfere with our plans. No one will believe such wild claims. Anyone who sees the grotto will know that it has not been created in this generation.' He nods at the captain. 'Besides, I do not believe this talk of looting. If there was money to be made from what the man found he could easily have bought the land himself. It would have sold cheaply enough without the house on it.'

'Holtum's a spendthrift, Newlove' says the captain. 'Men like that don't know how to make an investment.'

Mama is worried. She puts her hand to her throat and her fingers flutter-flutter there. 'My dear' she says 'what shall we do?'

'Nothing, Arabella' says Papa. 'Whatever the man may have done in the past, the grotto is mine now.'

'Ours, Newlove' says the captain. 'We shall speak of that, too.'

Papa looks at Mama and then at me. Mama nods.

'Fanny dear' she says 'go and ask the housekeeper to make some tea.'

'Yes, Mama.'

They want me to go. The captain looks at me with his horrid hard eyes and huff grunts. Put down my darning needle and my stocking and go to the door. Soft-close it behind me. *Pat-pat-pat* step down the hall. Ever-so-carefully tiptoe back again.

Well says the captain's voice very stern *why isn't it being done?*

They are very quiet.

PAPA'S VOICE: I haven't enough to settle him, Captain. I shall need more.

THE CAPTAIN'S VOICE: More? More, damn it? The man's a labourer, not a bloody architect!

MAMA'S VOICE: Oh Captain, please!

PAPA'S VOICE: The Spring floods were very damaging, especially at the entrance. I needed Wales to repeat some of what he had already done. Naturally, he will not take on any more until he has been paid for that.

Mr Wales is mending the shells. Mending the bits that *he* broke.

THE CAPTAIN'S VOICE: And how is it to be settled, sir?

MAMA'S VOICE: We were rather hoping, Captain, that you might assist us there.

THE CAPTAIN'S VOICE: *(Grunt grunt.)* Were you, madam? Indeed.

PAPA'S VOICE: We need to pay Wales to complete the task. If it is not done soon, we will not be ready for the beginning of the season.

THE CAPTAIN'S VOICE: You will be ready, Newlove. You *must* be. We cannot have it sitting there idle.

MAMA'S VOICE: Indeed, Captain, that is our intention.

THE CAPTAIN'S VOICE: Holtum has done his damage here, madam, mark my words. You'll need all the outside visitors you can get now.

They are quiet again. Mama *ahem-hems*.

MAMA'S VOICE: Will you kindly assist us again, Captain? We would not ask you, but you have been so very generous already.

THE CAPTAIN'S VOICE: So I have.

MAMA'S VOICE: We are *most* grateful to you for everything you have done.

THE CAPTAIN'S VOICE, HURRUM-HEMMING GRUNTING: It's not cheap in town, you know. I have a few debts to settle after the Winter season.

MAMA'S VOICE, VERY SOFT: Of course. Anything you might spare us, Captain.

THE CAPTAIN'S VOICE: That damned grotto had better be ready by May, Newlove. D'you hear?

PAPA'S VOICE, VERY QUIET: I do.

MAMA'S VOICE: We shall do all we can to ensure it.

THE CAPTAIN'S VOICE: I shall need it back, and soon. I've given you enough already.

MAMA'S VOICE: Of course, Captain.

THE CAPTAIN'S VOICE: Damn it. *(Grunt grunt.)* Damn it, all right then. Tell Wales to come to me, Newlove, I'll sort him out.

MAMA'S VOICE: Oh, Captain! Thank you, thank you. You are so very good to us.

He is not. He said he would do what he likes with us, and he means to.

Shuffle-shuffling of feet. *Mrs D!* Spring up and tiptoe-run from the door and meet her scuffling into the hall from the kitchen.

'Mrs D' say I 'Papa asked me to ask you for tea.'

'Did he now? I suppose it's for the captain?'

'Yes, please.'

'All right, all right.'

She turns and shuff-shuffles off again. The parlour door opens and Papa comes out, frowning and hand-rubbing. He looks up and stare-stares at me but he isn't looking, not really.

He puts on his big coat.

'Papa' say I 'I have asked Mrs D for the tea.'

'Tea?'

'Yes, Papa.'

He stares again, picks up his hat. 'Frances' he says. 'Frances.'

'Yes, Papa?'

'I'm going to the chapel meeting now, Frances.' Opens the door, turns back. The air comes in cold from outside. Papa's face is very long and dark and sad. 'Run and tell the housekeeper not to make any tea for me.'

'Yes, Papa.'

His coat looks too big and too black but it is the same coat as always. He goes out, thud closes the door.

Along to the kitchen and *tap-tap* the door. *Never* go in without knocking. Never. The cook's girl opens pink-pig-faced and stares at me. Her sleeves are rolled back right to her elbows. She smells of onions. The whole kitchen smells of onions, onions and tea and wet flour.

Cook chop-chopping turns with her knife and looks at me. 'What d'you want?' she says.

'Mrs D' say I.

Mrs D is setting out cups. She looks up and smiles. 'I thought I heard something' she says. 'Did he go?'

'No' say I 'it was Papa. He has gone to the chapel meeting. He said not to make any tea for him.'

'Ho' says Mrs D. 'Pity.'

Yes.

Cook wipes her knife on her apron and *tut-tuts*. The girl slam-shuts the door. *Missus wants t mind erself* her voice says. *That she does an all* says the cook's.

Ignorant ignorant ignorant.

Back *again* to the parlour. Don't want to sit silent tea-drinking with *him*. Mama will not let me go, though. Not now that Papa has gone out.

Stop at the door to listen but they are not talking. *Tap-tap* and open it.

He is next to Mama *very* close, sitting hand-holding. Her hand in his hand at his nasty whiskery mouth. Mama looks at me surprised and her hand drops into her lap. He stares at me, horrid and cold and blue.

'Papa has gone and Mrs D is bringing tea' say I.

'Good' says Mama.

She looks at the captain. He grunts and moves his chair away again.

Hate you hate you hate you.

Tap-tap on the door and Mrs D comes in with the tray. Mama looks at her and smiles her best brightest nice-Mama smile. 'Thank you' she says. 'How is supper coming along?'

'Fine, ma'am.'

'What are we having?'

Mrs D puzzled frowns at Mama. Mama never asks what is for supper.

'Onion pudding, ma'am.'

'Again?' says Mama.

Good. Sit down and pretend to look at my stocking.

Mrs D clatter-rattles the cups and saucers.

'Has the weather improved at all?' says Mama.

'Tolerably, ma'am.' She puts down the milk jug. 'Leastways it isn't raining now.'

'Oh good!' says Mama. She is trying to sound pleased but she isn't, really.

Mrs D bobs, goes out. Mama fusses with the cups.

'Well' Mama says 'perhaps as it is not raining now, I shall take a little walk. Some air would do me good, I think.'

'May I come too?' say I. 'I have not been outside all day.'

Mama looks at me. Her eyes are very sad. 'I do not think so, Fanny dear' she says. 'It is still rather damp. Perhaps you had better go home and practise the piano. We do not want you to disappoint Mr Mills, do we?'

She would not let me before but she wants me to go. *He* wants me to.

'May I go now, then?' say I. 'I do not want any tea.'

Mama sighs. 'Very well, take your things with you.'

I do, needle and basket and stockings and wool. Go to the door.

'Good afternoon, Captain Easter' say I. *I hate you I hate you.*

He nods. *I hate you too* his eyes say.

Miss Roke is very pleased with herself

I am glad that I do not have to have lessons with her. She goes *tra-la-la* singing for no reason along the corridor, smiling and singing and wearing very bright blue ribbons. I am never allowed to sing to myself in the house. Nobody tells Miss Roke to stop, though. *She* is the only happy person here.

Mary sad long-faced comes out of the music room. She has been teaching again, with the Toogood. Mama has put her in all the drawing classes with him, which is what Mary said she wanted, but it is only making her *worse*. Lizzy says that Mary is making a complete fool of herself but I cannot think that she is, for at least she can draw very well. Mary smiles a thin sad not-smile at me and watches Miss Roke go *trip-trippity tra-la-la*ing up the stairs.

'*Dear* Miss Roke' says Mary.

'Mary' say I 'Mama said could you take the first class in arithmetic because she cannot.'

'Oh' says Mary. 'Why can she not?'

'She has to see the captain.' *Again*.

Mary nods, turns to the music room. Sighs. Mr Toogould

is still in there. She will have to give up the rest of her drawing lesson. Because of *him*.

Mama said that we were not to disturb her unless it was *on a matter of great importance*. The captain is not a matter of great importance but he thinks so. Mama smiled her sweet-Mama smile when he arrived but she was not pleased, not really. He is always here now. He is always making Mama sit with him, even when she is meant to be taking lessons.

Lizzy comes bustling rustling down the stairs. She frowns at me. 'What are you doing, Fanny?' she says. 'Why aren't you in a class?'

'I had to take a message for Mama' say I.

'Well' she says 'now you've taken it you can get back to your work.'

She fusses with her bonnet ribbons. She has *new* gloves on, too. New grey ones.

'I haven't got a class now' say I. 'I am waiting for Mary. Mary is taking us.'

'Pooh' says Lizzy.

Mary comes frowning from the music room.

'Mary' says Lizzy 'I want you to spare Fanny for a few minutes.'

'All right' says Mary, not listening. She goes off to the classroom.

'Wales is in the grotto' says Lizzy 'and he has been down there for an age. Go and take him a drink, Fanny. Anne is at Papa's getting the dinner things and I've an appointment to keep.'

'What should I give him?' say I.

'Anne made some ginger beer. He can have some of that.'

She goes out, bonnet bobbing shawl swinging, slam-shuts the door behind her.

Go into the kitchen cold cupboard and there is the ginger beer cloudy and spicy-smelling in a jug. Pour some into a mug and take it outside.

Warm but damp. Not raining, though. Mr Wales by the dome standing leaning over, looking at the ground. He is laying out shells, brown and blue and white.

'Hello, Mr Wales' say I.

He looks up. His face long and bony and tired-looking. He *kha-kha-kha* coughs and his shoulders move up and down. They are very bony shoulders.

'I have brought you some ginger beer' say I.

He nods, takes the mug and drinks it. The lump in his throat goes *bump-bump-bump*. He tips back the mug and *argh ahh* gasps and gives it back to me. Empty.

He nods and looks back down at the shells.

'Mr Wales' say I 'what are those shells for?'

'Niches' he says. Even his voice is thin.

'What niches?'

'Entrance.'

'Oh.'

He lays them out into patterns but they are not the patterns from the walls. His hands are small and the skin on them is like paper. Thin and dry and chalk-dusty.

He has been inside many times, much more than I have. He is changing it and mending it and now he is even making new bits. I haven't been in for so long. Not since *he* came in and told me.

'Mr Wales?'

'Hm.'

'Will you show me? Will you show me the shells?'

He looks up. His eyes are watery shiny and there are red circles round them, and then black ones round those. He blinks and *kha-kha-khaaa* coughs again. 'In't you never been in?'

'Not for ages. Not since you came to mend it.'

He nods. 'All right then. Don't see the harm.'

Follow him to the tunnel entrance and there are steps now, going down. He goes ahead and lights the lantern. Lots of lanterns in spaces in the walls, sitting in little shelf arches.

'Did you make those?' say I.

'I did. That's what them shells is for, for making em pretty.'

We go along the tunnel, but it is not the tunnel *I* know. Joshua told me that it was much bigger now, since George's papa dug it out. Didn't imagine that it would be *this* big, though.

On and on twisting down, and there the *proper* entrance. No drop like there was before, no stepping down. All smooth and neat, just like a path leading up to the shells. The panel where the fishes were.

Mr Wales takes a lantern and gives me another. I hold it up high.

There they are, just as lovely as before, just as bright. Brighter, because of all the lanterns. Mr Wales holds up his lantern and *kha-kha-kha* coughs. The lantern goes up and down. He shakes his head.

'All this damp' he says *kha-kha* 'does an evil to me chest.'

'Are you all right?' say I. He doesn't look it.

'I am.' He nods to the shells. 'Come on, if you're coming.'

Cold damp-smelling but not like before. Not so dark. He was there behind me and he came pushing shoving squeezing hurting. He is not here though, not this time. He is with Mama, in the parlour.

'Come on' says Mr Wales.

Step in and put out my hand. The fishes sparkle shiny in

the lantern light. So pretty. Hold up the lantern and there are
the arches, high but not so tall as before. Or am I taller?
Fishes plants sunflowers vines. All like before but not chalk-
dusty, not spiderwebby.

'They look cleaner' say I.

'So I'd ope' he says 'I spent forever dusting em.'

He goes on and the light gets bigger wider and covers the
walls. He is lighting lanterns all along and the shadows go
splashing over the shells and disappear. So many shells and
all at once! Brown and orange and blue and white, plants
and shapes and trees. Beautiful shells, even more beautiful
than before.

'When I first came in' say I 'we could only see a little at
a time. We only had a candle each, and it was so dark.'

He nods, but he doesn't know. He thinks I mean the time
when we took the slab off.

Follow him round and to the dome. Not so pretty as
before. The shells at the top not the same – that is where
the captain broke it. He kicked it with his foot and it all fell
down.

'I had a job putting them new ones up' says Mr Wales.
'Show you the altar room, shall I?'

He goes on, past May's little girl, past the rows of hearts.
All mended now, all sealed where the sides were taken off and
the roof fell down. The arch not neat and smooth now but
stuck together like a broken pot. The plaster shows through
thick and grey, muddy.

He smiles. He is pleased with it, anyway.

He goes into the room. 'Come on, then.'

I can't, not in there. 'No thank you' say I.

'What?' He holds up the lantern. Darker there, darker and
louder. His boots shuffle scrape and make a noise. *Scraa-scrup.*

'Come on' he says 'it won't bite. I fixed it up all right where it got broke.'

'It isn't nice in there' say I. 'I don't like it.'

'It's nice enough now. Just put your head in and look.'

He steps back and I step forward. We hold up the lanterns.

No slates, no broken pieces. No chalk piles. The shell shelf patched and the roof all plaster pieces. Not much of it left any more. The little pillars stuck together again, not like before, not so pretty. Swept out and clean though, but dark still.

'There' he says. Holds up the lantern to the corners. 'Nothing here. You can come in.'

'No' say I. It goes round and round again, just like before. *No-oh-oh.*

'Suit yourself then.'

I go, quick-stepping past the hearts and the girl and the dome and the fishes. He puffs and wheezes, blows out lanterns behind me. It goes darker and darker. *Puff puff kha-kha-kha.* Into the tunnel and up and up and back into the outside light again.

Sit on the grass, damp and earth-smelling. No chalk on my shoes or my stockings and no holes from crawling. Not like before. It was better before, though, even so. Blow out my lantern and he comes up, *kha-kha* coughing.

'Mr Wales' say I 'who made the shells?'

'I did.'

'I mean, the first time?'

He shrugs and his shoulders look even bonier. 'Don't know' he says.

'I used to think it was fairies.'

'Aye.'

'I used to think there were shell fairies that would come back and finish it, one day.'

'Well, they didn't. You got me instead.'

He is more like a goblin than a fairy but he *is* small. He is not much bigger than Joshua, but older. Older than James, even.

'I don't think it could have been fairies' say I 'not now.'

'Well, I'd say that was a fair guess.'

'It wasn't Mr Holtum, though. Was it? He couldn't have done it.'

Mr Wales rubs his nose. 'I couldn't tell you' he says. He looks at the shells on the grass again and *kha-kha-kha*s. 'Best get on' he says.

'Thank you for showing me' say I.

He shrugs again, pointy. 'Don't you fret about that room, my girl' he says. 'It in't haunted.'

It *is* though. Just not by anybody who is dead.

Even Mary writes letters now

'Come on, Fanny' she says. She dips the pen. 'You always *used* to write to him.'

'Miss Roke writes to him now' say I. 'She tells him everything.'

'Miss Roke wasn't there' says Mary 'so she cannot tell him.' She puts the pen in my hand and it drips *blob blob* on to the page. 'Just a few lines, Fanny. You know how much he always enjoyed your letters.'

No I don't.

'Why are you writing to him anyway?' say I.

'Because Miss Roke asked me to.'

Of course.

'What did you tell him?'

'Oh' she says 'just local news, you know.'

'Did you tell him about Courtenay and the rebels? Joshua says that the ones they didn't shoot will be hanged.'

'I don't think that is the sort of thing he wants to read, dear.' She frowns, nods. Stands over me. 'Come on, Fanny, write something about the grotto.'

Dear James,
  Mary says that I am to tell you about the opening of the grotto.

'Yes' she says 'go on.'

Papa invited lots of people to come and look at it. Even the mayor was there and the bellman who says everything in rhyme. He was very loud.

He was very rude, too. He said that Papa had made the shell patterns and that Joshua and me and the schoolboys had helped him to stick them on. He said it was a *pedigree quilly* and Mrs D called him a *good for nothing nabbler*. May said that means he thinks the grotto is a prank, and that Mrs D called him a gossip. May said that Mrs D gave the bellman *a piece of tongue pie*, which is what she gives the cook's girl sometimes.

The bellman believes that Mr Holtum made our shell place. So do lots of other people. They don't like it because it is ours and not theirs, and because we don't come from Margate. Stupid stupid stupid.

The visitors drank cordial and fruit punch and looked at the shells. Some of them asked Papa questions about it.

And some of them laughed.
'Oh Fanny' says Mary looking over my shoulder. 'You can do better than that!'
She didn't notice the people that laughed. She wasn't looking at *them*. Papa did, though. He was very quiet.

Miss Roke did not come to the opening. If she had she would have told you about it and then I wouldn't have to.

Mr Davidson gave a speech about the grotto being an ancient place of worship. There is a sign over the entrance made of tin that says 'Subterranean Druidical Temple'. There are lanterns all the way through. Mr Wales made places to put them.

Mr Wales says that Papa hasn't paid him enough for his work and that he has got a bad cough from being underground all the time. Papa says that Mr Wales will not make trouble, but Mama is afraid. Mama is afraid of everything now. Papa said he would ask for more money again, to pay Mr Wales, but Mama cried and cried and begged him not to.

Perhaps now that the grotto is open to visitors you will come and look at it too. I am sure you will not take such a long time to visit us again.

Different, being inside with so many people, shoving nudging moving about. Prodding poking and picking at the shells. When they had gone I went into the shell room with Mrs D and Anne, to gather up the cups. Mrs D's eyes went big and she said *bless me this is a rare thing*. She thought it was beautiful. Anne's mouth was wide open and she couldn't say a word. I stood in the corner, where the captain had been. I made myself do it, made myself stand there and close my eyes while Anne and Mrs D were there, gasping and stroking the shells.

He was there *of course* pouring something from a little silver bottle into the visitors' cups. Papa didn't say anything. He could have lit a cigar and Papa would not have said anything. He stood next to Mama while Papa was busy and held her arm. Mama tried very hard to smile.

Mary stands leaning over my shoulder. 'Aren't you going to write anything else?' she says.

'No' say I. Put down the pen. 'There's nothing else to tell.'

When everyone had gone I heard them quarrelling. Mama said *there must be another way* and Papa said that there isn't. *We are ruined, Arabella* he said and Mama said, *no we are not, but I certainly shall be*. Then she started crying again.

They will hang the rest of the rebels because they said what they thought was right. It isn't good to do that, even if you *are* as mad as William Courtenay.

Not enough again

Papa was very disappointed, but Mama said *more will come, dear.* They will, for it is only a little after Midsummer and the season will go on and on for weeks yet. Papa is worried. Mr Wales said that people wouldn't come, that he'd *make sure of it.* Papa offered him a share of the visitors' money but he laughed, and his laugh was dry and hard like his cough. *Kha-kha-kha.* He said Papa could keep his money for all the good it would do him. *Unker-money* he called it. Dirty money, for a dirty deed.

Warm and light and the birds not resting in the trees yet, even though it is past supper. Shan't go in, not yet. Lizzy high and haughty and Mary sobbing wailing and hair-tugging. *He has gone he has gone* is all she can say now. Poor Mary. Poor moaning mooning spooning Mary.

Hallo, Miss Frances.

George!

He comes quick and jump-stepping over the garden and stands there, grinning. His face not long-looking any more, his body longer bigger to match it. He is almost as tall as a man now.

He pulls a knife from his pocket, wipes it on his trousers. Puts it back again.

'What are you doing here, George?' say I.

'Pa asked me to take a look at the garden' he says.

His knees buckle, legs fold and he sits, one leg sprawling one leg kneeling on the grass. Pick-picks at the ground.

'What do you think of it?' say I.

'It'll keep.' He looks out over the vegetable patch. 'Need to put the timnels in soon though or it might be too dry.'

'What are timnels?'

He grins again. 'You'll know when you have to eat them in your stew every day.'

'Oh.'

'What's the matter with you, anyway?' he says. 'You've a face long as a timnel yourself.'

Everything. Everything wrong but it doesn't look that way. The sun still warm and slow melting, disappearing. The bat *flut flut* swooping in from the roof, diving for his supper. The shells mended.

'Papa is sad' say I. 'I have never seen him sad like this before.'

'It'll be all right' says George. 'Always goes right in the end.'

It won't. Papa owes money, lots of money. Mr Davidson said that people would come to see the shells, and pay well for it, but they don't. They aren't coming. The ones that come laugh and go away grumbling. They don't believe.

Nor do I. Not Mr Davidson's little statue of the foreign god that he stuck up over the archway. Not the shiny tin sign over the steps that people point at and giggle and nudge each other. Not the silly spinning piece of glass that twists and slithers and is meant to look like a snake. Serpent Worship. Druidical Temple. Milksop Moonshine.

'What are you doing out here anyway?' says George. 'Shouldn't you be inside?' He *ho-ho* laughs, a man's laugh. 'Sewing, like a girl should. Making a flag to wave tomorrow.'

Mary was going to make the flags but she is too busy sobbing.

'I can't bear it' say I. 'They are quarrelling.'

'That in't new' says George.

Is not.

'Mr Toogould has gone' say I 'and Mary says that her heart is broken.'

'Oh Lor.'

'She sits in her room sobbing and reading poetry.'

> *When we two parted,*
> *In silence and tears –*

He didn't part in silence and tears. He handed in his resignation and went off to marry a woman called Margaret who draws pictures for a fashion-house. They are going to give drawing classes together in a gentleman's school in Deal. *The artistic young couple will take a hoy to Southampton and after the ceremony, honeymoon in France.* Poor Mary.

'Why do people do it, George?' say I.

'What?'

'Courting.'

He *ho-ho*s again. 'I tried to teach you that, remember? You were a bit young for it.'

'I am older now' say I.

He shrugs, looks at his fingers.

Courting makes you sad. Makes you cry. Sorrow, sorrow. *Silence and tears.* Lizzy with da Costa and Mary with the Toogood. (Too *bad.*) Even Miss Roke. She said *I want you to call me Jane now, Fanny* and her eyes were all wet and brown, like a dog's. She had been crying. I shan't call her that though, for she is *not* my sister. Not yet.

George's fingers lift up and go flickering past my face, *flut flut* like the bat.

'If you were older' he says 'I would teach you.'

'I am older' say I.

Flickering bat fingers flying past my nose and back again. *Flut flut, flut flut.* They hover and hang there, his nails little shells of dirt on the finger ends, long fingers brown and bony. Earth and grass-smelling, green sap stains deep in the swirly patterns, too deep to scrub out. He puts them ever-so-gently on my mouth.

'Not old enough' he says.

It only ever makes you sad so why do it?

The bat fingers swoop down and drop into his lap. 'It'll get cold soon' he says. 'Sun's going. Best go inside.'

'I'm not going in there' say I 'not with all that sobbing. I'll go to Papa's.'

'I'll walk you then' he says.

Get up earth pushing and skirt shaking. The sun lower and the birds quieter and the grass damper. George holds out his hand. I take it, long and bony and solid, not fluttering any more. Pull him up.

'I'll do the timnels on Friday' he says. 'Can't work tomorrow, can we?'

He brushes the grass off his knees and walks past the vegetable patch, nodding. Follow him up to the back door.

He puts his hand on the latch.

'Let's go round' say I. 'Let's not go in.'

He shrugs. 'All right.'

Follow him round the house and along the path. His steps longer than they used to be, quicker. He must be able to run very fast now, maybe even faster than Joshua.

'I'll race you' say I.

'No' he says 'not today.'

'You don't play with me any more.'

'You're grown too old for me' he says. Sly-grins.

'I'm the wrong age for everything then.'

'Not for long, though.'

Off the path into the road. George waits, *craa-eek* creaks shuts the gate behind us.

'What are you doing for tomorrow?' he says.

'I don't know' say I. 'I should like to see the fireworks. Mary said she would take me but I don't know if she will. Are you going to watch?'

'Course.'

Perhaps he will take me with him then. Lizzy will be busy fussing and dressing. Captain Meuer the mewing officer asked her to the big Coronation ball. Mama said she may go for Miss Roke is going too, but Mary isn't. Lizzy said she didn't want Mary there *tut-tutting* and sulking all the time. Mary wouldn't go now, anyway.

George walks on, arms long-hanging, hands swinging. 'Me and some others are going to the pier' he says. Looks sideways at me. 'Fassum and Hudson, Tom Gore, of course. Maybe little Fred Miller, if he can get out. Joshua, too.'

'What for?'

'You won't say aught, will you?'

Shake my head. *Of course not.*

'There's to be free beer' he says 'and a dinner on the pier. Roast beef and plum pudding they say. We've got no tokens for it but we're going anyway, see what we can get.'

'Oh.'

They are *always* hungry.

'Don't tell your pa' says George 'especially about the beer. He wouldn't like it.'

We go up to Papa's gate and stop. George nods towards the house.

'I won't tell' say I.

'You're good at that' he says. 'Well, g'night then.'

'Goodbye.'

He goes off along the road, long and tall and *fwuh-fwuh* whistling.

Darker now and colder. Clouds over the farm and the cows already in. Mama will not mind my coming even though it is late, not if it is to sit in the parlour and sew flags. Open the gate and on to the path and there someone sitting – sitting on the doorstep. *Mrs D.*

Mrs D, head in hands. She doesn't look up. The door open a crack and voices, noises behind it. Go up the path and Mrs D's cap moves and bobs and she sits up. She looks at me red-eyed and shakes her head. 'Not now, Miss Frances' she says.

Thumping banging behind the door and Papa's voice, low and loud. *A little longer* it says. *That is all.*

Pum-pum krapum thudding on the back of the door and the door shakes. *Please!* says Mama's voice. *Please don't!*

'Mrs D?'

'No, child.' She puts up her hands. 'Leave them be.'

Pum pum pum.

'Is it him?' say I.

She puts her head in her hands again.

It is him. Thudding thumping crashing. *Pum-pum kra-pum* crashing and his voice roaring. *Bloody well shall damn you! Damn you all damn your family to hell!* Mrs D's cap shakes and sinks. The door shudders. Thud thud *pum-krapum*. His voice *aaaargh damn you! damn you!* raging and Mama's voice *oh-aho-oh-oh* sobbing. *You will give me what you owe* his voice shouts. *You will give it or I shall take it – yes! Take it, madam!*

Mama makes a long sad moaning noise. Cattle lowing, ship's horn blowing. Sorrow sorrow sorrow.

Mrs D sits up, her hands on her face. She looks hard at me between her fingers. 'Go home now, Frances' she says, cross. 'Go on. Go away.'

The bells start

Ding ding ding ding da-ding da ding. On and on. Roaring shouting cheering and everyone waving and singing. Ribbons and flags and noise and May and Frances laughing. May waves, and her flag and dress and face disappear in the crowd of other flags and dresses and faces. Lizzy tug-tugs on my arm.

'Come on' she says. 'I promised I would be there by six o'clock.'

Never patient but at least she is not cross. Even *she* couldn't be cross today.

'What are you going to wear?' say I.

She smiles. (Smiles!)

'My fine *white* muslin, Fanny' she says. 'Not the sprigged one, with the blue on, but the fine white. Jane says that plain is best to start with, then adornments.'

Jane.

Lizzy chatters and smiles. *Jane's gloves – Frank gave me some satin ones – rose pink! can you imagine? – so pretty – wear my hair loose.* Her voice goes in and out of the cheering and singing and calling – *another glass, Ned? God save our gracious.* Pushing shoving bustling but all smiling, all happy.

'Goodness' says Lizzy 'it *is* hot. I shall be glad to get out of here again.'

Push and shove and on and on. Stalls in the streets, flags, more flags, cups of lemonade, gingerbread. Bonnets and hats and feathers and baskets. Past the market and a man grinning stale-smelling lifts his hat and bows to Lizzy. Lizzy pulls my arm and we go faster, tripping dragging hand tug-tugging up the hill, past the shops, along the street and out to the old cottages and the quiet again.

'Thank goodness' says Lizzy huff-sighing, brushing at her dress. 'I thought we should be crushed to death.'

Up the road and past Papa's. Mama and Papa still at the chapel, thanksgiving. Nobody there, not now – no boys no Woods no Mrs D. All out in the streets, drinking beer waving flags eating cakes. Celebrating.

Lizzy tugs quick-walks and pulls me to the gate.

'Now, Fanny' she says 'in you go. I must be away.'

'Aren't you coming in to get your dress?'

'Oh no' she says frowning. 'I took everything I need to Jane's this morning.'

'Oh.'

Lizzy opens the gate, waves me in.

'I hope you have a nice ball' say I. 'I hope your officer wants to dance and not get drunk.'

She stare-stares at me. Her mouth goes flicker-twitching in the corners. She wants to smile but isn't sure if she ought to.

'Fanny?'

'Yes?'

She shrugs, looks at the house. 'Nothing. Be a good girl, don't get too much sun.'

'All right.'

Go through the gate and she closes it behind me, hurries back down the road again.

Up to the door and push. Locked.

Squeak-bang squeak-bang the knocker and wait. No Anne for she will be out too.

No noise no steps.

Nap-nap-nap knuckle-knock the wood.

Nothing.

Mary must have gone to the chapel too. Dried her eyes and gone to pray, gone to ask God for another Toogood.

Round the house and to the back door and push but it doesn't move. Lift the latch and it creaks and push again, against the door. Nothing.

They have gone out and locked the house. Anne said that they should, said that *high days an holy days is best fer robbin.*

I shall wait in the garden.

Past the vegetable patch and over to the grass. Lizzy said not to get too much sun but it cannot matter, not really. Not so *very* hot, not where the shells are. Take off my bonnet and tuck my skirts under and sit, pick-pick at the grass. Like George yesterday.

Birds singing bells *ding-da ding* ringing. Shouting cheering and music from the town and the harbour, not so loud but still there. Rumbling. And a voice, nearer. A man's voice.

Papa?

A man's voice, low. Mumbling.

'Papa' say I 'is that you? Papa?'

The voice goes on rumbling mumbling, speaking very low. *And let not thine enemies prevail O Lord let them not prevail.* Close but strange-sounding, buried.

Underground. Papa. Papa is in the shells.

Mustn't speak mustn't disturb him, not when he is praying. Crawl slow and quiet to the place above the dome. Lie down grass poking tickling in my ear. An ant big and long-legged marching past my nose. Earth and grass and hot green sap smelling. Listen.

you allowed it yes – uh ahuh – you allowed them to prevail – ahuh ahuh ahuh – O Lord the devil has taken me he has dragged me down – I have failed I have fallen I am cast down – ahuh ahuh – the pit of my own making, Lord –

Papa is not praying. Papa is crying. And shouting.

– and what of you why did you let me? – where was your strength – ahuh – your sign? all I have done – you are not everywhere you are not –

'Papa!'

Say it to the grass, shout it to the shells. 'Come out, Papa! It is Frances, Papa.'

– you are not here – you are not everywhere! this is a place of devils – you are not here –

Slam-banging of a door. Look up to the house and there is Mary. Wave at her to come but she does not move.

Papa mumbling praying crying shouting underground. Jump up and run to Mary past the shells and the flowers and the vegetable patch. She opens her arms out and I run and she pulls me tight against her dress.

Poor lamb her voice says.

'Papa is in the shells' say I. 'He is crying, he is shouting at God!'

Mary pushes me back and stares hard at me. Hot nose hot eyes burning and hers burning too. Red and dry and burning from too much crying.

'We are born to weep' says Mary. (Sigh sigh.) 'If I had

thought thou couldst have died, I might not weep for thee.'
She sniffs, *sa*-sobs. 'Oh! Silence, silence and tears.'

'Stop it, Mary!'

'Must we but weep o'er days more blest?'

'Stop it! I think Papa is not *well*, Mary.'

'I water my couch with tears. Like David.'

Red-eyed and sniffing, hopeless helpless Mary.

'Papa is sick, Mary' say I. 'We must do something. He is
not himself!'

'Who is?' she says. Her fingers shaking fluttering push at
my hair. 'Who am I? We are none of us ourselves any more.'

Papa crying shouting Mary shaking. Where is Mama?

'Mary' say I 'is Mama still inside? Where is she?'

'Oh no.' She sniffs, tucks my hair behind my ears. 'No,
my lamb, she has gone.'

'Gone? Gone where?'

'To see Captain Easter.'

'Him? Why?'

Mary sniffs, sighs. 'To talk to him about some money. To
reach an agreement. She said that she must, for dear Papa
cannot.'

Hate him hate him hate him.

Run and run round the house up the path along the lane.
Bells *da-ding-ding* ringing and then a *baoom* bang. Not the
fireworks yet – the *cannons. The chiming of the bells of Holy
Trinity* the notices said, then *the royal salute with cannons.*

Run and run, feet *thud-thud-thudding* up the lane round
the long wall up the hill to the horrid hateful house.

He cannot hurt Mama he must not. God is everywhere.
He is He is He is.

Baoom. Baoom.

Up the lane and there the hateful house, hateful pretend

castle. *Scra-scra-scra* run over the gravel and up to the house and *nap-nap-nap nap-nap-nap* hard with the knocker.

Nothing.

Nap-nap-nap. Nap-nap-nap.

Baoom.

Scuffling scratching behind and there is his horrid dog, sniffing looking at me. Its mouth open, tongue lolling, *ya-*yawning. Its horrid long leg goes up scratching scuffing at its chin.

'Where is he?' say I. 'Where's your horrid master?'

It looks at me. Scratches. *Waa-aaa* whines.

'Where?'

Nap-nap-nap the knocker again.

Nothing. Nobody.

'Where is Mama?'

Look at the dog and it looks at me. *Ka-ka* clap my hands at it.

'Go away! Go away, you horrid creature!'

Ka-ka clap them again. It jumps, crouches.

Ka-ka. Ka-ka. Ka-ka.

The dog *graa*-growls grumbles and runs away, long lean over the gravel and into the garden.

If it is here then so is the captain, so is Mama.

Follow it.

Over the lawn past the fountain. It stops, crouches, *graaas*. Thinks it is a game and I am playing. Clap my hands and it springs up again, runs.

Flowers grass paths trees. The dog stops at the avenue, points its nose into a bush. *Waaa*-whines and lies down, tail *thud thud* thumping the ground.

Rustling shuffling and scuffling, very close. The dog not looking at me, looking at something further in. A rabbit?

Scuffling rustling and *huh-huh-huh*. Not the dog though, tail-thumping tongue-lolling. *Huh-huh-huh* and another sound, something else. *Uww a-uww*. Fox? Leaf rustling and wet sniffing and the sound again, a choking sound, a covered twisted stopped-up strangled sound. *Huh-huh-huh*. Peer in through the leaves and dark and rustling and the noise again, *uw uww*.

Him. His boots black on the ground. His hands. White skirts white petticoats caught up twisted and Mama kneeling shaking eyes shut *uw-uw* sobbing, her hands stuffed hard into her mouth.

March 1897
Masonic Institute, London

Dear Mr Goddard,

I received your letter quite safe this morning. I must tell you that I would much rather see you and talk it over than write. It is some years since you first looked me up and as I told you then, the place is nothing to me. I'm not interested in it any more. I lost my right in it many years ago.

I am the only one of my family left now and the only reliable person living that can tell you about the place. My brother died some years ago and it was he who found it. We were brought up very strict and he was afraid to tell his father.

You can ask people in Margate but they will tell you all sorts of stories about it. The truth is that they envied us the place. When I had it, and my father died, and even after I married Mr S, they still said the same. They said we had built the place, or that Prinny Wales did it. People would come in and say come now, didn't you make this all up yourselves? and I would say, oh yes, all for your amusement. Then they would pick the shells off for souvenirs. I used to make a nice little thing of it though, and had money to give my brother and sister, without anyone knowing. They are dead now, of course. Mr Stoddard, who used to show it before I had it, he paid

325

£30 rent. I heard later that it was let for £70 per annum and now it has been sold again. A private sale and for quite a price too, I gather.

I shan't say any more as I don't hold much to letter writing. If you do want to come and see me you can find me easily enough. You needn't think I shall tell you anything different from what I said before, though. You can't catch me out. I've a sharp memory still.

Frances Schmidt

I ought to say I wasn't completely honest with you last time and there is still something I have to tell you, if you want to hear it. I swore once I'd never say, but that was all a long time ago. It can wait.

P.S.

Ideas,
interviews
& features . . .

Q and A with Sonia Overall

What was it in the Margate junk shop that inspired you to write *The Realm of Shells*?
The plan was to go to Margate to look in the junk shop for some furniture. The junk shop was closed (well, it was Sunday) but I remembered hearing about the grotto nearby and decided to have a look there instead. An hour or so later, sitting on Broadstairs beach, I realised I had the plot of another book. The main inspiration for the story was a short description, in the grotto's museum, of Joshua Newlove's 'discovery' of the grotto in 1835.

The image of a boy climbing down a rope with a lantern round his neck, and finding an Aladdin's cave at the bottom, was where it all began.

What is the grotto like today?
The grotto now has a very careful owner, which has not always been the case. The shells have sadly been covered with a layer of soot as a result of the oil lamps used to light it in the past, which means much of their colour is lost. Despite this, the mosaics are breathtakingly beautiful. Whatever its purpose or provenance, the grotto is a treasure and well worth visiting. There really is nothing else like it.

The sense of time and place comes through in the tiniest details such as the rhymes the children sing or the excerpts Fanny reads out from the *Kentish Gazette*. How do you do your historical research?
I approach research from the outside in.

I began by reading about the murky 1830s, before Victoria but after George. It's an interesting embryonic period. Writers and thinkers of the time are increasingly outspoken about issues of poverty, education, rights and so on. There's a slide away from Regency decadence and hedonism towards Victorian asceticism. William's reign is like the hangover in between.

Historical detail comes from reading texts of the time as well as modern biographies, histories and so on. I plundered the local studies collections of Kent libraries for guidebooks and maps of the period, as well as archives of the local newspaper. A trip to the Bethnal Green Museum of Childhood was invaluable for detail on childhood games that Fanny and her classmates would have played.

The Realm of Shells is told from Fanny's point of view: why did you choose to write from a child's perspective?
Children are constantly overlooked and underestimated by adults, even by their teachers and parents (both, in Fanny's case). Fanny is the youngest in the family, and therefore best placed to be ignored, while noticing everything the adults get up to. It takes someone like Captain Easter, who needs to cover his tracks, to realise how observant she is. The relationship between Easter as manipulator and Fanny as observer gave me the central point of antagonism for the book.

Once I had worked out Fanny's character and role I had to write it in her voice. ▶

> ❛ The image of a boy climbing down a rope with a lantern round his neck, and finding an Aladdin's cave at the bottom, was where it all began. ❜

Q and A with Sonia Overall *(continued)*

◄ I relished the challenge of writing in the present tense too – a child's mind required that immediacy. It was also a good excuse to regress a bit.

Does she move from innocence to experience?

Fanny learns a lot about adult behaviour over the course of the book, as any child of her age does. I don't think current notions of innocence would have made much sense to the Newloves and their contemporaries. Besides, children are much crueller, and cleverer, than we care to believe.

Fanny is constrained because she is a girl; her sisters and her mother are used by men in different ways. Can you say a bit about gender in the book?

I didn't write the women in this book with any gender agenda. Having said that, it's impossible to ignore nineteenth-century attitudes towards women. The blanket view of the period is that women were considered by men as either saints or whores, but the truth is always more complex than that, as even the smallest research will show. The Newlove women certainly don't fit this pattern, although their unconventional attitudes cause them problems. Arabella is a businesswoman, and the older girls are expected to work and study responsibly, and to be useful rather than ornamental. Fanny's father believes that girls should be given a good education. He treats his wife as an independent individual, and it is partly because of this that he expects her to

❝ I began by reading about the murky 1830s, before Victoria but after George. It's an interesting embryonic period. ❞

share responsibility for solving their problems with Easter, however undignified or immoral.

The Realm of Shells **looks at a particular type of evangelical Christianity. Did you have a religious upbringing?**
No. I was exposed to Anglicanism as a child through church choir and Sunday school, but I was always left to make up my own mind about how seriously to take it.

'The realm of shells' is described by Mr Davidson as 'the hidden world of the demonic that exists about us, yet cannot be seen' but Fanny calls it a 'fairy palace'. Who is right?
Both of these characters describe the realm of shells in the way that makes most sense to them. One doesn't necessarily preclude the other.

Fanny is keen to help George learn to read. Do you believe in the power of reading?
Yes, very strongly. When Fanny teaches George to read she gives him a very valuable tool, and those that disapprove do so because they are afraid of how he, and people like him, might use it.

Do you think of yourself as an experimental writer?
I certainly don't consider myself a historical or genre writer, but then there's nothing in this book that much better experimental writers haven't done before me. I just write in the way that I think will best tell the story. ▶

6 When Fanny teaches George to read she gives him a very valuable tool, and those that disapprove do so because they are afraid of how he, and people like him, might use it. 9

Author photo © Monica Curtin

LIFE
at a Glance

BORN

Ely, Cambridgeshire, 1973

EDUCATED

Ely Community College; Cambridge Regional College and Anglia HEC; University of Kent at Canterbury (BA and MA)

CAREER

Served time behind the counter as a bookseller, then as a reviewer. Written one previous novel, *A Likeness*, and working on a third. When not writing, organises community events and works as a puppeteer with The Theatre of the Small.

FAMILY

Married to James Frost, puppeteer and artist. Two black cat familiars.

Q and A with Sonia Overall *(continued)*

◄ **The dramatic interludes are often very funny. Are there comedians or playwrights you particularly admire?**

I don't set out to be funny – if I did it probably wouldn't work. I enjoy the understated, dry humour of writers like Michael Frayn.

There are echoes of Jane Austen in the novel. Are you a fan of her work and which other writers inspire you?

I love Austen. Underneath the romantic packaging she is a very shrewd social commentator and deliciously acerbic. She never resorts to caricature like Dickens, or preaches like George Eliot, but she stills manages to expose the hypocrisy of her characters and the world they exist in. I'm inspired by many different writers of fiction and non-fiction – too many to mention without missing someone important out!

Your previous novel *A Likeness* was also set in the past. Will your next book be a historical novel too?

My third book is a contemporary novel, but history plays an important role in it. I'm very interested in how the past influences and affects us. ■

A Writing Life

When do you write?
Best in the mornings, with strong coffee. Once I start I keep going for as long as I can.

Where do you write?
When it's planned, in my study at home. Future books are often sketched out on the backs of envelopes and napkins.

Why do you write?
I can't help it. I'd never sleep otherwise.

Pen or computer?
Pencil notes first. Prose is typed straight into the computer.

Silence or music?
Silence.

What started you writing?
Learning to read.

How do you start a book?
With one strong idea and a first sentence. Then I plot it out on sheets of paper and work up a synopsis.

And finish?
At the end. Once I get started I tend to write in sequence.

Do you have any writing rituals or superstitions?
Not really – just the coffee. On good days it sits next to me and goes cold. ▶

❛ Future books are often sketched out on the backs of envelopes and napkins. ❜

A Writing Life (continued)

◄ **Which living writer do you most admire?**
I think Ian McEwan does exactly what should be done with the modern novel. I admire his precise, clinical style of writing. He can turn subjects that would normally leave me cold into compelling, complex dramas – he also writes malice, and the threat of it, more powerfully than anyone else I can think of.

What or who inspires you?
Reading, walking, overheard snippets of conversation, places, people, history, chance discoveries ...

What's your guilty reading pleasure?
Henry James. It's very unfashionable to like Henry James. I don't care much for fashion. ∎

Facts into Fiction – *The Realm of Shells* and the Margate Shell Grotto

by Sonia Overall

FIRST-TIME VISITORS to the shell grotto may find it impossible to imagine that a subterranean treasure is hidden beneath this part of back-street Margate. At first sight, the entrance on Grotto Hill looks like part of a private house. There is a small shop and café, and beyond these, a room of artefacts and pieces related to the grotto. The opening of the chalk tunnel to the grotto sits in the corner of this museum, breathing cold damp air into the room and eerily amplifying the sounds of visitors walking about within.

In one of the display cases is a potted history of the shell grotto's 'discovery', in 1835, by Joshua Newlove, son of the schoolmaster who owned the site. I read this, as most visitors do, before going into the grotto. It was a good story, but it didn't mean much without seeing the place. Then I went into the chalk tunnel and saw the scale of the site and quality of the shell work. I looked up at the central rotunda, in which Joshua had dangled suspended on a rope, and imagined him hanging there, taking in what he saw. It was the central image for a story that unfolded over the next few months of research, planning and plotting.

The Realm of Shells is essentially a novel about place, about how a place can influence and manipulate people. The grotto exerts a fascination on the book's characters, who all want a piece of it for themselves. This is still ▶

Facts into Fiction – *The Realm of Shells* and the Margate Shell Grotto *(continued)*

◄ the case today, with historians, Templars, New Age enthusiasts and folly fanciers all trying to claim the site as their own. When people want something to be true they can easily persuade themselves it is so, and twisting the facts to make a theory fit is a theme that runs throughout the grotto's history. It is also something that the characters of the novel do consistently – consciously or otherwise.

After another good look in the grotto's museum room, I began research for the novel by trawling local libraries, archives and the internet for references to the site. I read numerous guidebooks on Margate, from the beginning of the resort's fame as a sea-bathing destination in the 1700s to the present day. I studied old maps and engravings and used them, while wandering around modern Margate, to imagine what the town would have been like in the 1830s.

I also began looking into the Newlove family. Searches for present-day Newloves in the area drew a blank, which helped me to decide that the family should arrive from elsewhere in the country. I obtained a copy of the schoolmaster Mr Newlove's will: this gave me his age, the names of his children and in some cases their spouses, his social situation and, most importantly, something of his voice and attitudes. I looked into the evangelist sect that he belonged to and visited the sites of his church and Sunday school. Then I struck lucky: in the archives of Canterbury Cathedral I found a file full of Mick Twyman's research articles on the grotto itself. In amongst the

6 When people want something to be true they can easily persuade themselves it is so, and twisting the facts to make a theory fit is a theme that runs throughout the grotto's history. 9

various papers on the grotto's meaning and provenance was a mine of information on the Newlove family, their acquisition of the land, and even correspondence between the schoolmaster's daughter Frances Schmidt and historian Algernon Goddard in the 1890s, when Frances was in her seventies.

Until then I had planned to write the novel in Joshua's voice, but once I had read Frances's letter I couldn't get her out of my head. It occurred to me that this spirited lady would have been a bright and inquisitive child. Her short letter was hugely revealing, dangling the promise of information to her correspondent but maintaining an air of mystery and secrecy. She informs Goddard that her brother Joshua overheard two visitors – a Captain Easter and Mr da Costa – dropping hints about the land his father was leasing and suggesting that he buy it instead. Joshua's curiosity was pricked and led to his discovery of the grotto, which he shared with his sister but kept secret from their strict parents. Frances also suggests that there is more to the story than she is prepared to put on paper, even sixty years on. It was this knowingness and wariness that intrigued me, and made her exactly the kind of unreliable narrator that I wanted for my novel.

From Frances's letter I had the seeds of the book – the relationship between the children and adults involved, the secrecy and duplicity of the characters, and the atmosphere of distrust and bitterness that surrounded the grotto and its ownership. It also helped me form the plan to write the novel in two ▶

> ❛ From Frances's letter I had the seeds of the book – the relationship between the children and adults involved, the secrecy and duplicity of the characters. ❜

◄ voices, balancing the narrator's internal monologue with her more formal letter-writing style, and her desire to sign herself Frances, even though everyone else referred to her as Fanny.

I then began filling out the characters that would inhabit the story, using real names and places from the time. The census of 1840 provided me with a list of pupils and teachers from both the boys' and girls' schools, as well as the domestic staff. Some of these are used in the book, being the closest I could get to the names of those resident in 1835–8. An advert for the boys' school, reprinted in Twyman's research and tracked down on the microfiche records of the local newspaper, gave me a list of the subjects these tutors would have taught. Pigot's Directory, a 'yellow pages' of the time, gave me details of trades in the town and their owners, as well as listings for both Newlove schools.

I had many useful conversations with the grotto's owner Sarah Vickery, and Mick Twyman generously supplied me with a complete copy of his research for use at home. Plundering these sources introduced me to Stephen 'Prinny' Wales and his work on the grotto; to Davidson, the esoteric teacher; and to the shadowy figures of Mark Holtum and Bowles the builder, who had previous connections with the land. I was also given the invaluable information that Captain Easter was a gambler with large debts, who could barely pay for the upkeep of his grand house Chateau Bellevue. When I decided what Easter's role in the book would be, I was able

> ❛ I then began filling out the characters that would inhabit the story, using real names and places from the time. ❜

to trace his grave in Essex and went to apologise in person. His headstone also named his widow, Sarah, many years his junior. It was another opportune discovery that helped to shape his personality and created the minor character of his mildly impudent housekeeper.

More than anything else, the grotto itself informed the writing and essence of the novel. The truth about who built it and why, how and when it was really discovered and what purposes it has served are still unknown. Frances seemed to know more about it than most, growing up on its site, watching its effect on others, acting as live-in caretaker when she married and eventually growing bitter about its fate in old age. Whatever secret she planned to tell Goddard about the grotto, and her role in its story, is lost, as Frances died before his intended visit could take place. In light of the grotto's history, this is perhaps as it should be. ■

> The grotto itself informed the writing and essence of the novel. The truth about who built it and why are still unknown.

Have You Read?

A Likeness

When a young artist sees the royal pageant of
Elizabeth I pass through his home town, he
longs to capture its glory in paint. But as
Robin finds out on arriving in the teeming
city of London, it is far from easy to gain
access to the Royal Presence, talent or no.
Meeting the legendary Kat, a delicious
courtesan with a peculiar taste for paint, he
makes a dark bargain, a deal which will not
only enable him to fulfil his artistic ambitions
but also finally gain access to the Court. But
the repercussions of his lust for success will
eventually demand a high price indeed.

A Likeness is a sensual and intoxicating
evocation of a world as enthralling in its
beauty as it is savage in its passions.

'A vivid tale, part political thriller, part potent
account of the perils of ambition and desire . . .
its plot is pacy and Overall's rich language
intoxicates'   *Observer*

If You Loved This,
You Might Like . . .

Mansfield Park
by Jane Austen (1814)
This is a seminal Austen work, looking at issues of morality in an intense and claustrophobic family setting. Fanny Price is the shy and modest heroine who remains strong in the face of mounting dramatic crises.

What Maisie Knew
by Henry James (1897)
With much subtlety and humour Henry James shows us a corrupt adult world from a child's perspective. Maisie is neglected and exploited by her divorced parents, and the effect this has on her makes for a powerful and complex novel.

The Secret Garden
by Frances Hodgson Burnett (1911)
A widely admired children's classic about an unhappy orphan and her sickly cousin discovering an abandoned garden.

The Go-Between
by L. P. Hartley (1953)
An elderly man recalls the summer he spent in Norfolk as a child when he was used as a messenger to take love letters from his friend's sister to the farmer with whom she was having an affair. A masterly tale of an illicit sexual relationship and its disastrous aftermath, all told in exquisite elegiac prose.

If You Loved This, You Might Like . . . *(continued)*

Oranges Are Not the Only Fruit
by Jeanette Winterson (1985)
The Whitbread Award-winning autobiographical novel of a young girl's upbringing in a working-class Pentecostal family in a small Northern town. When Jeanette reveals her feelings for another girl, her mother tries to 'save her soul' . . .

The Observations
by Jane Harris (2006)
Set in the nineteenth century in a large run-down house in Scotland, this is a funny and original novel about secrets and hidden histories, told in the exuberant voice of serving girl Bessy Buckley. ■